MW00942769

What the Dog Ate

Jackie Bouchard

This book is a work of fiction. Names, characters, businesses, organizations, places, events, and incidents either are the product of the author's imagination or are used fictitiously. Any resemblance to actual persons, living or dead, events, or locales is entirely coincidental.

Copyright © 2012 by Jackie Bouchard

All rights reserved

ISBN: 1478100052
ISBN-13: 978-1478100058

Printed in the United States of America

Cover by Click Twice Design

Dedication

To paraphrase a Julio Iglesias and Willie Nelson song that makes me want to poke my eardrums out: I dedicate this book to all the dogs I've loved before.

Acknowledgments

First of all, I want to thank my hubby, not only for being an inspiration for Maggie's hard-working character, but for causing me to take a writing class to fill some of my alone time waiting for him to get home from work at night. In all seriousness, a big thanks to him for putting up with me when I was so often in dreamland thinking about my characters, and for when he'd come home from work, starving, and I'd look up, frenzied, and say, "Let me just finish this scene!" He never once grumbled when I would wake up in the middle of the night with an idea and start madly scribbling in the dark. I will be forever grateful.

I also want to thank the folks at UCSD Extension for the classes I've taken, and especially Nicole Vollrath for encouraging me to turn my short story that read "more like a novel" into one. Thanks to everyone at San Diego Writers Ink and notably Judy Reeves whose class helped me add a pivotal scene to the book.

To my early readers Patricia, Gayle, and Louisa: bless you for sticking with me through the various iterations of this book. A huge thanks to my sister, Terry, for searching diligently for my typos and misspellings through every. single. draft! I also very much appreciated the fact that she missed some edits the first time through because she was caught up in the story.

Cheers to my entire family for being hilarious and inspiring me to try to be my funniest. It would be nice if they were dysfunctional, so that they'd be ripe material for plot lines and character ideas, but functional is good and makes for pleasant holiday get-togethers.

Thank you to Andy Brown at Click Twice Design for the

wonderful cover. I am also grateful to Ellen Venturella-Wilson and her husband Joe for the photo of their beautiful chocolate Lab, Charley, used in the cover art. I "met" Ellen and Charley through Bone Cancer Dogs (www.bonecancerdogs.org) and Tripawds (www.tripawds.com), online communities for people like us whose pups got bone cancer. We lost our beautiful tripawd Abby, who is now one of Charley's angels, looking out for him and helping him keep kicking cancer's butt!

Thanks to the La Jolla Writer's Conference, where I had the chance to read the bacon scene with Dave and *That Woman* in front of the wonderful person who would ultimately become my agent.

Which brings me, finally, to a huge thanks to my agent, Taryn Fagerness, for all her help and for believing in me. This book would not be what it is today without her amazing support.

Chapter 1: Otherwise, His Bowels Look Great

The vet handed Maggie Baxter a plastic specimen bag containing a pair of size-tiny, lavender thong panties extracted from her dog; but they were not hers. Or rather, they were hers now since she'd just paid $734 to have Dr. Carter surgically remove them from Kona's gut.

She'd come home late the previous night from a three-day conference. When she crawled into bed, Dave had muttered hello, but was snoring again within the minute.

Then, this morning, she'd awakened to the muted foghorn sounds of Kona heaving. As she'd hurried down the hall to the living room, knowing that was where the chocolate Lab would be, she wondered two things: how could Dave sleep through that horrid noise; and why, in a house ninety percent floored with hardwood and tile, did the dog always throw up on the carpet?

She'd made it in time and pushed the big brown dog out back. Standing stiff-legged on the lawn, he had heaved several more times but nothing came up. When she'd offered him breakfast and he wouldn't even look at it, she'd known a vet visit would be on the day's agenda.

When Dave got up she'd told him Kona wouldn't eat. "I'll drop him at the vet on my way in, but can you pick him up?"

"Sure." Dave had poured coffee while she filled two bowls with cereal. They'd eaten in silence, reading the paper, until he looked up and said, "It's a bad sign that he's not even begging for our eakfast-bray." After being called for his breakfast, dinner and treats countless times, Kona knew those words meant his favorite thing: food. He went nuts, barking and jumping when he heard them. They'd tried to train him out of it, then given up and taken the lazier route of using Pig Latin for those words or spelling them out.

"I'm not sure he'll even react to his trigger words today, the poor guy," Maggie had said, while wondering if Dave would ask how her conference had been. He only seemed interested in his paper and the dog. But then, she couldn't blame him. No one but the keenest accountant wants to hear about a financial reporting conference; she couldn't even work up any excitement about it herself.

She'd finished getting ready and pecked Dave's cheek as he rinsed their coffee cups.

"OK, we're eaving-lay," she'd said. Leaving was another trigger word. When they went out they'd call, "We're leaving; be good!" and toss the dog a peanut butter filled Kong toy.

"You be a brave boy." Dave had kissed the top of Kona's head.

At the vet's office, Dr. Carter joked, "With stomach problems in a Labrador, you have to rule out three things: dietary indiscretion, dietary indiscretion, and dietary indiscretion."

Maggie had smiled, but thought, it's easy to make jokes when you're on the receiving end of the bills.

An x-ray had confirmed a bowel obstruction, and Dr. Carter said he'd call when Kona was out of surgery.

Later, he'd reached Maggie at work and told her Kona had come through fine; she could pick him up at four. Maggie exhaled, realizing she'd been holding her breath.

"I've got the panties he ate right here in a specimen bag. I'll save them for you. I guess it's like traffic accidents or something; people always want to see what I pull out of their dog."

"No, really, that's fine. You can throw them away."

"You would not believe this boxer I had in here last month. Pulled six of those plastic stuffed animal squeakers out of him. Family left him home during that freak thunderstorm we had, and he went crazy, pulling his toys apart and eating the squeakers."

But Maggie wasn't listening. Her mind had rewound and hit pause on one word: panties. She'd pictured the white cotton Ladies'

Fruit of the Looms under her khakis, her standard issue, and thought, these are *underwear*, not panties. She owned a few skimpy pairs, but she only wore them when she and Dave dressed up to go out, and they hadn't done that in a while.

"Actually, yeah, could you save them for me?"

"See, you can't help yourself. No problem."

Maggie had emailed Dave: "Dr. C called. K's all good. I can pick him up after all. See you at home."

Maggie had given up pretending to work and left the office at half past three, drawing looks from her staff since she never left early. At the vet's, the receptionist had led her into the windowless examination room where Kona, lying on the yellowed linoleum floor subdued from the anesthesia, had given her a single thump of his tail. Dr. Carter had begun praising Kona for his bravery, but she'd spotted the bag with its delicate lavender contents lying on the gleaming stainless steel table, which winked at her as the fluorescent light flickered, and stopped listening.

THE KEYS JANGLED as Maggie put them in the ignition. She'd held it together while the vet tech put Kona in his plastic cone and processed her credit card, but now, in the car, her hands wouldn't stop shaking. She wanted to scream down the freeway at the maximum speed limit (hell, she might even go a few miles per hour over) so she could get home and scream at her husband. But when she turned up the 805 onramp, the traffic was terrible. She hadn't driven home this early in ages; she almost never left work before seven or eight o'clock, sometimes even later. She'd forgotten how bad San Diego rush hour could be. She noticed the skin stretched taut over the knuckles of her hands, at ten and two on the wheel. She took a deep breath, released it, and loosened her grip. On the crawl home, she'd have plenty of time to plan the best approach for confronting Dave, time to think about how they'd gotten to this point, and to contemplate how she could have been so clueless.

In her wildest nightmares, she never thought Dave would cheat. The very thought was so foreign that they used to make jokes all the time. She'd call to say she needed to work late and he'd pretend to click into a waiting call and whisper in a deep voice, "Hey, Babe, I'll be right over; the wife's gotta work late. Oh wait, uh, Maggie?" They also had a running routine where she would "let slip" references to their imaginary pool boy, Fabian. Dave always replied that he couldn't understand why they needed Fabian when all they had was Kona's plastic kiddy pool.

It's been a long time since we joked like that; a long time since we joked about anything.

She used to make him laugh, asking if it bothered him that both her paycheck and her butt were bigger than his. She'd stopped asking when he gave her only a wan smile in response. Of course, the differences loomed larger now. Sure, she'd always earned more, but now she won much bigger bread—huge, hearty loaves compared to the slim baguettes he brought home.

And she'd had to drop working out. Each day held only so many hours, and work and sleep hogged almost all of them. Meanwhile, Dave had been cycling, running with Kona and going to the gym more than ever. She'd told him she was working her ass *on* for them. He used to grab at what he called her "handfuls of love," but when was the last time that happened?

Not only had they stopped joking, they were barely talking beyond the basic necessities. She'd get home from BioHealth and Dave would mute the TV to suggest an appropriate nuking time for her dinner in the fridge. Then the volume blared back on. That had been going on for, what, weeks? A month? But she'd been too stressed to deal with it. At work, the usual quarter-end madness shoved all other projects aside; at night, their personal tax return beckoned. She'd barely finished it by April fifteenth. Exhausted, she'd put no effort into coaxing him out of his pouting about her crazy hours. But now, she began to realize the depths of the problems at home.

Has he been feeling like he's at the bottom of my to-do list? When was the last time we had Date Night? When was the last time we . . . ? Oh, God, it's been ages. I've been working too much, way too much, for . . . She tried to pinpoint when work had gotten out of control. *Months ago? No, wait, it was last spring.*

Thirteen months ago BioHealth listed its shares for the first time on the NASDAQ, its Initial Public Offering. Yes, the IPO lay at the root of her stress. But, stress aside, it fit with the plan. *Their* plan. They would both work, work, work and save enough money to start up the bicycle-tour traveling company they always fantasized about. They'd run that for ten years or so, as long as they still enjoyed it, and then retire early. Ride their bikes, travel, cook gourmet meals, learn Italian, have sex on random Wednesday mornings . . . afternoons, even . . . or whenever; it was going to be fantastic.

At first, they both signed on, committed to the plan. Dave had chugged along at his job as Marketing Director at PETCO; she'd wowed them at BioHealth. The company rewarded her with a bonus of 50,000 shares and promoted her to Vice President of Accounting—a huge boost to their plan. She'd not only gotten a raise, but if the stock price climbed to $20, they'd have a million bucks. A million! Of course, it wasn't a sure thing, but the researchers and execs at BioHealth were banking on it. And, even if it didn't reach a million, it would at least pad and protect their nest egg, providing a soft landing if their bike tour business didn't succeed.

As she merged from the 805 freeway to the 163, she remembered the night of her promotion. They'd popped open a bottle of champagne; even splashed some in Kona's bowl, and he'd lapped it up. The plan's pieces started to fit together. The IPO work drained Maggie, with its seventy- to eighty-hour weeks, but Dave hadn't complained, since the end appeared in sight.

Only, it didn't end. The promotion meant work days that slogged on into the nights and work weeks that spilled over, making a mess of their weekends.

Dave told her he was fed up, but she begged him to hang in. They needed to be patient and wait for the good old Federal Drug Administration folks to come through for them. As soon as the FDA approved BioHealth's diabetes drug, the stock price would soar and they'd sell. The complex approval process would take time, but meanwhile, they'd work on their business idea. What was another twenty-four months or so in the greater scheme of things? It was a perfect plan.

At least that's what she kept telling him. But Dave no longer sat aboard the little boat sailing them into the sunset. He wasn't even hanging on to the edge or dog-paddling alongside. No, he'd swum for shore and yelled at her to bail out too. He'd asked her repeatedly to quit and find something else; she countered that there was no point. High-level accounting jobs always involved long hours and pressure from the constant deadlines. As stressful as it was, she might as well stay with the devil she knew. The pay was good, and it was only a couple more years.

As Maggie inched along in traffic, too distracted to enjoy the tall sycamore and eucalyptus trees standing sentinel over the 163 like she usually did, she turned the pages of an imaginary calendar. It was easy to conjure memories of their various fights, since they'd fallen on major holidays or events. A particularly bad one raged on Dave's forty-first birthday last July, when she'd been an hour late for their dinner reservation. Another hit on their seventeenth wedding anniversary in September. She'd tried to tell him they should wait and celebrate on the weekend, but he was "sick of living on the weekends." On New Year's Day, he couldn't believe she had to go to the office and called it a "bad omen" for the year ahead. She'd told him she couldn't ask her staff to work and then not show up, and that he didn't understand. She realized now she might have made it sound like her VP position carried greater responsibilities than his job as Marketing Director, which of course it did, but she'd never say that to him. Valentine's Day there'd been no fight, but it had come and gone with barely an acknowledgement. Maggie had worked late, eating pastel-colored antacid tablets in place of candy hearts.

I've been so stressed at work; I come home tired and crabby. I guess I could see how he might look for some . . . fun, some attention . . . from someone else. But I'm doing this for us. How could he do this to me? To us? I'm gonna kill him.

She turned the car off the freeway toward her North Park

neighborhood as she turned her mind from the past and imagined the imminent scene at home. She practiced opening lines in her head: *"Your lover must have left these behind."* No, *that's no good. I should at least give him a chance to explain.* Maybe: *"Exactly when were you planning to let me in on this little secret of yours?" Too accusatory? It's possible this is just a crazy misunderstanding, right?* She wanted to try to stay calm. Not lose it until she knew what had happened. After all, it wasn't outside the realm of possibility that he'd bought the panties for her, maybe as a let's-spice-things-up present. ("I must have bought the wrong size, Mags. I mean, I know *now* that they're three sizes too small, but honestly, honey, this is how I picture you in my mind.")

But, no, that didn't add up. Kona wouldn't eat a new pair of panties, with that fresh-from-the-factory chemical smell. As disgusting as it was to contemplate, Kona liked things that were lived in . . . sweaty . . . soiled.

Please, please, please let there be some explanation. Maybe a neighbor flung the panties over our fence? Yeah, that could have happened . . .

But she knew, by the twisted, vice grip squeezing her gut, that there was only one explanation. And she knew that, in the end, Dave would have to break down and confess.

She imagined him kneeling and sobbing uncontrollably into the hem of her skirt. (She wore slacks, but in her mental staging of the scene, sobbing into her khakis didn't look right.) He'd tell her he lost his mind; it was a stupid affair that didn't mean anything. He would explain that when she put her work above his needs, he'd turned to this other woman in a moment of total insanity and spineless weakness. Then he'd beg for forgiveness.

She pulled into the driveway as she tried to decide whether she should let him stay or throw him out for a time. She leaned towards throwing him out, for what, a week?

Is that enough?

She hadn't decided how long was appropriate, when she walked into the house. Kona gingerly followed behind, bumping the wall with his cone. Dave stood at the kitchen counter, sorting the day's mail.

He'd still been in his T-shirt and boxers when she left that morning, so she hadn't seen that he'd worn her favorite shirt to work, the pale pink one. The color complemented his olive skin, dark eyes and black hair. His temples seemed grayer than she remembered. Although Maggie knew Dave felt self-conscious about his ever-growing bald spot, she thought he was gorgeous. How could she find him so painfully handsome when she was so upset with him?

Worse still, she knew she looked like hell. The heavy marine layer had blanketed everything that morning, including her hair, as she walked from her car to the office. It had exploded into even wilder curls than usual. Total clown hair day. And she knew what she looked like when she got angry; her fair complexion turned to splotchy pinks and reds. She knew bright, ugly patches spanned her forehead, surrounded her nostrils. Perfect.

Dave's eyebrows wrinkled at the sight of the forlorn dog in the cone. "Hey, Buddy," he said in a soft voice. He crouched down. "Hey," he added as he glanced at Maggie. "How's Daddy's big boy?" He scratched the spot between the dog's eyes. Kona leaned into the rubbing, then eased himself down onto the floor with a groan.

Dave shook his head. "Kona. Back in the cone. He's in one of these so often we should have named him Cone-head."

Maggie did not speak. The specimen bag hung at her elbow, under her crossed arms. The lines she'd practiced in the car vanished. Her tongue stuck to the roof of her mouth.

Dave stood up. "So, what was it this time?" he asked, pointing at the bag. "A dish cloth again? Remember the time he ate that cassette tape and we were pulling it out of his mouth like a ticker tape machine?" He waited for her reply, but she still did not say a word. "Remember?"

At five-nine, Maggie stood one inch shorter than Dave. She blinked, then drew herself up to her full height, looked into his eyes, and placed the bag on the counter, in amongst the junk mail: pizza delivery ads and beachwear catalogues, and the daily detritus of life: a dry cleaning ticket, a grocery store receipt.

Dave stared at the panties for what must have been five seconds but felt like five minutes. He licked his lips, swallowed and said, "Those are Jessica's." He paused a moment, a lifetime, and added, "Maggie, there's no easy way to say this. I'm . . .," he glanced in Kona's direction and lowered his voice, "eaving-lay . . . ou-yay."

"What?" *Did he say . . . leaving?*

Maggie fainted once as a child. She remembered the sensation. It was not her body that fell, but instead, the angry ground yanked itself out from under her and rushed up to hit her in the face. Now, it was not the ground, but her whole world that tilted on end. She grabbed at the kitchen counter and anchored herself to its cold, granite surface.

"Wait . . . What?" she said again. "You're telling me this in . . . Pig Latin?"

"I didn't want to upset Kona. His stitches—" Dave gestured toward the dog, concern etched in the lines around his eyes.

"I can't believe you. You're more worried about the goddamn dog's reaction than mine."

"I didn't want him to hurt himself. You know how he gets. And, I am concerned about you. I've been trying for weeks to think of how I could tell you that . . . that I want a divorce."

"For weeks? And this is how . . ." With a sob, she shoved the panties and junk mail onto the floor. Her head fell down onto her arms, outstretched across the counter. Kona, startled, jerked his head up.

"It's OK, boy." Dave knelt by the dog and stroked his side. He looked at Kona, and back up at Maggie. He sighed. His voice wavered. "Of course, Kona can stay here."

"Of course he will," Maggie swung on him. "And you . . . Get the hell out of here. Now."

Dave lowered his head; put his hand over his eyes.

"Jesus, Dave. You don't get to cry." She knew, then, that she was right. He was more concerned about Kona; sadder about leaving his dog than his wife.

Chapter 2: I Know How Humpty Feels

"I'll pack a bag." He walked out. He didn't look at her.

Maggie couldn't reconcile any of this in her head. The man she'd loved for twenty-two years had cheated on her; no longer loved her; was walking out on her. *Sure, things haven't been great lately, but . . . leaving? Uckin-fay eaving-lay?*

Now tears came. Maggie made no effort to wipe them away; just stood and sobbed. Kona lifted his head, again, at the strange animal sounds she made. She dropped to the floor, her head in her hands. He poked her elbow with his nose; the edge of the cone jabbed Maggie's arm. He tried to get up, but whimpered.

"No, Buddy." She pushed him back down. When he'd settled, she cupped his chin and looked into his soft, sad eyes.

From their bedroom, she heard the clattering of hangers, drawers being pulled open and thrust shut. She took several deep, shuddering breaths and wiped her face on her sleeve. She changed her mind; she didn't want Dave to leave until she had some answers.

He tossed clothes onto the bed—a few pairs of dress slacks and some shirts, his workout clothes, a stack of T-shirts.

"I'll come back later for the rest of my things." He pulled his suitcase from under the bed and shoved clothes into it. "We're going to need to talk about how we want to handle everything. I don't care about the furniture or the art or any of that, but we'll need to figure out what to do about the house."

She realized he'd given this a lot of thought. He was trying to talk future practicalities, but Maggie wanted past details.

"Who is she?"

"I met her at the gym."

"How long have you been seeing her?"

"About four months." He did not slow his packing as he spoke. She did the math: January. For New Year's, he'd resolved to go to the gym more often. Chicken or egg, she wondered. "How did it happen?"

"We were just friends at first, but then—"

"But what? You couldn't help yourself? You accidentally started having sex with her?"

"It wasn't like that. I can talk to her."

"I don't want to hear it." Maggie closed her eyes. She held up her hands as if he threw things at her, rather than into his bag.

"You asked me."

"I changed my mind."

She opened her eyes as he added his Nikes to the suitcase. The bottoms, sandy from runs on the beach, landed on top of his best slacks.

She focused on random details: a thread poked out of the shoulder seam of his dress shirt; Kona's once-stuffed Humpty Dumpty lay eviscerated next to the dresser, his braided-rope arms and legs spread-eagle; her white cardigan hung over the footboard covered in dog hair—it must have fallen on the floor and Dave had thrown it there. It registered in a dark corner of her brain that he'd pulled the bag from under the bed. Normally they stored their luggage on the top shelf of the closet. This was no spur-of-the-moment act.

"Has she been pressuring you? Did she leave her . . . underwear" (the word "panties" now too intimate, too horrible) "here on purpose? She hoped I'd find them, didn't she?"

"No, she's not like that. I'm sure it was an accident."

"What kind of slut accidentally forgets her underwear?"

"She's not—" Dave glanced at Maggie, took a deep breath and started again. "Look, she stayed here for a few days. I guess she missed that pair when she left."

Now his behavior while she was at the conference added up.

How he'd rushed her off the phone each night; his interest in finding out exactly what time she'd be home. He'd asked for her flight information, even though she'd told him she'd just catch a cab.

Maggie tried to process everything. Her husband, her best friend, was leaving. What about the house? Would she lose it too? They'd lived here twelve years. Even if she could make the payments herself, she couldn't afford to buy out his half. She felt like Kona's Humpty Dumpty, her insides ripped out.

"What does she do? How old is she?"

"Thirty-three. She teaches second grade."

"A home-wrecker influencing young minds. That's lovely."

Dave moved to his underwear drawer and threw two handfuls of briefs into his bag. He yanked the zipper shut and hefted the suitcase.

Maggie watched as if through a fogged window but still noticed he had not packed any socks. She did not intend to tell him.

Maggie followed as Dave headed for the door. He looked back at Kona and chewed his bottom lip. "Goodbye, boy." His voice cracked.

"He's not your boy anymore. Just get the hell out." She wanted to be cruel, to hurt him, but her voice wavered, knowing she couldn't cause him anything like the crushing pain she felt.

As soon as Dave drove away, Maggie called her younger sister, Shannon. Although she lived on the other side of the country in Connecticut, she was Maggie's closest confidant.

Maggie hoped Shannon would pick up instead of her husband, Michael. When she answered, the news rushed from Maggie in a hiccupping flood.

"Slow down." She heard the concern in Shannon's voice. "Dave did *what*?"

Maggie paced the house while they talked. She hashed through every detail, everything Dave had said or done, or not said or done, for the past few months. She searched for the signs she'd missed or hadn't wanted to see.

"Do you want me to come out? I can be on a plane tomorrow."

"No, Shay, you don't have to." Maggie knew it would be a huge burden for Michael if Shannon left. With his busy dental practice, he couldn't drop everything to care for Beth and James. She blew her nose on Dave's favorite T-shirt, which he'd forgotten on the floor of the bathroom. "I'll be OK. I've got Kona for company. But, there is one thing you could do. Can you call Mom and tell her?"

"Of course. Anything. You know she's going to want to talk to you though."

"I know. I'll call her. Just not today. I can't deal with her right now." She pictured Mom's face when she heard the news. It would slide into that odd combination of stretched, yet pursed, lips. Her "duck face" Maggie and Shannon called it. The look that signaled there was plenty more she wanted to say, but she locked the words behind her teeth, knowing her girls wouldn't listen.

"You want me to call Kev too?" Kevin, their younger brother, lived only ten miles from Maggie. They saw each other once or twice a month. She and Dave would invite Kevin and the Girlfriend of the Month over for barbecues or they'd catch a Padres game. Maggie felt silly having Shannon call Kevin long distance, but she didn't know what she would say. He'd rather have a tooth pulled without Novocain then have an emotional discussion, and she knew she couldn't tell him what happened without breaking down. *Would it be bad to send him an email? Or text him? "Rat bstrd lft me. Dtls l8r."*

"I guess so. I'm sorry, Shay . . ."

"You don't have to apologize. I want to do whatever I can. I'm so sorry you have to go through this. I never thought Dave could be like this."

"I know. I didn't either."

Maggie apologized again for keeping Shannon on the phone so late. They'd talked for almost two hours. Shannon didn't want to hang up, but Maggie insisted.

Her face burned from crying; her hand hurt from gripping the phone. On her way to splash water on her face, she passed their bed. The bed where he'd slept with another woman. The image that plagued her now was not of them sleeping. She shut her eyes, tried to stop the pictures from coming, but couldn't.

The tears started again as she tore the sheets off the bed. She marched outside to throw them in the trash. She could hear Mom saying, "You should wash those and donate them to Goodwill. They're practically new." It stopped her in her tracks, the bundle of bedding hovered over the can, but she got over it and dropped them in. She put clean sheets and a fresh blanket on the bed and spent hours flipping like a fish washed ashore. She finally fell asleep, where a nightmare waited.

It started as one of her typical work-stress dreams. She was late and nothing she did helped her move toward the door. It took forever to put her clothes on. The zipper on her pants broke; her blouse refused to button. She hunted for her keys and briefcase. When she finally got in the car, she realized she was supposed to be going to her wedding, not work. She couldn't get married in khakis and a blue oxford button down. She ran back inside. A gorgeous wedding dress lay on the bed, but when she put it on, the sleeve tore at the seam. She took it off and searched for a needle and thread. The only spool she could find was lavender and so thick she couldn't get it through the eye of the needle. While fighting with the thread, the phone rang. Dave. He yelled, "Why the hell aren't you here?" His words became indistinct, as if he were *barking* at her.

She woke in a sweat. Kona's soft woofs were amplified by the megaphone he wore; his feet twitched. She wondered what he chased in his dream. *Daddy?*

Should she have chased after Dave? Begged him to stay and work things out? No, she decided, it was better this way. *He* screwed up. If anyone was going to do any begging it was going to be him, along with serious amounts of crawling, crying and groveling.

Fresh, hot tears slipped onto her pillow. She put her arm over Kona and lay her head on his sturdy shoulder, careful to avoid his stitches and his cone.

"Oh, Buddy," she said. "You're a mess. *We're* a mess." She wept into the dog's soft fur.

Chapter 3: Cost-Benefit Analysis Comes Up Short

Maggie gave up at five, her usual time to get ready for work, and got out of bed. In the gray light, she shuffled to the kitchen and made coffee for two before realizing what she was doing.

Kona, who normally slept until six with Dave, lumbered down the hall. Anchoring himself on the living room rug, he stretched from the tips of his paws to his hips. He let out a protracted yawn, then sat by his bowl. One ear, not yet awake, stuck straight out, framed by the plastic cone. Maggie fed him, knowing he could manage even in the cone, which he plunked down around the bowl; it looked as if he ate under a lamp shade. Afterwards, she let him out without speaking; she wanted that craggy, first-words-of-the-day voice when she called in sick.

Thank God it was early enough that she could leave William a voicemail. She knew her boss would be annoyed, since she'd already been out most of the week for the conference. Too depressed to feel guilty, she still rationalized, *I've never taken a sick day. They owe me.*

As she poured her coffee she noticed the wall calendar. Friday, May first. May Day. *More like Mayday.* She scuffed across the living room to the sofa.

She lay around all day, alternating between crying, raging in her head at Dave, and berating herself for being so clueless. Shannon called that night and offered words of comfort while Maggie cried and raged and berated herself all over again.

The routine repeated itself over the weekend, with two additional phone calls on Saturday. The first was from her mother.

"Maggie?" Mom hated to talk to the machine. "It's your

Mother." *Yes, Mom, I recognize your voice.* "I guess you're not there. I wanted to talk to you, about Dave. Your sister said—"

She thought about not picking up, but opted to get it over with. "I'm here."

"Oh, honey, I'm so, so sorry," Mom sighed into the phone. "Such sad news. But . . ."

"But?"

"But, well, I . . . I just can't really say I'm all that surprised."

"What's that supposed to mean?"

"Well, I was there. At Christmas. I saw Dave's face every night when you called to say you'd be late again. And then you'd come home and practically never put down that Blueberry."

"It's a *Black*Berry. And we were getting ready for year end. That's an incredibly busy time. You don't understand what it's like working for a public company these days. Dave never did either. There's no room for error. The SEC—"

"Honey, this isn't time for excuses."

"Oh, but it's time to point fingers?"

"I wasn't pointing fingers. I'm just saying it's time to figure out a plan to fix things. Now, when are you going to talk to Dave?"

"I don't know. I don't have a . . . Look, I've got a migraine. I need to—"

"Wait, don't hang up. I could come out there."

"No. I mean, thanks, but it's not necessary. I'll call you later. I'm not feeling well."

"Try some saltines."

Saltines. Mom's answer to all ailments. But maybe she's right about the plan thing.

The second call was from Kevin. He left a message saying he hoped she was "doing OK" and offered to take her out that night or maybe Sunday for brunch. She didn't call back.

She stayed in her sweats all weekend. She never once looked at her BlackBerry; although she thought a lot about her job, and how much it was costing her. All for a job she didn't even really care about, a job she thought of as nothing more than a paycheck and a means to an end. An end that was supposed to involve Dave.

She'd become an accountant because it seemed perfect for her in college; she found memorizing the rules and standards easy and earned straight A's. As an added bonus, she knew decent-paying jobs would be plentiful. But she didn't *love* it. *Who could love accounting?* Sure, she had liked it at one point. Enjoyed it even. But it had been years since she looked forward to going to work. She used to like the analysis, the logic, the fact that you could work your way toward a right answer. But, as she excelled and moved up the ladder, the stress got worse and worse. She felt like a New Orleans levee and there was only so much more she could take. It had been one thing when she was only responsible for her own work, but now she had to be sure her staff were doing their jobs correctly as well. As the number of people reporting to her grew, she couldn't personally review everything. She'd tried to build an excellent management team, people she could rely on, but even the best and brightest make mistakes now and then.

It was more than that though. After Enron, the SEC instigated more and more regulations. Rules she could handle, but these were impossible to stay on top of. They filled volumes thick enough to press leaves with, and, worse yet, were sometimes contradictory. There was more gray area than the mosh pit at a Neil Diamond concert. Often, external auditors and audit committees had to be consulted. Misinterpretations of the rules, missed deadlines, an over-looked glitch in a spreadsheet—any of these could cost the company hundreds of thousands of dollars.

No, work was no longer fun. Especially when you added in the fact that she worked for William, who'd proved time and again to be a Type A, Grade A ass. On top of her other stresses, Maggie felt the need to buffer her team from him as much as possible.

It boiled down to two reasons she kept going to work every day: the money and their plan. And now the plan's blueprints had gone up in a lavender-tinted flame.

She briefly considered that maybe she needed work right now. Throw herself into long, exhausting hours; forget everything else. But that was how she'd gotten into this mess in the first place. She decided that when she went back on Monday she'd tell William that she couldn't keep such insane hours anymore. She needed her life back.

Maybe, if she did that, if she showed Dave she had changed (and once he came to his senses about this stupid slut), maybe they could work things out. She could find them a counselor.

But William's not going to be cool about this. She knew he couldn't fire her for working fewer hours. (She had a stack as thick as Kona's tail of excellent performance reviews.) But he might try to make her life miserable; drive her out of the company. What would she do then?

I'll call Janice first, to cover my bases. Maybe she'll have something. She thought back to the last time she'd used Janice's accounting placement service, when her payroll clerk quit. Janice, who knew the profession well, helped her find someone. She and Maggie had become acquainted over several phone calls and a lunch meeting.

I kinda hope she has something for me.

With that simple thought, Maggie realized she dreaded going back to work Monday. Having to smile and act like everything was normal; playing the human shield between William and the team; trying to pretend she gave a rat's ass about the acquisition they were pursuing. It all sounded so . . . tedious, meaningless.

ON THE WAY to work Monday, Maggie imagined what it would be like to quit.

Pros: show Dave I'm serious about changing; get away from William; maybe something new would get me excited about accounting again . . . doubtful, but maybe; new job means new people who don't know me and won't be gossiping about what an idiot I am for being so oblivious about my stupid, cheating bastard of a husband.

She slammed on the brakes as a traffic light changed to red. *Calm down. Think about trying to work things out with Dave. The stupid, cheating, lying bastard.* She took a few shallow breaths. *OK, move on. Cons: My staff might miss me, but they'll get over it. Probably less money. On the other hand, it would almost certainly be fewer hours. And if things don't work out with Dave, I have to get home in time to feed Kona and let him out. And I'd have my shares, so even if the pay is less, I'll still have the stock squirreled away for the future.*

The future. The F-word. She couldn't bear to think about a future without Dave. Every scene she'd imagined of the years ahead—the bike traveling business, retirement, growing old, even on her death bed, hell, especially on her death bed—every last one included Dave.

She started to cry as she turned into the parking lot. Please don't let anyone see me, she thought as she pawed through her purse for a tissue. *Oh hell . . .*

William pulled into the space facing her. She blew her nose with a loud honk and got out of the car.

He nodded in her direction and called out, "Maggie, enjoy your long weekend?"

"I was sick, William," she said as they walked toward the building.

"Oh, right, sick. Well, we saved a pile of work for you, so hope you're feeling better."

Maggie shifted her briefcase to her other hand and dug in her purse for her security card, while William told her about a meeting she'd missed regarding the potential acquisition. He stood, talking and watching as she fumbled to swipe the card and open the door. He droned on in the elevator. Maggie heard snippets, a phrase here, an expletive there. She pictured Janice's business card in her desk drawer: Covington Accounting Placement in raised bright blue type; she saw it glowing in her drawer like a beacon. She planned to call as soon as she got a chance.

FOUR HOURS LATER (having ignored the majority of the ninety-six unread emails in her inbox), Maggie had spoken to Janice, twice, as well as to the CEO of Clean N' Green, a pleasant-sounding man with a British accent named Stephen. Some quick research showed the company had launched a line of environmentally friendly cleaning products. Stephen told her they needed someone with good business acumen, but couldn't afford someone full time yet as they were only selling online. But, if things went well and they liked her (Maggie knew they would; she worked hard and knew her stuff), it could become full time later. For now, the hours were flexible and she'd get health benefits. She told Janice she'd think about it and call her back.

Backup plan in place, Maggie went into William's office and shut the door. She asked if he had a minute.

"Oh crap." He threw his pen down on the papers scattered across his desk. "Don't tell me. You're pregnant. We don't have time for you to be pregnant."

"I'm not pregnant." *Total ass. True to form.*

"Thank God. All of sudden, I thought maybe that was why you called in sick. But, come to think of it, you're too old to be getting pregnant."

"I'm only forty-one, William." Why did she never carry a tape recorder when she dealt with him? "I need to talk to you about my hours, about cutting back."

"Cutting back? You can't. This couldn't possibly come at a worse time. Uh, hello? We're going after our first acquisition. We need everyone giving a hundred and ten percent right now."

Maggie hated when William said that. It was so illogical. Why not a hundred and twenty percent? Or thirty? Why not one thousand percent? It was one of the many trite phrases he thought motivated the team, but which they all made fun of behind his back.

"Look, it's personal. I need to get my life back."

"Get your life back?" He chuckled and shook his head. "Maggie, you're just like me. People like us don't have lives. We have work."

Ohmygod, I am not like you. An image of William getting home late to his empty condo flashed into her head: she saw him on the sofa in his work clothes, eating an Angry Man dinner while watching ESPN. He often complained about his alimony and child support payments, but she'd never heard him talk about hobbies, a girlfriend, siblings, a goldfish, anything. He didn't display pictures of his kids in his office—only his Masters degree and accounting certificate. The only things he seemed interested in were his job and his nightly fix of sports news.

She thought about her own life. What did she have now besides her job and her dog? *No. I am not like him. I have hobbies. I mean, I used to have hobbies. And I have my family. I . . . have other options.* She had brought Janice's business card along for strength. She put her hand in her pocket and fingered its dog-eared corner. Her heart began to pound.

"If I can't work fewer hours, then . . . I quit."

"You're not quitting." He said it as if he'd handed out any other assignment.

"Yes, I am."

"No, I don't think you are."

"Yes, William. I am."

William stood and began to pace. "No. You can't leave now. We have an acquisition coming up. How can you do this to us? To me?" He stopped and yelled at her over the top of his desk. "After everything I've done for you. I got you that promotion!"

He's taking credit for my promotion? I am so outta here.

"Hey," he sat back down, "I know what this is about: money. I can give you a five percent raise, but no more. OK, maybe seven and a half. Eight tops."

"No, money's not the issue at all."

He put his head in his hands. "I can't believe this. I can't believe you are leaving now, when we really need you. When I need you. You women. You always know how to kick a guy where it hurts. You're just like my ex."

Ohmygod, please tell me he is not going to cry. As Maggie looked around for a box of tissues, he suddenly sat up. He dug out a legal pad and began drawing boxes connected with lines; he scribbled names into the squares. "If I move Tom into your job, and promote Yukiko into his job. Yeah, that could work."

Maggie watched him hit himself repeatedly in the head with his ballpoint pen. *Did he just go through the five stages of grief, in like one minute flat? Denial, anger, bargaining . . . I'm pretty sure they were all there. I think he's even forgotten I'm still here.*

He put pen to paper again. "Then split Yukiko's job in two and give Treasury to Carlo and Tax to . . . what's that girl's name in accounts payable?" He snapped his fingers at Maggie. "The one with the glasses and the black hair down to her butt?"

"Are you referring to Bindira?" *Oh yeah, he's in trouble without me. He doesn't even know their names.*

"That's the one!"

"She's actually in accounts receivable." *Doesn't know their positions either. And that's way too big of a jump for Bindi. And Carlo doesn't want to do treasury. Oh well, it's William's problem now.* "OK then. I'm officially giving you my two weeks' notice." She walked out.

Once on the other side of the door, she found that the hallway had become an anti-gravity chamber. Her feet seemed to barely touch the worn gray carpet as she floated back to her office.

She thought about what Dave would say when she told him she'd quit. She'd done it—the thing he'd been begging her to do for so long. And it felt good. She decided to call him.

It was lunch time, so she tried his cell since he almost never worked through lunch. Instead, he'd go out to eat with people from work or to the gym. After several rings, she heard the call connect and, then, rustling.

"This isn't the best time," Dave said, without even saying hello. A woman giggled in the background. "Is it Kona; is he recovering OK?"

"He's fine," she heard herself answer.

"Thought you might be calling about him. Uh, is this urgent, or can I call you later?"

"Don't bother."

Gravity flooded back in a rush; it pounded her against her chair. It was an effort just to get the phone in the cradle.

THE REST OF the week, Maggie went to work on autopilot. She was committed to fulfilling her notice period, but she put in half her usual hours. What could they do; fire her? Mornings, she came in late, wearing the same khakis she dragged from the heap she'd left them in the day before. At lunch time, her staff offered to take her out, but one day she used Kona's appointment to have his stitches taken out as an excuse to not go. The other days, she'd claim a doctor's or dentist's appointment. She'd drive to the beach and stare out her closed car window. She didn't want to feel the sand under her feet; be rejuvenated by the fresh sea air. She just wanted to be away from the office, away from everyone. At five each night, she headed home while her staff looked up from their desks like prisoners watching a fellow inmate being paroled.

The few minutes when she first got home were the highlight of each day. Kona, happy to see her and even happier to be free of his cone, would wiggle his way to her and cover her with kisses. After she fed him and changed into sweats, they'd squeeze onto the sofa together. She channel surfed; tennis matches, disasters, talking heads, people selling diet aids, car chases—it all passed by in a disjointed blur.

One evening she lay there, marveling at the fact that while her world imploded in slow-mo, someone somewhere was engrossed in a rerun of *The Golden Girls*. She studied Kona, sitting, staring at the door. He leaned against the sofa, near where her bare foot dangled off the edge. His nostrils flared as he let out a loud exhalation.

Wonder if he's thinking about Daddy; wondering why he doesn't come home. Kona lifted his back leg and began to lick his crotch.

"Kona, stop it. You kiss your mother with that mouth?" *Well, maybe that's not what he's thinking. But really, where is Daddy? I can't believe he didn't even fight for Kona. I mean, he wouldn't have a leg to stand on; Kona was* my *birthday present. Still, I thought he loved Kona. But then, I thought he loved me, too. What the hell do I know?* She snorted in disgust and changed the channel.

HER SECOND WEEKEND without Dave paralleled the first, but with the addition of pasta bowls full of ice cream. The phone rang Sunday and Maggie lifted her head from the sofa to hear if it was Shannon. She listened to the outgoing greeting, which she'd let revert back to the computerized "leave-a-message," after deleting the cheerful hello she and Dave had recorded.

"Mags?" Kevin again. "I know you're alive, cuz I talked to Shay. In fact, I bet you're standing right there." *Ha, shows what you know. I'm lying here.* "Could you pick up? Or call me? Thinking I'll swing by tonight with In-N-Out burgers and we can stuff our faces. Unless I hear from you, I'll assume we're on for inner-day." *How come I can train my brother about the trigger words, but not my dog?*

Maggie waited an hour, then emailed to say she'd been out walking Kona when he called and wouldn't be home tonight; thanks anyway.

MAGGIE TRIED TO finalize her remaining projects during her last week at BioHealth, but she found it hard to concentrate—or care. Wednesday afternoon she claimed a migraine and left early holding her hand to her temple for effect, thinking: *Just two more days of this place.*

She wanted to go straight home, but knew the refrigerator held nothing more than a half-eaten jar of kosher dills and some marmalade. She didn't need much. She planned to whip through the store, grab some cereal, milk and ice cream, and then zip home to her dog and pajamas. This would be so much easier if someone would just invent Human Chow, she thought as she grabbed a cart and pushed it, with its rattling wheel, into the store.

She'd already hit the dairy section and stood in the cereal aisle analyzing all the different options. Oat Squares were on sale. The cost-per-ounce was less than her favorite granola, so she opted for two boxes. She flung them into the cart, contemplating the simplicity of a product named for its main flavor and shape. She tried to think of other examples; pineapple rings came to mind. *What else? Orange Slices. Those sugarcoated jelly candies Dad used to buy.* She hadn't had one in forever. Her mouth watered as she imagined sinking her teeth into one, the burst of orange flavor, the crunch of the sugar crystals. Orange Slices would be the perfect snack for the ride home. She started to swing the cart back toward the candy, when she glanced up and saw Dave with *That Woman* at the end of the aisle. She stared in horror and fascination. She flip-flopped between the urge to run the opposite direction, or to get a good look at That Woman who stole her husband. It was like watching a slasher film. She couldn't look away, even though it made her feel sick to see Dave and the easy, comfortable way he stood with That Woman, his hand resting at the small of her back. The way he used to stand with Maggie.

They were heading down the back aisle and hadn't seen her. The lighting was bad, with only every other florescent strip light on, and Dave had his back to Maggie, but after so many years together she would have recognized the back, side, top of the man's head at fifty paces in any light. That Woman stood in front of Dave, next to the meat case, so Maggie could only see a sliver of her long wavy hair, jeans and sweater.

They had stopped in front of the bacon.

Dave doesn't eat bacon.

They had shifted now; Dave still had his back to Maggie, but she could see That Woman's face. She danced a bacon package back and forth in front of Dave, as if to entice him with it. She was not at all what Maggie had envisioned in her tortured thoughts.

When she'd seen the lavender thong panties, less substantial than the pink velvet cord Gram used to keep her reading glasses around her neck, she'd known That Woman was small. Impossibly petite. Maggie pictured a slim comic-book vixen with long legs, no hips and a flat stomach beneath Zeppelin breasts. She'd also imagined thick blond hair and too much makeup. But *This* Woman was skinny—boyishly so. Her figure looked like she could act the part of a slice of bacon in a school play on agricultural products; it didn't look like she ever ate bacon. She didn't seem to wear any makeup. She wasn't plain, but she certainly was not gorgeous. Her hair was long and thick, but frizzy and a mousy brown color. She was . . . normal.

They laughed as That Woman flipped the package over to read

to him. They huddled together as she pointed at the words, and Dave appeared to read along.

He won't eat that. It has too many nitrates.

Dave took the package out of That Woman's hand and tossed it in the cart. She giggled, bumped him with her twelve-year-old boy's hip, and they moved on.

Maggie stood rooted to the spot. Her brain shouted: *Dave doesn't eat bacon.* But her gut whispered: *He's not coming back.*

She drove home, barely noticing where she was going. She shoved the groceries into the fridge, still in the canvas bag, even the cereal. Her wedding band caught her eye. She fingered it with her right thumb and index finger. She yanked it off and pulled open the junk drawer. She dropped the ring into an old Altoids tin that still smelled of mint and held a few paperclips. She slammed the drawer shut.

She went to her closet and grabbed a laundry basket. Methodically, she scoured every room looking for things Dave had been too forgetful or too lazy to take. The shelves under the TV yielded a testosterone-fest of DVDs; the office closet coughed up a collection of musty college texts; his half of the bathroom cupboard held an assortment of near-empty toiletries. She pulled photographs off the walls and out of bookcases.

In their room, she stopped in front of the large, abstract painting over the bed: a stylized seascape they'd bought years ago on a trip to Maine. One of Maggie's favorite vacation pastimes was wandering local galleries looking for a special keepsake. This particular piece had been their biggest splurge. Sometimes they would lie in bed and tilt their heads up to look at it, especially if one of them had been through a particularly bad day. They'd snuggle together and remember their "Happy Place" where they'd taken long walks on the windswept beaches. It hurt to look at it now. She thought about taking it down. But she thought the giant empty space on the wall would only make her feel worse; remind her of the gaping hole in her life.

She turned away from it and was confronted by the eight-by-ten from their wedding, hanging on the opposite wall. She pulled it down and studied it. They were so young. Dave's jet black hair hid his ears; her auburn curls cascaded over her shoulders. They were so happy. When a fat tear splattered on the glass, she dropped the picture into her collection basket, and then bundled all of it into bags in the garage. She resisted the temptation to set the lot of it on fire and decided that, for now, just having it out of the house would have to do.

Back inside, she went into the office and turned on the computer. She plugged in her iPod, found "their" song, *I Got You Babe*, and deleted it. *What a stupid song.* But at least it was the UB40 and Chrissie Hynde version; much cooler than the original by Sonny & Cher. And it had seemed appropriate at the time. They were young and didn't know. And they couldn't pay the rent. And they did grow. Apart.

Maggie sighed. *Need to pull myself together. I've got shit to do. I've gotta cancel the cleaning service. Need to save money and I'll have time to do it myself now, anyway. And I need a lawyer, a real estate agent . . . a new life. What do I look under in the Yellow Pages for* that*?*

HER LAST DAY at BioHealth, Maggie made it through her goodbye party with only a few tears as she hugged the members of her team. She tried to be oh-so-professional while shaking William's hand. *Never know when you might need a reference. Don't burn those bridges. Fight those pyro desires . . .* She gritted her teeth and thanked him for "everything."

She walked out of the building for the last time carrying the paltry remains of all the time, energy, and life blood she'd put into the place. It amounted to a wedge of carrot cake wrapped in foil and a cardboard box of crap: a mug, ceramic coaster, and baseball hat, all with the BioHealth logo; a framed photo of her staff hamming it up at the Christmas party; and an assortment of goofy "from all of us" birthday cards that marked the passing years she'd spent there.

She sat in her car, unsure what she was feeling. Regret? Excitement? Relief?

God, I hope I'm doing the right thing. This seemed like a great idea when I thought Dave might come back. But now, I'm going to have all this free time . . . and no one to spend it with. She looked back at the building as she started the ignition. *No. It's better this way. That job was sucking the life out of me. I'm going to make a new life now. Right?* She watched the lights of the office recede in her rearview mirror as she drove away.

On the way home, Maggie replayed William's "greatest hits" of irritating moments, to reassure herself she was doing the right thing. She snapped out of it when she saw a glowing Safeway sign and remembered that after seeing Dave at the grocery store she'd left without getting the last, yet most important, item on her list. She couldn't get through the coming weekend without it: ice cream.

After picking up several pints of her favorites, an idea struck her. She strode to the meat section and grabbed a package of thick center-cut bacon. She hadn't bought bacon in seventeen years because Dave had stopped eating it shortly after they got married. She went home and made herself a gigantic BLT for dinner. She even cooked two slices for Kona.

Damn Dave. Poor dog's never even tasted bacon.

Chapter 4: Is There Nothing You Won't Eat?

Maggie spent most of Sunday morning lying on her favorite roost, the sofa. It beat being upright and trumped the bed, where she felt the keen absence of Dave from "his side." She could lie still on the couch for hours. Although sometimes she tried different positions, to break things up: feet on the arm, feet off the edge, face down, fetal, laid-to-rest.

What if I lay here and never got up? She stared at the ceiling, hands folded on her chest. *Pros: Dave would feel guilty when he saw my name in the obits.* He'd *have to deal with selling the house. It's one way out of accounting . . .*

Kona ambled over and snuffled her ear.

Cons: Dave would get Kona. It might be a while before anyone found me. Would Kona eat my dead body?

"Would you, Kona? Would you eat your momma?"

He trotted away and rummaged in his toy basket. He came back with his ball. She rested her hand on his head, said "Sorry, Buddy," and rolled over to face the back of the couch. She was nodding off when the phone rang.

"Mags, come on, pick up." Kevin. "Please? OK, that's it. I'm coming over there."

She'd better answer. Better to talk to him than have company. "Sorry, I was outside."

"Hey, you're there. Good. I, uh, wanted to see how you're doing." He paused and when she didn't say anything, went on. "I've got Padres tickets for this afternoon. I know it's kinda last minute, but what do you say? Come have a dog and a beer with me?"

"I'm not feeling too good. I was just taking a nap."

"Oh, OK. Well, maybe we could go out to dinner this week?"

"I'm starting a new job, so . . ." She trailed off. She didn't want to lie outright and say she'd be busy. She was starting a new job—but not for two weeks. He didn't need to know Clean N' Green asked her to start June first. "I'll call you when things are calmer. But, thanks."

It was sweet of him, but she didn't want to go. Didn't want to get dressed, wash her hair, abandon her slippers. Didn't want to chat or pretend things were normal. And she couldn't really talk to him. Not at a ballgame. And not without crying.

Maggie and Shannon had analyzed their brother many times, mainly trying to figure out why he never stayed with the women he dated. They hadn't come up with an answer. But one thing that was easy to pinpoint was the reason for his extreme discomfort around crying women.

When Dad had died so young of a heart attack (Maggie always thought of it as a "heart ambush," since they might have seen an attack coming), she'd been a freshman, living in the dorms at San Diego State, two hours away from home in L.A. Shannon had been spending her last semester of high school in Paris on exchange. She'd come home for two weeks but they'd all decided that Dad would want her to go back. That meant Kevin, only thirteen, was left home alone with Mom. They knew he'd tried to help, but she was devastated. How could she not be? And Kevin was just a kid, ill-equipped to deal with their mother's grief. He'd seen enough of a woman's tears to float an armada; enough to last his lifetime.

Maggie remembered a time he showed up for dinner without his latest girlfriend.

"Where's Cindy?" she'd asked.

"We went to a matinee of *Happy Gilmore*. And she cried."

"She cried at an Adam Sandler movie?"

"Yeah. You know the part where his dead mentor, the alligator and Abe Lincoln all wave at him from the beyond? She said it was 'so touching.' I took her home and broke up with her."

As Maggie hung up, she thought, that's why he thought of

baseball; there's no crying at Adam Sandler movies and there's no crying at ballgames.

She took advantage of her momentum and gathered a load of whites. She couldn't put it off, having pulled on her last clean pair of underwear that morning.

Something caught her eye as she shoved clothes in the machine. A dress sock of Dave's hid between the washer and dryer. Even after her purging, reminders of him lurked everywhere: the switch plate in their bathroom, cracked because he'd tightened it too hard; their dark leather sofa (she'd wanted the sage green velvety one, but Dave hated it; she'd had to settle for velvet throw pillows); the monolithic TV in their bedroom (she'd have let him take it if she hadn't been so angry; she planned to put it on craigslist). Maybe it wouldn't be so bad to sell the house; escape the memories. Easier though to just trade places with that sock; crawl into a dark nook.

I'm reduced to feeling jealous of a sock.

She threw it in the trash and started the washer. She leaned against the cool metal machine, gathering energy for the trek back to the sofa. Kona peeked around the corner with his favorite stuffed rabbit in his mouth, eyes wide with the hope of a game. The corners of Maggie's mouth flitted upward, a brief happy blip on the radar of her face.

She squatted down and he offered her the rabbit. She tugged at it gently. "I'm sorry I've been ignoring you, Buddy. How about a walk?"

His ears perked up. She didn't feel like it—out the window to the west San Diego's "May gray" afternoon clouds rolled in off the ocean, matching her mood—but she felt guilty. Kona would race around the yard now and then, but mostly he moped around the house with her.

Although it was cloudy in the west, the sun still shone in the neighborhood. She hunted for her sunglasses, but couldn't find them. An old pair would have to do. She grabbed her Padres cap off the shelf of the closet, pulled it low, and they headed out.

She heard kids screaming "not it!" in a backyard; the whir of a lawnmower. The cut-grass scent wafted toward them. Maggie normally loved this type of quintessential spring Sunday. But today she searched the western sky, ready for the clouds to smother everything in a damp blanket.

As they walked past the oleanders bordering his property, Maggie saw her neighbor, an old man in a seersucker shirt and plaid Bermudas, stop short with his mower, watching them.

"Hello Mr. Gunderson. Hello, Pip." She greeted the poodle who sashayed over and rubbed noses with Kona through the fence.

Mr. Gunderson opened his mouth. He seemed flustered. Was it possible he knew about Dave, was he going to say something?

I don't want to talk to this man about my personal life. She tugged at Kona's collar, but he sniffed furiously at the fence post. *Damn dog. Knew we should've stayed home.* An abundance of pee-mail must have built up in his absence from his route, and Kona seemed determined to catch up on all of it.

"You, um . . ." Mr. Gunderson pointed at her, then moved his hand, with its gnarled tree root fingers, to his straw hat and tipped it at her. "Enjoy your walk."

Kona added a reply to the post and pulled Maggie in search of further correspondence.

Odd. Thought he was going to say something more.

The Freedmans, who lived across from her, drove past in their minivan. Mrs. Freedman pointed and her husband turned to look at Maggie.

What the heck? She walked behind Kona, distracted. *Wait a minute; I bet they all know. They must have seen That Woman coming and going while I was away.* Maggie imagined that skinny stick, mincing up to the door in a mini skirt and cropped T-shirt that read, "I'm just here for the adultery." *For God's sake, Dave, the neighbors knew before I did! I bet they've all been gossiping about what a fool I am.*

Once home, Kona headed to his water bowl; Maggie went to the powder room to wash her hands. In the mirror, she found her missing glasses. She must have set them on top of her cap last time, then pulled off the hat, along with her shades, and tossed it in the closet. Her reflection showed a pair of sunglasses over her eyes, while a second pair sat on the brim of her hat.

Ohmygod. That's what Mr. G. was gonna say; that's why the Freedmans pointed. They weren't feeling sorry for you or gossiping, you idiot. She laughed at her ridiculous image for a second, then watched her face crumple into sobs, realizing it didn't matter whether the neighbors knew or not. The truth was that *she* knew what had gone on in her house.

Repulsed by the pathetic figure in the glass, she snapped out of her crying jag faster than usual. She resolved the next time she started to cry to go stand in front of the mirror.

MONDAY MORNING, HER first official day without a job, Maggie woke at five. She wondered why the alarm hadn't gone off; then remembered she hadn't set it. Didn't her body know she had nowhere to go? No one waiting for her? She'd hoped to sleep through most of the morning, but now, here she was awake. And aware that no one was concerned with her whereabouts. She wanted to go back to sleep, but knew there'd be no returning to sweet unconsciousness without the siren song of some serious sedatives.

Who am I kidding? I don't have any sedatives, any drugs in the house. She'd never taken recreational drugs. She thought about what an odd phrase that was. *What exactly are you supposed to be trying to "re-create" while on these drugs. Oh, right, happier times, I suppose.*

She didn't even have any medicinal drugs in the house, at least, nothing stronger than ibuprofen. *Why aren't I taking Ambien like everyone else . . . or . . . what's that other one? The one with that creepy talking beaver in the ads?* Those ads that were so pervasive she sometimes felt like the only non-medicated person in America.

But, there was alcohol in the house, definitely a drug, a sedative. Was she desperate enough to have a drink—at five a.m.? She got up and trudged to the kitchen. Kona followed. He sat next to her, looking sleepy-eyed, as she opened the liquor cabinet and studied the bottles of clear and amber liquids for a full minute. Mandarin-flavored vodka stared back. *Hmmm. I could add OJ. That would make it slightly less pathetic. If I had some tomato juice and Worcestershire, I could make a Bloody Mary. Perfectly acceptable to drink a Bloody Mary in the morning. Or champagne. People drink champagne in the morning.* But that had too much of an air of celebration. She didn't need a glass of bubbly irony. She needed hard oblivion.

"Fuck it."

She grabbed the bottle of silver tequila they'd bought on their anniversary trip to Cancun two years ago. It was almost empty. She yanked the cork out with her teeth, and looked down at Kona. His ears stuck out in what Dave had always called his "bat-wing look;" his I-just-got-up-and-can't-do-a-thing-with-my-ears look.

"What are you staring at?" she said to him, then tossed the last of the clear liquid down her throat. It burned like drinking Vicks VapoRub. She shuddered and they trooped back to bed. She slept until eight and didn't get out of bed again until 9:45.

"HI SWEETIE . . . I guess you're not there, so—"

Maggie picked up. She hadn't talked to her grandmother since Dave left; hadn't had the energy. But when she heard her on the answering machine, she realized what a mistake it had been. Gram's voice wrapped around her like a cozy quilt. Maggie apologized for not calling.

"Darling, how can I get along without my weekly call from my favorite granddaughter?"

"I'm sure Shay's been calling you every week like always." It felt good to joke with Gram. Maggie had no doubt Gram went through the same "favorite granddaughter" routine with Shannon (and maybe her cousins too, although, really, she and Shay had to be the true favorites). "Things have been . . . kind of crazy around here."

"I know, sweetie; your mom told me." *Great. Mom's version.* As if reading her mind, Gram added, "I also talked to Shannon, of course." *Oh, good.* "I'm worried about you."

"I'm OK." The OK squeaked out. For about the hundredth time since Dave left, tears stung the backs of her eyes. *If I made myself really dehydrated, would it stop these damn tears?*

"I know you've hit a bad patch. You need a break; why not

come to Jacksonville?"

"I don't know . . ." The thought of running away for a while tempted her. She still had ten days before work started. But visiting Gram meant seeing Mom. *No thanks. I need a vacation, not The Inquisition.* "I'd love to go, but I'm starting my new job soon, so it's not great timing."

"No pressure, dear. I just thought I'd suggest it."

"I'll come soon." She should go, she thought. At eighty-eight, Gram wasn't going to be around forever. "Maybe you could come see me. We could have a lot of fun, just us two single ladies." She'd said it. She'd called herself single. It was like getting a job at a high-powered office and having to suddenly wear dressy heels again. It might be the way things had to be, but it was damn uncomfortable and going to take some getting used to.

"Speak for yourself."

Had her grandmother giggled? "Do you have news? Do you have a . . . boyfriend?"

"At eighty-three you can hardly call him a boy." She chuckled. "I prefer to call him my gentleman friend."

"Wow, a younger man. Way to go, Gram." Competition was fierce at the assisted living complex; Gram had told her once that single octogenarian males were as "scarce as people in line for seconds on 'tuna surprise' night at the cafeteria." Yet Gram had managed to find one. Maggie wasn't surprised. "I didn't know you were looking."

"I wasn't! You know it was hard for me when your grandpa passed. After sixty-five years with one man, you get pretty set in your ways. And I've got my friends and classes here at the center, and, of course, I see your mother several times a week. I thought my life was very full."

"So, what happened? How did you meet?"

"Well, he moved in on my floor recently, and we started chatting one day waiting for the elevator. He asked for some cooking advice. Poor dear. His wife passed away last year, and I guess she was a wonderful cook, so he never learned. He was so funny. He told me he made split pea soup, and spent forever slicing the peas in half! He really had me laughing, so when we got to the bottom floor, I asked him to go for a cup of coffee."

"You picked up a man you just met?" Maggie pretended to be shocked.

"At my age, nobody's 'picking up' anything or anybody. I'm lucky if I can pick up my dirty laundry."

Maggie laughed. "Is he cute?"

Gram half-whispered, "Let's just say he can hang his cane on my bed post any time."

"You're so bad. Tell me everything. What's his name?"

"Humphrey. Isn't that adorable? Your Great Aunt Lyda used to have a basset hound named Humphrey, and my Humphrey sort of reminds me of him. That dog was so regal; high forehead, intelligent eyes. And, well, I have to admit, my Humphrey's ears are rather long. But if that isn't the pot calling the kettle black. My ears are in some sort of crazy race with my breasts to see which can hit my knees first."

Maggie laughed again. It felt good.

"He's a snappy dresser too. I love a man in a sweater vest. Oh, there's the door; hold on."

Maggie listened to muffled noises; then heard the phone being picked up.

"Hello, Maggie."

"Mom." Maggie got a small jolt, hearing her mother's voice.

"Grandma said it was you. Didn't you get my messages? I called twice."

"My answering machine's acting up." Although she'd generally been screening her calls, Mom had caught her off guard one night when she'd been expecting Shannon. Mom had hounded her some more about working it out with Dave and ended the call with an exasperated, "Well, at least I guess it's a good thing you two never did give me a grandbaby." After that, Maggie stuck strictly to her screening rule.

"We didn't finish our conversation last time. Have you talked to

David?"

Here we go again. "Briefly. I called and told him it's going to be a while before I'm ready to put the house on the market. There's a ton of stuff to do to get it ready."

"You're selling the house? Aren't you going to even try to work things out? You can't throw away all those years together. Marriage isn't always easy; it takes work sometimes."

"I know that."

"Marriage is a sacred vow." *Oh hell, the "sacred vow" guilt trip.* After doing hard time, serving a full twelve-year term in Catholic school, Maggie'd walked free of her religion. But not Mom. She went to church on Sundays and every day during Lent. "You two stood in front of the priest, God, your family and friends, and swore you'd stay together through the good and bad."

Figures Mom would list the priest first, even before God.

"Yes, Mom, I remember. I'm sure Father Tim would be appalled. But Dave's living with his girlfriend now. I'm pretty sure she wouldn't want me talking to him."

"I don't care what she wants." Mom's voice tightened. Maggie could *hear* her lips sliding into duck face formation.

"I don't either. I was being sarcastic."

"This is no time for jokes. This is the time to think about how to work things out."

Maggie heard the mailman jiggle the gate latch. Kona barked like a repeating rifle and beat his paws on the window. This was the escape hatch she needed.

"Someone's at the door. Gotta go. Tell Gram I said goodbye."

I wonder if I could train him to go nuts like that on command. Could come in handy. She went to the kitchen for a biscuit.

"Kona, treat. Come here, you brave guard dog, you."

Kona barked one last time and raced to the kitchen for his reward.

IF I WON the lottery, I wouldn't have to go back to work, Maggie thought from her prone position on the sofa. Only a handful of days remained of her stint as an unemployed person. She would miss staying in her pajamas all day. *But if I'm going to win the lottery, I have to play the lottery. And that means getting up and going to the store.*

She thought about walking Kona to the store, but that exceeded her ambitions. It was over two miles. She did need to walk him though. He'd become impatient with the infrequent exercise and developed the habit of sitting at the front door and whining. He sat there now, head tossed back in full pathetic cry.

"What have you got to whine about? You totally won the doggie Lotto. I'm the one with something to whine about around here." She decided to give it a try. "Hhyyymmm."

Kona stopped and tilted his head. He walked toward her.

She whined again. "Hhyyymmm." He wagged his tail and climbed up with her. "Can't beat 'em, join 'em? That your plan?" He sat on her chest. "Oooof. OK. Get off. We'll go for a walk."

Hearing the last word, he jumped down and ran to the door, barking. His back end wagged. Maggie decided they'd go to the park. If she felt up to it, they'd swing by and get a lottery ticket on the way home. "OK, in the car, Buddy."

The park smelled of wet grass. The morning May gray hadn't burned off yet, but Maggie still hid behind her sunglasses. Kona dragged her to the edge of the park, where he sniffed determinedly at one particular bush. She stretched his leash to its maximum length and flopped down on a bench to wait, her back to him.

Several mothers shadowed their toddlers playing on the swings or climbing on the green sea monster that bobbed up and down out of the sand. Maggie was vaguely aware of the laughter of the children as she pondered her growing to-do list for putting the house on the market. On top of the routine cleaning and gardening, there were dozens of repairs to make: the dining room ceiling fan wasn't working, the office needed repainting, the—

"Aaaagggghhhhhh!"

The piercing scream came from a little girl in off-kilter pigtails, who pointed at Kona. He was devouring something. He had that "Mine!" stance, hunched over a small, gray blob. She ran back to him and heard furious crunching.

"Drop it!" She tugged his leash. He ignored her, lunged at the last of whatever it was and, showing his lupine ancestry, wolfed it down. Maggie turned back to the playground.

A woman scooped up the crying girl and stroked her hair. "Your dog flushed a baby ground squirrel out of its nest, and ate it! In front of the kids!"

"Oh, gosh, I'm so sorry. He's never done anything like that before." Kona had eaten many things, but never something living. Well, maybe a few spiders and some moths, and a bee once, but never a . . . mammal. She dragged him back towards the car. He twisted and bucked, trying to get back at what was left of the squirrel's nest. It was like walking a marlin. Maggie began to sweat as everyone watched her trying to reel in her beast.

"Kona, how could you?" She scolded him and pointed at the back seat. "Get in." He hopped into the Honda, licking his chops. *I just know this is coming back to haunt me. What goes down, usually comes up—or ends up with a trip to the vet.*

SURE ENOUGH, THE next morning, Maggie was cleaning up bits of dead baby squirrel in the pre-dawn light. "Couldn't you at least give me some warning so I could put you outside?" She glared at Kona, who surveyed the action and appeared to grin at her.

She turned her head away and, using Dave's old beach towel, swiped at the dark lumps on the rug. There was another small spot on the hardwood floor. *Thank God it's too dark in here to really see what I'm doing.* She glanced to see if she'd gotten all the . . . pieces and felt her gag reflexes kick in. When the gagging passed, the tears came. Dave had always cleaned up after Kona because Maggie couldn't stomach it. *I'm on my own now when it comes to cleaning up dead baby squirrel bits.*

Afterwards, Maggie went back to bed, but couldn't sleep. She kept thinking about being on her own. She also thought about the liquor cabinet. The tequila had worked pretty well before, and she'd managed to turn off her brain and get a few more hours sleep. In fact, it also worked well on several other mornings, when she woke before dawn and her mind wouldn't stop asking the same annoying questions over and over—like, how are we going to get through the next days, weeks, months? Now she knew how to make the little hamster wheel in her brain stop spinning.

She got up and went out to the cupboard for the big bottle of Cuervo. It smelled like fermented green olives. She hated green olives. She plugged her nose and drank a shot like it was medicine. It tasted bitter; she shivered as it burned a path down her throat. She wondered how something that tasted this nasty alone could be so delicious when you added margarita mix or lime juice. She thought about how Dave loved margaritas, his favorite drink. They'd even served them at their wedding reception, the bartender squeezing the limes fresh. Even with the nasty taste, a second shot didn't seem like a half-bad idea just now. She shuddered again.

"Take that, brain cells."

She went back to bed and crawled in. She realized her feet were cold and reached into her nightstand drawer for socks. She drifted toward sleep as Kona came in. His stomach was empty from earlier events, and he sat next to the bed and whined.

"Go away." He whined louder. "Go *away*, Kona."

He emitted a frustrated half-sigh, half-yowl.

"Oh, all right, you beast. If I feed you, will you leave me alone? God, you're a pain." She threw off the covers and stood up. "Whoa." She'd underestimated the effect of two shots on her empty stomach. Once back on solid legs, she stomped down the hall to get Kona's breakfast. She hit the damp hardwood floor at just the right speed and angle with her cotton-covered heel. Her left leg flew up, and she landed with a sharp pain on her right side, her foot turned under her.

"Shit!" She lay back, panting and feeling even woozier than before.

Kona stood over her, apparently wondering what fun new game this was.

"This is your fault. Did you have to wake me up so damn early? Did you have to eat that poor baby squirrel?" Kona crouched and backed away as she yelled at him, which made her feel even worse. She'd foolishly thought that was not possible. "Did your dad have to leave us?" She started to cry. *This is all his fault.*

THAT NIGHT ON the phone with Shay, after telling her about the squirrel murder and gruesome clean-up that followed, she said, "On top of that, I slipped on the wet floor and fell and sprained my ankle." Kona slept on the sofa next to her; she grabbed his ear and squeezed it.

"Yikes. You've got to be more careful. What if you hit your head when you fell?"

"You mean now that I live alone? Who would find me if I cracked my head open? How long would I lay here? Trust me, I've thought about that. God, I'm so pathetic."

"No, you're not. Did you get an x-ray?"

"It's just a sprain. It'll be fine in a few days. I'm icing it." She looked at her ankle, propped up on the coffee table with a bag of frozen peas over it. She leaned forward and rolled her glass of vodka and orange juice back and forth against the cold bag of peas. "I'm taking something for the pain." She swallowed the last of the drink.

"Well, you need to be more careful."

"I am. It's just the floor was wet, and it was still kinda dark, and I was a little tipsy."

"I thought you said this was at like five this morning?"

"I meant . . . light-headed."

"You said tipsy. Were you drinking?"

"No . . ." It came out like a question. *God, I'm a terrible liar. But, really, I wasn't drinking . . . at that particular moment.*

"Had you been drinking *earlier*?"

When did Shannon start to sound like Mom? "Maybe. A little. Just to get back to sleep."

"Mags, if you're not sleeping, you need to go to the doctor. Get some proper sleeping pills. And take them *at night*. And, maybe you need something . . . for depression."

"No. I'm fine. I don't need to go to the doctor. I don't need any pills. I just drank a couple of mornings, just to get back to sleep. To get me over the hump."

"I could come out there for a few days, a week."

"I don't need you to come out here."

"I'm worried about you. You don't sound like yourself."

"You don't sound like yourself either. You sound like Mom."

Maggie heard a sharp intake of breath. "I'm just trying to help," Shannon said. She sounded close to tears.

"I don't need any help. I'm fine. I can take care of myself."

"I know you can. I just thought maybe you could use some company."

"I've got Kona. When he's not being bad, he's good company. Really, we're . . . OK. I've gotta go. I'll talk to you later." She hung up and Kona squirmed, still half asleep. He pushed against her to make more room for himself on the sofa.

Although some of us are more OK than others.

Chapter 5: Little Brother, Big Favor

The next day, the last Saturday in May, Maggie opened the door to find Kevin on her porch, suitcase in hand. He wore baggy, faded blue shorts and a T-shirt that read, "Golf Naked."

"Annie and I broke up. And I'm sorta between jobs right now." He ran a hand through his beachy-blond hair. He needed a haircut and a shave.

"That sucks about Annie." Maggie was not surprised about the job (Kevin moved from one company to another), but she was surprised about Annie, who'd been Girlfriend of the Month for a record nine months. They'd even moved in together. Maggie learned early on not to get attached to Kevin's girlfriends, but at thirty-six, she thought he might finally settle down, and Annie seemed perfect for him. She knew better than to ask what happened, though. Kevin turned stone deaf when asked about his personal life. "But I kinda wish you'd called first."

Kona ran to greet Kevin, who thumped the dog on the side like a watermelon. Kona maneuvered his behind under Kevin's hand. Kevin obliged, scratching the spot where tail met dog until Kona's legs sank beneath him and he sat on Kevin's foot.

"Somebody's gained a few pounds," he said, looking up at her.

He better be talking about the dog, Maggie thought as her eyes narrowed.

"Can I crash here?" He strode through the door and added, "You look like hell."

Well, I feel like shit, so I guess that's a step up.

"Thanks. Come on in," she said to his back as he dropped his bag. He bent his tall frame and shuffled the meager contents of her fridge with his praying mantis arms. "Make yourself at home." She tried to sound sarcastic, uninviting; maybe he'd get the hint and leave.

He grabbed the orange juice and took a swig. "Geez Mags, you're still in your PJs? It's almost eleven."

"I'll have you know I was up really early this morning, but then . . . I went back to bed."

He studied her with a look she couldn't read, as she pushed a tangle of auburn curls out of her eyes. She knew he was right; she looked like crap. Her roots, streaked with gray, cried out for their usual touchup of Midnight Mahogany. Bags, large enough to exceed the carry-on limit, drooped beneath her eyes. She wore a stain (chocolate sauce?) like a brooch on her oversized T-shirt. Her lower legs stuck out of her capri-length pajama bottoms like strawberry-blonde Chia Pets. The ace bandage wrapped around her ankle hung loose. The house fared no better. It smelled of too few windows opened and too many bags of microwave popcorn consumed. Newspapers and junk mail hid the top of the dining room table; dirty dishes, mainly ice cream and cereal bowls, covered the kitchen counters; and crumpled tissues, like autumn leaves, blanketed the floor around the couch.

At least Mom couldn't drop by. And friends weren't an issue either. Her best friend had moved to Dallas two years ago and they'd been reduced to infrequent emails. As for the rest, she'd been so out of touch (canceling lunch, happy hour and dinner invites at the last minute because of work), that she figured they'd given up on her. Which was fine. She didn't feel like talking to anyone. In fact, she'd been thinking about going to a hotel to get one of those Do Not Disturb signs to hang on her front door. Better yet, get two and wear them like earrings.

Yet, here was her brother, the only person she knew who would drop by unannounced, wanting to be her roomie. Except for two men named Ben & Jerry, she did not want a roommate. But she could never say no to Kevin, whom she always thought of as her "little" brother, even though at six-three he'd towered over her since his growth spurt at age sixteen.

He'd just better not expect me to feed him.

"You eat eakfast-bray yet?" he asked, still hanging onto the fridge door.

She picked up a box of cereal lying on the counter under a half-eaten bag of stale popcorn and said, "You're looking at it." She grabbed a handful and stuffed it into her mouth.

"Why don't you make some of those yummy waffles? Or, no, wait, how about one of your awesome smoothies?"

The nerve. "I don't think so," she said. "I'm out of flour and the milk's questionable at best. Go ahead and take the spare room. I'm going back to bed."

She walked out, weighing the pros and cons of having him there. *Cons: have to make civil conversation. Or not. Need to clean the house. Or not. Have to stop lying around on the sofa all the time. Or not. Pros: he can pick up any dead baby squirrel bits.*

MONDAY WHEN MAGGIE came home from Clean N' Green, which had been a typical first day of filling out forms, learning names, and figuring out where the coffee and bathrooms were, she was shocked to find that Kevin had straightened up and washed the dishes.

He wasn't there, but breezed through the door a few minutes later with a pizza and Caesar salad. They spent the evening eating pizza, drinking beer and watching the Padres lose to the Astros. Other than, "Another beer?" and comments on the pitching, they didn't speak much.

At ten, Maggie yawned and said, "Well, some of us have to work tomorrow." As she and Kona got up to head down the hall to bed, she added, "Thanks for dinner."

"No prob. Hey, tomorrow I'm golfing with my buddy, but after that, I thought I'd try to fix your ceiling fan. I noticed it's not working."

"That'd be great. Thanks. Again."

Two days later, Maggie had the day off. She'd planned to sleep late, but awoke at five. She groaned at the glowing green numbers on her clock. She lay there, trying to ignore the broken record asking her what she was going to do with her life now. She thought about sneaking out to the liquor cabinet. *I don't have to sneak. This is my damn house.*

She got up and walked down the hall. There at the bar, reading the paper, sat Kevin.

"Hey, you're up. Good. I was about to make some coffee but didn't want to wake you. You sit. I'll make pancakes."

She sat and stared at him as he whipped up a stack of fluffy pancakes. *I don't feel like pancakes at five a.m. It's too early to eat. Oh . . . but not too early to drink? Just eat the damn pancakes.* She dutifully cleaned the plate he set in front of her. Then, full, went back to bed and slept for three more hours.

When she finally got up, he was gone. She decided to go grocery shopping and make chicken piccata for dinner. That afternoon, she called Shannon while she cooked and apologized for accusing her of sounding like Mom the last time they spoke. Shannon said it was "low," but forgave her. Kevin came in with a six pack while she was on the phone. He took over cooking the chicken and also made a salad.

As they sat down to eat, he handed her a flyer for a yoga class at the neighborhood rec center. He said he'd seen it at the grocery store, while picking up the beer.

"You should go. You might like it," he said. She dismissed him, but he continued on, his mouth half full. "Annie used to drag me along to her class sometimes. It was kinda cool."

"I dunno," she said. She'd wanted to try yoga, which seemed to be the perfect combination of relaxation and exercise. Two birds with one stone; efficient. But, after twenty-two years with a man she'd shared most of her hobbies with, it had been a long time since she tried something new on her own. "I'll go if you'll come with me."

"Can't. Tuesdays are poker night."

"I don't really wanna go by myself."

"What are you, twelve? I double-dog dare you to go."

"OK. I'll try it."

And so, the following Tuesday, she found herself practically being pushed out the door, with a purple rubber mat in hand. Kevin told her he'd found it in his trunk; Annie must have left it behind.

When she walked into the hall at the rec center, she considered pretending she was in the wrong room. Lean, lithe, confident-looking people, mostly women, filled the room. They sat cross-legged on their mats and watched the instructor, waiting for class to start. Maggie felt like everyone was looking at her; the large pendant lamps felt like spotlights. Noticing they all wore earth-toned halter tops and yoga pants, Maggie played with the hem of her cotton gym shorts and tied a knot in the extra-large T-shirt she'd pulled on over her jog-bra. *They should tell you what to wear, and where to shop for this stuff, on the stupid flyer.*

Maggie moved to the back. She bumbled through the opening moves, hoping no one noticed, but when they progressed to the more challenging poses, they must have seen the instructor correcting her posture: helping her place her feet just so or her knee at the proper angle. She glanced at the stretching jungle cats that surrounded her and felt like a three-toed sloth.

God, this is hard. She'd expected a lot of gentle movement and deep breathing, but her T-shirt stuck to her sweaty back. Her arms shook while she held some of the poses. An unbelievable cramp gnawed at her right buttock. *I swear this is never going to end.*

The woman in front of Maggie, who looked to be in her late forties, had a gorgeous, athletic figure. *Didn't expect to see Madonna here. What a hard body. Wonder if that's just from yoga?* Madonna's forehead touched her shin when they did the forward bends. Maggie rested her head on a blue foam block the instructor gave her, stood up on end the long way. For the seated poses, Madonna folded herself along the length of her slim leg and clasped her hands beyond her foot; her white-blond hair, silky and fine as a doll's, fell along her cheek. Maggie held a strap wrapped around her arch; wisps of hair that had flown free from her lopsided ponytail snaked across her face.

The last part made the rest worthwhile, though. They hugged

their knees to their chests, then stretched out on the floor.

"These final poses will guide you to deep relaxation," the instructor said. "Breathe deeply; focus on relaxing each part of your body. Your hairline, your forehead. Feel the skin of your face relax. Let your eyes descend into their sockets." The instructor's voice soothed her, like tea and honey on a sore throat. This part she could do! She actually felt her face relax, her ears and cheeks slid toward the floor; her eyes dropped into their sockets. *Wow. Who even knew that was possible?* Her forehead unfurrowed for the first time in weeks.

After class, as Maggie rolled up her mat, Madonna whispered, "It gets easier. See you next week."

When she got home, she was surprised to find Kevin, lounging on the couch with Kona, watching baseball. Kona climbed over Kevin and ran to greet her.

"I thought this was poker night."

"Oh, yeah. Uh, it got cancelled. How was class?"

"OK." Maggie flopped down on the overstuffed chair across from Kevin. Kona wedged his eighty pounds in with her. "You should see the women in there."

"You gonna go back?" Kevin asked; his hazel eyes never leaving the TV.

"I sorta have to. I stupidly bought a three-month pass. Each class was like half-price if you did it that way." The cost-per-use would be outrageous if she never went back.

"Safe? He was out by a mile." Kevin jumped off the couch and ranted to Kona about umps who suffer from severe myopia.

Maggie walked out. No sense trying to talk to him while he was watching sports.

SATURDAY MORNING, MAGGIE slept in. When she got up, she told Kevin she'd make him a smoothie for breakfast. She'd planned ahead the night before and put a well-ripened banana in the freezer, knowing it would add a nice creamy texture. She poured vanilla soy milk into the blender, then cleaned two handfuls of fresh strawberries. She noticed their deep red color, their perfect ripeness, as she pulled off the leaves and sliced them in half. She couldn't resist the smell and popped one in her mouth. The burst of sweet juice contrasted with a bitter memory of Dave telling her she made the "best smoothies on the planet." I guess that's not the kind of talent that helps you hold onto a man, she thought as she plopped the rest of the fruit into the carafe. She broke the frozen banana in half and dropped it in, then sprinkled some wheat germ on top.

While she blended her concoction in the kitchen, Kevin rummaged in the garage. He'd moved in enough sports equipment to open a shop. He'd also brought his collection of over forty Smurfs. He'd been collecting the small bright blue and white rubber figurines ever since he and Dad had gotten hooked on the cartoon when Kevin was nine. When Maggie saw him heading into the house with the box marked SMURFS, it led to a discussion that started with, "How long are you going to be staying that you feel the need to have your little blue friends in the house with you?" and ended with, "The Smurfs stay in the garage." (Although she noticed when she put clean towels in his room, that he'd smuggled in his "lucky" Golfer Smurf.)

He came in as she was pouring the thick, pink smoothie into two tall glasses.

"That looks good," he said. "Nice shirt, by the way."

She leaned against the counter and handed him a glass. She wore an over-sized black T-shirt with red lettering that said, "I'm a witch, OK?" It was from a Halloween party she and Dave had gone to last year. She hadn't had time to figure out a costume and grabbed the shirt on a last minute dash to Target. Meanwhile, Dave had spent hours, days turning himself into a bottle of Corona, complete with lime wedge. She'd wanted him to make her a matching Corona Light, but he wouldn't do it. *Had he already stopped loving me? If your husband won't make your Halloween costume, is that one of those signs you're supposed to notice?*

Kevin sat at the bar and sucked on his straw. "As awesome as I remembered them being. But maybe a little heavy-handed with the wheat germ." She frowned at him, but realized he might be right when she took a sip from her own glass. "It's good, though. Really.

Hey, let's finish these up and go for a bike ride. It's a beautiful day out there."

"I don't think so." She held the empty blender for Kona to lick. She hadn't biked in ages. For years, Dave and Maggie had gone for long Sunday rides and then she'd whip up a big batch of smoothies for them when they got home. But then, as work consumed her, she'd started sending Dave on his own. It gave her at least three hours to get some work done. At first Dave objected, but eventually he told her he'd met a guy from their neighborhood and was riding with him each week.

Now she wondered if he'd ridden over to Stupid Slut's place every Sunday. He'd started to stay out longer each week, saying he'd gone for coffee or lunch with his bud. *Yeah, right. I'm an idiot.* She sighed and told Kevin she didn't need him dragging her on a fifty mile ride-from-hell, razzing her about how out of shape she was. Besides, the idea of forcing her now-flabby butt into spandex shorts called the phrase "bag of cats" to mind. *No, thanks.*

"Not that kinda ride," he said. "We'll go to Mission Bay; it's nice and flat. We can stop at Bandito's for lunch and margs." He waited for an answer, but when she silently continued wiping the counters he added, "Truth is, I'm supposed to meet my buddy, Russell. Sometimes he's a bit much, and I figured if you were along, you could be my excuse to leave early."

"This is supposed to entice me to come along?"

"Come on, it'll be fun. Besides, what could you possibly have planned for today that beats the ocean and margaritas?" He sealed the deal by promising he'd owe her one; she could drag him along the next time she wanted to go somewhere.

So she tossed Kona a Kong full of peanut butter, and she and Kevin drove to Mission Bay with their bikes loaded on his car. They pedaled along the boardwalk, dodging the other bikers, walkers, teenage girls in skimpy bikinis, joggers, rollerbladers, tourists, gawkers and a drunk yelling about the end of the world and the rising price of grain alcohol.

Russell waited for them on the deck of Bandito's, which smelled of hot, spilled beer and suntan lotion. He stood up when Kevin introduced them. He was almost Kevin's height, maybe six-two. He pushed his sunglasses up into his wavy brown hair as he said hello. She liked the way his smile wasn't just a flash of teeth, but his whole face took part: his tan cheeks, the crinkles around his bright blue eyes, his pointed devil's eyebrows.

Was that an extra flex of his bicep, she wondered as he shook her hand. *Surely he's not trying to impress me. I've got major bike-helmet hair and I'm all sweaty.* Although the ride had been flat, the day was sunny, and keeping up with Kevin had been an effort.

They sipped margaritas while waiting for their food. Russell still worked at the same firm Kevin left two jobs ago. It sold administrative software for doctors' offices and clinics across the western states, and Russell was head of sales in California and Oregon. He filled Kevin in on the latest gossip and told Maggie funny stories about Kevin, including an episode where Kevin suggested to a client they go to a tapas bar for dinner, but the client thought he said "topless."

The food arrived and the men bantered and bragged while they ate their quesadillas.

"I'm glad you quit, man," Russell said to Kevin. "Since you've been gone, I've been top sales dog five of the eight quarters."

"Only five?" Kevin said.

This led to a debate over who was the better salesman, with boasts of the "I can sell heaters to Arizonans in August" variety. Maggie missed the connection, but somehow this evolved into an argument about whether surfing or fishing was the better sport. She laughed at them as this segued into a discussion over whether Mel Brooks' best movie was *Young Frankenstein* or *Blazing Saddles*.

When she tired of this, she said, "You're both idiots. *The Producers* is his finest work."

"Ah," Russell toasted her with his margarita. "A woman who knows her Mel Brooks is a woman after my own heart."

"Speaking of women," Kevin asked, "what's up with Pam? You break up with her?"

"Yeah, man. I told you. She had that fatal flaw."

Alcoholic? Champion nag? Jealous type?

Kevin said to Maggie, in mock seriousness, "She has an outie."

Maggie looked at Russell. "An Audi? And you, what, only date women who drive American-made cars?"

Kevin laughed, and Russell said, "No, an outie belly button." He shivered. "I couldn't get past it."

Oh dear. Kevin was right. This guy is a bit much. But funny. And cute. Definitely cute.

In the end, Kevin did not use her as an excuse to leave early. They sat all afternoon. They drank (after the margs, the men switched to beer and Maggie to iced tea, not wanting to pedal drunk), and they laughed until Maggie's sides hurt.

THE NEXT TIME Maggie went to yoga, Madonna, whose name was actually Helen, invited her for a drink afterwards. A flight attendant who worked first class on trips to Spain and France, Helen asked for a glass of water along with her glass of pinot noir. She told Maggie about the ravages of dry airplane air on her fifty-one-year-old skin.

"I thought you were in your forties. You look great." Maggie decided she'd ask for some water too. "Your job sounds so glamorous."

"It can be fun sometimes. I just qualified as a Spanish Speaker, so that's been kind of interesting . . . and challenging."

"Spanish speaker?"

"On international flights we try to have a person who speaks the local language. You get paid more if you're the official designee. I decided to study up and got qualified."

"That's great. Must be fun to learn something new—and useful—for work." Maggie thought of the financial reporting conference she'd been to. Not much use for that knowledge in everyday life. "What a cool job."

"Well, it can be pretty un-cool sometimes." Helen went on to amuse Maggie with drunken businessmen horror stories. When you work in accounting, it is seldom that a drunk gropes your ass. Maggie realized it was one thing in the "pro" column for accounting, but still, she couldn't think of any funny stories that could compete with Helen's.

By the time their second round of drinks arrived, Helen mentioned her divorce three years ago, and suddenly Maggie was pouring out her story, and a tissue's worth of tears.

Maggie found Helen easy to talk to, maybe because of her practically-a-stranger status or because of the alcohol. She liked how Helen didn't offer platitudes or advice, simply frowned or smiled sympathetically while Maggie talked. *It's sort of like talking to Kona.*

Maggie dabbed at her eyes and said, "I don't want to be one of those bitter women who end up hating men. I mean, I realize it wasn't all his fault." She started to cry again, "I . . . I didn't make him happy anymore. If I'd made him happy, he wouldn't have . . ."

Helen handed Maggie a napkin, since her tissue was on its last legs. "My ex cheated on me too." She shook her head. "I'm not going to lie. Divorce sucks; it's damn hard to get through. And I'm no Liz Taylor, but, I'd like to at least put my limited experience to good use. You call me anytime you want to talk." She wrote her number on a second napkin and pushed it across the table. "And you'd better call me, or I'll call you."

MAGGIE PHONED HELEN two days later, clutching the crumpled napkin. "I have Friday off, so I thought I'd see if you wanted to go to lunch or something?"

"I'd love to," Helen said, "But I'm working the Barcelona flight."

"Oh."

"How about taking yourself out shopping instead? When my ex left, I bought a whole new wardrobe. You know what they say, when God closes a door, he opens a charge account."

Maggie couldn't help but laugh. "I'm not much for shopping. Or are they offering charge accounts at Baskin Robbins now?"

"Wait, I've got a great idea. And it won't affect your bottom line, if ya' know what I mean. You know the modern art museum?"

"MAMA reopened?" Maggie remembered reading about the Museum of Abstract and Modern Art when it closed last year for remodeling, but hadn't heard it reopened. She missed a lot of news these days. It hit her one day after back-to-back stories on the Middle-East crisis, the plight of the polar bear, and a local murder-suicide that she'd had enough. She'd quit cold turkey. Kevin read Sports, she read Business, and after a quick scan of the front page to make sure she wasn't missing any major world crisis, she'd toss the paper in the recycling.

"It reopened last week and it's fantastic. You've got to go, and then next week when I'm back, we'll go to lunch and compare notes. Sound like a plan, *mi amiga?*"

"OK, it's a plan." Maggie smiled hearing Helen call her "friend" and at Helen's idea as well. Maggie loved modern art; with her color-inside-the-lines ways, she liked to imagine the free-spirited artists, unconstrained by convention. At work, everything was rules and numbers; perfectly aligned columns and rows of little digits, soldiering toward totals that would lead to strategic plans, tactical decisions, investments, divestments. God forbid someone might forget to carry the one; misplace a mere decimal point and all hell could break loose. But abstract art was the antithesis of all that. The seemingly haphazard colors and designs somehow came together; there simply to be looked at, to be enjoyed, to provoke thought or emotion. There could be no mistakes; no way to get it wrong. No dire consequences. No stress.

Kevin, unfortunately, did not share her opinion and objected when she told him her plan.

"Tough," she said. "You promised you'd come along wherever I wanted."

He tried to convince her they should go somewhere else. "Shopping? Get pedicures? Anything but that. Modern art's weird. It looks like something a kid could do. An annoying kid."

She sweetened the deal by offering to buy lunch, and on Friday morning, they headed out. It was a perfect cornflower-blue-sky June day. Maggie flashed back to waking up as a kid on the first glorious day of summer vacation.

As they stepped into the light-filled, soaring entryway, a faint smell of sawdust hinted at the recent renovations.

Leaving Kevin flirting with the woman at the information desk, pretending he was oh-so-very interested in contemporary art, Maggie strolled through every quiet corner of the museum.

She had the main exhibit room to herself: a huge space with white walls, twenty foot ceilings and pale bamboo flooring. Massive, somber canvases in blue and gray oil paints covered the walls. They raged around her like winter storms at sea.

The sound of her sandals striking the wood floors reminded her of going with Mom to help clean the church when she was a girl. They'd be the only ones there; every step echoed off the walls. Only, where the church was dark and gloomy, this room was open and bright. And whereas she always felt guilty in church (she didn't go often enough, didn't pray with enough conviction, wasn't good or pious enough), here she felt peaceful and calm. It occurred to Maggie that perhaps this was what people who enjoyed going to church felt.

She lingered in the last room. It was filled with tall sculptures, tilted at odd angles, defying gravity, made out of everyday objects: buttons, snaps and zippers on one, another with kitchen gadgets. Old, rusty measuring spoons, whisks and worn wooden rolling pins were mixed in with brand new gleaming ones. Her favorite, called "Busy Work," featured office supplies: thousands of paper clips, rows of shiny new staples and binder clips painstakingly fused together in a column that teetered over her head.

She walked out thinking, is it over already? She wanted to come back as soon as possible.

"Come on, I'm starving," Kevin said, waiting for her in the foyer. He tapped his watch.

On the way out, she picked up a pamphlet about volunteering.

That afternoon she went into her home office and picked up the phone, Kona by her side. She looked at the flyer, the phone, the dog.

"I know you think Momma's brave," she said. Kona tilted his

head as if hanging on her every word. "But, really, I'm a big chicken like you." He put his head in her lap.

She stroked his head while she dialed. The volunteer coordinator set up an appointment for her to come in the following week for an interview.

Smiling, Maggie marked the appointment in ink on her calendar.

Chapter 6: Paint Fumes and Poems

"Did I wake you up? I didn't think it was too early to call." *Dave. Swell.* At nine in the morning, Maggie still lay in bed. *Talk about your rude awakenings.*

"It is too early," she yawned loudly into the phone. "What do you want?"

"I decided I want to come get my TV—today."

"Oh, *you* decided. Just like you decided to cheat? You decided to leave? I'm sick of your decisions, Dave. Know what? *I* decided to sell the stupid TV on craigslist." She looked over her shoulder at the behemoth in question. *Need to get on that.*

"You can't just sell the TV. Come on. That was my TV."

"No, it was our TV." *And you left it behind, just like everything else that was ours. Our life, our plans . . .*

"Look, I just want what's rightfully mine. I didn't even take any of the furniture, for Pete's sake. And I'm not trying to take advantage of the fact you made more money than me, but I think you owe me—"

"Owe you? I don't owe you anything. You'll hear from my lawyer." She hung up. *Stupid portable phones; can't even slam the damn thing down. And what an ass. You want what's yours? I was yours, you idiot.* She threw the blankets off. *I've gotta ask Helen about her lawyer.*

There was no point staying in bed. She got up and decided to take Kona for his walk, try to "exercise" her demons.

As a kid, when Maggie heard people mention exorcising demons, she thought they were talking about exercising them; make them so tired they'd leave you alone. Even now, she liked to picture the demons, miniature red men with black eyebrows and horns, dressed in bright '80s-style Lycra leotards soaked with sweat as they slogged through a grueling aerobics class. She still thought her phrasing made more sense, since she usually felt better after a workout.

When she called for Kona, he didn't come. She found Kevin in the kitchen making coffee. He said he'd let the dog out to pee and hadn't seen him since. She ran to the front window; the gate was open. It must not have been latched properly last night. She knew where he'd be.

She marched out to the sidewalk in her bare feet. Sure enough, he was there, rooting in the neighbor's flowerbed, hunting for cat poop snacks left behind by their tabby.

"Kona." She made her voice as deep as she could. "Bad boy. Go home."

He yanked his head up, then let it hang low as he slunk toward her. When he reached her, head still down, he lifted his eyes up to her.

"I mean it. Get inside." She pointed at the house. He trudged past her, then picked up his pace and skipped through the gate.

She went in and found him waiting for her with a broad smile on his face. She shook her head. *No guilt. What must that be like?* She knew she should probably ignore him as punishment, but wanted to get his walk over with so they set off.

She hoped she'd feel better after a long march, but the walk began with a full view of the crack of Mr. Freedman's ass as he picked up his paper. Not a good start. And it was close enough to July that there was no June gloom; it was even oddly muggy. By the time they got home, she felt hot and cranky. But her demons remained cool and comfortable, settled in for the long haul.

"Let's paint the office today." Kevin emerged from the kitchen and handed her a cup of coffee. He'd already tackled several projects on her To Do list for the house, either while she was at work or lay on the sofa watching him. "It won't take that long if we do it together."

"Wouldn't you rather be out golfing or something?" Kevin had not seemed at all stressed about his lack of employment. He'd dedicated himself to improving his putting.

"No. Come on. We can blast some Bob Marley and get into a groove."

"Wow. You make it sound like you think this could actually be fun."

"It will be, and think how much better you'll feel when you scratch it off the list."

She wasn't in the mood, but she didn't even have the energy to try to dissuade him, so she handed him two fifties and a list and sent him to Home Depot.

After he left, Maggie pulled books off the shelves and stacked them in the hallway so they could move the furniture. On the top shelf, she found a volume of classic love poems Dave had given her. She'd missed it in her previous purging.

The slim volume seemed heavy as a stone. She dropped it on the desk. She stared at it. She didn't need to open the cover; she remembered what Dave had written. She could see his crabbed handwriting in her mind's eye. It said:

"Poetry is painting that is felt rather than seen." Leonardo da Vinci
Maggie, I hope these poems will show you how I feel about you. I love you.
Dave.

She remembered the flush of joy she'd felt when he'd given it to her after Dad's funeral.

She'd met Dave the first week after she moved into the dorms at San Diego State. They'd only been dating a few months when she got the call from home that Dad had had a heart attack. Dave had been great; taking care of her; driving her home to L.A. Mom had been in a daze and barely said two words to Dave, until it was time for him to drive Maggie back to school. Mom had hugged Dave that morning and Maggie had overheard her ask him to "take care of my girl."

"I promise, Mrs. O'Connell," he'd said.

Maggie had realized as she watched him drive, at the end of that exhausting week that had been like wading knee-deep through mud, that she loved Dave and wanted to spend the rest of her life with him. She'd cried a new batch of tears, realizing her dad would never meet him.

A few days later, while she tried to find a new sense of normalcy, Dave had given her the book of poetry and told her he loved her.

Maggie blinked, returning to the present. While she clearly remembered the first time Dave said he loved her, she could not remember the last time. And now he loved someone else.

She flung back the cover of the book and tore at the pages. She crumpled them and threw them to the floor, crying. At one point she grabbed too many pages at once and struggled in a rage to rend the pages from the binding. She let out a half-scream, half-groan of frustration and dropped the book; her legs folded under her and she sat heavily on the floor next to it. She picked it up and threw it across the room, then held her head in her hands and sobbed.

As she calmed down, she heard Kona bark at the sound of Kevin's car. She scooped the paper trail of her meltdown into a trash bag and ran to splash cold water on her face. She heard Kevin walk to the back of the house. Her skin was blotchy. It would be a while before it was back to normal. Could she paint in her biggest, darkest sunglasses?

"Hey, you're not even done clearing everything out of here," Kevin called from the office. "Were you dorking around while I was gone?"

"I started," she yelled back. She dabbed powder around her eyes. She pulled her pony-tail holder out and fluffed her hair, hoping her wild curls would hide some of her face.

"Come on. I need you to help me move the desk out from the wall."

"OK. I'm coming." She knew they'd be face-to-face over the desktop.

She walked into the office and bent over to examine the paint, under the pretense of making sure he'd gotten the semi-gloss like she'd asked.

"It's everything on the list. I got the rollers and the stupid tape."

"It's not stupid. You can't paint without taping off the windows and ceiling."

"Uh, you can. And I do. But whatever; it's your house, your rules." He stood by the desk, ready to hoist his end. "Come on."

She went to the opposite end of the desk. His usual omnipresent grin faded.

"Are you—" he started to ask, but she looked down and cut him off.

"Yes, I'm strong enough." She hefted her end. "Let's move this stupid thing."

All afternoon they taped, prepped, primed and painted. Ready for the second coat, Maggie stood waiting with her roller as Kevin cut in along the ceiling. She marveled at her brother. He was always so calm. He didn't seem to have a single tense muscle in his whole body, whereas she could feel her own stresses piling up like a topographical map of the Rockies.

"I envy you, ya' know?"

Kevin scoffed. "Yeah? My good looks? Or you mean my status as an unemployed, single, homeless person?"

"No, really. I mean the whole unemployed thing. How you quit, and you don't have anything else in the works—and you don't even seem concerned about it."

"I think most people wouldn't see that as enviable."

She worked her roller in the prescribed W pattern. "Maybe not, but that's what's so great about you. You don't care what other people think. You didn't like the job anymore, so you left. Cut and dried. No stressing or whining. I think Dad would be impressed with that."

"I dunno; I can't see Dad being impressed by my quitting. Remember how mad he got when I quit soccer? Always felt bad about that. He'd just given me the Soccer Smurf."

"The way I remember it, it was mostly Mom who was mad, and that was only because they'd just bought you new cleats. Dad just said, 'For a ten-year-old, the kid knows his mind.'"

"Really?" Kevin paused in his painting. As much as Maggie had felt cheated by their father's death at such a young age, she felt worse for Kevin. He'd had five less years with Dad than she did.

"Yeah, really," she said. They both turned back to their painting in silence.

After many hours, and a stack of rock and reggae CDs, they finished. With Bob Marley still ringing in her ears, and with the room looking so much brighter, Maggie did feel better. Being a bit high on paint fumes didn't hurt either.

They were pulling the painter's tape off of the window casings when the phone rang. She'd been unable to convince Kevin to agree to her screening policy, so he grabbed the phone and answered it before she could say anything.

"Hi, Mom," he said, turning to look at Maggie. She slumped her shoulders and held up her hands to wave him off.

"I'm not here," she mouthed.

As she wadded the tape into a big blue sticky ball, she listened to Kevin's side of small talk about the weather. She heard him say, "Yeah, she's right here."

He held the phone out to her and she glared at him. She grabbed it and held her hand over the mouth piece. "Kevin. I told you I didn't want to talk to her."

"Hey, no worries, mon," he said in the same fake Jamaican accent he'd been talking in since they started playing the first Bob Marley CD. He grinned, picked up the trash bag, and left.

Maggie sat on the floor.

"Hi, Mom," she said, trying to sound chipper. Mom preferred her children chipper.

"Hello, Maggie. How are you doing? I haven't heard from you in a while."

"I'm fine. I've been really busy; you know, starting my new job and all." Now that Mom was finally beginning to accept that Dave wasn't coming back, she'd moved on to work, grilling Maggie about her future. So Maggie hadn't bothered to tell Mom that her new job was a part-time position. It was just easier that way.

"I hope you're not falling into that same trap again and putting all your time and effort into your work."

"I'm not. This place is much more reasonable. I haven't worked any overtime yet." *In fact, I'm not even working full time.*

"Well, that's good. Speaking of jobs, what's Kevin doing? Is he looking for a job? Are you helping him?" She interrogated Maggie, wanting to know what Kevin did with himself all day and whether or not Maggie encouraged him to search the Want Ads in the paper.

"People don't look in the paper anymore. Everything's online. Besides, I'm his sister, not his career counselor. Look, I've got to go; we're in the middle of painting the office and Kev's waiting for me. I'll talk to you soon."

She hung up as Kevin walked back in, followed by Kona. Frustrated, she let out a loud sigh. The mood-boost she'd gotten from Bob Marley and the "no worries" vibe Kevin had been pushing long gone.

Kevin tried to pick up the drop cloth, which Kona had stretched out on.

How is it possible that he has such a free and easy relationship with Mom?

"How come she grills me about *your* job hunting?" Maggie asked.

He gave her his answer-to-everything shrug. "I'm the baby. You're the oldest. I'm a boy; you're a girl. Sucks to be you, but she's never going to change. You need to get over it already. You're forty-two. Are you always going to let her get to you?"

"I'm not forty-two; I'm forty-one. And she just really knows how to push my buttons."

"Did it ever occur to you that maybe you have really big buttons?" He held up his hands indicating a square large enough to toss a basketball through.

She chucked a roll of tape at him. "It's these painter's pants; they make my buttons look big."

Kevin caught the tape and walked out laughing, tossing it in the air. She watched him go and hoped his happy-go-lucky vibe might be contagious.

Then she studied her dog. He lay on his back in the center of the room, frozen in the position Kevin had rolled him into while pulling the drop cloth out from under him.

Look at him. Not a care in the world.

"How's my silly puppy?"

He twisted to look at her, but remained on his back. His tail whacked the floor.

I'm sure he's completely forgotten he was in trouble with me this morning over the cat poop caper. But, maybe he's got the right idea. Forget the past. Live in the moment. Hmmm. Maybe I could try to be more like him.

"Wish I could trade places with you, just for a day or two."

Kona yawned, a long, noisy protracted harrumph.

"You're right. I'm bored with being too introspective, too. And we don't need to trade places. I'm just going to try to go with the flow more. You can be my guru! And I'll follow your lead, or . . . your dogma, as it were."

Chapter 7: Poker Face

It had been five weeks since Kevin moved in, and Maggie was settling into her new routine. She worked three or four days a week (the job was OK; not exciting, but not stressful either); she walked Kona almost three miles each morning; Tuesdays meant yoga and sometimes tea afterwards with Helen (she felt too guilty going for drinks after being so healthy at yoga, and convinced Helen decaf green tea was the perfect post-class beverage); she rode her bike one day during the week and again on Sundays; and she had recently started volunteering at MAMA every Thursday evening. She and Kevin were working their way through the house To Do list (although sometimes adding a new item for every two or three they scratched off), and she repaid him by treating for lunch or dinner. Russell often traveled for work, but if he was in town he joined them. He always made her laugh, so she liked it when he came along.

This weekend was Russell's birthday, so she and Kevin had invited him for a combined birthday-and-July-Fourth barbecue. While Kevin stayed home marinating the steaks, Maggie picked up a cake at her favorite bakery, Baked Greats, the place where she liked to say her butt wanted its ashes sprinkled. There, she ran into Kevin's ex, Annie.

Maggie wasn't surprised to see her; after all, Annie had introduced them to this out-of-the-way shop that always smelled of yeast and buttercream frosting. She was as beautiful as ever, with her toned legs and thick blonde hair. The July afternoon, combined with the bakery ovens, warmed the shop, but Annie looked as perfect as a magazine cover in her ivory linen shorts and salmon-colored silk tank top. She stood at the back of the Saturday crowd. Maggie waved as she took a number. When Maggie walked over, she noticed shadows under Annie's pale blue eyes.

"I can't believe I ran into you," Annie said after they exchanged polite greetings. Annie turned away, poked in her purse, counted the people ahead of her in line.

"What do you mean?" Maggie asked, wondering why Annie was acting so distant. Sure, she wasn't part of the "family" now, but she'd always been warm and friendly before.

"I'm only in town for my parents' anniversary party."

"What do you mean?" Maggie repeated. "You moved?"

"Didn't Kevin tell you I moved to Boston last month?" Maggie looked at her with a blank expression. Annie rolled her eyes and muttered, "That is *so* Kevin."

She told Maggie how her brother, Jeremy, whose graphics software company in Boston had taken off, had offered them "great" jobs around the end of May. Kevin would have been in charge of North American sales.

"But he told me he 'couldn't possibly move to Boston right now.' It didn't make sense, because he'd already quit his job here. But I knew he said it to get me to go alone because . . . because he didn't love me. I mean, I knew he'd had a million girlfriends, but I thought things were different with us." Tears welled up in her eyes, and she looked at the ceiling as if to will them back behind her cheeks. She fanned herself with her hand. "It's really hot in here. Anyway, when he said he couldn't move, I . . . kinda lost it. Called him a coward and . . . said he had less 'relationship balls' than any man I've ever met; that he's a 'relationship eunuch.' It got ugly; I started sobbing and he stormed out. Other than a couple of text messages about getting his stuff out of my apartment, I haven't talked to him since." She ran her fingers through her bangs. "And, that's it. A couple of weeks later, I moved. End of story."

Maggie was spared thinking up something to say when Annie's number was called.

Maggie watched her place her order. *That's Kevin for you. They fall in love with him, but he just cannot commit. Poor Annie.* She wondered how two siblings could be so different when it came to relationships: she'd been with Dave her whole adult life, whereas Kevin had had so many girlfriends she'd never be able to name them all. He probably couldn't either.

Maggie had thought that if any woman could stay in the picture, it would be Annie. But when Kevin told her they broke up, Maggie figured she'd been wrong and it was the same old story. She chalked it up to his being, well, not so much a "commitment-phobe," since Kevin didn't fear anything, but rather commitment-intolerant. It didn't seem to agree with his system.

Annie turned from the counter, pink cardboard box in hand.

"Wait up. Let's go for coffee," Maggie suggested, then asked the girl at the counter for a carrot cake. She wanted to try to cheer Annie up; try to make up for her brother in some way.

"No, I've gotta go," Annie said. "My family's waiting for me. Or, for the cake anyway." She held up the box by its twine bow and gave a tired smile.

"Are you sure?" Maggie asked. "At least come to my car with me. I've got something of yours." She handed over her money and hefted the box.

"What could you have of mine?"

"Kevin gave me your yoga mat to 'borrow,'" she made air quotes with her fingers. "If you want it back, it's in the car. I was just at my class the other night." She pointed to her Civic across the lot and walked toward it. "I'm really enjoying it."

"I have no idea what you're talking about." Annie stopped, head to one side.

"It's not your mat?"

"I don't do yoga." Annie said. "Look, I've got to go. Tell Kevin I said, I don't know, just . . . tell him I said hi."

WHEN MAGGIE GOT home, Russell was already there. He'd come early and was out back with Kevin and Kona. She could see them, drinking beers at the patio table while Kona eyed the meat sizzling on the grill. She set the cake box on the counter and went to the fridge for a beer of her own. Her stomach growled when she smelled the steaks through the open patio door.

She heard Kevin saying, "So, what do you make, like doilies or something?"

"No, that's crocheting, you moron. You don't knit doilies."

Maggie slid open the screen door. "What are you guys talking about?" she asked as she joined them at the table.

"Sports," Russell said.

"Uh, yeah," Kevin said. "You entertain our guest while I go make the salad."

When he'd gone inside, Maggie scooted her chair next to Russell's and whispered, "What do you know about Kevin and Annie breaking up?"

"Not much. Just that Annie wanted to move to Boston and Kevin said something like he couldn't go then, which I thought was weird. He'd quit his job. I didn't understand that."

"Did you ask him why he didn't go?"

"Hello? We're men. We don't mine our deepest feelings over cosmopolitans."

"Of course. Forgive me. Heaven forbid you should discuss your actual hopes and desires." She peeked at Kevin through the window, tearing up lettuce into her big wooden salad bowl. "Maybe he just didn't love her. Maybe he was trying to get rid of her."

"I don't think so." Russell shook his head. "With Annie, he was different. I've seen Kevin with some of his gals before. He didn't say anything after she left, but he's got about as good of a poker face as Kona does. I think he really misses her."

"Huh, that's odd." Maggie told Russell about seeing Annie and having the same feeling: that she missed Kevin and still loved him. "Hey, did you say he doesn't have a poker face?"

"Oh yeah. It's terrible. You know how he's always smiling and laid-back? Well, when he's got good cards, he gets all serious. It's pretty entertaining, actually. It was the same with Annie. With other gals, he'd sort of joke around when he talked about them—not mean, but just guy stuff. But with Annie, he'd get real serious when he talked about her. She was good cards."

Maggie mulled this over. "Must make him easy pickings at his poker game."

"Kevin's in a regular game? That's news to me. I've got to get in on that; relieve him of some of his money."

"Yeah, every Tuesday."

"No. You must have the day wrong. Tuesdays we go out to eat or grab a beer. We went to that new sushi place in La Jolla this week."

"This past Tuesday?" Maggie asked.

"What's that look for? Yeah, this Tuesday. Oh, I get it. You're mad because we didn't invite you. Look, I wanted to. Lord knows you're softer on the eyes than that mug," he jerked his head toward the window, where they could see Kevin tossing the salad. "But he said I shouldn't ask you because that's your yoga night, and we shouldn't tempt you away cuz it's good for you."

"Oh, did he?" She sat up straight and put her beer down with a thunk on the glass tabletop. "First of all, my brother is not my social director. And if you want to ask me to go somewhere, you should just ask. It's not up to him how I spend my time. And second of all, why the hell would he lie and tell me he's got a running poker game on Tuesdays?"

"Did I say Tuesday? I meant Thursday. Sometimes on Thursdays we go out."

"Do *not* try to backpedal and save your friend's ass. He has some explaining to do."

Kevin walked out with the salad and flashed his best contract-closing smile at them. "Am I interrupting anything here?"

Maggie stood up. "Would you mind telling me why you've been lying to me about your supposed Tuesday night poker game?" She could feel heat creeping up her face like a rash. "And why the hell would you tell me Annie took you to yoga, when she doesn't even do yoga?"

"How do you know she doesn't?" Kevin, frozen in place,

continued to hold the salad bowl out to them, like some sort of romaine-wielding mannequin. "Did you see her?"

"Yes, I saw her. Don't try to change the subject. I want to know what the hell's going on. And what is up with telling Russell not to 'tempt' me away from yoga? You are not my frickin' babysitter. You better start telling me what is going on, or you can just get out of my house."

"Um, I'm, uh, going to go . . ." Russell rose from his chair and slipped sideways toward the house.

"I don't know, Russell," Maggie railed on. "Better check with the puppet master here; he might have plans for you and me."

Kevin nodded at him. "Yeah, probably best if you just go."

Maggie watched Russell walk toward the back door and saw the pink cake box on the counter. *Shit. It's his damn birthday.* "No, wait, Russell," she stormed past him. "You stay. I've gotta get out of here for a while."

Maggie grabbed Kona's leash and yelled, "Kona, come on, we're going to the park." Although he appeared torn for one moment (steaks or park?), he opted for the park since it was rare to be offered two walks in one day.

Although they sometimes drove the two miles to the park, tonight she needed to walk. Walk and think. The things she'd heard today struggled to add up in her head as they strode down the block. The sun sank in the west, but Maggie was in no mood for Mother Nature showing off her pinks and purples. She looked down at the sidewalk as if the concrete replayed a movie strip of the last few weeks and all the hoops Kevin had had her jumping through.

She guessed now that he'd made up the Tuesday poker date so she'd go alone to yoga. And Russell was his best friend; he must have known she'd like him, but scrambled for a reason to get her out of the house that day so he'd said she'd have to be his excuse to leave early. Even his needing a place to crash made no sense now that she thought about it; he'd been making good money and could afford his own place. She realized he'd manipulated her from the day he showed up on her doorstep.

Like one of those cheap marionettes you buy in Tijuana. "Dance, Maggie."
When they reached the park, she still pulled Kona along at a clipped pace. She wouldn't let him stop and sniff for picnic remnants, in his usual the-world-is-my-smorgasbord way. At one point he tried to lift his leg on a tree, but she yanked his leash and stormed down the path.

How dare he? Does he think I'm so pathetic I can't take care of myself? I don't need my baby brother holding my hand. I can't believe he lied. Why couldn't he just be straight with me?

After forty minutes of marching, she dropped onto a bench. Kona leaned against her legs, panting. With the cool early evening air tempering the fever of her anger, she sat and thought.

She had sort of lost it when Dave left. She'd shut herself up in the house; moped around for days, weeks, in her PJs; done tequila shots when she couldn't sleep. She'd become like Dave's sock she'd found in the laundry room, the sock she'd envied; tried to hide from it all. If Kevin had been "straight with her," telling her point blank she needed to get on with her life, she'd have told him to get lost. No, instead he'd pulled her out of her dark hiding place and pushed her out into the world, back into circulation. And he'd done it in his own way.

If Shannon had come out, they'd have had long talks, late each night, psychoanalyzing every move she and Dave had made for the last several months before the marriage ended. But that wasn't Kevin's style. Of course he wasn't going to show up on her doorstep with hugs and tearful sympathy. But he'd been there for her. She wondered now if he'd gotten up early on purpose those first few mornings, urged by Shannon to make sure Maggie didn't pay any five a.m. visits to the liquor cabinet. And all the lies he'd told, well, she was still angry at the thought of them, but she could see how that was his way of getting her out her slump.

Now she realized how much he'd done to help her and how much she had needed him.

How is it that poor Kev always ends up taking care of the ladies in this family? First Mom, now me. Reluctant nurse-maid to the broken hearted. I'm sure that's a role he'd rather not play. Wait a minute . . . Am I part of the reason he told Annie he couldn't move to Boston "right now"? I'm going to have to grill him about that.

She asked Kona, "What shall we do, Buddy? Go home and make up? Eat cake? Good idea, let's go." They started to walk back under the yellow street lights, after a short detour to check out the picnic area.

BY THE TIME they got home, Maggie could hear the whistle and pop of fireworks in the distance. She poked her head through the front door, a bit embarrassed about her own earlier fireworks display, and ruining Russell's birthday. *Shoot. I owe that man a birthday dinner.*

Kevin lay on the sofa watching ESPN.

"Russell gone?"

He shut off the TV. "Yeah, he left a while ago. Look, if you'll just let me explain—"

"Oh yeah, you've definitely got some explaining to do. I finally clued in to what's going on around here, and I don't appreciate being lied to. But, what you did, it was sweet . . . mostly sweet, anyway."

Kevin opened his mouth, then closed it again with a short exhalation through his nose. Maggie moved toward him with her arms open, determined to wrangle a rare hug out of him.

"I really am sorry, Mags." He sounded contrite as he squeezed her.

Maggie thought she might cry, but instead laughed as Kona wedged himself between their legs. Kona, a big fan of open displays of affection, demanded a piece of the action.

"Don't worry; we've got hugs for you too, Buddy," Maggie said, wrapping her arms around her broad, faithful friend. She looked up at Kevin, "You're not off the hook with me yet, though. We are going to have a long talk right now. And then, first thing tomorrow—"

"I know. You want me to start looking for my own place."

"No," she said, "I want you to call Annie."

Chapter 8: Upward-Facing Dog

The next morning, Kevin sat at the bar while Maggie made buttermilk waffles. Kona stood at her knee, watching her every move. Kevin held his cell phone.

"You're sure it's not too early to call?" he asked.

He looked like he hadn't slept. They'd stayed up late the night before, eating carrot cake, sipping Gentleman Jack and talking. Maggie had told him about running into Annie and insisted Kevin tell his version of their break up. He relayed a story similar to Annie's: he'd told Annie he couldn't move to Boston right then, and they'd gotten into a "brutal" fight. She'd started sobbing and he "couldn't deal" and headed to Russell's. The next day, he'd moved to Maggie's. He hadn't talked to Annie since.

"You can't recover from a fight like that," Kevin had said, shaking his head.

"Yes, you can. You just don't know because you've never tried." Maggie'd let Kona lick the remains of the cream cheese frosting off her plate. "I could tell Annie regretted that fight. I'm sure if you put a bit of effort into this, you can work it out. Think about it, OK?" She'd known better then to try to finagle another hug out of him. She'd settled for patting his shoulder as she'd said goodnight and headed to bed.

Now, this morning, Maggie turned to look at him for the third time. "Call her already." She'd never seen Kevin stressed like this. *I'm the chicken around here; the one that's got to weigh every option, the waffler.* She smiled at her pun and gave the batter a final stir. Then she cupped Kona's chin in her left hand and with her right moved his floppy upper lip. "Call her," she said in a gruff voice. "See, even Kona says so."

As Kevin got up and started to walk into the other room, Maggie asked, "Wait, don't I get to listen to your side of the conversation?"

He muttered something she didn't catch as he walked away, head bent over his phone.

"I want to know everything you guys say," she called after him as she put a steaming waffle in the oven to keep warm. Kona followed its trajectory intently.

As she scraped the last of the batter into the maker, she heard Kevin return and pull out the barstool. She turned to see him put his head in his hands.

"*That* went well. Great idea. Call early, wake her up. She's not a morning person, did I mention that?"

She ran around the bar and put her hand on his shoulder. "Oh no. What happened?"

He grinned at her. "I'm totally messing with you. It really did go well."

She swatted him with her kitchen towel. "Alright, weasel, tell me every single word."

"We're meeting for lunch."

"Details. I need details," Maggie pleaded. "What did she say? What did *you* say?"

"I didn't say much. I told her I was stupid."

"Well, she had to have agreed with that."

"Shockingly, she did. And I told her why I didn't want to move when she first asked me."

"Yeah, you kinda glossed over that last night. Why didn't you want to move?"

Kevin sighed. "Right around the time Annie first told me about the Boston idea, Shannon started calling me, like every day, telling me I had to do something to . . . help you. I was stressing out, cuz I didn't know what to do. Then Annie and I fought, and I left. That's when I got the idea to move in with you—I needed somewhere to go, and you needed, well, someone to be here."

Maggie twisted the towel in her hands. It was as she'd guessed last night at the park. He'd moved in to help her, not because he needed a favor.

"Kev, I appreciate what you did for me. Really. But . . . now I feel guilty about you and Annie. Why didn't you tell her what you were doing? You . . . you big dummy." She hit him again with her towel.

"Well, I'm glad we're all three in agreement that I'm an idiot." He rolled and unrolled the placemat she'd set on the bar. "It's not like I thought I was picking my sister over my girlfriend. It all just happened so fast. It wasn't like I had this well thought out plan. Annie was bugging me to move—and, ya' know, it's kinda scary to think about making a big commitment and moving across country with someone. And then Shay started bugging me; and Annie and I had that big fight. I just kinda moved over here and figured it'd all work itself out."

"It's not going to just work itself out though, Kev. You need to put in some effort." She went into the kitchen and pulled the waffles out of the oven and loaded up their plates.

"I *am* making an effort." Kevin buttered his waffle. "I called her. I apologized."

"So, back to your call. You explained why you hadn't wanted to move, and then what?"

"And then she said I was *really* stupid, cuz if I'd just explained all that in the first place, she would have understood and she would have waited for me. She said I've never been any good at articulating my feelings or my plans."

"I thought you said this call went well? When does it start to go well?" Maggie sopped a bite of waffle in syrup.

"Just shut up and listen. Anyway, I told her I was going to try hard to work on that particular flaw of mine, starting with articulating the fact that," he paused and wiped his mouth on his napkin, looked down at his plate and rushed out, "that I love her and need to be with her."

Maggie gasped and froze with a second waffle in mid-flight to her plate. "You did?!" Kona picked up on the excitement and danced from paw to paw as if sensing a waffle in his immediate future. "What did she say? Did she say she loves you too? Because I know she does!"

"She said we should talk."

"She wants to talk about how much she loves you." Maggie pointed her fork at him. "And she wants to start making plans for you to move to Boston."

He smiled at her, shook his head, and went back to eating.

She bounced in her seat. "I am so happy for you. This is so great. Let's give Kona a waffle. He enjoys a good celebration."

She tossed one to the dog and they watched as he inhaled it like a furry Pac-Man.

They turned back to their plates in silence.

As she ate, it occurred to her that soon she might not have anyone to make waffles for. Besides Kona. She would be alone, again. She felt a bit of panic rising up in her. She hadn't done so well, living alone before Kevin moved in. She didn't want any more practice at it.

KEVIN DIDN'T GET back until almost half past four. As usual, he held back on the emotional details of their conversation, but filled her in on the practical ones. Annie had confessed that she'd called her brother, Jeremy, as soon as she got off the phone with Kevin. Jeremy still wanted to hire him, so there was no problem there.

"The guy who's heading up sales isn't working out, so Jeremy'll move him to tech-support." He hunted in the junk drawer for paper. "He wants me to start right away."

Annie was flying back tomorrow morning, and Kevin would join her as soon as he could.

"Which will be soon," he said as he started making a list. "I can probably be there by early next week. I just need to sort out my stuff; figure out what'll fit in the car." He bent over the paper. "Get car tuned up," he said to himself. His plan was to drive cross-country, which he figured would take four days. "Go online for maps," he muttered, scribbling.

Maggie watched while Kevin darted around. He'd start one task, drop it, move to another, stop to laugh at himself. He was so happy. *Well, he's always happy, but now he's insanely happy.*

"Wow, a week," she said. "Can I do anything to help?" *Help you get out of here and on to your new life so you can leave me all alone that much sooner?*

She'd gotten used to having Kevin around. It had been fun to have someone to do things with, someone to cook for. Again, she felt tears sneaking up. *Come on, Maggie. You've got a new life to be excited about too. There's your job and your volunteer position and yoga. And Helen and Russell. It's going to be . . .*

She didn't want Kevin to see her cry. She got up and started heading out of the room.

"I need to call Mom. You want to talk to her?" Kevin asked.

"No, not right now." She knew she sounded like Minnie Mouse. She kept walking.

"Mags, you OK?"

"I'm fine," she squeaked and scurried to her bedroom.

Get a grip. She tried her mirror trick and went straight to the large one over her dresser. Her chin stopped wobbling. But, tears or no, she was still depressed.

She decided to try putting some of the yoga money she'd been spending to use. Try to calm down. She stood on the hardwood floor and practiced some of her favorite poses: Downward-facing Dog, Upward-facing Dog, Exalted Warrior. These were the moves she liked best, not because she was particularly good at them, but because the names alone usually lifted her spirits. She was best at Tree Pose, and could easily balance on one leg with her hands in prayer position over her head all day. And Tree Pose was a nice enough name; but, for feeling powerful, Exalted Warrior beat Tree Pose any day.

She was still feeling down, so she decided to pull out the big guns and end with her favorite, Happy Baby Pose. *More like Morose Baby Pose today, but let's give it a shot.* But she couldn't lie down and bend her knees into her chest to grab hold of her feet while lying on the hardwood floor; it would be murder on the spine. She went to the closet for her mat, where she found Kona fast asleep on it. One end was ragged and bits of purple rubber littered the floor around his large, square head.

"Kona, bad dog!"

He woke with a start, then assumed his caught-in-the-act, peeking up sadly from under his eyebrows, look.

She yanked the ruined mat from under him. "Get out of here, you bad boy. Go outside."

Alone in her room, she avoided the mirror, and curled into fetal position in bed.

Chapter 9: They Should Try to Bottle That Smell

Several days later, Maggie found herself struggling, yet again, to keep from crying as she said goodbye to Kevin. He drove off, his car loaded with clothes, Smurfs and golf clubs. She held back the tears until he turned the corner. Her cheeks still damp, she had to smile when she went into his room to pull the sheets off the bed—he'd left his Handy Smurf behind for her with a note saying it would bring her good luck. She picked it up and fingered the little blue figurine's gray overalls and toolbox. *Leave it to Kevin to say it with Smurfs.*

In the days after Kevin left, she tried to get used to his absence. Actually, she could get through the daylight hours well enough. She went to work, worked out, or puttered around the house and yard. She played her eclectic CD collection (American musicals, alternative rock, opera, reggae, punk, French accordion music, whatever) and rather enjoyed the fact that Kevin wasn't there complaining about the majority of it.

But dinner time was tough. She tried watching baseball while she ate, just like they'd done most nights while he was there. Even though they'd hardly talked during the games, it wasn't the same. It felt lonely, sad. She tried reading during dinner, paying more attention to her book than she did to what was on her plate, pushing the food around with her fork. She thought she'd try making comfort food one night and cooked up a big pan of cheesy, melty tuna casserole. It cheered her up the first night. The second, it was still tasty. By the fourth night she was sick of it. Kona offered to finish it, but she put the rest in the freezer.

Tougher even than dinner times, though, were the last few

hours of each day. Somehow those hours took on a palpably different feeling from the daytime. When she got back late from the museum or from being out with Helen or Russell, the quiet of the house seemed to have its own physical presence, waiting for her. It tried to smother her.

Until Kona realized she was home and came running; his high school cheerleader energy chased away the gloom. If it wasn't for him, she might have considered getting a roommate.

She was especially glad to have Kona there with her when it was time to crawl into bed each night. She was glad now that they'd been bad owners and let him sleep in their bed.

They'd intended to crate train him as a puppy, but that had lasted all of three nights, well, technically two and a half. Of course, back then he took up minimal space, his brown bean-bag puppy's body flopped between their pillows. Once grown, however, it was a constant struggle for mattress real estate. As with all such dealings, the key was location, location, location. Each night, he started out stretched along the foot of the bed, their legs bent around him in a horizontal game of Twister. But slowly, throughout the night, he'd slink his way up toward the head of the bed, burrowing in between them. Then he'd push against them until he had enough room.

Now, with just the two of them, they each had plenty of space. But some nights, when she felt especially lonely, she was the one bothering him. She would scoot over until they were back-to-back. Or sometimes she'd rest her head on his sturdy side, soothed by the metronome of his slow, rhythmic heartbeat.

IN ADDITION TO Kona's company, Maggie took comfort in knowing Helen and Russell were both keeping an eye on her. It helped, knowing they were thinking of her. Some days a simple message on her machine ("*Hola.* Wanted to see how you're doing. Call me.") pulled her out of the mild undertow of depression that often lurked close by. And Helen had insisted they add a weekly weights workout to their routine. Maggie suspected Helen only suggested it to make sure Maggie got out of bed on Saturdays, but she'd had fun the first couple of times and hoped they'd stick to it.

It was the same with Russell. He'd email her almost every other day, often including a link to a funny dog-related video he'd found on YouTube; his emails always made her giggle. He had come by, twice, armed with his toolbox. When she'd treated for the combined Kevin's going away/Russell's do-over birthday dinner, Kevin ceremoniously handed the house To Do list over to Russell, who'd crooned a few bars of James Taylor's *I'm Your Handyman*. She'd had to intervene though, when Russell started a debate over whether DeWalt or Craftsman made the best tools.

One night a couple of weeks after Kevin left, she invited Helen and Russell for dinner. She didn't say it outright, but she wanted to thank them for looking out for her. As they dug into their grilled salmon, she imagined her new friends as her own personal lifeguards. *No, they're my get-a-life-guards, my own little Bay Watch team.* She saw them running in slow-motion on the beach in red swimsuits. Of course, she knew from yoga that Helen would look fantastic, but she wondered about Russell. He'd probably look fantastic as well. She knew he'd been on the swim team in college, and he still had a swimmer's broad shoulders and narrow waist. She'd seen him in shorts before. *Nice legs, but what does he look like without his shirt on?*

She shook her head as if she could rid herself of the image on the Etch-A-Sketch of her brain. *Best not to think that way about your new buddy.* She excused herself to go get the peach cobbler she'd made for dessert.

But Maggie did think about him "that way" the following Sunday. Russell, having bought Kevin's bike, suggested they ride to Bandito's.

They sat on the deck under an umbrella to escape the July-afternoon sun and talked about how happy Kevin had sounded when they each talked to him earlier that week. Then as they finished their beers, Maggie told him she was changing her name back to O'Connell. Russell offered her his large, strong hand to shake and said, "Pleased to meet you, Ms. O'Connell."

Back at her house afterwards, he'd loaded his bike on his car, and then walked her to the door. He leaned against the doorjamb while they said goodbye. The sun, low in the sky, peeked under her porch and pointed out the fine gold highlights in his brown hair. In an effort to keep her fingers from reaching out to touch them, she played with the jade pendant on her necklace.

Kona burst through the front door between them, happy to go out and relieve himself after being home alone for hours. Maggie smiled to herself, thinking it would have to have been a seriously hot and heavy moment not to be disturbed by the musical accompaniment of Kona peeing on the liquidambar tree in her front yard.

They laughed as Kona, done with his business, rolled over on the grass and shimmied and twisted, scratching himself and grunting. He kicked at the air like an upturned beetle.

"Well, I'd better go. Gotta get the dog his inner-day," Maggie said, closing the door on any further thoughts she, or Russell, might be having about him crossing the threshold.

"Yeah, OK," Russell said. Maggie wondered if that was a look of disappointment in his eyes. "This was fun, Ms. O'Connell. We'll have to do it again some time."

A FEW DAYS later Russell called to see if she wanted to catch *Young Frankenstein* on Friday. A theater in town was having a Mel Brooks retrospective. They arranged to meet up and go from his place.

After Maggie hung up, she thought how relieved she was that nothing had happened between them after their bike ride. It was just a weak moment—a desire for a man's touch—that made her want to run her fingers through the fool's gold of his hair.

I can't think about men right now. I'm a mess. Rebound central. Besides, it would never work out between us. He's too young for me.

Maggie thought about that. He was actually only three years younger. And she guessed that anyone who saw them together might think he was older than her. She didn't look her age, thanks to her Midnight Mahogany touch-ups and her fair skin, which she'd hated as a young girl. But now, all that hat-wearing, sunscreen-slathering, and general sun-avoiding she'd put up with as a kid meant she had very few lines on her face. Whereas, Russell's temples held the first hints of gray and the laugh lines around his eyes gave away the fact that this Southern Californian had not been tied to his hat and sunglasses. Of course, Maggie also knew that in the world's eyes, as well as her own, this only made him look distinguished, not old.

I guess it's not that he's too young, per se, but just . . . well, a little immature. More like a twenty-eight-year old, rather than thirty-eight; just wanting to date and have fun. Not that there's anything wrong with fun—I could use some fun myself. Still . . . I wonder if he's ever been in love, or would even want to be. She shook her head. *I hope he doesn't think I'm his next conquest, especially after that . . . moment on my porch. Or am I crazy?* Was *that a moment?*

At any rate, she was glad he wanted to go see *Young Frankenstein.* No chance he was thinking of that as a date movie.

EVEN THOUGH SHE'D seen it a million times, Maggie still laughed all through the film. On the way back to Russell's condo, where Maggie had left her car, he asked, "Who do you think was sexier in that, Madeline Kahn or Teri Garr? I enjoy a good debate, but I really can't pick a side in this one. Madeline was damn hot, but Teri Garr as Inga . . . What man doesn't want a blond, Swedish assistant? I really can't decide." He shook his head.

"That's a tough one," she said, tapping her forefinger on her lips. "I'm going to have to think about that." But what she thought was: *Cool. I'm pretty sure a man who finds a woman attractive, doesn't ask her to weigh in on the sex appeal of other women. Clearly, we're on the same page here. We're just buddies.* "I'm going to have to say: Cloris Leachman."

Russell looked thoughtful. "Of course. How could I forget the lovely Frau Blücher?"

Maggie whinnied and he laughed.

"Want to come up for a bit? Have a glass of wine?" he asked as he pulled into his parking space in the underground lot.

"OK." She wanted to check out Mr. Bachelor's pad. "I can't

stay long though. Gotta get up early tomorrow and go to the gym."

She expected it to look not unlike a dorm room, but it actually turned out to be rather nice. Bare, but nice. Except for scattered sports, travel and software magazines, and a few beer bottles by the sink, it looked similar to a Pottery Barn ad: wood floors, a tan sofa with fat red throw pillows, and a rug of reds and browns set on an angle. The kitchen was small, but with a beautiful tiled backsplash. The half-empty living room shelves held a golf trophy; a picture of Russell, sunburned and smiling, holding a huge bass; and some paperback books, their bindings cracked, mostly of the Bond or Bourne type. A pale green hardcover caught her eye: *101 Knitting Patterns*.

Huh, she thought. She hung her sweater on the back of a barstool and looked around for the accompanying basket of wool. Aloud she said, "Cool place. Love the tile work."

"Thanks. I did that myself." He pulled a bottle of wine out of the pantry.

"Is that an Xbox?" she asked, pointing at the TV cabinet. *Aha, there it is.* She spotted a large coffee tin next to the television overflowing with yarn in soft blues, greens and grays. Knitting needles stood up out of the can, stuck into the balls of wool like chopsticks.

"*Combat Fighter* totally rocks. Wanna play?"

"No, that's OK. So, you're a knitter, huh?"

"Yes." He uncorked the bottle with a satisfying "thock" sound. "I like to keep my hands busy. And it's relaxing."

"You don't have to sound defensive. I think that's cool." She watched him pour the wine. "So, what kind of stuff do you make?"

"Mostly scarves and hats. Easy stuff. We're not talking works of art here. Once I get a decent-sized pile together I just donate them to Goodwill."

"That's sweet."

"Nah. Like I said, I just like to keep busy. Can't sit still and watch TV." He shrugged and handed her a wine glass filled with what looked like liquid wheat. "Anyway, if you won't let me beat you at *Combat Fighter*, how about I show you my ocean view, instead?"

"Sure." He led her out to the balcony, lit only by the light he'd left on in the kitchen. But when she stepped outside into the summer evening air another block of condos, a softball lob away, dominated the view. She raised her eyebrows at him.

He waved her over to the right side of the balcony. "You've gotta lean out." He stood behind her, one hand on her arm as she stretched over the metal railing.

"Oh yeah, there it is." Between two buildings, she saw a column of black, touched with pockets of silver as the ripples in the water caught the light of the three-quarter-full moon. "Very nice." The heat of his hand warmed her bare upper arm. She looked down at the ground, four stories below. "Makes me a little dizzy. Better sit down."

They sat in his Adirondack chairs and Maggie said, "It must be nice, being this close to the ocean. Even if you can't really see it."

"Sure, if you like parking hassles and traffic, it's great." He took in a deep breath. "Seriously, though, I do love it. Smell that."

She breathed deeply too, filling her lungs with the cool, briny air.

"Sometimes in the summer when I have my windows open, I can hear the waves late at night," he added. "And I like to go down and run on the beach. Speaking of working out, that was fun riding to Bandito's last week."

"Yeah. But, that's not a workout."

"No? I broke a sweat. Doesn't that count for something?"

"If your replacement drink is a beer, it's not a workout. If you really want to go for a serious ride, you should come with me some time. I go almost every Sunday morning."

He bobbed his head side to side. "Hmmm. I guess I could do Sundays, although sometimes I'm out pretty late Saturdays. Technically, it's already Sunday when I get in."

"Are you setting up your excuse for when I kick your butt on Torrey Pines hill?"

"Them's fightin' words. You're on. This Sunday I can't; golfing. But next week's good. What time?"

Before Maggie could answer a gust of wind tickled the back of her neck; she shivered.

"Let's go inside," Russell said. "That's another thing I love about living on the coast. No matter how hot it is during the day, it cools off at night." He waited at the sliding door for her to pass through and patted her shoulder. "And there are so many fun ways to warm up."

He's joking, right? She put her hand up to bat him on the arm and laugh it off with a light-hearted, "That's what I brought my sweater for," but he grabbed her raised hand and pulled her to him, before she could say anything. He kissed her.

He smelled amazing, a combination of a worn leather jacket, rain on the ocean in winter, and . . . something else, something inexplicable . . . maybe ginger snaps? *Ohmygod, that's it. He smells edible.* His lips were warm and soft and tasted like fresh grass from the Sauvignon blanc they were drinking. A wave of heat tried to sweep her legs out from under her.

"Wait, Russell . . ."

"Mmmmm. Wait for what?" His voice resonated deep is his throat. Her heart rattled the cage of her ribs. He nuzzled her ear. She resisted the urge to cling to him. He felt so . . . solid. She felt like Jell-O salad. *OK, pros: good grief, what a kisser. It's been a while. Cons: It's been a while. A long while. Oh God, too nervous. Hyperventilating; breathe. What would Kona do? No, don't even think about that. Remember, you're just friends . . .*

"I don't think we can do this." She put her hands to his chest and looked down to hide the fire she felt on her cheeks.

"Oh, I'm pretty sure we can do this."

Mustering her resolve, she pushed away from him like a swimmer off the wall of a pool.

"I want us to be friends." She went to the kitchen counter and grabbed her sweater. She was no longer cold, but she needed something to do; somewhere safe to put her hands.

"We are friends, Maggie." He came up behind her and caressed her shoulders. "But we could be friends *with benefits*."

She faced him. "Yeah, we *could* . . . but I really value our friendship and don't want to mess that up."

"We're not going to mess that up." He played with a lock of her hair.

"We might. What if the . . . ya' know, sex is awful?"

"You obviously don't know who you're dealing with." He licked his forefinger and made a show of smoothing one cocked, devilish eyebrow. Then he put his hands on his hips, stuck out his jaw and struck a male-model pose, looking into the distance.

She scoffed at him. "OK, then, what if it's mind-blowingly good?" she asked.

He dropped his exaggerated pose and turned to look at her. "You say that like it could actually be a bad thing. I'm not following."

"Well, you know, that just . . . It . . . it wouldn't be any good, because we're not in a relationship. And we're never going to be."

He chuckled. "Mind-blowingly good sex can be a darn good basis for a relationship."

"Maybe at first, but that sort of thing never lasts," she said.

He shrugged and turned toward the sofa. "I don't know," he said as he sat and patted the space next to him. "I've been in relationships built on a foundation way flimsier than great sex. Mind you, there was great sex, lots of it." He crossed his arms and put his feet up on the ottoman. "But that wasn't the foundation."

She sat next to him, pulled her feet up and hugged a big red pillow. "Like what?"

"Like . . . mind-blowingly good ravioli."

"Excuse me?"

"I dated this Italian gal a while back. She was very pretty; not the sharpest knife in the block, but man could she cook. And you know how I loves me some chow. She made everything from scratch—the sauce, the fillings, the pasta. It was amazing."

"So what happened? You got her to stock your freezer and then dumped her?"

"No, I'm not that insensitive." He put his hand over his heart and looked at her as if wounded to his core. "I gained ten pounds and then I dumped her."

Maggie laughed, "That's a switch."

"What do you mean?"

"I thought pigs like yourself," she fluttered her eyelashes, "were the type to dump a woman when she gained ten pounds. I never heard of a guy breaking up with someone because *he* gained weight."

"You think I'm terribly shallow don't you?"

"I know you're terribly shallow. At least when it comes to women. For Pete's sake, you told me yourself that you dumped a woman because you didn't like her belly button."

"Well, there might have been a little more to it than that."

"Yeah? Well, either way, I still like you." She patted him on the knee and stood up to go. "I'm gonna head out. It's late."

He walked her out. "Look, I apologize. I hope you don't think I was totally out of line."

"Well, you wouldn't be the shallow pig I know you to be if you didn't at least try."

"Right you are. Now give me a hug and get out of here."

"I'll even give you a kiss." She pecked his cheek and left without looking back.

At home, Kona ran to greet her. He jumped up and pinned her to the sofa, covering her in wet licks. She held her head up, directing his aggressive kisses away from her face.

"Not you, too. This must be my lucky day, fighting off two boys on the same night." She smiled and hugged him. "But you win, Buddy. *You* I'm going to sleep with."

Chapter 10: Reviewing the Pass

The following Tuesday at Tea Time, Maggie waited patiently to tell Helen about Russell. Helen's hair shimmered and fell back into place while she shook her head, complaining about the heat in Paris.

"It was *muy chaud*, over one hundred both days. There's a reason they don't sing about August in Paris you know."

"Don't you mean *'tres chaud'*?" Maggie asked.

"Oh, *merde*. I was doing that the whole time I was there. I get used to flying to Barcelona, and then I get all screwed up every time I switch over from Spanish. Everyone on the crew makes fun of me and my 'Sprench.' And it doesn't go over very well with Parisians when you say things like *'bon jour, señor.'*"

"The French just don't appreciate you like I do. I'm happy to have you back. Something happened on the weekend, and I've been dying to talk to you." She took a deep breath. "I went to a movie with Russell on Friday, and he, uh, sorta hit on me afterwards."

"Russell made a pass at you?" Helen asked, leaning in closer.

"I never understood that phrase," Maggie pretended to read non-existent leaves at the bottom of her tea. "A man must have come up with that one. You know how they always love to turn everything into a sports analogy?" Now that her friend was finally back, and Maggie could hash through the event with her, she enjoyed making Helen wait.

"What happened? Tell me everything. I want every juicy detail of this pass." Helen raised an eyebrow. "Was it in your end-zone?"

Maggie laughed. "There are no juicy details. The pass was deflected."

"What?" Helen looked at her as if she were a book with the pages of a steamy sex scene torn out. "Start at the beginning and tell me everything."

"We were drinking wine on his balcony and chatting, and when we got up to go inside, he kissed me."

"And?"

"And nothing. That was it."

"So, wait a minute. It was like a peck?"

"No, it was a *kiss*."

"*En français?*" Helen's eyes widened over the top of her tea mug.

"He*len*, I'm not telling you that."

"Oh, *oui*. I have my answer." She set her mug down.

"Anyway, it was pretty clear he was hoping for more than just a kiss."

"And please explain to me why you didn't want to give that gorgeous man some of what he was hoping for? Is he a bad kisser?"

"Uh, no." Maggie waited while a passing waiter asked if they'd like refills, then continued. "Let's just say, if kissing were an Olympic sport, he'd make the podium. His lips were so soft."

"How soft? Please. You're talking to a woman who hasn't had any lipular contact in way too long. I'll take my vicarious thrills where I can get them." Helen rested her chin in her hand.

"They were like . . . You know when you buy a half gallon of ice cream—"

"I don't buy half gallons. I can't be alone in the house with a half gallon of ice cream."

"OK then, ya' know when you buy a *pint* of ice cream," she paused and Helen nodded for her to continue, "and by the time you get home and take the lid off, the top part's all melty? Kissing him was like that."

"Oh, man." Helen pretended to wipe a bit of drool from her bottom lip, then sat back and folded her arms. "So . . . why would you stop kissing a man with melty-ice-cream lips?"

"Well, we're just friends for one thing."

"You could be friends with privileges." She wiggled her

eyebrows. "That's the beauty of having an attractive male friend."

"That was Russell's basic argument. But, I'm not so sure. Besides, it's just . . . too soon."

"Too soon? What do you mean? You know Russell. You know he's a good guy."

"It's not about him." Her voice was quiet. "It's Dave. It's too soon after Dave."

"Oh honey, I know it's been hard. But it's been like, what, three months since Dave moved out? And, I don't mean to overstep, but from what you've told me, I'm guessing you two weren't exactly going at it before D-Day."

"I know. It's . . . crazy. *I'm* crazy. It's been ages since I—" she glanced around to make sure no one in the quiet shop was listening and, to be on the safe side, mouthed "had sex." She turned her stir stick over and over. "And Russell is very attractive and when he kissed me I went all . . . wobbly. You know when you see a newborn colt on TV, trying to get up on those spindly little legs? That was me. It took all my will power to walk away from him, but . . ."

"Yes?"

"This is going to sound pathetic, but I just knew that if I" again she mouthed the next two words, "*had sex* with him I'd be comparing him to Dave. And that's no fun for anybody."

"That is not pathetic. It's only natural." Helen patted Maggie's hand. "Dave's the only man you've" she looked slowly left, then right and mouthed with exaggerated lip movements, "had sex with" eliciting a smirk from Maggie, "for like twenty-plus years. So, of course it's going to be a big deal for you to uh, get back up on the horse, so to speak."

She earned a full smile from Maggie with that comment and Maggie repeated her last words. "So to speak."

But the smile slid away and Maggie snapped the stir stick she'd been tormenting in half.

"What is it? Is there more?" Helen asked.

"It's . . ." She rested her forehead on a tripod of her fingers, then glanced up from beneath her bangs. "It's not just that it was a long time that I was with Dave. It's that . . ." She picked at a spot on the table where the varnish had worn thin. "Dave's the only one I've ever been with."

She wondered what Helen was thinking. She knew Helen had had many lovers, both before and after her marriage. She'd told Maggie once that she had no problem with sex as recreation, liberation, or celebration. She accepted that it was also handy for procreation, but she'd never personally been interested in employing it that way.

Maggie felt like a schoolmarm standing in the center of a raucous saloon.

"Wow," Helen said. "That's—"

"I know; it's crazy." Her hand sought her heart-shaped jade pendant she often wore. Her dad had given it to her when she turned sixteen. She rubbed it like a gambling addict fingering his last coin.

"I was going to say special."

"It's not special. It just happened that way. I mean, I fully expected to have some hot, casual sex when I went away to college. I'd had boyfriends in high school, but no one special, ya' know? No one I was even remotely serious about." She sighed. "I started college thinking I was so ready; going to sow my wild oats, or whatever. But then it turned out, I had these very tame oats on my hands. I mean, these were some seriously domesticated oats."

Helen smiled, her hand over her mouth.

"I met Dave right away and I thought we were having casual sex, but, who knew? He turned out to be my first and, so far, only love."

"Maggie, that *is* special."

"Yeah. So special that my so-called one and only love started boinking another woman."

"Well, that part's not so special. That part sucks. Total *merde*."

"You said it." They sat for a minute in silence, Maggie studying her cuticles. When she looked up again, she said, "Let's change the subject."

"Sure."

"So . . . I'm attempting this new thing, where I try to think more like Kona. I ask myself what he would do in any given situation, and then try to act like him."

"You're planning to sniff people's crotches and eat everything that isn't nailed down?"

Maggie laughed. "OK, maybe I won't act a *lot* like Kona, but, you know, try to go with the flow more. Don't over-think everything."

"Sounds like a good idea." Helen nodded her head in approval. "So, you'll be following his *dog*trine? Get it?"

"Yes, you're very clever. But, I'm wondering then . . . if I'm trying to think like Kona, maybe I made the wrong decision, saying no to Russell?"

"You're saying Kona would have slept with him?"

Maggie smiled. "Not exactly. What I meant was, Kona's always up for some fun. In fact, with the exception of going to the vet, he sees potential for fun in every situation. And he never worries about the consequences."

"I'm sure that's true, but dogs also only do something if it feels right. And I know you didn't think sleeping with Russell felt right."

"You're right," Maggie said. "Right, right, right. I really do just want us to be friends." She pictured that kiss again. *Right?*

MAGGIE HAD TWO bikes, the old beater of a cruiser that she rode for bayside jaunts and a sleek road bike that Dave had given her for Christmas five years ago. She hadn't realized how much she'd missed riding. She loved the wind in her face, working up a sweat, the freedom. She timed herself on the hill at Torrey Pines each week. She liked seeing the times drop.

The second Sunday after their moment-that-was-definitely-a-moment, Russell joined Maggie on her ride. They'd exchanged a few emails, but it was the first time she'd seen him. She felt awkward at first, but he acted as if nothing had happened, so she soon felt normal again.

As promised, she kicked his butt up Torrey Pines. She pulled away on the steep incline and then made a show of waiting for him at the top. She looked at her watch and tapped her cycling shoe on the asphalt as he rode up behind her, panting. She suggested they ride a bit further to a spot with a view of La Jolla Shores where they could rest and eat an energy bar.

When they stopped, overlooking the beach below, he took his helmet off and fluffed his brown locks.

"There's no primping on bike rides, Mister," she said.

"I wasn't primping. I was cooling my head." He gnawed at the bar she gave him. "Mmmm, yummy," he'd said, deadpan. "Just like momma used to make."

"I know they're not great, but eat it. You need it, if you're going to keep up with me."

When they got back home, Russell confessed to being beat. "You were right. You kicked my ass. But, you wait. I'll get in better shape. I'll beat you up that hill one day."

They agreed to try and ride every Sunday and made a deal that whoever lost on the hill each week had to provide the energy bars for the next ride.

"Just be sure whatever you bring me is either some sort of chocolate or peanut butter flavor," Maggie said. "I don't like the fruity ones. And you might want to pick up a box at Costco. I'm pretty sure you're going to need to buy them in bulk."

"We'll see," Russell said, wiping the sweat off his face and smoothing his eyebrows.

ON THEIR THIRD Sunday ride, Maggie and Russell stopped at their now standard rest spot to enjoy the view. He pulled off his helmet and rifled his fingers through his hair. He swallowed a bite of the PowerBar (which he had supplied) and said, "So, I'm seeing this gal."

"Oh, since when?"

"I dunno. Almost three weeks, I guess. Her name's Natalia."

Hmmm, shortly after that kiss. Guess he didn't lose any sleep over it like I did. "That's good." She fastened and unfastened the Velcro strap on her cycling glove. "But, are you trying to tell me I'm about to lose my riding partner?"

"No, she's not into biking, although she's not crazy about my biking buddy being a gal."

"We're just friends."

"I know that, but she doesn't know that. You should meet her, and then she'll see that we're just buds. You need to find a man so we can go on a double-date."

"I don't know any men. I mean, not that I'd want to date." Again she wondered if she'd done the right thing in stopping him when he kissed her. Maybe she should have had sex with him. Gotten it over with. After all, she was no romantic.

But even to a practical person like herself, she admitted that "getting it over with" didn't sound very nice. It was more fun to think about meeting someone, not to fall in love with, but just to be excited about, to look forward to seeing. She'd begun to warm up to the idea of getting out there again. She was even assessing most of the single men she encountered as potential date, or even crush, material. *Might be fun to have a good, healthy, borderline-obsessive crush on someone.* But no one had piqued her interest; not at work, or at the museum, or at yoga (especially not at yoga where there were usually only two men—both in their seventies).

"I thought you might say that. Because, let's face it, once you've kissed me, any other man is going to look like chopped liver."

She punched his arm. "You think you're such a stud? I'll race you home." She clicked into her pedals and started off down the hill before he could even put his water bottle away.

Being heavier, he caught her on the downhill and they took turns riding in front in the wind. But when they rode up the hill on her street, she left him in her wake.

"I kicked your butt again today," she said, when he pulled up next to her.

"No fair. I feel like I'm catching a cold."

"Excuses. Come on in and I'll make you a Fuzzy Navel smoothie. It'll fix you up."

Kona greeted them and tried to lick the sweat off Maggie's legs while she gathered the orange juice, a bag of frozen peach slices and a frozen banana for their drinks.

Russell picked up where he'd left off. "Anyway, like I was saying before, I knew you wouldn't be able to find a man that could compare with me, so I've found one for you."

"Excuse me?" She paused in the act of pouring orange juice into the blender.

"There's this guy at work, Mark. I don't know him real well, but he's not bad looking. I know he got divorced last year and he's an accountant, so there you go. What else do you need?"

She got the brewer's yeast out of the cupboard. "What are you saying?" she asked as she shook a tablespoon or so worth of the musty golden flakes into the mix.

"What is that?" Russell turned up his nose. "Healthy junk?"

"It's packed with vitamins. You won't even taste it, you big baby." She snapped the lid down on the carafe. "So, did you talk to this guy about me or what?"

"No. I just invited him to a Labor Day barbecue this coming Saturday."

"I hope you didn't say anything about me," she shouted over the whirr of the blender. A feeling of dread coursed through her as she watched the ingredients swirl together. She'd thought she was ready to date again, but now faced with an actual possibility, she felt as if he'd put her stomach in the blender and set it on pulse. She filled two glasses with the pale orange smoothie and handed him one, while Kona watched and hoped for spillage. "Seriously, did you?"

"No, I was cool. Just told him I was having a few people over." He took a drink and his eyes widened in surprise. "Oh, damn. That's good. I thought you were ruining it with that brown stuff, but I think I'm hooked. I'm going to need one of these after every ride." She watched with pleasure as he gulped it down. Her pleasure turned to panic when he added, "Anyway, I just told him there'd be this one particular gal there."

"Oh, God." She set her glass down on the counter with a thud.

"What? It'll be super casual. You come over, you eat dinner—"

Kona lunged at Russell, barking at him. The dog caught Russell off guard, knocking him against the counter.

"Kona, off!" Maggie grabbed a tin canister painted with fire hydrants and pulled out a biscuit. When Kona heard the schwoop of the lid, he left Russell alone and ran to Maggie. She tossed the biscuit in the air and Kona snapped at it like an alligator.

"Did you just reward your dog for going ballistic on me?"

"*No*. I mean, well, I guess it kind of looked that way. But, I told you about his trigger words. You can't just say the D-word. Anyway, I'm sorry. Now, go on with your terrible plan."

"As I was saying, before I was so rudely accosted, you come over for d-i-n-n-e-r; you talk to him. If you don't like him, no harm done."

"Why did you do this without telling me first?"

"I knew you'd say no."

"Hey, you didn't even invite me to any barbecue yet. How do you know I'm even free?"

"Maggie, I don't want to be mean, but you're always free on the weekends."

She dropped her arms to her sides; she had no retort. She looked down and noticed Kona begging for their empty glasses; it reminded her: *Think like Kona. Go with it. Maybe it will be fun.* "Can I bring Helen? That way it won't be like you're shoving the two single folks together."

"Yeah, I was assuming Helen would come. Isn't she your wing-woman?"

THAT EVENING MAGGIE invited Helen to go to dinner. They decided on Helen's favorite Mexican restaurant, Alfonso's, in La Jolla. It was an upscale version of Bandito's with more ambiance and less grease. Maggie sipped a strawberry margarita, while waiting for Helen.

"Did I see you flirting with that bartender?" Helen asked without saying hello. She hopped up on a barstool as she indicated the well-muscled man in a black T-shirt behind the bar.

"No, I wasn't flirting." As she said it she wiggled her fingers to get the bartender's attention and called out, head tilted to one side, "Could you bring one of these for my friend?"

He winked at her and walked off to the blender. "He can tend to me anytime," Helen said in her best Mae West. Then added, "Yes, you were flirting. And look at this sexy ensemble." She looked Maggie up and down.

"Oh, well, I went shopping. My old jeans were getting a bit baggy." She wore a halter-style handkerchief top, with black-on-black flowers embroidered on it, and slim low-rise jeans with strappy black sandals.

"*Buenas noches,*" Helen said into Maggie's cleavage. "Nice to finally meet you, girls." Helen had told Maggie more than once that she should show off her figure.

The bartender brought the margarita in time to see Helen talking to Maggie's breasts. He grinned as he set the drink down and asked if they needed anything else. "Anything at all?"

"Um, not right now," Maggie said as a blush cascaded down her cheeks and chest, which he openly stared at. Her hand went to her jade pendant, her usual nervous habit, but also to hide her cleavage. "Thanks," she dismissed him, then whispered to Helen, "You are so embarrassing."

"Sorry. I'll be good. But, really, you seem different. Ready to get back up on that horse."

"Russell said the same thing."

"You talked to Russell about riding?" "Horses" and "riding" had become code for sex.

"Noooo. Not about *riding*; just dating in general." She told Helen about Natalia and Russell's plan to set her up with Mark. "So, will you come along? Be my wing-woman?"

"Sure. I'm back from Paris on Friday, so I can make it. Might be a little jet-lagged, but, what the heck. And if you don't like this Mark guy, maybe I will."

Maggie almost said, "Hey, back off. He's mine." Then realized she hadn't even met Mark yet. Kona wouldn't second-guess a friend's motives. In fact, Kona would just order nachos.

"Let's order nachos." Maggie held up her margarita in a toast, "Here's to having fun. Now get that cute bartender back over here."

Chapter 11: The Mark

Maggie and Helen arrived first at Russell's barbecue, which he was holding at Natalia's. Compared to his condo, her place had ample parking and a big backyard. He'd asked Maggie to come early to get to know Natalia.

She was, as Maggie had expected, gorgeous. Maggie thought she looked like everything round from Sophia Loren—dark eyes, full breasts and buttocks—tacked onto Olive Oyl's frame.

"Nice to meet you?" Natalia said, shaking Maggie's hand with all the authority of a butterfly. *Oh dear, she's got Olive Oyl's voice and upper body strength too.*

Russell fetched everyone a beer and asked if they'd help cut up veggies for the skewers.

"Sure," Helen and Maggie answered together, and the four of them gathered in the kitchen around the butcher block island large enough to function as a helipad.

"We've got a bit of time," Russell said, pulling a plate of raw, cubed beef from the refrigerator. "The Mark won't be here until around five."

"Stop calling him 'the Mark,'" Maggie said. Russell had been teasing her all week via email, causing her to threaten to not show up. "It's not like we're out to con him. Are we? Am I that awful that we have to try to pass me off on this unsuspecting man as something I'm not?"

"No, you're not that bad," Helen said, lopping the top off a zucchini. "I mean, come on, if they can put a man on the moon, we ought to be able to put one in your bedroom."

Russell laughed while Maggie glared at them both. "Real nice, you two," she said.

"We're just messing with you," Russell said.

Maggie pointed her knife at him, "Well, knock it off. You're making me nervous."

"There's nothing to be nervous about. Drink your beer and chill out."

"He's right," Helen said. "Chill." She clinked her beer bottle against Maggie's.

Maggie decided to ignore them. She surveyed the gleaming counters and appliances. Either Natalia was a clean freak or the kitchen didn't get much use. Judging by the way Natalia methodically dissected a bell pepper, Maggie figured it was the latter. *At least Russell won't have to worry about her fattening him up.*

Helen and Maggie finished chopping their assigned veggies and watched Natalia wipe her slender, French-manicured fingers on a towel and then drag a basket of cherry tomatoes to her cutting board. She held one up, examined it and laid it down as if about to operate.

"I think you can leave those whole," Maggie offered.

"Yeah?" Natalia said in her sing-song voice. "Maybe one of you could help with the salad?" Maggie had noticed Natalia's tendency to end every sentence as a question. OK, but maybe you could cut her some slack, she chided herself. *That one really was a question.*

"I'll help," Helen said.

Maggie went to open the screen door for Russell as he headed out with the tray of meat. Since the salad prep looked under control, she followed him outside. She heard Helen ask Natalia how she and Russell met and heard her reply, "Rollerblading?"

She stepped out into the warm September evening air and the smell of jasmine.

Russell lowered his voice as he lay the skewers on the sizzling grill, "So, what do you think of my gal? She's gorgeous, isn't she?"

"She's almost as pretty as you."

"Hey, be nice."

"I am. She's beautiful. And she seems nice. But I haven't talked to her all that much yet."

"Well, you should because she's sweet."

"She's got a sweet house, that's for sure," Maggie took in the large yard with its inlaid stone patio and built-in barbecue. A fountain gurgled in the corner and a wind chime that hung from the redwood pergola overhead struck a single low note as a slight breeze passed.

"Divorce settlement," he whispered.

"Oh. Does she work?"

"Yes, she works. She's not just a pretty face, living off her alimony. She's a sales rep for a pharmaceutical company. And she used to be a Charger Girl."

"Oh. Cool." Maggie peeled at the label on her near empty beer bottle.

"Is that how you're going to wear your hair?"

Her hand went to her bare neck. She'd twisted her hair up into a loose French knot and fastened it in place with a banana clip and a serious dose of hair spray.

"Well, obviously I'd planned to wear it this way. It's hot . . . I thought it'd be cooler this way. Why? Do you think I should take it down?"

"I just think you have really beautiful hair. You should show it off." They heard voices inside. "Gotta go welcome The Mark." He left her, twirling a loose tendril around her finger.

Does this look stupid? Maybe he's right. Maybe I should take it down. God, I never wear my hair up. Why did I try a new style tonight?

She pulled the clip out and bent over to shake the style out of her curls. They resisted, having been lacquered into place with too much spray. She heard the back door open and Russell say, "Mark, I'd like you to meet Maggie."

She stood straight, knowing her hair must be sticking out like some sort of Vegas showgirl headdress. Blond-haired, green-eyed Mark moved toward her, his hand outstretched. She stuffed the banana clip in the front pocket of her long rayon skirt, where it stuck out like an appendage no woman should have.

They shook hands and she heard herself saying hello and nice to meet you, while her mind screamed: *Well, this is going great. And he's cute. Make up an excuse to get in the house. Hurry; come up with something.*

"I need to go to the bathroom." Her mouth folded under the pressure from her brain.

"Oh. OK. Uh—" Before Mark could say anything else, she left him standing there with Russell and bolted for the house. She ducked into the powder room, avoiding Helen and Natalia still in the kitchen.

Her imagination had been too kind. Her hair stood out in tufts as if a bird had built a nest in it. In fact, it seemed possible the bird might still be in there somewhere. She blinked several times at her reflection, then pawed at her insane headdress. There was no helping it; it was going to have to go back in the clip. She fought the stiff locks back into place and reinserted the clip with such ferocity it felt like she'd put an industrial clamp into her hair.

"Hey," Helen said through the door, "What's going on? Come out; 'the Mark's' waiting."

Maggie yanked the door open and glared at Helen. "Not you too."

"Sorry. I was trying to lighten the mood."

"You couldn't lighten my mood with a thousand-watt bulb."

"How about this then?" Helen pulled a sweating beer bottle from behind her back. "*Una cerveza pour vous?*" She held her free hand under it like Vanna White displaying a prize.

"I was thinking of something a little stronger. I hear Natalia's a pharmaceutical rep."

"Yeah, she told me? That that's what she does for a living?"

Maggie had to smile at Helen's impersonation. "What do you think of her?" she said.

"She seems harmless, I guess." Helen lowered her voice. "I'd like to have her on all my cross-Atlantic flights. In the event of a water landing, she could double as a flotation device."

"Shhhhhh." Maggie stifled a giggle. "Seriously, though, do you think she could maybe set me up with something? Like a Valium or twelve?"

"Malted courage is all you need." Helen pressed the beer into her hand. "Come on, let's go outside. He's just a guy. He puts his pants on feet first like every other man. We hope. I mean, maybe he prefers skirts at home. Let's go feel him out, so to speak." Helen winked and Maggie followed her outside.

Throughout dinner, Mark told of his harrowing adventures: rock climbing, caving, back country camping. Stories flowed one after another, each with a greater risk of imminent death. Rising to the challenge, Russell wedged in a few stories of his own: caught in a sudden storm while deep sea fishing, a close call while scuba diving in Belize. The three women barely got a word in edgewise.

Maggie asked Helen to pass the salt. As Helen handed her the shaker, she and Maggie exchanged, "Can you believe this guy?" glances.

This is a total drag, Maggie thought. *It started off so semi-promising. He's good looking. He's definitely not a nerdy accountant. But good grief, the dare devil routine is getting old. I'd take a nice, quiet dork over this guy any day.*

Mark cut off the end of one of Russell's stories and addressed Maggie. "So, Russell tells me you're into biking."

I thought Russell said he didn't tell Mark anything about me?

"Yeah. I am. Russell and I ride along the coast every weekend."

"Oh. Road biking. I didn't realize you guys were gutter bunnies." He laughed and cut a piece of meat vigorously. Maggie noted that when everyone else cut theirs it didn't require quite so much bicep action. "You ever mountain bike?" She shook her head and he continued, "My friends and I were in Moab last year on this epic ride, and about five hours in, my buddy totally bonks and does an endo off this ridge." He told of climbing down, rescuing his friend with his now broken leg, and scaling the ridge again with his friend riding piggy back. He went back a second time for the bike. Maggie noticed he never mentioned the height of the ridge, but told the story as if it were a fifty foot drop.

The story ended, greeted by a "wow" from Natalia and a "No way, man" from Russell. Maggie stood and offered to clear plates. She took Mark's and he smiled at her. She escaped to the kitchen. *I can't believe I was so looking forward to this. I even bought new eye shadow and lip gloss, for Pete's sake.* She unloaded the dishes into the sink.

"It's nice to finally get a minute alone." Mark's voice startled her and she spun around to see him leaning against the butcher block island. "Now we can really chat a little." *You mean I might get to speak?* "So, Russell tells me you're divorced."

"Yes." She nodded. "Or, well, it's in the works anyway. You too, huh?"

"Yeah, twice. It gets way easier the second time."

"Oh?" *I don't plan to have a second time. Maybe by your third, you'll hardly notice.*

"So, I was serious out there," he said.

"Sorry, about . . . ?" *What the heck is he talking about?*

"About taking you mountain biking. I could show you the ropes."

"Oh, uh—"

Before she could answer he added, "It's great for the love handles." He pointed at her. *Does he think I have love handles?!* He mimicked crouching over handlebars and twisted this way and that as he descended an imaginary hill. *Hope he does an "endo" over an imaginary rock.*

"Sounds a little scary." *Maybe if he thinks I'm a chicken he'll drop the idea.* "I better stick with riding in the gutter." She turned and stacked plates, hoping he'd get the hint, but he moved closer, backing her into the corner formed by the L of the counter.

"It is a little scary, but that's the thrill of it. I could show you some thrills." He reached into his back pocket and pulled out a card. "You should know something about me." *No, really, I don't need to know anything more about you.* "I'm the kind of guy who goes after what he wants. I can't help it. It's my Scandinavian ancestry. Got a little Viking in me." He raised his eyebrows at her. *Well, you should keep him in there. Don't let him out.* "And I think we had a little connection out there . . ." *What connection? I'm pretty sure what you're referring to is called passing the salt.* "Which is weird, because I'm usually not into redheads. They can be so freckly, you know? Anyway, I'm going to give you my number." He still held the card aloft between them, like she might hold out a treat for Kona. "And I'll expect to hear from you by, let's say Wednesday. I don't go for all that game playing, so don't think playing hard to get is going to work with me. Unless you get hit by a car while you're out on your bike or something, if I don't hear from you by Wednesday, all bets are off."

She was spared having to answer when the screen door slid open. They both turned to look. It was Russell, carrying the rest of the dirty plates.

"Hey, you two."

"Hey," Mark said. He turned back to Maggie. "Wednesday," he mouthed. Then he set the card on the counter and went back outside.

"You two are hitting it off, huh? What's that? His card?" Russell came over and picked it up to check. "I knew it. Suh-weet." He waved the card in front of her.

"Oh, no. Not suh-weet. Stoo-pid." She plucked the card out of his hand and ripped it in two. She lowered her voice and glanced out the kitchen window to the backyard. "Seriously, what the hell were you thinking? Why would you think I would like a guy like that?" *Do you know me at all?*

"What's wrong with him? He's good looking; he's fit."

"Some of us are interested in a little more than what a person looks like. The guy is so full of himself I'm surprised he had room for the shish kabobs!"

Russell laughed. "He's just confident. And he's showing off a little. You should call him."

"No thank you. I'd rather be alone." She tossed the pieces of the card into the trash and went back out to whisper with Helen about how soon they could leave.

ON THE WAY home in Helen's canary yellow Beetle, Maggie asked, "Why did I let myself get so worked up over a blind set-up with such a pompous jerk? I shaved my legs. I ironed. I went online and looked up small-talk tips—as if there was a chance for anyone else to talk. I even tried this stupid new hairdo."

"That hairdo's not stupid. It's cute. Besides, welcome back to the wonderful world of dating. This is what it's all about: dashed expectations."

"Swell."

Helen laughed, "He was something else. I never heard the words 'spelunking' and 'belay' so many times in one night. My favorite was that one rock-climbing story: 'There I was, hanging by two fingers and I said to myself, Mark, you've got too much to live for!'"

In unison they finished, Maggie adding in the reenactment while Helen drove: "And I clawed my way, hand over hand, back to the top."

After they finished laughing, Maggie asked, "What do you suppose the 'too much' was? His accounting job? Or his soon-to-be-second-ex-wife?"

"Don't know. All I know is *he's* too much."

"I shouldn't be so mean." Maggie got quiet and looked out the window. "I mean, anyone could say the same about me." She stared at the houses rushing past. What was going on inside them? Were the people happy? "What have *I* got to live for? My accounting career? My dog?"

"Maggie, you have tons to live for. You don't have to have a husband or kids to have a meaningful life."

"Yeah, but a career I'm excited about might help."

"Then find something else."

"I know. I should. I'm just worried about money and retirement and all that stuff. I mean, who's going to take care of me when I'm old and drooling?"

"Tell you what, when we're both old single ladies, which you know we eventually will be, even if we remarry, since women usually outlive their men, we'll take care of each other. Deal?"

"Deal."

"But don't drool in my car." Helen shifted gears and they merged onto the freeway.

TUESDAY MORNING MAGGIE sat drinking coffee and

reading the business section. Page two always had brief items about local companies, and when she turned the front page the word BioHealth caught her eye as if in huge, red type. The short paragraph said BioHealth had received Fast Track approval for its diabetes drug. Since the drug appeared to have fewer side effects than existing therapies, the FDA would make an effort to get it to patients sooner.

Maggie knew that would send the stock price up. It was only 7:30 in San Diego, but 10:30 in New York. She ran to her office and Kona followed, grabbing his tennis ball on the way.

"Hang on a sec, Buddy. Momma's busy." She fired up the computer.

There it was on her stock-watch list: up $3.50 already this morning. The price was almost $8. Almost $400,000. It was tempting to sell, but there was no reason. This was just the start.

As she sat at the computer, a thought hit her like a dog's cold nose on a bare belly. A shiver of excitement ran through her.

The plan didn't die on D-Day. It was alive; its pulse was strong.

She'd been so depressed about Dave leaving that she'd given up on their plan; worried the shares would never be worth much. But now it looked like the BioHealth scientists were right. The drug could be a blockbuster. The shares were still the answer; the crux of a new plan.

She'd work hard and save up as much as possible for the next year (with Fast Track status that was likely the longest the approval would take), waiting for the big payoff. The stock could easily go to $20, and she'd have her million bucks. Sure, it would be less after taxes, but it would be enough to quit her "safe" career and do something else. Something fulfilling. Goodbye, accounting. Goodbye, retirement worries. She'd work for the fun of it, while her ostrich-sized retirement nest egg waited, growing bigger every year. God bless you, compound interest! No worries about Social Security going bust. No worries about not having children to care for her in her old age. She'd be entirely self-sufficient.

OK, minor detail that she didn't know what her dream job was, but she'd figure that out. It wouldn't be the bike tour travel idea. She loved the thought of starting her own business and not being tied to a desk, but that particular idea had been Dave's from the start. She'd take some time to figure out what she wanted to do, and then create a business plan. Everything would be in place by the time she cashed in on the stock.

"Come on, baby, keep climbing," Maggie said to the computer screen. Turning to Kona, she said, "We're gonna be OK."

He put his paw up on her lap and she shook it.

Wait a minute . . . Is Dave still going to mess things up? She knew legally she could be forced to give him half of everything. *But he claimed he'd be reasonable. Of course, he'd said that while being unreasonable about the TV.*

They'd been waiting for the sale of the house to finalize everything, but she wondered if it was possible to start getting things in writing.

She needed to call her lawyer, but it was too early. Maggie had decided to use Paul Dickson on Helen's recommendation. Helen warned her not to be put off by his "baby-*merde*-brown" polyester suits. Maggie hoped he was too caught up in his love of the law and getting his clients the best deal possible to worry about making any fashion statements. He reminded her of a bulldog, with his barrel chest, wrinkled brown suits and heavy jowls.

Maggie killed some time looking up *Entrepreneur* magazine online and subscribing. She had research to do. She poked around on Amazon and ordered a five-starred book that would supposedly help her find her dream job.

Later, she called Paul and asked him to set up a meeting on Friday, her day off, with Dave and his lawyer. "Let's get this ball rolling," she said, hoping it wouldn't be a wrecking ball.

Kona must have heard her say "ball" into the phone. He pressed the now-soggy sphere insistently against her leg. It made a "schlock, schlock" sound as he re-situated it in his mouth.

"You think we're gonna be OK?" she asked. Grabbing the bit of ball that protruded from his jaws, she nodded his head up and down while he hung on with his teeth. "I sure hope you're right."

Chapter 12: Generally Accepted Dating Principles

Maggie dabbed a bit more powder under her eyes. She'd taken a full fifteen minutes to put on her makeup, in contrast to her usual three minute routine.

Got to look perfect, she thought as she pulled on her new steel gray, form-fitting dress. *Make that rat see what he's missing.* What Maggie was missing was someone to do up her zipper. She danced around the bathroom, contorting herself until she finally managed. She slipped on her burgundy three-inch heels, knowing they would make her two inches taller than Dave.

An hour later she paced Paul Dickson's conference room. He invited her to have a seat, but she said she preferred to stand. She wanted Dave to see how tall and powerful she looked. When he finally walked in, followed by his gawky lawyer, she noticed the sweat on his forehead. It was blisteringly hot that September day.

Dave looked at her. She held his gaze; pushed her shoulders back. He dragged the back of his hand across his beaded forehead as he sat down. She sat and crossed her legs. She felt confident in her steel dress. After all, Dave had said he'd be reasonable and, besides, she was certain her bulldog-look-alike lawyer could eat Dave's whippet-of-a-lawyer for lunch.

But the whippet turned out to be a biter.

After discussions of grounds and timing, Dave's lawyer, whose wrists reminded Maggie of the stir sticks at Tea Time, suggested they move on to the "disposition of marital assets." He read from the notepad in his leather binder. "My client is willing to concede the furniture and paintings to Ms. O'Connell." Of course he is, Maggie thought. *The paintings only have sentimental value, and I'm sure that's worth nothing to him.* "But will be seeking half of all the remaining assets, including the proceeds from the sale of the house, the savings and the 50,000 shares of BioHealth."

"The shares?" She lurched forward. "You said you weren't going to go after me just because I make more than you. Those are *my* shares. You know what I had to go through to earn those." She tried to stay calm but could feel herself rising, almost against her will, out of her seat. Paul put his weighty paw on her arm and she dropped back into her chair. She dug her nails into the armrests while she envisioned sliding across the conference table's glossy surface, coming to rest with her hands firmly around Dave's neck.

"Yeah, believe me, I remember. I earned them, too." Dave pointed at her. "They're as much mine as yours. Besides, I am not 'going after you.' Tell her," he said to his lawyer.

"Against my advice, my client," the whippet turned his long thin snout toward Dave, "is not seeking spousal support."

"Spousal support?" Maggie looked from her lawyer to Dave and back. Her mouth tasted like she had chewed an aspirin without water. She threw her hands up. She waited for her lawyer to leap out of his chair and cut them down with his rapier knowledge of divorce law. But he sat, taking notes in his loopy cursive writing on his yellow legal pad.

Dave's lawyer continued, "As would be well within Mr. Baxter's rights, since he worked and supported Ms. O'Connell while she obtained her MBA."

After graduation, Maggie had worked for two years while getting her accounting license. After that, she and Dave agreed an MBA would make her more marketable, so Dave had worked while she took eighteen months off to get her Masters. She couldn't believe he was throwing that ancient history back at her. She glared at Dave.

He returned her stare and said, "And I'm not pushing for shared custody of Kona. I'm being very reasonable."

"Of course you're not pushing for it. You said yourself when you left he would stay with me. He's *my* dog. You gave him to me for my birthday!"

"Technically," Dave's lawyer said, "since my client can prove that he paid for the dog, we would have a strong argument for the dog being his property."

Dave gave her a curt nod as if to signal, "So there," but she couldn't believe it. *He just sat there and smiled like a smug bastard while this idiot referred to our fuzzy baby as "property!"*

She could not glare at him with enough venom. Her left eyelid began to twitch. Dave squirmed, looked down at his hands in his lap.

When does it become justifiable homicide? Who decides that? The judge? Or the peers? You get me a jury full of divorced women, and they'll see my killing him as justifiable.

She stood and went to the windows; she crossed her arms to keep Dave from seeing that her hands shook. She couldn't look at him anymore. *How did we get here?* She wondered what the shortest distance was between loving someone more than yourself, and having them make your insides curdle with anger. Paul said something, concluded the meeting, but all she heard was her blood pounding in her ears. She looked at the parking lot below, where the sun beat down on the cars. The glare hurt her eyes, but she didn't look away. She felt the heat radiating off the glass. Or was that off of her?

When they were gone she asked, "Is it true; can he take half my shares?"

"I'm afraid so. He is entitled to them."

She watched out the window until Dave drove off. She limped to her car, a blister eating at her heel; her feet weren't used to these stupid pumps. The lining of her dress clung to her sides.

At home, Kona greeted her. Not in the mood for kisses, she pushed him down.

"Get down. I'm sorry you have to hear this, Buddy, but your daddy's a dick."

She filled the tub with cool water and climbed in with a beer. She closed her eyes and slid down into the bath until her head was underwater, then scrubbed away the mask of makeup.

When she came up with a gasp, Kona stood next to the tub, lapping up her bath water.

THE NEXT MORNING the phone rang before seven, waking her from a nightmare that Dave was driving off with Kona while she screamed obscenities at him. Her heart pounded as she reached for the phone. Ever since that morning her freshman year when Mom had called with the horrible news about Dad, she'd always hated waking up to a ringing phone. *Oh God, Grandma's in the hospital . . . or worse . . .*

"*Hola*," Helen whispered. "I can't go with you to the gym this morning."

"Are you sick? What's with your voice? Why are you calling so early?"

"No, I'm not sick. I'm in Raul's bathroom. Don't want to wake him."

Raul? Who the hell's Raul?

"I know you're wondering who Raul is; we just started dating."

"Since when?"

"Since a couple of weeks ago. I should have told you, but I didn't want to jinx it. Anyway, I wanted to let you know about the gym. I'm going back to bed."

"Wait—"

Helen hung up.

Now Maggie was wide awake, picturing her friend crawling back into bed with a hunky, naked man, while she—she glared at Kona, as if this were his fault—lay in bed with an overly large chocolate Lab. Kona looked at her and thumped his tail on the mattress. She knew that look. It was his "Feed me?" face. She reached over and scratched his belly while studying her ceiling.

She was happy for Helen. Really. Happy. She knew Helen had been trying to meet someone for a while. But she wondered what this would mean. Was Helen going to cancel their standing Saturday morning trip to the gym? What about their weekly yoga date?

OK, you're getting ahead of yourself. Calm down. Might as well go work out anyway.

As she fought her way into her workout bra, she replayed yesterday's meeting in her head. *He thinks he earned half of my shares. Un-freaking-believable.*

"*Earned* them," she said aloud to Kona, who galloped after her to the kitchen. She slashed at the peanut butter with a knife and stuffed his rubber Kong toy full of it. "I'm leaving," she said, as she flung it to him.

On the plus side, she must have burned 2,000 calories, taking her aggravation out on the elliptical trainer. While she sweated white hot anger, she tried to decide if she'd rather the stock became worthless, so she wouldn't have to give anything to Dave, or if it would be better to have the price go through the roof, so she'd still have a good chunk left over after giving both her rotten ex and Uncle Sam their respective portions.

When she got home, she checked her email. There was a message from Russell: "Can't make our Sunday ride. N and I decided to drive up to Santa Barbara for the weekend. R."

Great. What a fabulous twenty-four hours this has been.

She didn't want to be jealous, but she couldn't help it. *I wish I had someone who'd whisk me away for a fun, wild-sex weekend. I like Santa Barbara.*

God, I'm surrounded by nothing but couples now: Kevin and Annie, Russell and Natalia, even Grandma has Humphrey, and now Helen's met this Raul person. I don't necessarily feel the need to be part of couple, but it's going to suck being the only single person.

She reached for the men she knew she could always count on, the two there for her in her freezer.

I don't need a man. I have ice cream. And I have work to do. A boyfriend would just be a distraction right now. I need to figure out what kind of business I want to start. I don't have time for a man. If she repeated it often enough, would she believe it? *I don't have time for a man. I don't have time for a man. I don't have time for a man.*

She flopped down on the sofa with her ice cream and her book,

Five Rules for a Dream Career! The phone rang.

"Are you mad at me?" Helen said. "Ditching you for a man I hadn't even told you about?"

"No. Yes. But I'd forgive you if you took me out to lunch and told me every last detail."

AND THAT WAS how Maggie found herself several days later on the "women's side" of the private dining room of Giuseppe's Italian restaurant, about to take part in her first round of speed dating. Helen had been holding out on her. Sneaking off to speed dating sessions, embarrassed to admit she was going; but, she told Maggie, the third time was the charm and she'd met Raul (whose name she liked to pronounce with a roll of the R and a throaty growl). After margaritas with their lunch, Helen had made Maggie promise she'd give it a try, at least once. *I shouldn't have had that marg. If I'd been stone sober, I'd never have agreed to this. And so much for my no-time-for-a-man theory.* But Helen had insisted there was always time for a man, or at least time to "enjoy the ride."

So here Maggie sat, in her new jeans, sandals and a soft emerald-colored short sleeved sweater that Helen helped pick out saying it brought out the green flecks in her brown eyes, wanting to get this the hell over with so she could go home.

Maggie decided the one consolation was that most of the others appeared as uncomfortable as she felt. Men and women of various shapes and sizes filled the chairs pulled to either side of the room. (The sexes had been asked not to fraternize prior to the official start.) In the center of the room stood twelve tables, in a large circle, and their moderator for the evening.

Betsy, a curvy mid-forties-ish woman wearing a satiny hot-pink shell under a black polyester suit, fussed over each table: pushing the white vase with the lone daisy a few centimeters to the left on this table, squaring the tablecloth on that one.

While most everyone had their eyes on Betsy, Maggie glanced at the other women. She thought back to the online registration form that read "for ages thirty-five through fifty." *Wow, if that one's under fifty, she's seen some hard mileage. Smoker?* The woman, with a face cross-hatched like parched earth, wore a leopard print wrap-dress and her hair teased up to a height that reminded Maggie of some of the wilder '80s New Wave bands. *Wonder whatever happened to Flock of Seagulls?* Two other women, who'd come in together, and were apparently going clubbing if this didn't pan out, sported silky, low-cut halter tops, hoop earrings large enough to pass a fist through, and lots of smoky eye makeup. *Not that there's anything wrong with that look. Don't be mean. Anyway, the type of guy who's attracted to that look is not the man for me.* She smelled the chemical cocktail of their perfume and hairspray from four chairs down. It overpowered the odor of sautéed garlic that permeated every other corner of the restaurant.

Then Maggie did a quick inventory of the men: *No. No. No . . . God no. Maybe. No. Eh? Maybe . . . Hello, what's this? No. NO.* The most interesting one had thick salt and pepper hair and charcoal slacks with a pale blue dress shirt unbuttoned at the neck. Mr. Maybe #1 wore khakis and a chambray shirt, while Mr. Maybe #2 looked shy and had his hands in the pockets of his jeans, accompanied by a simple T-shirt and beat-up tan cowboy boots. Maggie'd always had a weakness for men who could pull off the cowboy look in the "big city."

Maggie turned back toward Betsy, whose head swiveled from the door, to her watch, to her clipboard for the third time.

"We're waiting for one other gentleman," Betsy said. "But it is getting a bit late."

The dating was supposed to begin at 7:30. It was now 7:45. Maggie had calculated that with a dozen people at ten minutes each, she'd be home and in her PJs by 9:45, cuddled up with her dog and her copy of *Entrepreneur* that had arrived that afternoon. This late gentleman was screwing up her plan.

"Let's start without him," said a dark haired man in a maroon shirt that shone with each pose he struck. As some of the others murmured their assent, Maggie heard him mock-whisper to a man with a bad comb-over next to him: "More ladies for the rest of us that way, eh?"

"OK, everyone," Betsy motioned for them to gather around. Her perma-smile never wavered. "I want to go over the rules. The women take the outer seats," she pointed to the seats like a flight attendant pointing out exit rows, "and the gentlemen will draw a number from my bowl." She paused and held the bowl aloft in a move Maggie found disturbingly reminiscent of a priest with the chalice. "The numbers match the chairs, so that's where you'll start. When the bell sounds after each ten minute interval, the men will move one seat to the left. Since we're one man short, unfortunately each lady will have one turn where she'll just have to wait, OK?"

The women found seats while the men selected numbers. The man with the comb-over came to her table, and Maggie noticed what appeared to be mustard stain on his wide, brown tie.

She tried to introduce herself while the others took their seats, but he shushed her.

"We're supposed to wait for the timer," he said and twisted in his seat toward where Betsy sat off to one side.

Wow, this guy's even more of a rule nut than I am.

When Betsy called out, "OK, begin," he turned back to Maggie.

"I'm Maggie." She tried to sound excited about handing out this information a second time.

"Hi Maddie. I'm Dennis," he said in a flat tone.

"No, it's Maggie."

"Oh, sorry . . . Maggie. Uh, what do you do, Maggie?"

"I'm an accountant."

He sat up straighter. Dennis was an accountant as well. He told her about an article he'd been reading and launched into his thoughts on globalization of the markets and the virtues of GAAP versus international reporting standards. Maggie hadn't come here expecting to discuss Generally Accepted Accounting Principles. She could barely work up any excitement about GAAP at the office, let alone care to discuss it outside of work. She tried to sway the conversation in another direction, but he was a pit bull of public accounting and wouldn't let go.

She was expecting him to pull out a PowerPoint presentation of his ideas and wishing there were Generally Accepted Dating Principles people were held to, when the bell finally rang.

"It was great talking to you, Maddie." He pumped her hand as he stood to move on. Maggie, fully aware she'd barely said a dozen words, nodded her head and turned to Mr. Maybe #2, Mr. Cowboy Boots, moving toward her table.

"How do you do, Ma'am?" He held out his hand to her. "My name's Floyd."

"You can call me Maggie."

"Yes, Ma'am." He nodded. The ma'aming continued throughout their conversation. He was very polite, but nothing like being called ma'am over and over to make you feel old and undesirable.

Shiny-maroon-shirt man sauntered to her table next. After about fifteen seconds of introductions, he asked her what she did to keep herself in such "fine shape."

"I ride my bike, and do weights and yoga."

"Ooohhh. Yoga." He said it as if she'd said pole dancing. "I bet you're very flex-i-ble." He raised one eyebrow and rolled the last word in his mouth like a piece of hard candy.

Ewwww. She longed for the previous few minutes when she'd felt undesirable. Maggie tried to steer him to a safer topic. "So, what do you do for a living?"

"I own a bar." Maggie wondered if he meant a strip club. "You?" he asked.

"I'm an accountant." There was a safe answer; nothing sexy about being an accountant.

"You can audit me any time," he leaned in, crossed his arms on the table and stared at her.

She leaned back as far as possible and pretended to misunderstand. She launched into a long explanation of auditors actually being quite different from accountants that she was sure could cool any man's ardor. Sure enough, in no time at all, he leaned back in his own chair, craned to check the official clock, and looked ahead to examine the woman at the next table.

There was the bell. *Thank God.* The man with salt and pepper hair moved to her table.

Mr. Interesting, whose name was Robert, asked if she was the one he'd seen pull into the parking lot in a brand new convertible BMW.

"No, that wasn't me. I drive a white Honda Civic."

"That's my car right there," he said. He pointed across the room and out the window. "The red one." There, in the row of cars, was a red BMW, shiny as a brand new fire engine.

"It's nice."

"She's a beauty." He spent the rest of the time trying to regale her with the merits of German automotive engineering. Finally the blessed bell sounded again.

The next guy, Jamie, exhausted her. Where Floyd had called her "Ma'am," Jamie called her "dude." He drummed his fingers on the table, rocked in his chair, and jumped from topic to topic: energy drinks and which one got him the most "amped," his "idiot" boss, the "totally bogus" price of gas, his ex, mountain biking, and how iguanas made the best pets "by *far,* dude." It was like conversing with a pinball machine.

Most of the rest of the men were a blur. One man in torn jeans might have invited her to go outside and get stoned, although she wasn't certain since smoking a "blunt" was not a term she'd ever heard before. She declined as graciously as possible. One knocked over his wine glass, and a drop landed on her sweater. She had to put up a block with her hand as he targeted her breast with his napkin. The rest of them were nice enough, but there was no spark, no sizzle, no chemistry of any kind. Her Bunsen burner was stone cold. Her Petri dish inert.

She welcomed her turn for the ten-minute break when it came. She looked around. Some couples desperately grasped at gossamer conversational threads. *You never realize how long ten minutes is until you're stuck talking to someone you have nothing in common with. If we were dogs, we'd just sniff each others' butts and move on. Efficient, I suppose . . . but if that was the only option, I guess I'd pick the speed dating any day.*

A few couples appeared to hit it off. Dennis-the-Accounting-Menace seemed interested in Ms. Leopard Dress. One of the big-earring ladies was in an intimate *tête-à-tête* with Maroon Shirt Man, and her friend exuded the necessary enthusiasm as Beemer Bob pointed out his little red pride and joy.

Maggie only had one more man left, Mr. Maybe #1 in the chambray shirt. Ready to give up and go home, she still felt a glimmer of hope as the bell rang and he walked to her table.

He was a dentist. He had perfect teeth.

"Oh, my brother-in-law's a dentist," she flashed her own pearly-whites back at him.

Either he was appalled by her smile, or he'd come for business, not pleasure, since he whipped out his card. "You've got a slight chip there in your front tooth." This was news to her. "I could fix it in a jiff. And I've got a new whitening system in. You might want to check it out."

She spent the rest of the time talking with her hand half over her mouth, then went home, intent on further staining her teeth with large amounts of red wine.

On the way home, she fantasized about how much better it would be if finding a new man was like getting a dog. You could go online and research the type you wanted. Would you prefer one who'll be a couch-potato with you? Or one that would fit into an active life-style? Toy or worker? Purebred or mutt? More influenced by scent or sight? Guard or companion?

I'll take an active, worker mutt who's more into scent to be my companion, please.

With her spec's nailed down, she'd go to the Hu*man* Society website and search for an appealing picture. She'd go meet him and if they hit it off, bring him home. And he'd be grateful and love her for saving him from a life spent alone in a cage. And he'd be loyal and never stray.

Chapter 13: MAMA's Boy

Maggie stood on the steps of MAMA waiting for Helen, her date for the museum's annual fund-raising gala. She had fantasized earlier that week that her date this evening would be some wonderful man she'd met at the speed-dating session, but, of course, that hadn't worked out. She was irritated with herself now for even entertaining such a silly idea and irritated with Helen for being over fifteen minutes late. When Maggie called her cell, she got voicemail.

"Where are you? I'm gonna be a big girl and go in by myself. Call when you get here."

The museum looked beautiful. Delicate white lights wound their way around the pillars and staircase railings, huge Asian-style floral arrangements stood at either end of the appetizer-filled table in the foyer, and a projected spray of constellations danced across the ceiling.

Maggie said hello to Vanessa, the volunteer coordinator, and a few of the other volunteers and went to the bar to get a drink.

In addition to the usual beer, wine and champagne, there was a martini bar. Maggie chose a blood-red pomegranate concoction, reasoning that the antioxidants would counter the negative nutritional effects of the alcohol, and wandered through the halls to revisit some of her favorite works while waiting for Helen. She'd wandered into a room displaying the work of a new artist, who happened to be an elephant, where she overheard a woman describing to her companion how she could truly feel the artist's angst.

Good grief. Some of these people are too much. Obviously she didn't read the panel explaining these were painted by a pachyderm. She rolled her eyes, then snuck a peek at the woman who droned on. She saw an older woman with a perfect hairdo, tailored black designer suit and chunky turquoise necklace. The woman had a face only money could buy: porcelain forehead, eternally surprised eyebrows, and oddly elongated upper lip. *Ohmygod, she's been youth-anized.* Maggie bit her lip to keep from snorting out a laugh at her joke. The woman posed like a Grecian statue, only with an Appletini where a vase or cluster of grapes should have been.

After observing the woman for a moment, Maggie noticed she was surrounded by what seemed to be nothing but wealthy museum patrons. And all of them in couples. She tugged at her $30 cocktail dress. She'd been so excited when she'd gotten such a deal. And even though she thought the dress flattered her figure, she felt that the mannequin-matrons around her knew she'd gotten it at Target. She might as well have been a modern day Hester Prynne, only with the trademark red bull's-eye on her chest. She wanted to say aloud to anyone who would listen, "It's designer. Isaac Mizrahi. And I paid full price for this pashmina." She'd treated herself to the gorgeous pale pink cashmere shawl to celebrate the deal on the dress and the fact that her stock's price had gone up after the Fast Track news. But instead of baring her soul and dress label to the room, she sighed and headed for the rooftop deck. She could hide there while waiting for Helen.

"I SEE I'M not the only one who had this idea."

Maggie turned to see a nice-looking man with dark blond hair in a crisp, white shirt and navy blazer. She smiled as he walked over to where she stood looking at the city lights, her martini resting on the wall that ran around the rooftop patio.

"It's a bit stuffy inside," she lied. She couldn't tell him the real reason she'd escaped to the roof. *"I'm socially inept and intimidated by the thought of a little cocktail party banter."*

"I know what you mean. Some of those folks are definitely stuffed-shirts."

"No, I didn't mean—"

"Oh, I wasn't accusing you of anything. I just needed a break; running low on witty repartee." He flashed a warm smile, a lone dimple creasing his left cheek, and set his own clear martini next to hers. It was a man's martini; its olive turned a disdainful red eye on her decidedly girly drink. She guessed he was not the fruity-concoction type. It struck her as sexy; but, lonely as she'd been, she had to admit that, similar to Kona and his definition of "edible," she had a wide definition of sexy these days.

"Me too." She returned his infectious smile and hoped there was no stuffed mushroom in her teeth. *Oh, is he cute.* He was fairly tall, probably six feet, with a hawkish nose balanced by his firm jaw. His hair, thinning on top, made Maggie wonder about his age. He looked familiar, but she figured she'd remember meeting such a handsome man.

"I'm Brian."

"Maggie." They shook hands, and then both leaned into the wall and admired the view. They agreed it was a beautiful night. The museum was only three stories tall, but sat on a hill at the outer edge of Balboa Park, with a view of downtown, sparkling a short distance away.

"So, do you work at the museum?" He asked.

I must not look like a rich art patron. "No, I'm a volunteer," she said. "I started a couple of months ago. What about you?"

"I just started recently as well. I mean, working here though, not as a volunteer."

"Oh, that's nice." *"That's nice." So lame. You weren't lying about being out of witty conversation. Besides, you're pathetic. A minute ago you wanted to leave, but now here you are, all happy just because a cute man is talking to you.* She was about to ask what he did at the museum when he beat her to it, asking what she did for a living.

"Well, I'm trying not to define myself by my work at the moment." She was about to add "but I'm an accountant," when he spoke first.

"You know, I think you have the right idea. Everyone's too wrapped up in their work in this country." He sipped his drink. "So, if you're not defining yourself by your work, how are you defining yourself?"

"That's the hard part. I'm trying to figure that out," Maggie played with the pendant on her necklace. "Actually, that's part of why I started volunteering here. I'd sort of turned into a . . . a workaholic I guess, but now I'm trying to figure out what I really want to do. What my passions are." She shrugged.

"Ah, our passions. They make life worth living."

"Yeah, that's why I really need to find some."

"What sorts of things are you interested in? What do you love?" He stressed the last word and pantomimed squeezing something in his hands.

"I love art and music. I'm not creative though. I don't have talent for those things; I just enjoy them. I love food; I used to cook a lot. Although now about the only 'cooking' I'm doing is blending smoothies and nuking Lean Cuisines. And, honestly, I prefer the eating over the cooking." *Dream job idea: ice cream taste tester. That'd be great. Probably not a lot of call for that though, and I'd weigh three hundred pounds* . . . Maggie had started mentally trying on various occupations in her quest to find her ideal second-career. "Oh, and I love biking and I love dogs." *Dog walker? Definitely don't want another office job; it would be great to be outdoors all the time. But, no. Too much poop, too little pay.*

"We have a lot in common. I love art as well. I guess that's obvious since I work here. And food; what's not to love? Music too—classical is my favorite. I haven't been on a bike in ages, though. I prefer running, although I cannot say that I love it. But, dogs. Dogs are the best."

"Do you have a dog?" Maggie asked.

"I do." He didn't volunteer any further information.

"What do you have?"

"I have a Chihuahua." He looked at her as though he'd admitted he would have preferred an Appletini.

"Oh." She tried not to sound surprised. "How cute."

"I know what you're thinking."

"No, no really. I'm not thinking anything."

"Yes, you are. You're thinking, why would a big guy like him have a tiny Chihuahua?"

She laughed. "That's not what I was thinking. I was actually thinking about how people say dogs look like their owners, but I can't imagine that's the case with you." Her eyes played over him, in search of Chihuahua comparison points. "What's its name?"

"Her name is Peaches."

She stifled a small giggle. "I'm sorry. I didn't mean to laugh. That's just so cute."

"It's fine. I know. Trust me, I get this a lot. But, I'm secure in my masculinity, and I have no problem with owning a Chihuahua named Peaches. For the most part."

Maggie was surprised at how comfortable she was with him, comfortable enough to tease him a bit. "So, does Peaches get dressed up?"

"Peaches has a sweater that she wears when it's cold." His voice took on the slightest edge. "But I would not call that 'dressing up,' per se. She has zero body fat, so she trembles if I don't put her sweater on her."

"Is that what makes you two look alike, the no body fat thing?"

He patted his stomach and took another swig of his martini. "No, not quite."

His stomach looked pretty flat to Maggie. "So, how long have you had Peaches?"

"Let's see, we got her when we moved to Philadelphia, so she's two and a half now."

Damn. There's a "we." You're so stupid, Maggie. No ring, but of course a good-looking, charming guy like this is a "we."

"So, does your girlfriend take her everywhere in her purse?" She tried to sound as cheerful as she'd been a moment ago.

"No—"

"Good. I have to admit, I hate when people treat dogs like accessories."

"What I meant to say was 'no, I don't have a girlfriend.' We broke up. But when we were together, she did carry Peaches in her purse."

"Oh. Sorry. I didn't mean to say I *hate* that. I'm sure she carried her around because she wanted to be with her all the time. I'm sure it wasn't like a fashion statement or anything . . ." *Hmmm. No girlfriend. But you put your foot in your mouth there and now you're rambling.*

"It's OK. Believe me, I never liked it either. In fact, that's partly why I insisted I get Peaches. I think she just wanted the dog to be trendy. She didn't love her like I do."

"Aww, that's sweet. I'm sure Peaches was happy about that."

"Well, you know, breakups are never easy on the little ones," he joked.

"I know what you mean." Maggie hoped the conversation would veer away from breakups.

"So, I assume you have a dog that you do *not* treat as an accessory," he said

"That's correct. I've always tended to have dogs that a purse could fit inside, rather than the other way around. In fact, I'm sure my pooch could eat this thing in one bite if I smeared it in peanut butter." She held up her tiny evening bag, big enough to hold only the bare essentials for an evening out, which in Maggie's case included her driver's license, credit card, AAA card, proof of insurance, a bit of cash, keys, phone, and her Blistex lip gloss.

"What do you have?"

"A chocolate Lab named Kona. He's three. Kind of a meathead, but I love him."

"And how is it that you resemble Kona?"

"Well, other than the shedding and the bad breath and the stinkiness . . . that's pretty much it I guess." They both laughed. "OK, really, hmmm," she thought for a second. "We both have brown eyes. And in the summer he gets red highlights in his hair from the sun. Only he gets them on his butt."

He laughed again. "He sounds lovely. Maybe we could get them together for a play date. We just moved here and don't know too many people yet. Peaches would enjoy a little friend. I mean, a big friend."

"Does Peaches like other dogs?"

"Well, it depends—" A tinny rendition of *Beethoven's Fifth* came from his pants pocket.

"Oh, you do like classical." She thought of her own ring tone and reached into her purse to turn down the volume. Kevin had swiped her phone one day while he still lived with her and downloaded *The Sun'll Come Out Tomorrow*. She still hadn't figured out how to change it back.

"Excuse me one second," he said, as he turned to the side.

She gazed off in the distance, trying to at least look like she wasn't listening.

"Yes, of course I'm still here. I'm on the roof getting some air . . . OK. I'll be right down and we'll do this thing." He hung up and leaned on the wall next to her. "I've got to get back." He gestured over his shoulder and smiled his disarming smile again. "Are you going back in?"

She was suddenly aware of a snapshot of her senses. She saw the blue flecks in his gray eyes; felt the rough fabric of his jacket against her bare forearm; heard the slightest noise as he swallowed and parted his lips; smelled the musky scent of his . . . aftershave? Deodorant? Lovely self? Whatever it was, it smelled good. *Let's see, what am I missing? Oh yes, taste . . . I wonder . . .* A shiver trilled down her spine. She pulled her pashmina tighter around her shoulders. "Um, yeah. It's getting a bit chilly out here anyway."

"I've got to do this thing," he explained as they walked toward the door. "But afterwards I'd like to buy you another drink."

Back on the main floor, a microphone stood under a spotlight; people gathered around it.

"Will you wait for me here?" They stopped near the bar. "This shouldn't take long."

Maggie nodded. She assumed he was needed to help set up whatever announcement they were about to make. She watched him disappear into the crowd, then saw silver-haired Mr. Van Zant, the museum director, walking to the microphone. The staff held Mr. Vee-Zee, as they called him, in high regard, but she knew he was retiring and a new director had started.

The crowd quieted. He thanked everyone for their generous support and spoke about the renovations, saying the museum itself was now a work of art. The audience applauded.

"Now that the museum has a new face," he continued, "it's time for her to have a new heart as well. As many of you know, I'm retiring and we have a fantastic new director who's taking over the reins here at MAMA. And, with that, I'd like to introduce: Brian Benatti."

Now Maggie realized why Brian looked familiar. She'd seen his picture in last month's MAMA newsletter. The thinning hair had thrown her; the picture must have been an older one. She remembered reading that in art circles he was known as Golden Boy Benatti. He was a *wunderkind* who'd gotten his graduate degree at an early age; then convinced a museum in London to hire him. It was new with a small budget; they agreed to hire him at a low salary and give him a chance. He'd turned it into a success, and then been head-hunted back to the U.S.

Maggie missed most of Mr. Vee-Zee's speech but tuned back in as he said, "I must admit this young man makes me feel very old. When I started here in 1977, he wasn't even born yet."

There were some chuckles from the crowd, and Maggie's mind spun while Mr. Vee-Zee handed the microphone to Brian.

Wasn't even born yet? Maggie barely heard Brian as he thanked Mr. Van Zant and said "what an honor," blah, blah, blah. *I was flirting with a man who's at least eleven years younger. Not only that, but he's a shooting star in his profession. How could he be interested in me?*

She felt ridiculous, still standing where he'd asked her to wait. He was going to have more important things to do, like meeting and greeting the upper echelon of patrons, than to come back and buy her a martini. She was wondering if she should leave when she saw Helen.

"There you are. I've been looking everywhere for you. You didn't answer your cell."

"Sorry . . ." Maggie reached for her purse. "I guess I turned the volume too low."

"Where were you?" Helen asked. "Hey, what's wrong? You look funny."

"Can we get out of here?" Maggie looked back as the crowd applauded one last time. The spotlight went dark and Mr. Vee-Zee, hand on Brian's shoulder, introduced him to a handsome older couple who had come forward. Brian flashed his crooked smile at them.

"Sure, as long as you tell me what's going on."

As they left, Maggie did some math in her head. She worked out that she'd been on the planet thirty-seven percent longer than Brian.

Maybe our age difference wouldn't seem as bad if I calculated it in dog years?

Chapter 14: I'm Gonna Need To See Some ID

Maggie and Helen sat at their usual table at Tea Time.

"Sorry to make you leave," Maggie said as she stirred her tea. She looked at the worn furniture. "We're a little overdressed for this place, huh? You look really pretty by the way." Helen's hair was slicked back in a wide black headband that matched her strapless little black dress. A strand of oversized pearls circled her slender neck. "Like a blond Holly Golightly."

"Holly Golightly, the AARP years, you mean. I can see it now, *Early Bird Special at Tiffany's.*"

"Don't make me laugh. I'm not in the mood."

"Alright, tell me what the heck happened back there."

Maggie told her everything: about the flirting, the doggie-play-date invite, the fact that Brian turned out to be the new museum director—and probably under thirty years old.

"I meet this nice looking, interesting guy, and he's way too young for me."

"What are you talking about? He's not too young for you."

"Uh, yeah, he is. If I asked him, 'where were you when John Lennon was shot?' his answer would be, 'I was in diapers.'" *Pros of dating a* much *younger man: um, . . . drawing a blank. Stamina maybe? Oh God, OK, come back to pros. Cons: Will I look totally foolish? What will people think? I'd have to be really vigilant about my roots.* Helen interrupted her analysis.

"Aren't you supposed to be going with the flow? Thinking like Kona?"

"Yes." Maggie looked down at the table, her curls falling like a curtain over her face. "I forget when I get stressed."

"Well, stop stressing. Look, does Kona focus on the journey, or the destination?"

"The journey," she said, in the voice of a teenager answering a nagging mother. She hated that Helen was so right, but she could see that this was basically the same reason things went wrong with Dave. She'd been so focused on the destination, the All Powerful Plan, that she hadn't noticed the journey had started to feel like a forced march. She pushed her hair out of her face. "You're right. I'm overreacting. Besides, we don't even know if he's interested in me."

"From what you said, it sounds like he is. I'll bet you a margarita he asks you out next time you see him at MAMA."

"If he does ask me out, how do I work my age into the conversation?" Maggie knew it was possible Brian thought she was only a bit older. People often guessed her age as low- to mid-thirties. She'd even had a grocery clerk make her day, hell, her whole month, last year when he carded her while buying tequila.

"Uh, you don't. You just accept his invitation, and then you call me and ask me when and where I'd like to go for my margarita."

Helen sat back and crossed her arms, confident in her prediction. Maggie's hand crept toward her pendant.

AS MAGGIE WALKED across the foyer at MAMA to the information desk, she heard a familiar voice behind her say, "Miss, I'd like some information."

She turned and Brian beamed his lop-sided smile at her. She'd known she might run into him tonight, but now that she had, the butterflies in her stomach fluttered in earnest. Although she pictured whatever trampolined around in there not as delicate butterflies, but fat, beige moths instead. She also wondered if she should tell him she was not a "Miss" but more of a "Ma'am." *Oh well, just go with it. Think like Kona. Besides, when's the last time you felt moths in your stomach over a man?*

She pushed the corners of her mouth up into a smile. "What can I help you with, sir?"

"I'd like some information on where you disappeared to the other night."

"Sorry about that. I was at the party with my girlfriend, and . . . she wasn't feeling well so we left. I wanted to say goodbye, but you looked busy, meeting people and . . ." she trailed off.

"I accept your apology, if you'll agree to that doggie play-date we talked about. How's Saturday? The dog park here at Balboa. Say, eleven? We can get some lunch afterwards."

Guess I owe Helen a margarita. And I've got to go shopping. I need new shorts. Wonder if they can fit me in for a cut and color tomorrow? OK, calm down. Start by answering the man. What would Kona say? Probably: "Hell, yeah!"

She settled for a simple, "OK."

"YOU DON'T HAVE to look so smug," Maggie said to Helen.

"I'm not. I'm just enjoying my margarita. My marg that you *owed* me, because I was right. Did you hear about our bet?" Helen asked Russell.

Maggie had called Helen when she got home from MAMA. When Helen heard about the date, she'd suggested they go to Alfonso's on Friday so Maggie could pay up. They'd decided to invite Russell too since Natalia was out of town on a Girls' Weekend. When Maggie called to invite him she'd told him she had news that would make Natalia happy.

"Yeah, I heard," Russell said. He turned to Maggie, "But let's hear about this guy. What's he like? Artsy-fartsy-type?"

"No, he's smart and articulate . . . handsome." Maggie studied her menu, even though she planned to order her usual.

"He *is* handsome," Helen said. "I can vouch for that. Tall, blonde. He's *young.*" Maggie shot Helen a look and Helen added, "But very mature."

"He sounds dreamy." Russell picked up his menu.

After they ordered, the two pros offered to share their tried and true rules with the rookie, once again acting as her personal lifeguards, as she prepared to jump back into the dating pool.

"Rule number one," Helen said, "is never accept an invite immediately. Always act as though you have to check your calendar first."

"You should have told me that sooner; I already broke that one," Maggie said.

Russell said, "That is not the number one rule of dating. The number one, most important rule is a little thing I like to call: The Twelve-Hour Rule." He sat back as though waiting for the choir of heavenly angels to quiet down so he could continue. He held up a finger, "Unless you're going away together, you should never spend more than twelve hours at a stretch with a date. It's been my experience that the ladies begin to put down roots after that."

Maggie laughed, thinking he must be joking; Helen called him a numbskull. He started to expand on his theory, but the food arrived. Then Russell started a debate on whether blended or "rocks" margaritas were better, and they never got back to the rest of the rules.

AS MAGGIE PULLED into the parking lot, she drummed her fingers on the steering wheel. *Wonder what the rest of those rules are. Could use some rules right about now.* She wanted to sit and gather her courage, but Kona saw the other dogs and whined, beating the door with his paw.

"OK, we're going."

Brian stood at the edge of the park, in a navy linen shirt with the sleeves rolled up and tan shorts with a crease ironed into them, sharp enough to slice brie. A pale golden Chihuahua stood next to him. Balanced on three legs, it eyed a gray schnauzer that had come over to say hello.

Maggie called Brian's name and he looked up, his crooked smile stretching across the left side of his face. The smile disappeared when Peaches growled and snapped at the schnauzer, which had circled around in an attempt to sniff her petite posterior.

Brian looked down at the canine hurricane that raged in front of his Italian leather sandals and tried to extricate his dog. The schnauzer's owner shrieked and ran over. Kona, ready for a game of spin-the-schnauzer, trotted over to stick his big brown nose into the action. Maggie tried to grab his collar and restrain him.

When all three dogs were back under their owners' control—Peaches in Brian's arms, the schnauzer on his leash, and Kona leaning against Maggie as she held his collar—the woman dragged her dog away. She muttered about "people who can't control their dogs," while Brian apologized to her back.

"She doesn't like to have her, uh, hind end sniffed," he said to Maggie.

"Can't fault her for that."

"Well, this is an excellent start to their date. I never even said hello to you." He nodded at the little dog. "This is, obviously, Peaches."

"Hello, Peaches." Maggie reached out and stroked the dog's fine, tawny fur. Maggie still held Kona's collar, but he struggled to pull free. "This is my beast, Kona."

Brian patted Kona's head, but Kona was busy watching two mutts that wrestled nearby. He wagged his tail frantically, while Peaches looked down from her perch in Brian's arms.

"Maybe I'll let him burn off some energy before we introduce him to Peaches." Maggie released Kona, and he took off like a sprinter hearing a starter's pistol.

They watched him join the melee, and the three dogs raced across the park, mouthing each other's ears and collars. They yipped and growled in mock ferociousness.

"I see Peaches is much too dignified for that sort of behavior."

"She can be a bit of a diva."

"So, how are you guys doing? Adjusting to life in a new city?"

"We're doing fine. It's so quiet here, though. I've got a condo near the museum. Unless there's a baseball game or it's the weekend in the Gas Lamp district, the sidewalks roll right up at night downtown."

"Oh, um, I didn't know. I'm not much for the downtown scene. Gas Lamp and all that."

"I don't mean the Gas Lamp, per se. There are some great restaurants, but I'm not one for the bars either. I meant culture. Big City life. The thriving metropolis. I guess I'm just used to Philadelphia, London. And I went to college in Chicago. It's just a bit 'small town' here."

"Well, for culture, there's the Old Globe. Have you been there?"

"I saw a play there that they billed as 'Broadway bound,' but I'm not so sure."

"And there are a lot of galleries in La Jolla, and I think there are usually a lot of people down there at night. I, uh, don't really know though. I haven't been out much myself lately."

"Maybe we can change that. Do some exploring together. Don't get me wrong, it is nice here. The weather's ideal, of course." He indicated the sunny sky and trees swaying in the breeze. It was a perfect September day, low seventies; white, puffy clouds dotted the deep blue sky.

"I don't think you can beat the weather here. Of course, I've always lived in Southern California, so I don't really have anything to compare it to. How about you? Where did you grow up?" *Are you a grown up? You talk like one, but let's see some ID.*

"In Philadelphia. That's how I ended up there after London. My mother's a violinist with the Philadelphia Orchestra."

"Wow. Very cool." Maggie wondered how much older his mother was than herself. *I've got to work my age into this conversation. And find out exactly how old* he *is.*

"She's been a huge influence on me. She introduced me to art and classical music." He also told her about his father, a history professor at Penn State. "But, enough about me," he said as he set Peaches down. She pranced through the grass like a miniature Tennessee walking horse. "What about you? I know you're a So-Cal girl, but what about family? Do you have siblings?"

She told him about her family; how Mom had owned a gift shop, and that they all lived on the East Coast now. She told him her dad was an engineer and realized this was her chance.

"But he died when I was pretty young; I'd just started college."

"I'm terribly sorry to hear that."

"Well, it was a long time ago. I can't believe he's been gone more than twenty years." She poked a thick tuft of grass with the toe of her white Ked.

"I can imagine. I bet it feels like yesterday."

He seemed not to have noticed she'd just said she'd been in college twenty years ago; when she looked up, his eyes studied her face.

Now she didn't care about their ages either. She thought about her dad; wished she could talk to him about her career, Dave, everything. *Would he be disappointed in me?*

"Hey, lady, is this your dog?" an irritated voice called out.

She spun and saw Kona, his legs and head plastered in mud, tongue hanging out the side of his mouth, and then noticed the corresponding splatter-pattern of mud on the man's khakis.

"Ohmygod, Kona." She ran toward him, fumbling with the clip on the end of his leash.

"Your idiot dog got into a broken sprinkler head over there and shook mud all over me." He gesticulated wildly and pointed at his Jackson-Pollacked pants.

"I'm so sorry. I'll give you my address; you can send me the dry cleaning bill." She tried to snap Kona's leash in place while another muddy mutt tackled him. The two dogs tumbled into her, streaking her legs and pink plaid Bermuda shorts with dirt. A wall of wet dog smell hit her.

"Kona! Bad dog." He dropped to the ground, in happy exhaustion; he panted heavily. Slobber dripped off his lolling tongue onto her shoe.

"I can throw these in the damn laundry; but I was supposed to go somewhere, and now I've got to go home first." He swore and set off for the parking lot at a clipped pace. "Thor, come!" he yelled to a German shepherd in the distance.

As with Brian and the schnauzer's mother, all Maggie could do was call out another apology to the man's hunched back.

"We're not making any friends here today are we?" she said.

"At least these two are getting along." He pointed at Kona who still lay at Maggie's side. Peaches had approached and they sniffed one another, broad black nose to pointed, pink one.

"I guess that's something." Maggie looked down at her dirty legs and dog. "We're a mess. We'd better go home."

"I'm sorry this was a bit of a fiasco."

"It's my fault. I should have been paying attention to Kona. He can get a little out of control. Maybe next time we could take them to Dog Beach in Del Mar." *Was there going to be a next time?* "Everyone expects to get wet and dirty there." *Oh God, did I suggest we get wet and dirty next time we go out?*

"Or next time we could leave them home."

"It's tough to have a doggie play-date without the dogs."

"I thought perhaps we'd have a real date, maybe after your shift on Thursday."

"Oh, a real date. Of course. Duh." Maggie smacked herself in the forehead with her palm in the universal sign of "oh-dopey-me," realizing too late her hands were as filthy as her legs. "Good one," she rubbed her forehead with the inside of her wrist, which was not much cleaner.

"Let me help you out there." Brian moved closer to her and tilted her chin up with his right hand as he wiped the splotch of dirt away with his thumb. "There you go. You're perfect."

Maggie felt a surge of heat at the touch of his hand and bent down to fuss with Kona's collar to hide her red cheeks.

Brian and Peaches walked them to her car. Maggie opened the passenger door and pulled out an old towel. She started at Kona's haunches, cleaning the mud off as best she could.

"So, how about Thursday after your shift at the museum?" Brian asked. "We could go for that drink I owe you, or maybe get a late dinner—"

"No!" Maggie yelled and tried to hold Kona by his back legs, which she still had wrapped in the towel, but he was too strong. Hearing one of his favorite food words, he charged Brian, leapt up and hit him squarely in the groin with his muddy paws.

Maggie scrambled to pull a Milk-Bone out of an emergency stash she kept in the glove compartment. Out of the corner of her eye, she saw Kona continue to jump at Brian, who was doubled over and groaning. Peaches had backed away and, from a safe distance, yapped nonstop.

"Kona, here, treat!" She tossed the offering on the ground and he devoured it.

Brian groaned again. "What just happened?" he asked through gritted teeth.

"I'm really sorry." Maggie put her hand on his shoulder and bent down to search his face. "Are you OK? I'm so sorry. He's just got these trigger words that make him go nuts." She rattled off the forbidden words in Pig Latin. "I always spell those words, or say them in Pig Latin."

Brian looked at her as he began to unfold. He grimaced as he supported himself on the open car door. "I'm going to need to hear those again, when I can think straight."

"I would've warned you before, but I didn't think they'd come up. You can't say those words unless you have a t-r-e-a-t at the ready."

"I see . . . I guess." Brian looked down at the streaks of brown on his tan shorts.

Maggie offered him a semi-clean corner of the ratty towel she'd been using but he held up a hand to refuse.

"We'd better get going." He bent, tried to stifle a groan, and picked up Peaches.

"Of course. Yeah. OK. I'm sorry again. This was . . . fun." Maggie gave up on the idea of rubbing Kona down anymore. She draped the towel over the passenger seat. "Get in Kona." She tugged his leash and he leapt into the car. "I'll see you Thursday?" She wondered if they were still on for their date. "At the museum," she added lamely. "Bye."

Brian held up his free hand. She thought it felt more like a dismissal than a wave.

She smiled and mouthed goodbye again as she backed out. She watched him in the rearview mirror as she drove off; saw him look down at his shorts and shake his head.

She turned to Kona. "You totally blew that. We could still be out there, having fun. Instead, you're going home for a bath. He'll probably never ask us out again. I'm sure he thinks you're a beast, which you are! And thinks I'm a terrible dog owner."

Kona just smiled at her.

Chapter 15: Modest Midas

As Maggie climbed the museum steps Thursday afternoon, she chewed the inside of her lower lip. Would their date still be on? She doubted it. *And who could blame him? My dog nailed him in the balls on our first date. Not exactly an enticement to go on a second one.*

Still, just in case, she'd put on a bit more makeup than usual and dressed up. There was no uniform for the museum staff or volunteers, but they did have a "black, gray or white only" dress code. Maggie usually wore black pants and a white blouse with flats (and got very annoyed whenever Vanessa wore red; *Come on, red? That's not even close. And she's the volunteer coordinator; she should set an example!*), but today she wore her steel-gray dress and black peek-toe pumps.

Inside the still museum, she saw Brian talking to Vanessa at the information desk.

"Great, you're here," Vanessa said. "I need to do something in the back." She hurried away while Maggie locked her purse in the drawer under the desk.

Maggie stood up. Brian had said a quiet hello when she'd walked in, but now he just looked at her.

"I'm really sorry again about Saturday," she said. "I realized after, I should have offered to buy you some new shorts. I hope—"

"It's OK. I soaked them when we got home and washed them, twice, and they're fine."

"Oh. Good." *Is he going to say anything about our date? Or rather our cancelled date?* She rushed to fill the silence. "We tried to train him to not do that, but then we started the whole Pig Latin thing or spelling. It was just easier. And then . . . we got used to it." She shrugged.

"You could hire a trainer."

"Yeah, I'll think about it." Maggie had thought about it. Many times. But she loved Kona as he was—an exuberant, dive-in-with-all-four-feet, carefree spirit. She didn't want to inflict her rule-obsessed, buttoned down ways on him. He was the bad boy yang to her good girl yin. She'd allowed, no *wanted*, him to be her wild thing, her alter ego.

"Anyway, enough about Kona," he said. "Let's talk about Kona's mom and how pretty she looks." Maggie blushed, excited that maybe he wasn't as angry as she thought. "I hope you're dressed up like that for our date."

"Oh, well, I wasn't sure . . ."

"Did you think I'd cancel over some muddy shorts?"

Well, yeah, that and the fact that my dog tried to neuter you.

He didn't wait for her to reply. "As far as I'm concerned, we're still on for d-i-n-n-e-r."

Maggie smiled and they made plans to meet out front after closing.

Since the summer tourist season was over, the museum was nearly empty. At seven Vanessa told Maggie to go ahead and take off. Maggie called Brian and said she was ready to go.

"Have a good evening." Vanessa smiled a Cheshire Cat grin as Maggie headed out to wait for Brian on the steps.

"Yeah, uh, goodnight." *Odd. Vanessa looked as if she knew what was up.*

She wondered if there were rules against museum employees dating the volunteers, but then convinced herself it was fine since she wasn't an employee. Still, if things worked out, it could be awkward around the staff; and even worse if things didn't. *You're getting ahead of yourself again. The journey. The journey . . .*

Brian came out, pulling on his blazer, and suggested The Prado, since it was so close.

"Perfect," she said. "It's one of my favorite restaurants." They set off across the park in the fading light. "I just realized I never told you what I do for a living."

"I already know." She looked at him. "You caught me. I asked Vanessa about you."

That explains the grin.

"Oh, did you now? And what did she tell you?" She pretended to be annoyed, but wondered what Vanessa might have said. Had she told him her age, her marital status?

"She told me you're an accountant. And a huge help, both in the gallery and in the back."

"That was nice of her." She waited a beat. "Did she tell you I'm getting divorced?"

"Yes, she mentioned that."

"And that didn't . . . scare you off?"

He leaned towards her. "Apparently not. Besides, why should that scare me? Lots of people are divorced."

"I know, but, it's not final yet."

He asked her if there was any chance of reconciliation, and she assured him there was not.

They walked on; the only sound that of their footsteps on the cobbled walkway, echoing off the buildings. *Good grief. Heard of small talk? Couldn't you comment on the Spanish architecture or something? Maybe point out the topless babes holding up the Casa de Balboa? No, you dive right into the big talk. Monstrous freakin' talk.*

"So, it's just a matter of finalizing everything on paper?" he asked.

"Yeah. I've got several weeks to go on the six-month waiting period. And I need to sell the house."

They reached the restaurant and he opened the heavy wooden door for her.

After they were settled at their table and had ordered dinner and martinis, a Lemon Drop for her, "dirty" for him, she planned to change the subject, but he picked up where they'd left off.

"That must be hard to come to terms with, the end of such a fundamental part of your life. Not to mention moving out of your house."

"I'm dealing with it." She waved her hand as if shooing a fly.

"Let's talk about something else. I think I'm revealing a little too much baggage here, aren't I? Like steamer trunks full."

"We're not high school kids on our first date; everyone our age has baggage. Besides, I like it that you're so open. You don't play games like some women I've dated." The way he said it, Maggie wondered if he had a specific woman in mind.

"When you say people 'our' age, you do realize I'm a lot older than you, right?"

"I wouldn't say 'a lot.' When we first met, I thought you were mid-thirties, but then I figured from what you said about your dad the other day that you must be thirty-eight or so."

"I'm forty-one. I'll be forty-two at the end of December." She waited for shock to register on his face but he was impassive, fishing the olive from his martini. "How old are you?"

"I turned thirty last month."

Thank heaven his age starts with a three and not a two. Still . . .

"Don't you think almost twelve years is kind of a big difference?" she asked.

"It's just a number. Besides, my mother's been saying I was 'going on thirty-five' ever since I turned four. And since forty's the new thirty that actually makes you younger than me."

"That's some kind of crazy math you're doing there."

"Tell me, do you really feel different now than you did at thirty-five? Or thirty even?"

"You've got me there. I don't. In fact, I have to keep reminding myself what my age is. Sometimes I honestly forget I'm over forty." She forced herself to stop staring at his full lower lip. She sighed and said, "In a way, getting divorced makes me feel younger too. I thought I'd be on this . . . set path by now. But instead, I'm starting over; questioning my career; needing a new place to live. Like a kid out of college." She took a drink of her sweet, citrusy martini. It was like a liquid SweeTart. *Is this the drink of a grown up? I need to develop a taste for gin and tonic.*

She thought for a moment and continued, "What does make me feel old, though, is when I think about any one individual body part.

Like, for instance, my thighs. For Pete's sake, between them they're eighty-four." *Did I just say "between my thighs" to my date? Quick. Come up with a less titillating body part* . . . "Or, say, my spleen. I think, 'holy cow, my spleen is forty-one.' What if you found a spleen that had been, I don't know, kept in a jar in your office for *forty-one* years? That's a helluva long time."

"But your cells are constantly regenerating themselves, so your spleen is, in fact, only about two weeks old."

"Huh. Well, here's to regenerating ourselves." She held up her glass, then leaned back as the waiter served their food. After taking a bite, she said. "So, I was hoping Golden Boy Benatti could give me some career advice; help me figure out what to be when I grow up."

Brian groaned. "I was hoping you hadn't read that."

"Why? It was a great article."

"It was excessive."

"Did you or did you not graduate from college very young?"

"Not that young. I was hardly a boy genius. I skipped kindergarten because I could already read. In high school, I took AP classes and tested out of some GE courses. In college, I piled on the units and finished in three years. I did my Masters right after so I had that by twenty-three, which is *not* that young. I mean, you hear about teenagers getting their Masters degrees."

"All right, then, what about your huge success at that museum in London?"

"Again, there was a bit of hype in that article. You can't believe everything you read." He agreed that, yes, the museum was new and unknown when he started, but said he wouldn't label it a "huge" success. "It was making money, but not because I'm this Midas of modern art. It all started with one particular exhibit."

She looked at his long fingers. *Hmmm, Midas . . . Touch . . .* She snapped out of it as he told a story of falling in love with an artist's work at a gallery. When Brian looked into exhibiting the work, he found out the man was serving a life term for a murder he swore he didn't commit.

"Wow." She set her fork down and leaned in.

"When the museum got interested in him, so did the media. This non-profit group picked up his case—one of those groups that works to free wrongly convicted people. They uncovered some new evidence, and the guy was exonerated. It was big news. Tons of free publicity; everybody wanted to see his work. He does these gorgeous mixed media pieces. I have one at my place; I'll show it to you sometime."

She smiled at the subtle implication that there would be more dates in their future and said, "So, you not only made the museum profitable, you saved this poor guy's life?"

"No, not *me*. The group, they saved him."

"I think you're being way too modest, Golden Boy. Think I'll start calling you GB."

"Please don't. I only told you to show it was a fluke, this so-called 'huge' success."

"I suppose you're going to tell me the museum in Philadelphia was a fluke as well?"

"They didn't print everything I said." He dragged his hand down the side of his face. "It's embarrassing. My mother got me in the door. She's friends with a museum board member."

"Maybe they interviewed you as a favor to her, but they wouldn't give you the job if you didn't deserve it. And the museum was on the verge of closing before you took over, right?"

"That was just pure mismanagement. I didn't do anything your average first-year business student couldn't have done."

"Man, you don't cut yourself much slack." She wiped her mouth, set down her napkin, and decided continuing to be open was the way to go. "But, I'm glad you told me all that. I have to admit, I was feeling kind of intimidated by you."

"Honestly?"

"Yes, honestly."

"Well, I'm no Golden Boy. I'm just . . . me." Although thinning, his ash-blonde hair glowed under the amber glass shaded lamp that hung over the table. The light warmed the smooth apples of his cheeks above his eight o'clock shadow. She thought he was right about being "no boy," but he was definitely golden.

He pointed at her empty glass, "How about another?"

"Better not." *Or I'll be in your lap.* "I've got to drive home. I'm a cheap date, aren't I?"

"Another thing to like about you."

Brian picked up the check, waving off Maggie's attempt to split it with him, and they went out into the night. The temperature had dropped, along with the sun. Maggie shivered in her sleeveless dress and Brian slipped off his jacket and draped it around her shoulders. *How gallant.* It was deliciously warm from his body heat.

"I could walk you back to your car," Brian said. "Or we could go to my condo and see that artist's work. I'm just a few blocks from here."

Kona would go; but he's a slut. OK, pros: possibly replace warm jacket around me with warm arms. Hmmmm. She thought how wonderful it would feel just to be held. *Cons: Totally not ready for anything more than that. And mustn't appear too easy on first official date.* The cons won. "I should head home. Maybe you could show me some other time."

"I'll look forward to that."

They walked to her car, discussing places he'd been to so far in San Diego. He admitted he hadn't been to the zoo yet, adding that he hadn't been to any zoo since he was a kid.

She resisted the urge to say, "You mean last year?" and instead said, "San Diego's is the best." They reached her car. "We could go on Sunday, if you're not doing anything."

"That's sounds great."

He opened her door for her. She was tempted to linger and wait for a kiss, but decided a first kiss in the parking lot was not how she'd imagined it. She reluctantly handed back his jacket and got into the Honda. She lowered the window.

"We could go around one," she said. "Maybe grab dinner there and stay until closing."

She gave him her home number. His hand rested on the door frame and he tapped it three times. Was he figuring out the logistics of kissing her while she was in the car and he stood beside it? It wasn't going to work.

"Thanks for dinner," she said. "I'll see you Sunday."

"See you then." He rapped the car a final time, then waved as she drove off.

SUNDAY, BRIAN WAS on her doorstep at the agreed time, holding a plant wrapped in pink cellophane. She noticed he backed up a step and held the pot protectively over his crotch when Kona ran to say hello. Kona was good and stayed down while Brian patted his head.

"I brought you a begonia." He was wearing perfect khakis and a pale blue Oxford shirt.

A bit much for the zoo, but he looks handsome.

"Thanks. How sweet." She wondered how he knew she preferred the practical gift of a living plant over dead-in-a-week cut flowers. She put the pot in the kitchen, and they headed out.

As she got into his silver Lexus, she smoothed her skirt. She spotted a small scuff on her sandal. She looked at Brian as she directed him toward the zoo. He was so perfect and wrinkle free. I'd like to muss him up a little, she thought, then blushed and looked out the window.

At the zoo, they hit all her favorite animals: the hippos, gliding through the water like obese trapeze artists; the polar bears, asleep but still fascinating to watch, their huge paws twitching as they dreamt of chasing who-knew-what, perhaps a sweaty tourist; and the gorillas, strutting like bar bouncers. They ate dinner and then set off again in the dusky light.

Brian pointed out a sign with an arrow for the elephant exhibit. He grabbed her hand. "Let's go see the elephants. They're my favorite."

She wondered if he would drop her hand after the change in direction was complete, but he continued to hold it, lacing his fingers through hers. His hands were soft and warm, and he stroked the back of her hand with his thumb. Her nerve endings tingled like lit sparklers.

As they walked, they noticed a strange bleating sound coming at semi-regular intervals from beyond the elephants' habitat.

"Something's going on over there." She tugged his arm. "Let's go see."

They passed the elephants, gamboling along like old ladies in baggy hose, and saw the noises had attracted a small crowd. Groups in twos and threes gathered along the pen's railing.

"Ohmygosh . . . is that . . . a tapir *ménage à trois*?" Maggie said as they drew closer.

Three tapirs, something like an odd mix of a long-legged panda and an ant-eater with a truncated trunk, were humping in a conga line across their enclosure. The female at the front of the line was the source of the intermittent honking. She appeared to be trying to get away from the attentions of the large male that had mounted her, who continued to walk and thrust his way along behind her, his front feet resting on her back. The third tapir appeared to want to join in the fun. It walked along on its back legs, its forefeet up on the large male.

Brian bit his lip, and Maggie put her hand over her mouth.

"Three? How does that work with tapirs?" Maggie asked.

"Someone in that threesome is confused. Is that a male on the end or a female?" Brian bent to try to check out the apparatus on the last tapir in line. They reached the railing and leaned against it, as a zoo employee whirred up behind them in a camouflage golf cart.

"Oh, interesting," she said, standing tiptoe on the cart's runner for a better view.

"What's going on in there?" Maggie asked. "Besides the obvious." The conga line stopped and the third tapir dropped off the back. It hadn't lost interest in the proceedings, however, and stuck its almost prehensile nose in between the legs of the male, an unwelcome move, judging by the honking sounds he added to the bleating of the female at the front.

"That's a male and two females," the woman answered.

"Every male tapir's fantasy," Maggie whispered to Brian.

He laughed as the employee went on, unabashedly keeping her

eyes locked on the large male that continued humping the female in vociferous fashion. "That's a five-year-old-male. The females are four and twenty-six. I heard them, so rushed over here to see who he's interested in."

"And, who is the lucky lady?" Brian asked.

"It's the twenty-six-year old."

Huh. Maggie kept her eyes on the zookeeper who continued on, "She doesn't look too impressed." Maggie looked back at the animals. The older female was lying down, apparently to ward off further advances from the male, who continued to try to scale her. He thrust ineffectually at her side. The smaller female stood immobile watching them, as if dumbstruck.

"Looks like he hasn't quite got this figured out," the woman said. "And the little girl's not too sure what's going on either. Oh well, they'll work it out eventually." She jumped in her cart and took off again.

"Let's leave them alone." Maggie said.

They went and watched the elephants for a few minutes. Maggie, lost in thought, wondered if it was a bad sign that, although the young tapir seemed to prefer the older female, he clearly did not know what he was doing.

Afterwards, back at her house, Maggie invited Brian in for a drink. She wasn't ready for the evening to end yet, but hoped he wouldn't see the offer as an invitation to try any young-tapir-in-lust moves.

Trying to make her intentions clear, she told him, "It will have to be a quick one though . . . I mean, a quick drink . . ." She hoped he couldn't see her cheeks flush pink under the car's yellowy dome light. "I have to get up early for work tomorrow."

"Me too. I promise I won't stay long."

They went in and received a warm welcome from Kona. Maggie was relieved when he didn't put his nose, or front feet, into Brian's crotch. She fed Kona, apologizing to him for the late hour, and then put him out back. Then she and Brian settled on a bottle of pinot noir and upon the sofa. Maggie worked herself into the corner of the couch and tucked her feet up under her. She thought it would be a safe distance. Brian relaxed in the middle of the couch, his arm along the back of the overstuffed cushion, his legs crossed in front of him.

He complimented her charming Craftsman-style house and said he thought it would sell in a heartbeat.

She wasn't so sure. Even though she, Kevin and Russell (well, mostly Kevin and Russell) had done a lot of work, the market had cooled. She had no idea how long it might take to sell. He asked what her plans were once it did. She told him she leaned toward renting. She wasn't ready to buy another house, especially if she still hadn't figured out what her dream job was going to be and where she might be working.

When he finished his wine, he stood up to go and she walked him to the door.

"Thanks for a great time. I saw some things tonight I've never seen before." He raised his eyebrows for emphasis.

Maggie giggled, "I have to confess, I almost always see animals doing it at the zoo."

"Oh, that's why you enjoy it so much."

"It can be pretty entertaining. You should see the giant tortoises doing it." Her eyes darted up to an image playing in her mind and she laughed. "It's very . . . methodical."

When she looked back, Brian wasn't laughing. In fact, he was rather serious. She frowned, thinking, I hope he doesn't think I get my kicks watching animals do it.

"You are so beautiful," he whispered. He pulled her to him and kissed her.

She kissed him back; but then unbidden images rushed in: kissing Dave goodbye each morning as they left for work; laughing as they rolled across the living room rug in a tickle fight and Kona tried to join in; Dave carrying her across the threshold when they first moved in.

She stiffened, pulled away from him, and looked down.

"I know; you think I'm about to try to back out on my promise to leave early. But, I'm good as my word. I'm going," he said. She smiled up at him. "Right now. Gone. Unless you wanted to try to entice me to stay?" The left corner of his mouth crept upward into the crooked smile she found almost irresistible. Almost.

She knew there was no way she'd feel comfortable doing anything with him in this house. There were too many memories, gathered in every corner like cobwebs.

"No, you'd better go. School night and all," she stepped partly behind the door.

He said goodbye and kissed her once more, lightly on the lips, then left.

She let Kona back in. She was glad he'd been outside so he couldn't try to wiggle his way between them when Brian kissed her. There'd been enough kinky animal action for one day.

She sat on the couch and invited Kona up. She surveyed the house she had lived in and loved for the last twelve years. It was ready to go on the market.

She rubbed the dog's ear and said, "What do you think, Buddy? I think *we're* ready too."

Kona sighed with pleasure at the ear rubbing and gave her a look that was a combination of "I love you" and "Please keep doing that." He collapsed across her lap. She knew he didn't care where they lived, as long as they were together.

Chapter 16: The Sequel

After their workout Saturday morning, Maggie asked Helen to come along and help pick out new towels. It was the last thing she needed to do to finish sprucing up the master bath.

As they walked through the bed and bath section of Macy's, Helen grilled Maggie about her upcoming date with Brian.

"So, you think tonight's the Big Night? Ready to get back up on that horse?" Helen whispered as they shopped the shelves stacked with rainbows of fluffy towels.

"I guess so. I mean, he invited me to his place, so I'm sure that's what we're both thinking." Maggie chewed her lip. "God, why didn't I suggest we go out instead? Do you think it's too soon? How many dates are you supposed to go on first? This is only our third."

"First of all, this is your fourth date: dog park, dinner, zoo, tonight." Helen counted them off on her fingers. "Count 'em. *Quatro*."

"Dog park doesn't count."

"It does." Helen held up a finger to silence Maggie who had opened her mouth to argue. "And that brings me to my second point. It's not about keeping some scorecard of dates and hitting a predetermined number. It's about doing what you feel comfortable doing. So, how about it? Are you ready?"

"I guess. I'm excited about tonight, but I'm also nervous as hell. It's awful. It's this mix of anticipation and just wanting to get it over with. It's like . . . virginity all over again."

"Hmmm. I can picture the preview now." Helen said as if reading the words across a movie screen. "'Virginity: The Sequel.

Coming soon.' Get it?" She cracked up at her own joke.

Maggie twisted her pendant. "I hope the tag line is: 'The one sequel that's actually better than the original.'"

"At least this time you'll know what you're doing." Helen reached out and gently pulled Maggie's hand away from her necklace. "But would you mind if I give you a few pointers?"

BRIAN ANSWERED THE door in a white dress shirt and navy slacks. Maggie had dressed up too, knowing he would. She'd bought a new dress, a white flowing A-line, and pale pink, lacy underwear; although they were not having the desired effect of making her feel sexy. More than anything, she felt uncomfortable, as the lace scratched her left hip. She tried to surreptitiously rub at it with her arm as, with a sweeping gesture, Brian welcomed her to his "humble abode."

The condo was an inanimate extension of Brian—everything perfectly coordinated and perfectly groomed. It looked as if he either did not actually live there or had just ushered out the camera crew from *Interior Design*. Not a single dog-eared magazine, piece of mail, or old newspaper appeared within sight, let alone a Chihuahua hair or speck of dust. His love of art was evident throughout. The rich but neutral colors of the walls and furniture allowed the paintings and sculptures to be well-deserved focal points. A huge piece hung in the foyer.

"That one's from the artist I was telling you about," Brian said. "In London?"

"The guy who got out of jail? You're right; he's amazing." There were bits of fabric and metal on the canvas, expertly woven in with the thick strokes of vivid oil paints. "When you told me his story, I thought his stuff was going to be dark and depressing. But this is so . . ."

"Kinetic?"

"Yeah. It's really gorgeous."

He took her on a tour of the rest of his treasures, telling her stories about the artists and where or how he'd acquired each item.

Brian tactfully left the master bedroom off the tour. In the guest room, she said hello to Peaches, curled in her cozy basket. Peaches deigned to bestow a darting kiss on Maggie's hand.

A gleaming silver abstract piece stood alone on an oak end table above where Peaches lay. Maggie wanted to touch its shiny surface, but wouldn't dream of marring it with a fingerprint.

"That's an interesting piece," she said. "It's so sleek."

"That's my iron, actually." Brian rubbed the back of his neck. "It's from the Hammacher Schlemmer catalog."

"Oh, hell, I'm an idiot."

"No, you're right, though. It is gorgeous, isn't it? That's why I leave it out."

An antique brass iron sat on a shelf overhead. She pointed at it. "My grandma has one of those. I wouldn't actually have figured you for an antiques kind of guy, though."

"I'm not, usually. But, I'm sort of . . . into irons."

Maggie turned and noticed a tailor-quality steamer in the corner she'd overlooked before.

At the end of the tour, he escorted her back to his long, narrow kitchen, which smelled of roast chicken. He invited her to sit at a bistro table under the window while he finished prepping a plate of appetizers. He poured her a glass of cabernet and began describing the menu. She half-heard him talking about the problems he'd had finding decent looking fennel bulbs.

Her legs were crossed and her foot bounced like the tongue of a panting Pekinese. She fiddled with her pendant, until Helen's tips for "feel sexy, be sexy" came back to her. Number One was: "No fidgeting." Helen had noticed her tendency to play with her necklace when anxious. "Try not to be nervous," Helen had said, "But if you are, just be still; move slow-ly."

Be still, move slowly, she thought as she laced her fingers and put her hands in her lap. She glared at her foot. It stopped bouncing.

Within a minute her foot resumed its jig. She figured getting everything out in the open was the best approach.

"Look," she said taking a gulp of wine, "I need to tell you.

I'm . . . a bit nervous."

"About my cooking?" Brian stopped slicing and grinned at her.

"No." She forced a smile back at him, then took a deep breath. "About tonight."

"Tonight?" He raised an eyebrow at her.

"Yeah, you know. Tonight." Her hands waved in desperate circles, but she willed them back into her lap. "I was thinking maybe we need to talk about a few . . . ground rules."

"Ground rules."

"Yeah, ground rules. You know, lighting, that sort of thing."

"Alright, what sort of rules did you have in mind?" He grabbed his glass of wine and the plate of crackers and assorted cheeses, and went to sit opposite her.

"'Rules' doesn't sound very good. Let's call them 'guidelines.' I know this is sort of a spontaneity-killer, but I always feel more comfortable when everyone's on the same page."

"I'm all for doing whatever we need to do to make you feel comfortable, so what sort of guidelines did you have in mind?"

"Well, first of all, we should get the whole safe-sex discussion out of the way." Her hand went to her pendant again. She pictured the condoms in her purse. She wasn't sure, so she'd brought different sizes. (Two "trim," which she'd figured out in the store must mean "small," since she realized no one would want to buy small condoms, and, optimistically, three "XLs.")

"Certainly," he said. "And I want you to know, I've got a box of condoms in my nightstand drawer. And, as long as we're laying our cards on the table, I have had one in my wallet, like a hopeful teenager, ever since our first date."

"You brought a condom to the dog park?" She giggled and nibbled a cracker. Her mouth was too dry. She put the cracker down. "What were you thinking was gonna happen there?"

"I guess I anticipated that there'd be more than just the dog park involved, but, then, there was that whole scene." He shrugged.

"As long as we're being honest, I have to admit, I'm not really crazy about condoms. But we gotta do what we gotta do." *God, why did I stop taking my pills after Dave left? Why didn't I ever get my tubes tied? I'm not using them. I wonder . . . do they really get in there and tie them in little knots? They must, because otherwise wouldn't they call it "having your tubes snipped" or "soldered" or whatever? But then, where do the eggs go that drop out of your ovaries? Wouldn't they build up behind the knots?* The knots in her stomach brought her back to the discussion at hand. She'd missed a bit of what he'd said.

". . . none of my business, but when was the last time you used a condom?"

She thought for a moment. "Hmm . . . I was nineteen, so like twenty-two years ago."

He smiled. "I'm not exactly a prophylactic expert, but I'm guessing they've made advances in the last two decades."

She began to feel slightly nauseous, realizing the first time she used a condom Brian would have been seven. But she forced herself to focus on Helen's Tip Number Two: "No dwelling on age differences. *No math.* Remember to feel experienced, not older."

"No doubt." Her voice echoed into her wineglass.

"Anyway, what's next? You mentioned lighting. What's your preference?"

"None." She set her glass back down.

"You have no preference?"

"No, I mean, I'd prefer there was no light."

"No light? At all?"

"Right. Pitch blackness would be great. But if that's not possible, a bit of moonlight would be OK. Is that a problem?"

"Well, I like bright lights. The brighter the better." Her eyes widened in a look not unlike sheer terror so he added, "I'm teasing. But I was thinking maybe some candlelight."

"Urrhhh . . . I'm not sure." She shook her head.

"When I've pictured this in my head, you look exquisite in candlelight. Very sexy."

"You've been picturing this, huh?"

"Again, it's cards-on-the-table time. It would be a bald-faced lie to say I hadn't."

She bit her lip and looked down. Her eyes flitted back and forth, mentally comparing candle versus moonbeam wattage. "Would moonlight be a deal-breaker?"

"If you're looking for a deal-breaker, you're going to have to come up with something more drastic than that to back out of this. Moonlight it is."

"OK. How about music? I know we both like music, but what about . . . you know, *during*," she asked.

"I'm fine with anything, as long as it doesn't have words."

"Agreed," she clinked her glass against his. "Words can be very distracting. But . . . you're not thinking like *Ride of the Valkyries*, right?" *Who, or what, is a Valkyrie anyway? And what, exactly, are they riding?*

He laughed. "Actually, that could be very moving. But no, I was thinking of something a bit quieter."

"I'll trust your judgment there."

"What else? You mentioned words being distracting. So, what about talking? Where do you stand on that?" he asked.

"I'm not a fan of that. That makes me . . . sort of uncomfortable."

"OK, I can be quiet as a mouse." He winked at her.

"Oh, no, I don't mean total silence. I mean, a bit of talking is OK. But no play-by-play."

He chuckled. "Got it. No play-by-play. No color commentary."

She looked around the room as if playing I-Spy while he watched her, unblinking.

"Are we missing anything?" he asked.

"Let's see . . . Condoms, lights, music . . . I think that's it. I think we can, you know, try to pretend we're being spontaneous about the rest."

"Well then, why don't we change the subject." He stood up, unbuttoned his cuffs and rolled back his sleeves, revealing the golden hairs on his forearms. "Do you want to help with dinner?" He held out his hand to her.

She stood up and put her icy hand into his warm one, thankful to have the conversation over with and feeling much better for having brought it up. "Yeah, I can help."

"Excellent. But first, let me go put on *Ride of the Valkyries*."

AFTER DINNER, BRIAN suggested they sit on the couch and relax. He dimmed the lights.

"I can give you one of my famous foot rubs."

"That sounds fabulous." Maggie was glad she'd had a pedicure that morning. Every inch of her had been shaved, plucked, scrubbed and/or slathered in preparation. She was a living scratch 'n sniff replica of The Body Shop. "I've never had a handsome man give me a foot rub."

He began to work his magic on her left foot, which he held in his lap. "How about an ugly man?"

She laughed. "No, can't say that I have. Ohhhhh, that feels fantastic."

She took a deep breath in and let it out slowly. She could get used to this. She watched him concentrating on her foot.

"Why do you suppose women never give men foot rubs? Why is it always the other way around?" she asked.

"Hmm, I never thought of that before. I guess because women generally wear much more uncomfortable shoes than men. And since some sadistic man somewhere probably invented the high heel, we feel a sort of deeply ingrained guilt about that and a need for recompense." He'd stopped massaging her foot while he spoke.

"Hey, don't stop."

"Sorry." He went back to work. "Besides, men have troll feet. Women have sexy feet."

"You think so?"

"Definitely. In fact, I remember the first time I noticed a woman's foot." He looked up as if seeing into his past, but continued to knead her foot.

"You do? That must have been some foot."

"I was fifteen. I was at my friend Bradley's house working on a project for school. We went into the kitchen for a drink, and his mother was up on a step stool looking for something. She was on one leg, with her other foot pointed out behind her and I had this overwhelming urge to run my fingertip along the arch of that tiny, pink foot of hers."

"You were hot for Bradley's mother's foot?"

"I was fifteen; I was hot for many things back then. Right foot please."

While she changed position, she couldn't help but wonder if that was the start of a penchant for older women.

The foot massage, combined with the wine, turned her tense muscles into elastic bands. Her shoulders dropped and she rested her head on an oversized pillow and shut her eyes.

"Maggie, I need you." Brian said in a deep voice.

Her eyes snapped open.

"Get it? I *knead* you." For emphasis he ground his thumbs deep into the ball of her foot.

She laughed, but stopped when he let go of her foot, got on his hands and knees and prowled up the couch toward her. He held himself over her, lowering his head to kiss her.

Oh God, I hope my breath's OK. She might have pulled back, ever so slightly, if her head weren't held in place by the sofa cushion.

His kissing technique was . . . interesting. Mostly enjoyable, although every once in a while he would run the underside of his tongue back and forth across the front of her teeth. It left her with nothing to do but wait for the regular action to resume, and wish she'd snuck into the bathroom ahead of time and hunted for floss.

After several minutes on the sofa, he said, "It's too bright in here." He stood and held out a hand to her. "Come with me?"

In his room, moonbeams slipped through the plantation shutters.

He held up his index finger, "Wait right here." He picked his iPod up off the dresser. He slid the dial-wheel in circles; it clicked as he tried to land on what he was looking for.

"Looking for your sex playlist?" She giggled.

"For your information, it's called 'Mellow.'" Finding what he wanted, he put the iPod into the player. Slow strains of saxophone and keyboard washed over her.

This could work. She tried to concentrate, but random thoughts kept popping into her head, like why was saxophone music so perfect for having sex. *Is it the name—sax?*

She felt oddly disconnected from herself as her crazy saxophone thoughts ran through her mind and Brian trailed his fingertips across her shoulders, down her arms. She shut her eyes.

"Sax," she said, absentmindedly. It just popped out. *Ohmygod. I'm coming down with some sort of arousal-induced Turrets Syndrome.* She imagined the drug company ads: *"A*T*S is a real disease that affects tens of dozens of Americans. Don't let A*T*S spoil that special moment with that special someone. Just take our pink pill . . ."* No, *a pink pill would be too feminine.* But she liked the alliteration. *"Our purple pill . . ."? No that's taken. Puce? . . . Oh God. I'm losing it. Please let him kiss me before I blurt out something else nutty, like "Penis."*

She guessed Brian had no qualms about having sex with a crazy woman as he continued to caress her.

He pressed a finger to her lips and bent to whisper in her ear. "What happened to our guidelines? No play-by-play."

He put his arms around her, she thought to hug her, but then she felt a tug and heard the "zzzzzzettt" of her dress being unzipped. He gently pushed the straps off her shoulders and it fell in a pool around her feet. Seconds later, the scratchy lace underwear was no longer a problem.

She started unbuttoning his shirt at the top, while he worked his way up from the bottom. She was still fumbling with the second button when his hands met hers. She heard him unbuckling his belt as she pushed his shirt off over his shoulders. He let his arms down and the shirt floated to the floor to take its place beside her dress.

The bed creaked as they lay down on it. She sent her hands on a reconnaissance mission. *Oh good, no hair on the back. Pro. Nice smattering on the chest. Another pro . . .*

She'd lectured herself in the shower that day. *No comparing body parts with certain other males.* She didn't want to be derailed by thoughts of Dave at an inopportune moment.

So, now, with the subject at hand she concentrated on thinking only in generalities. *Men have such odd . . . parts. No control. Just . . . boom. What must it be like to suddenly have an appendage be three times its normal size? What if you saw someone you were attracted to on the street and, like, your hand puffed up three times as big?* She imagined trying to get something out of her purse with a fat-fingered, Mickey-Mouse-sized hand. Or fumbling with her keys to get in the car. She heard the attractive man of her imagination ask, "Is that a baseball mitt on your hand or are you just glad to see me?"

Brian kissed her neck at the tender spot just below her left ear— her major weakness. Her Achilles' ear. She giggled and felt a delicious shiver of pleasure run down her spine. *Ooooo, that's nice. OK, now we're getting somewhere. Now I can concentrate on the task at hand.* She giggled again as she thought, So to speak.

MAGGIE WATCHED BRIAN sleep. He lay on his stomach; his right arm anchored her in place. A stripe of moonlight fell across his face. The slight hint of his crooked smile was there, but his forehead was furrowed. Had he been worrying about her before he fell asleep?

If so, he needn't have. All the same, she was glad he was asleep so he wouldn't see the tear that crept down her cheek. She wouldn't want him to misunderstand this lone remnant of the stress she'd felt building as their date drew nearer. She'd been looking forward to it with a stomach-churning mix of excitement and dread. Now she felt light and free.

I didn't even think about Dave once. Until now . . . She wondered if Dave had felt any stress, trepidation, anxiety, the first time he was with Stupid Slut. Or was it just man-the-torpedo and full steam ahead.

Stop it, she told herself. *I don't care what Dave thought . . . or thinks.*

"Brian," she said, partly to drive Dave fully from her mind, but also because she needed to say goodbye. She had to go home and let Kona out. Besides, she needed to get some sleep so she could get up early and go biking with Russell.

"Brian." She said it again, louder, as she stroked his arm.

He stirred. Seeing her, the furrows on his brow faded and the hint of smile stretched to full-strength. "Hello, Beautiful." He shifted to his side and reached out to tug at a lock of her hair. He pulled it out straight and released it. It bounced back into place. "You ever think of straightening your hair?" he asked, sleepily.

"Uh, no. It'd be a lot work. Why?"

"No reason. I've got a flat iron, if you ever wanted to try . . ." he muttered as he turned away and picked up a glass of water on the nightstand. He took a drink and offered her some. "Since we're both awake, why don't you come over here?" He patted his side of the bed.

"I can't. I have to go home."

"You can't leave me."

"I don't want to, but Kona needs me."

"I thought we established that *I* need you."

"Well, Kona really needs me, because he might explode."

"What about me? I might explode."

She laughed and allowed him to pull her on top of him as he rolled on to his back.

Kona could wait.

BRIAN LET OUT a last cry and Maggie collapsed on him, her hair tumbling across his chest as she burrowed her face into his warm, musky neck.

Seconds later, she heard a soft whimper. *Good God, is this boy multi-orgasmic? I don't know if I can take that kind of competition.*

But then, there was the sound again—only more insistent this time. She realized it was coming from beside the bed and turned to see Peaches, staring at them with big, bug eyes.

"How long have you been standing there?" Maggie said.

Brian woke from his dozing and lifted his head to look over the side of the bed.

"Oh . . . Peaches." His head dropped back to the pillow. "Tina and I used to always close the door. Peaches likes to watch."

"Oh." As adorable as Peaches was, Maggie found it rather

disturbing to see the pocket-sized voyeur glaring at her with a look that seemed to say, "Why are you naked on my man?"

"We used to call it '*ménage à Chihua.*'" He yawned. "Was that too much information?"

"Yes," Maggie said. "I need to go, but she looks like she might bite me."

"She's not going to bite you, are you, Princess?" Brian let his hand flop over the side of the bed. The tiny dog took a step closer and pushed his hand up with her head, then sat under it.

"Awwww." Maggie held her hand out for Peaches to sniff, but yanked it back as Peaches' upper lip began to curl back. "Uh, next time, let's be sure to close the door."

Chapter 17: What Are the Rules About That?

On her ride with Russell the next morning, he beat her up the hill for the first time.

"Oh, yeah!" he yelled, reaching the summit seconds ahead of her. He raised his arms as if breaking through a finishing line tape.

"I'll beat you next week," she said. "I didn't get much sleep last night."

"I don't want to hear any excuses, Missy. I just want to hear you asking what flavor energy bar I'd like next time."

"OK. What flavor do you want?"

"Hmmmm. I dunno. What tastes like . . . victory?"

"Napalm? Oh, no, sorry—that *smells* like victory. How about vanilla?"

"Vanilla it is." Russell acted like he'd won the Tour de France. He was border-line insufferable, but kept her laughing. She was laughing so hard he beat her to her driveway.

After he left and she'd showered, Maggie decided to call Helen. She'd gotten home in the wee hours (wearing her freshly steam-ironed dress—Brian, rather adorably she thought, had insisted on ironing it before she left, since it had been "in a heap on the floor for hours") to Kona two-stepping in front of the back door, anxious to go out, and a blinking answering machine light. It was Helen: "Hi-ho Silver? Call me *mañana*. I want to hear everything. OK, well maybe not everything, but the highlights."

She decided to have a big decadent smoothie before calling—after all, she'd burned a lot of calories last night and this morning. Instead of adding a frozen banana like she usually did to her vanilla soy milk and strawberries, she blended in some of her favorite Ben & Jerry's flavor, Cherry Garcia. She put her feet up on the couch and got comfortable with her glass and a spoon (it was so thick her straw was useless), while Kona settled into begging-mode below her. When she was done, she gave him the glass to lick and dialed.

She was just about done giving Helen the *Reader's Digest* version of the evening when she heard another call coming in. "Gotta go. See you Tuesday?" She clicked into the other call.

"Guess who's getting married?" Kevin said without saying hello.

Maggie screamed. "Ohmygod, no way! When did this happen? Annie must be so happy. When's the wedding? Does Mom know?"

"One question at a time please." Maggie swore she could hear him grinning. "I've been thinking about it for a few weeks, but I asked her yesterday."

"Yesterday? When were you going to tell me?"

"We were in New York. We just got back a little while ago."

"Please tell me you didn't do the ol' 'Marry me, Annie' on the jumbo screen at Yankee Stadium thing."

"No. Come on. You know I hate the Yankees as much as you do." He waited a moment and added, "It was a Mets game. No, I'm kidding."

"Good. OK, let's hear it. And I want some damn details."

"Her brother, Jeremy, was in on it. Said he was sending us for some big meeting on Monday, and I said we should make a weekend out of it. Saturday we walked all over sight-seeing. When we got to Tiffany's, I told her we needed to go in and do some shopping. I did the whole one-knee thing right there on the sidewalk. Some people stopped and watched. They even applauded when she said yes."

"That's so sweet. She must have been shocked. Did she cry?"

"A little. But happy tears I can take. And . . . I might have cried a bit, too."

"Oh, you're going to make me cry. I'm so happy for you guys."

"Well, we owe you a lot."

"No, you don't. I almost royally screwed things up for you guys."

"No, really, we owe you big time. Annie says so too. If we hadn't broken up for those few weeks, I wouldn't have realized what I really wanted. We probably would've coasted along until she got tired of waiting for me to do something and dumped me." He paused and added, "Hey, the wedding's the Saturday after Thanksgiving. You'd better book your ticket soon."

"Thanksgiving weekend? Wow, it's early this year; that's less than two months away."

"I know, but we don't want to wait. And it's not going to be anything formal. No big church wedding or anything like that, just a civil ceremony with close friends and family."

"Oh, how did Mom take that news?"

"You know, I think she was so shocked that I'm getting married, it didn't faze her."

"That figures. Nothing you do fazes her."

"No, really. She was super happy."

Of course she was; Kevin could tell Mom the Pope's a cross-dresser and she'd smile and agree. Actually, he really is a cross-dresser. You never see him in slacks. She started wondering what the Pope wears under his robes when Kevin continued.

"She's going to drive up with Grandma and Humphrey. Can't wait to meet Gram's boyfriend. I've got to call Shay when I get off the phone with you."

"What about Russell?"

"I just got off the phone with him actually."

"Oh, you called him before me," she teased. "I guess I know where I stand."

"I had to call my best man first. But, get this; he doesn't want to be my best man."

"What? Are you kidding? Why not?"

"He wants to be the minister. Said he can get a single-use license on the Internet," Kevin laughed. "Won't that be great?"

"A single-use license? This isn't a fishing trip. Is that even legitimate?"

"I'm sure it's fine. But I'm still short a best man, so I was thinking of asking you."

"Me?"

"Yeah, come on." He convinced her it was going to be a non-traditional event, which was easy considering his choice of minister. He also told her that Annie was asking Jeremy to be her "Man of Honor" so it would work out perfectly; with the two most instrumental people in getting them back together standing up for them.

"OK. I'm in. But I'm not getting you a stripper for your bachelor party."

After she hung up, Maggie decided to call Mom to get her reaction to the no-church-wedding news. She guessed that Mom wouldn't care; her "baby" could do no wrong.

"Oh Maggie, have you talked to Kevin?" She could hear the excitement in Mom's voice.

"I sure did. That's why I'm calling. Pretty great news, huh?"

"Yes, I'm thrilled! But, I'd be more thrilled if all my children were settled down—"

"Mom," Maggie cut her off. "Could we not go there? Can we just both be happy for Kevin for like five minutes?"

"I'm very happy for Kevin, honey. I'm over the moon."

"I know you are, but . . . never mind." She rolled her eyes. Since Mom had already managed to make her crazy fifteen seconds into their conversation, she decided not to bring up the whole civil ceremony thing. She figured she'd try to move on as if her mother was not completely irritating her. She was usually pretty good at that. She'd had a lot of practice. "So, Kev says you're driving up with Gram and Humphrey."

"Yes, your Grandmother's very excited. It's been such a long time since we had the whole family together. And it will be nice for you to meet Humphrey. He's very sweet with her."

"I can't wait. They sound adorable. Gram told me she had to warn him she's not on the pill."

"Margaret Anastasia."

"Hey, I'm just repeating what *your* mother said." She was

pleased to hear Mom let out a small laugh.

"Hmmm. I just realized, you and I will be the only single ones there from the family," Mom said. "We can compete for the bouquet. We'll just be two old spinsters together."

"Actually, I'm bringing my new boyfriend, Brian." *I am? Is he my boyfriend? How many dates does it take to make a boyfriend?* It seemed early in their relationship. (Did they even have a relationship? Where was the line that demarcated the border crossing from "just dating" to "in a relationship?" Had they passed it? No one had asked for her passport. She was pretty sure her papers were not in order. They'd had the "let's be exclusive" discussion regarding sex. But, did that conversation also mean he qualified as her boyfriend? She figured it sort of did, but thought she'd ask Helen for a ruling.) And was she really going to ask him to travel cross-country with her, for cross-examination by Mom? "I mean, if he's not already going home for Thanksgiving."

"Oh, I didn't know you were dating someone."

Maggie told her a bit about Brian, then made up an excuse to hang up. She hadn't really been ready to talk to Mom about dating. It just came out.

After she hung up she wondered if she should ask Brian. It would be nice to have someone there with her. It was going to be odd to see her family without Dave. Except for Kevin, none of them had seen her single since she was a teenager. Dave had been such a long-term fixture in her life. She thought if she went alone they'd all be feeling sorry for her in her new sans-Dave state; looking at her as if she'd lost a limb.

She appalled herself. Had she just thought of Brian as nothing more than Dave-filler? Human-Spackle to fill up the hole in her personal life?

No, that's not it, she reasoned. *I really do like him. I'm not just trying to plug a hole . . .*

She needed to think seriously, and quickly, about inviting him. Thanksgiving weekend flights would fill up fast. If she was going to ask him, she'd need to do it soon.

Pro: I'll have a date; con: he might read too much into it. No. She shook her head. *Stop it. Go with the flow. Besides, I'm in too good of a mood today; I'm not going to worry about it . . . at least, not today.* In her best Scarlett O'Hara voice she said aloud, "I'll think about that 'tamarra.'" She got up, intending to flounce out of the room, but, before she could even learn that flouncing really only works in a hoop skirt, she stopped in her tracks. She'd put her bare foot down in a puddle of what, judging by its viscosity, could only be dog drool.

Ewwww. She peg-legged her way to the kitchen for a paper towel. *Scarlett never had these problems.*

She thought about how Scarlett could have benefited from a dog. After all, nobody but Rhett really understood her. A dog would have been a good friend. A dog would have advocated her I'm-not-going-to-worry way of thinking, and been fully supportive of that I'll-never-be-hungry-again stuff.

"DOWN TO THE last thing on the To Do list. Can you come by Saturday a.m. and help fix the fence?" Maggie emailed Russell from work on Thursday. Her realtor had said the house looked great, but suggested Maggie fix the back fence (where Kona had tried to tunnel under to eat the neighbor's cat) so that the place would be picture perfect for the Open House a week from Sunday. "Tried to fix it myself, but need a power saw. I already bought the boards. Shouldn't take long. You have a saw, yes? Hate to bug you again, but can you come by??"

She should have called, but email was easier when you were feeling a little guilty. For one thing, he'd already helped her with several projects and she didn't want to take advantage. She'd tried to hire a handyman this time, but the first one never called back and the second stood her up. It had led to another career idea: a handyman business that catered to single women. She'd pictured herself in tool belt and safety goggles. *That would probably be really popular. I could be my own boss. And if it really took off I could franchise it . . . Of course, I have no interest in home repair. OK, keep thinking.*

She'd also asked Brian if he owned a saw. He'd chuckled and

said, "Yes, it's right here, next to my jackhammer and steel-toed boots." So, she didn't have much choice but to ask Russell. Besides, she also needed to talk to him about skipping their Sunday ride, which was the other reason she felt guilty. But she could at least do that in person. Nice; ask the man to give up his Saturday morning, then tell him you're blowing him off on Sunday, she thought as she hit send.

A few hours later he replied: "Got the tools and the talent. I'm in San Fran right now. (Just closed a big sale for a new clinic here!) But I'm flying back this afternoon. So, 9:30 tomorrow? I'll bring donuts to celebrate the end of the To Do list."

Saturday, he was on her doorstep with a circular saw under his arm, his red metal box full of tools in one hand and a small white cardboard one full of donuts in the other.

"That won't take any time at all," he said when she showed him the chewed fence. "Let's eat first. I'm starving." Maggie was hungry, too, having just come from working out with Helen.

Maggie had made coffee and they carried their mugs and donuts outside. It was a sunny day, but cool under the covered patio. Kona followed along as though an invisible cord led from the cardboard box to his nose.

"I haven't eaten a donut in forever," Maggie said. The glossy surface of the chocolate frosting splintered like cracks on an ice-covered lake as she picked up her selection. "Going to undo all the good I did at the gym."

"Don't worry about it." Russell swallowed a bite of jelly donut, parentheses of powder at the corners of his mouth. "We can work these off on our ride tomorrow."

"About that . . . I can't make it." Brian had invited her to a play that night and, since she'd had to leave the last time because of Kona, he'd told her to bring the dog along and spend the night. He'd been very understanding about the fact that she felt uncomfortable having him over to her house.

"Why not? You and Brian going away or something?"

"No, we're just going to a play tonight, and then . . . ya' know,

I'm gonna spend the night." She tore a chunk off the bottom of her donut and tossed it to Kona who swallowed it without so much as a single chew.

"So what? Get your butt out of bed tomorrow and come biking with me."

"I can't jump out of bed and say, 'Gotta go. Things to do. People to see.'"

"Why not?"

"Well, I don't want to. And . . . I think that's sort of rude."

"It's not rude. I do it all the time." He finished his jelly donut and wiped his mouth with his napkin before reaching for a cruller.

"I know you do. You explained the whole stupid 'Twelve-Hour Rule' thing to me."

He glowered at her; it was the same face her mother had made when Maggie admitted she didn't go to church anymore. "The Twelve-Hour Rule is a time-honored, tried and tested system. It's not stupid."

"Whatever. Look, tonight's the first time I'm spending the night and I'm not leaving early. I promise I'll try to make it from now on, but not tomorrow, OK?" She closed the box of donuts and stood up. "Come on, let's get to work."

Russell whistled *Oh What a Beautiful Morning* while they carried his tools across the grass and set up shop next to the fence under the warm sun. White clouds streaked in thin wisps across the deep blue sky, as if a child had taken a swipe with the broad side of his chalk.

"I'm surprised you know the music from *Oklahoma*," Maggie said.

"What are you talking about?"

"*Oklahoma*. The musical." He stared at her. "You're whistling the opening song."

"I don't know nuthin' 'bout no musicals. It's just something my grandma used to sing all the time." Maggie knew Russell had lived with his grandmother for several years after his parents went through a nasty divorce when he was ten. "She taught me lots of things that I was too stupid to appreciate at the time. She's the one that taught me to knit. She was a great lady." He looked up at the sky. "I miss you, Grandma."

She smiled as he belted out the first few lines of the song while they took down the old boards.

While they used them to measure and cut the new ones, Maggie mentioned how excited she was about Kevin's news. She hadn't had a chance yet to talk to Russell about the wedding, other than a short email exchange earlier in the week. He agreed, saying he couldn't wait to go to Boston.

"Kev tells me you're going to be Mr. Minister. Is that . . . legit?" She wasn't sure how she felt about that. She and Dave had been married in the church, but that was back when she still felt some small connection to the religion she'd been raised in. She could understand Kevin's choice of a civil ceremony, but having a friend play minister-for-a-day didn't seem right.

"It's legit. I Googled it. For Massachusetts, it's fine to have a friend perform the ceremony. I downloaded the application from the Governor's office. It's twenty-five bucks and then I get a one-day license to—what was the word?—solemnize the wedding. Cool, huh?"

"Super cool," Maggie said, dead pan. "So, solemnize . . . as in 'to be solemn.' You're not going to be cracking jokes and whatnot, are you?"

"No, I am not going to upstage my best friend's wedding. I can *be* solemn."

"OK . . . For Annie's sake, I hope so." She tried to lighten her voice and changed the subject. "Anyway, you'll get to meet the rest of our family. You'll love my grandma."

They talked for a while about her family and the trip. He asked if she planned to bring Brian.

"Not sure." She'd asked Helen's opinion that morning at the gym. Helen had said, "What would Kona do?" and Maggie had said he'd obviously go for it. Kona always preferred to travel in a pack. On the phone last Sunday, Shannon had also voted in favor of Brian being invited. She wanted to meet Maggie's younger man. When

Maggie had emailed Kevin about it, he'd replied, "Sure, bring him. The more the merrier."

"We haven't been dating that long," she continued. "If the wedding was here in town it would be no big deal, but asking him to fly across the country and meet my whole family and, on top of that, not spend Thanksgiving with *his* family . . . Seems a bit much, don't you think?"

He set the first board in place and asked her to hold it while he nailed it in.

"Why don't you just ask him if he's planning to fly home for Thanksgiving?" he said as he drove the nails in with a few swift pounds of the hammer. "If not, you invite him."

"I suppose." She grabbed the next board and handed it to him. "Is Natalia coming?"

"No, she's spending the holiday with her parents in Maine," he lisped a bit due to the nails between his teeth.

"It's not that far. She could come down for the day or something."

"No. It's cool. I'd rather go alone."

"Do you think I should go alone?"

"I don't know. Depends how serious you are about this guy. Do you want him to meet your family?"

"We've only been dating a month. I'm not planning to get serious at all . . . I just thought it'd be fun to have him come along. It makes it so much more of a big deal since it's this whole cross-country trip. Wish they were getting married here. After all, her family lives here."

"Yes, it would be better if they planned their wedding around what works for you." He grinned at her, then positioned the last board into place.

She started to hold it for him, but then yanked her hand away.

"Ouch!" A fine splinter had embedded itself in her middle finger.

"Let me see that." Russell took her hand in between his large, rough ones and examined it. "I'm going to have to amputate. Let's move over to the saw."

"Let me go get my tweezers, you clown." She tried to pull away.

"No, I can get it." He bent his head over her hand and inspected it, then pinched at the skin. "The end's sticking out."

While he concentrated on the operation, she looked at the brown curls at the back of his tan neck. Like whorls of mocha cake frosting, it was tough to keep her fingers out of them. He was so close she could smell him, that leather-rain-and-ginger scent. She closed her eyes for the briefest of moments.

"Got it." He displayed the offending sliver on his fingertip. "You're good as new."

"Thanks." Her voice cracked. She swallowed and hoped he hadn't noticed. "Handyman, surgeon, donut delivery guy. Is there any limit to your talents?"

"You may never know." He winked and turned to hammer in the last board.

God, he's such a flirt. She blinked a few times, then started gathering up the old wood.

As he packed up his tools he asked about the play they were going to see.

"It's new. It's about the alienation we feel in our mindlessly consumerist society."

He laughed. "Oh, a comedy then? That sounds like fun."

"It will be . . . OK, maybe not fun, but . . . enriching. Why, what are you and Natalia doing tonight?"

"We're going to snuggle up on the couch and be enriched by a Will Ferrell movie while mindlessly consuming a pizza the size of your dining room table."

"Well, if that's your idea of a good time. Hey, I owe you big time for helping me *again*."

"No problem. My pleasure."

They turned away from the fence and saw Kona standing in the center of the patio table, his head in the donut box.

Chapter 18: Downward-Facing Dog

As Maggie pulled into the visitor parking at Brian's, she worried the security guard might not let her in with Kona, since he was over three times heavier than the building association's weight limit for pets. She called Brian on her cell and asked him to come down and let them in.

"Isn't Tony at the desk? He'll buzz you in."

"I don't know if he's there. I'm still in the car. You're sure it's OK to bring Kona in?"

"It's fine, but if it makes you feel better, I'll come down and help you smuggle him in."

"Should we smuggle him? Is there a back way?"

"I was joking. I'll be right down."

When Brian came downstairs, he took Kona's leash and walked across the slate-tiled lobby like he owned the building. Kona, wagging his tail and grinning like the ambassador from Labrador, garnered a "hey boy" and pat on the head from Tony, who came out of his glass-enclosed office to greet the dog.

"OK, you were right," she said when they got in the elevator.

"Do you feel like we just got away with something? It's exciting, huh?" He pulled her close. "If you really want a thrill, maybe later we could sneak into the laundry room and wash a load of whites after hours." He dropped Kona's leash and kissed her.

He was wearing his navy blazer with a pale lavender shirt. The outfit made his gray eyes a pale blue shade, like the sky on a hot August afternoon.

She pulled away. "Stop teasing. I know I get a little crazy, but are you sure the dogs'll be OK home alone? I'm a little nervous about it. Hope Kona's not picking up on my energy."

Brian laughed. "Wow, that sounded very California."

"It's true. Dogs do pick up on your vibe."

"Yes, he looks terribly concerned." He pointed at Kona, reclining against the back wall of the elevator, his mouth hanging open in his ever-present grin.

"OK, well, Kona's just not much of a worrier, but *normal* dogs pick up on their owner's energy," Maggie said as they reached the fifteenth floor.

"I'm certain you're right. But I'm also certain they'll be fine." He opened the door to the condo, calling out, "Peaches, your boyfriend's here."

Her toenails clicked down the hall like tiny castanets. Kona perked up at the sound. As she rounded the corner, he lowered his head to his front feet, rear end still up in the air in the traditional, "Hey, let's play" invitation. Peaches stopped short when she saw the big dog, lifted one paw and flattened her ears.

Maggie tensed. But then Peaches let out a yip, swung her ears forward like radar antennae, and wiggled her tiny whip of a tail.

The two dogs scampered into the living room where Kona surprised Maggie by playing very gently and never once even trying to put the Chihuahua's head in his mouth.

They had time before their pre-play dinner reservation so they decided to have a glass of wine before they left. From the sofa, they watched King Kong chase Fay Wray around the coffee table in a game of tag that alternated between fast forward and stop-action slow motion.

Maggie noticed that Brian had moved a blown-glass vase and matching shallow bowl that normally sat on the coffee table to the mantel piece. She checked the room, hoping there was nothing her sweet-natured but ham-handed hound could get into while they were out.

Twenty minutes in, the game was finally on pause.

"We should probably get going," Brian said. Maggie had finished her inventory and didn't see any potential problems. Still . . .

"You're sure you're OK with leaving them alone? Maybe we could have a neighbor check in?" she asked as he helped wrap her in her pashmina. It was a crisp fall evening, but not cold enough for a jacket. She'd decided her pink pashmina would do. Besides, she thought it was pretty with her white blouse and black pencil skirt. But now, when she caught a flash of her reflection in the mirror above the mantel, Good & Plenty candies came to mind.

"They'll be fine." He lifted the ends of her hair caught under the shawl and arranged them on her back. "I'm terrible. I didn't even tell you yet that you look good." He emphasized the last word with a kiss, while she thought, And plenty. She consoled herself with the thought that maybe the pink and white licorice candies were before his time.

The play was, as she'd figured it would be, deep. Very deep. She'd felt a need for scuba gear at one point. Brian thought the play was wonderful and thought-provoking, although he complained about the set direction. And about the fact that he'd counted "at least twelve people wearing jeans and one idiot in shorts."

"People are just super casual here," Maggie tried to explain. "It's a beach town."

On the drive to his condo she remembered the dogs. Home alone. Would his silk pillows be intact? His hardwood floors puddle free? Kona hadn't chewed a piece of furniture or peed in the house in years, but still, she'd never left him alone in a strange place before.

Kissing her as they rode up in the elevator, Brian seemed oblivious to the possible destruction that might await them. She didn't say anything, but held her breath when Brian opened the door. He returned to kissing her, moved her toward the bedroom, untucked her blouse. She took advantage of his concentration on her skirt's zipper to scan the living room. He'd left the accent lights on that lit his paintings and sculptures, so she was able to see that everything was fine. They'd come in so quietly, she assumed they hadn't woken Kona, and he must be sleeping soundly in the guestroom with Peaches. She let out a sigh of relief, which segued into a sigh of desire.

They worked their way into his dark bedroom, a tangle of

shirtsleeves and stubborn buttons. In their haste, they forgot to close the bedroom door. Free of their clothes, they tumbled onto the bed.

"Hrrmmph."

Three heads were silhouetted by pale moonbeams as they looked up in unison.

They had landed beside Kona, who had apparently been deeply asleep on Brian's pristine pale blue matelasse bed cover. His tail thumped when he saw them.

Brian reached to turn on the bedside lamp.

"No, not the light," Maggie yelled too late. She snatched her pashmina off the floor and wrapped it around her naked self.

Peaches ran in, yapping as if tattling, "I told him he wasn't allowed up there!"

Kona jumped onto all fours, jostling the bed, then lowered his head, inviting Peaches in on the game. He added his booming bark to the melee and hopped from side to side.

Maggie held her pink security blanket in place with one hand, while she pushed at Kona with the other, and scolded him, "Get off!" They'd made a nest for him in the corner of the guestroom next to Peaches' basket. He was supposed to have curled up on the old blanket where they'd set his favorite stuffed rabbit as the indicator that this would be his bed for the evening.

Brian laughed and rolled on to his back. He stretched his arms over his head as he surveyed the scene, then pulled them back. "Ewww. What the . . . ?"

They turned. There was Kona's rabbit, soggy with drool, lying upon the pillows like a gold-foil-wrapped chocolate left by the maid during turn-down service. And, trailing from the rabbit to where Kona had been, was a trail of blood; little red splotches, like rose petals, marked a path down the center of the pale blue bedspread.

"What the . . .," Brian said again. "Look at this mess." He got off the bed, and stood, hands on hips, in his Calvin Klein briefs.

They looked at Kona, whom Maggie had finally pushed off the bed. Dark, dried blood crusted the lower half of his left ear.

"Ohmygosh, what happened?" Maggie inspected his ear and

found a small puncture. "Poor baby." She turned to Brian. "I think your dog bit him."

"No." He walked to the other side of the bed where Maggie knelt next to Kona and flipped the dog's ear to inspect the underside. "Well, maybe. But he must have done something to her. She wouldn't bite him unprovoked."

So, you're saying this is Kona's fault, she thought, but did not say aloud. She picked up her underwear and wiggled into them under her pashmina-wrapper. *Although, I guess Kona can be pretty provoking. Suppose I should offer to buy a new bedspread, even though this is his dog's fault. Maybe I'll suggest* he's *the one that needs to hire a dog trainer.*

"Do you have a T-shirt I could put on while we clean this up? We could try soaking this." She started to pull the bedspread up. "If the stains don't come out, I could buy you a new one."

"You don't have to do that. It's Peaches' fault."

Darn right.

She was glad Brian had acknowledged this was his dog's doing, but things still seemed tense as they silently cleaned Kona's ear, wiped up more drops of blood they found on the hardwood floor, and moved Kona's blanket out of the guestroom and into the kitchen. But then, while they were scrubbing the bed cover in cold water in the tub, Brian playfully flicked water at Maggie. "Hey," she yelled and splashed him back. They laughed and tussled on the bathroom rug until he pinned her on the floor and kissed her, then helped her up and led her back to his bed.

Later, while the dogs snored at opposite ends of the condo, Maggie and Brian spooned in the dark in his bed.

"I'm sorry if I seemed a little . . . testy earlier," Brian said into her hair.

"You don't have to apologize. I knew I shouldn't have brought Kona over here."

"No, it's all good. They're fine now. Besides, if you hadn't brought him, you might not be here still, and then I couldn't do this." He brushed her hair off her neck and nibbled her earlobe. She giggled and snuggled closer to him. She wondered if she should ask him now about the wedding. Kona certainly wouldn't put off asking. And now seemed as good a time as any.

She rolled over to face him. "What are you doing for Thanksgiving? Are you going to your parents?"

"No. My mother wants me to come for Christmas, so I thought I'd stay here for Thanksgiving. How about you? Going to Florida?"

"No, Boston. Remember I told you my brother's getting married?" she fiddled with her pendant. "It's the Saturday after Thanksgiving, so my whole family's going to be in Boston. And . . . well, I wondered if you'd want to come?"

"That sounds perfect. I'd love to meet your family." He stroked her cheek. "Let's go online in the morning and book it."

"Now, don't feel obligated to go. Why don't you sleep on it?" *Doesn't he want to ponder this a little? I know I sure lost sleep over thinking about inviting him.* "Let's talk about it more tomorrow." She kissed him goodnight and rolled back over onto her side.

She lay thinking, listening to the steady sigh of his breathing. *Was that a mistake? Is it too soon? Oh well, the deed's done. Can't uninvite him. Kona wouldn't give it a second thought. Must remember to have no regrets. No regrets.* She repeated her mantra until she drifted off.

When she woke, Brian was gone. With the shutters closed, the room was still dark. She looked at the clock: 8:30. She'd slept later than normal. Then she noticed the tray by the bed. It held orange juice, a white china bowl bursting with fruit, a single red rose and the newspaper, along with a note from Brian that he'd taken Kona for a run. There was a P.S. that read: "I thought about it again this morning—I <u>do</u> want to go with you for the wedding. Let's look up flights when I get back!" *OK, I guess he's going.* She fluffed her pillow, and sat up in bed. Her stomach growled. She picked up the tray and noticed a small empty plate in the back corner, with a little smudge of . . . butter? *Hmmm. Something's missing. Maybe he made toast for himself before he left. Anyway, breakfast in bed! How sweet. And there's no reason to regret inviting him. He's adorable, and everyone will like him. It's going to be fine.*

She wondered, as she popped a raspberry into her mouth, if she should wait and share the fruit with him, but she was too hungry.

She'd make it up to him with a smoothie. Hopefully there was some fruit left. And maybe some yogurt. She'd have to see what he had.

She sat in bed eating (*He even sliced the grapes in half; how cute is he?*) and perused the Business section. BioHealth chugged along. Some days it would be up a bit, some days down. It moved with the general whims of the market; nothing to get excited about. She tried not to think about Dave getting half. *It is what it is and there's nothing I can do about it,* she told herself, tossing the paper aside.

When she finished, she put on Brian's lavender shirt from the night before and padded out to the kitchen in her bare feet. His spotless fridge contained a wonderful representation of the food pyramid: an abundance of fruits, lots of leafy greens, lean meats. She peeked in his cupboards, which were the same as the fridge. Everything was multi-grain, no trans-fat, preservative-free. *Doesn't he have any vices? Where are the PopTarts? The Mac n' Cheese? Well, it's good that he's so healthy.* She just hoped he wouldn't look in her cupboards, although they weren't *too* bad. There were a few boxes of Girl Scout Cookies, but come on. How could she not buy those? *Who can say no to a little girl dressed as a Thin Mint? Guerilla marketing at its finest.* And there was that five-pound bag of mini chocolate bars, but she could explain those too. Those were for Halloween. Of course, she'd have a hard time explaining why the bag was open when Trick-or-Treaters weren't due for another three weeks . . .

The door opened. She was caught standing on her tiptoes, looking through his cupboards.

"You already finished going through my drawers, I suppose?"

She slammed the cupboard door shut and spun around dropping to her heels.

"I was just . . ."

"I'm teasing. I'm an open book; poke away." He walked into the kitchen, glistening with sweat, hands on his hips. His T-shirt clung to him. Kona dropped, panting, to the tile floor.

"Seriously, I wasn't poking. I wanted to make you a smoothie. I was looking for your blender. And hoping you maybe had some wheat germ. How was the run?"

"Perfect. There's wheat germ in the pantry and fruit in the fridge. And yogurt or juice; use whatever you need."

"It's funny to see you in a T-shirt," she said as she opened the pantry door.

"My formal running gear is at the cleaners. Speaking of attire, I like you in my shirt." He filled Peaches' water dish, then set it down for Kona. Peaches ran in and Kona waited like a gentleman, or a dog afraid of being snapped at again, until she was done drinking.

"Doesn't Peaches get jealous when you go out with another dog?" Maggie asked as Brian pulled the blender out and set it on the counter for her.

"No, we have an open relationship. She's fine with it."

"I see. Cuz she looks a little jealous to me." Peaches stood in the center of the kitchen, staring at Brian, following his every move. Maggie put strawberries, raspberries, blueberries, wheat germ and low-fat vanilla yogurt in the blender. "Hold on, gonna make some noise."

When she was done, Brian said, "No, that's her 'where's my food?' face." Then he spoke to the dog, "Sorry, Princess. It's coming right up. Um, speaking of food . . ."

"Oh, gosh, I'm sorry. I forgot to thank you. That was so sweet. It was wonderful." She gave him a kiss as she handed him the tall glass of pinkish-purple goodness. "Here, try this; the perfect recovery drink after a hard run."

He gulped the thick liquid. "Wow, that's delicious. Thank you." He set the glass down and dug in the pantry for Peaches' bag of food. "I wasn't sure about the croissants, but, I reasoned that if you were worried about the calories, I'd offer to help you burn them off." He winked at her and set two bowls of kibble down for the dogs.

"Croissants?" Maggie asked. "What croissants?"

They blinked at each other, then looked at Kona in unison. His muzzle was buried in his bowl, while his eyes watched Peaches'.

Chapter 19: And You Should See My Asparagus Fern

After their Sunday ride, Russell and Maggie sat on her patio with the peach smoothies she'd made. Although deep into October, the Santa Anas dragged hot, dry air in off the desert and the thermometer read eighty-six degrees. The wind tore the tissue-paper-petal flowers of her bougainvillea loose, and they tumbled across the yard like miniature magenta Chinese lanterns.

"Damn. I'm going to need to clean those up before anyone else comes to see the place." Maggie licked her chapped lips. She hated this weather. The day they buried her dad, the Santa Anas had raged. The wind had whistled, jeering at them, as they lowered his coffin into the ground.

Russell asked how the Open House had gone the previous week.

"OK, I guess. A lot of people came through. Hard to say how many were Lookie-Lous." Maggie hated the thought of strangers pawing through her things, looking in her underwear drawer. "The realtor said one woman loved the house. She was supposed to come back with her husband, but no word so far." *Realtor? What would that be like?* She pictured herself in a designer suit and heels. She'd need to spend a lot more time on her makeup and nails. *It meets the non-office-job criteria, but nah. Too much competition out there. Besides, I'm no sales person. Definitely not dream-job material.*

She slumped down in her chair, throwing her head back against it. "What am I going to be when I grow up?" she asked Russell, herself, the career gods.

"Still haven't come up with anything, eh?" She'd told Russell weeks ago about her plan to try and figure out a new career while waiting to cash in on her stocks once the FDA approval came through. "You'll figure it out. And, whatever it is, you'll be great at it. You're brilliant."

"Thanks," she said, sitting up again. "But just because I can calculate the tip and everyone's share when we go out doesn't make me brilliant." She topped off his glass with the last bit from the blender, then held the glass carafe down for Kona to lick. He tried to stick his head all the way in to get every drop, but she frustrated his efforts and pulled it away when he got too far down inside.

"Watch the blades, Buddy," she said.

Kona gave his lips a once-around, looking for stray drops.

"Does it gross you out that I let him lick the blender?" Maggie asked Russell. "Not that it matters, because I'm still going to let him, aren't I, Buddy." She lowered her face so she was nose to nose with Kona. He sniffed her, then threw his head back for her to scratch under his chin, which she did after wiping away a smudge of smoothie. "Besides, it's green; saves water since I don't have to rinse stuff before it goes in the dishwasher."

"Doesn't bother me." Kona went to sit by Russell, who still had some drink left. "We used to have a beagle when I was a kid; fed him stuff right off our forks." He moved his glass away from the edge of the table, out of Kona's reach. "He's sure a fan of your smoothies."

"He's got a sweet tooth. He loves them." She watched Russell scratch behind Kona's ear. "You ever think about getting a dog?"

"Nah. Too much work. I need to be able to come and go as I please."

"Oh, right. I forgot. Heaven forbid you'd have some sort of commitment. But, come on; having a dog is great." She pushed a handful of hair back as another strong gust of wind blew.

"A dog would be great. But then I'd have to be home every night."

"But a dog plays right into your Twelve-Hour Rule. A dog's an iron-clad out. You've got to head home because you've got to let Fifi out. The ladies can't argue with that."

He held up his forefinger, "Except when the ladies want to

spend the night at my place. Then what?"

"So you get a mastiff or a Great Dane and you tell them the dog sleeps on the other half of the bed, so there's no room for three."

"Hmmm. You might be on to something. I might have to rethink my position on getting a pooch." He held out his empty glass to Kona who poked his long tongue into it, trying to reach the bottom. "So, what did you guys do last night?"

Maggie had convinced Russell to make their rides later so she could spend the night at Brian's on Saturdays, sleep in a bit and have some breakfast with him, then race home in time to hop on her bike and meet Russell.

"We went to the symphony. And cooked. It was nice." They'd had a lovely evening, even though Maggie could tell Brian didn't think the symphony compared to the Philadelphia Orchestra, but she figured that was only natural given the connection with his mom. "What did you guys do?" she asked as she got up and carried the dirty blender and her glass into the kitchen.

"We broke up." He followed her with his own glass. Kona trooped behind.

She spun around to face him. "You broke up? Last night?" *We just spent the last three hours together and he waits until now to tell me? Isn't this big news? He acts like he just told me the weather forecast.*

"Yeah, but really I shouldn't even call it a breakup. There was nothing substantial enough there to break. It was more of a 'snap up.'" He snapped his fingers for emphasis.

"I can see you're really torn up about this." She dropped her glass in the dishwasher. "So, what happened? No, wait, let me guess, she had the nerve to actually start caring about you."

"Are you mad at me for some reason?" He held his hands up in question. "Because, I didn't even think you'd care. I got the impression you didn't even like Natalia."

"I liked her fine, as a person. I just . . . I'm *not* mad." She knew she was talking louder than normal. *I'm not. I am not mad. I just can't believe he can be with someone for months though, and then act like it means less than nothing. I swear the man has no feelings. I bet he's got a Three-Month Rule in addition to that stupid Twelve Hour thing.* She kept her back turned to him and busied herself at the sink rinsing the blender, even though she'd just told him she didn't need to rinse things after Kona licked them. "So . . . what happened? You dumped her?" *Your relationship passed the "use by" date?*

"No, she dumped me."

Oh. Well, that's . . . surprising. "Why?" She looked at him over her shoulder.

"She started talking about us moving in together. And she got mad because she said I didn't have enough enthusiasm for the idea." He made air quotations with his fingers as he said the last phrase.

"Well, I'm guessing she was right." She put the blender in the dishwasher and shoved the door shut. She looked at him, leaning against her kitchen counter in his spandex shorts and Arrogant Bastard Ale cycling jersey. She knew he and Natalia had toured the local brewery the previous weekend and Natalia had bought him the jersey as a present.

"No, she was dead wrong." He'd taken his cycling shoes off and left them by the front door when they came in and she noticed now, when he crossed his legs at the ankle, that he wore matching Arrogant Bastard socks.

"Really?" She gave him a sidelong look as she reached for a towel to dry her hands. *OK, maybe I jumped to conclusions a little too fast there. Hear the man out. Maybe he is upset about this. He's just having a hard time talking about it.*

"Yeah, really. I didn't have *any* enthusiasm for the idea."

"I knew it." She made a tsk sound and put her hands on her hips. *Should have gone with my gut instinct. Mr. Shallow here isn't going to get serious about anyone. This is the same man who broke up with a woman over her belly button!*

"You knew what?"

"I guess I should say I know you, Mr. Eternal happy-*get*-lucky bachelor." The volume had crept up again in her voice.

"You *are* mad. I swear I don't understand women."

"Speaking on behalf of women everywhere, let me say that we

understand you. It's not hard to figure out a guy who has a Twelve-Hour Rule. A guy who can't even commit to a dog. Clearly, this is not a person looking to establish a connection with another living soul. Where do you stand on house plants?"

"Man, that's harsh. I *have* house plants. I have a spider plant in my master suite. And it's thriving, I'll have you know. I have connections. I thought . . . Never mind. I don't need this."

He put his hands up and lowered his head as he thumped loudly, even though only in his socks, across her hardwood floor.

"Fine then, leave." She still held the towel and twisted it in her hands.

"I will—as soon as your stupid dog gives me my damn bike shoe."

She stuck her head out of the kitchen in time to see Russell pry the expensive shoe out of Kona's mouth and storm through the door.

"Bad boy, Kona!" she said. She threw the towel back into the kitchen.

Hmmmph. Maybe that Natalia was smarter than I gave her credit for. Get out while the getting is good. Be the dumper instead of the dump-ee. Bet she could see that it was only a matter of time. But . . . why am I so worked up about this?

The phone rang and she snatched it up.

"Hey, Beautiful." It was Brian. "We're invited to a Halloween party on Saturday." He told her a gallery owner friend of his was having a big party at his house in Del Mar overlooking the ocean. "It's come as your favorite artist or subject. Won't that be fantastic?"

She sighed. "Yeah, that sounds fun."

"He said bring as many people as we like, so I thought we could invite Helen and Raul." The four of them had gone out to dinner the previous week. She'd been proud of herself. Things were crazy-busy at Clean N' Green that day, but she'd left at five so she could go home and get changed before their reservation. She'd been glad she hadn't cancelled, as she would have in her "former life" at BioHealth. The work had waited and, better yet, Raul and Brian had hit it off. Even though a good twenty years separated them, they'd bonded over their discovered mutual love of opera. Raul, an architect, volunteered his time every year at the San Diego Opera to help with set construction. He'd impressed Brian immensely when, in a discussion of their favorite operas, he'd rattled off Puccini's full name, said in an over-exaggerated Italian accent: Giacomo Antonio Domenico Michele Secondo Maria Puccini. They'd all applauded.

"I bet they'll come," she said. "Halloween is Helen's favorite holiday."

"Is everything OK? You don't sound like yourself."

"I'm fine. Just tired. And these stupid Santa Anas always give me a headache. I'm going to take a nap. I'll call you when I get up, OK?"

She and Kona got into bed, but she couldn't sleep. As Kona snored, she replayed the fight with Russell on a continuous loop. Maybe she had been a little harsh. *I don't even really know why that made me so nuts . . . I guess it just annoys me that a great guy like him wastes his time dating bimbos. But . . . whatever. If he chooses to stay in the shallow end of the dating pool, it's none of my business. Man, I am so glad we're just friends. If we'd gotten together that one time, that would have been a huge mistake. It wouldn't have meant anything to him, and I was way too vulnerable back then. So much better to just be friends . . . Some friend I am, though. He tells me his news and I jump all over him.*

She got up and went to her computer, but then decided apologizing via email was the chicken's way out. She picked up the phone and went and sat cross-legged on the sofa. She hugged a russet-colored velvet throw pillow to her chest.

She got his voicemail. "Look, I apologize for before. I was out of line. I, uh, I guess these Santa Anas make me a little crazy . . . OK, crazier. Anyway, I hope you aren't mad at me. And I hope your shoe is OK. Kona, um, he has this thing for sweat. Call me, OK?"

Then she called Brian back. "Do you think we could invite one more person? You know my friend I ride with, Russell? Well, he broke up with his girlfriend and I feel kinda bad for him." *Or . . . badly about how I treated him when he told me the news anyway.*

"Sure, go ahead and ask him. Did you give any thought to your costume yet?"

"Not really. My favorite artist is Matisse, but I have no idea what he looks like. I doubt anyone else does either, so I can't go as him."

"He actually always sort of reminded me of Freud. Similar white beard, glasses. So, no, you wouldn't want to go as him. How about a subject of his?"

"I love *Blue Nude II*." She pictured the image, a solid cobalt blue silhouette of a seated female figure on a pure white background. It was simple, perfect. "But, I'm thinking, stripping down and painting myself blue isn't really an option." She etched a pathetic rendition of it with her fingernail in the thick fabric of the pillow she still held on her lap, then rubbed it out with her palm.

"Maybe you can do that at the after-party at my house," Brian suggested.

"I wouldn't want to get your sheets all blue. I'll think of something. What about you?"

"Definitely *The Scream*."

"Perfect for Halloween, but is that really your favorite painting?" Maggie asked.

"It's one of them. Think about it; there are probably only a handful of paintings that are instantly recognizable by the masses, and since I don't want to go as *Mona Lisa*, *The Scream* is the next best thing. Did you know the killer in the *Scream* movies is based on the painting?"

"I didn't, but I can see that now." She pictured the elongated white mask from the movie.

She could hear the excitement in his voice as he told her about how hugely influential Edvard Munch had been and the many pop culture references to *The Scream*.

"It was even in an episode of *Beavis and Butthead*," he said.

She hoped she could come up with a costume that she could be as enthusiastic about. She told him she had some research to do and needed to call Helen and Russell and invite them, so they hung up.

Helen was excited and couldn't wait to figure out a costume. Maggie didn't tell Helen about the fight she'd had with Russell. She didn't want to make it into a bigger deal than it was. She'd just been crabby. From the Santa Anas. It was nothing.

Helen hung up to call Raul. As Maggie clicked the phone off, it rang. It was Russell.

They exchanged awkward hellos while she squeezed the pillow tighter.

"Look," the word rode a wave of his breath. "Let's not make a big deal out of this. I accept your apology so, let's move on and forget it."

"Is your shoe OK? I'll buy you a new pair."

"It's fine. A little damp."

She wanted to ask if he was mad at her, try to explain herself, but he was right. Get past it. Kona sure would. "OK, well, moving on then . . . Wanna come to a Halloween party Saturday with us and Helen and Raul?" He didn't say anything so she went on. "It should be fun. It's at Brian's friend's house. He's got a beach house in Del Mar and it sounds like he's going all out. I bet there'll be lots of beautiful, rich women."

"Beautiful, rich women could be interesting I suppose." He agreed to go, but then hemmed and hawed when she mentioned the art theme. She persisted until he relented.

"Alright, I'll go," he said. "I guess I'll finally get to meet your young stud."

"Please don't call him that," she said, but she was glad that he was already back to his normal teasing self.

"OK, but I'll be thinking it. Hey, I just thought of what I'm going to wear."

"What? It's not something to do with young studs is it?"

"I'll let it be a surprise."

After they hung up, Maggie leaned back on the sofa and closed her eyes. *Hmmm. Favorite artists.* There were many: Matisse, Chagall, Picasso, Kandinsky, Mondrian. The list could go on, but Chagall was definitely one of her all-time favorites and his colorful, dream-like paintings would be ripe with Halloween costume fodder. Her favorite Chagall came instantly to mind: *La Mariée.* It showed a young woman in a red wedding dress, "The Bride" the painting was named for, with someone hovering behind adjusting her veil. The vivid red and white of the bride jumped out from the painting's somber blue and green background. In addition to the expected church in the distance, there was a goat playing a musical instrument and a fish . . . She couldn't remember what the fish was doing. She'd have to look it up online. It had been years since she'd seen the painting. She used to have a framed poster of it in her college apartment, but at some point she'd sold it at a yard sale.

She got up. A quick Google search and there it was. The goat playing . . . a cello? *He's holding it upright like a cello, but it could be a violin on end. After all, it'd have to be a specially-made goat-sized cello. If the squirrel wasn't in front, you could see if it had that little spiky thing cellos have. Maybe Chagall put the squirrel there on purpose. Maybe he wasn't sure either. And, there's the fish . . . Playing a xylophone? No, maybe lighting candles, like in church. Those little red votives that you light to say a prayer. That's it—the fish is saying a prayer.*

She really wanted to go as the cello- (or violin?)-playing goat, but she wasn't creative enough to figure out *that* costume. The bride would be much easier. And she'd carry a stuffed goat. She could get an old wedding dress at a thrift store and dye it red. Would she have time one night after work, or maybe on a lunch hour, to hunt for a cheap wedding dress? It'd have to be just right, with long sleeves and . . .

Wait a minute. I've got a freaking long-sleeve wedding dress with a full skirt. She marched to her guest room and pulled open the closet door. There on the upper shelf was the special heirloom box she'd stored her dress in.

Huh. She snorted. *Heirloom schmeirloom.*

She reached for the box and set it on the guest bed. She yanked off the lid and the layer of acid-free tissue paper, like pulling off a Band-Aid. When she saw the dress, folded with such care on the day she'd packed it away, she wasn't so sure about her plan anymore.

She'd loved this dress. The memory of standing in the store, circling this way and that before the fan of full length mirrors while

Mom beamed and told her she looked lovely, rushed back. It was pushed aside by the image of Dave's face as she walked down the aisle. That was when she'd felt the most beautiful, seeing the look on his face. The little stab of sadness that Dad hadn't been there to walk her down the aisle came back, as fresh as on their wedding day.

Am I really going to ruin this?

She thought of all the symbols of their marriage: her ring, still in the Altoids tin in the kitchen junk drawer; the photos she'd stuffed unceremoniously into a garbage bag in the garage; the license—she'd forgotten about that as well. It would still be in their fire-proof safe, as worthless as the paper it was printed on. The dress was just one more token, once a treasured keepsake but now a useless reminder, of their love that hadn't lasted.

Maybe if we'd had a fish say a prayer for us things would have been different.

There was absolutely no reason to keep this dress, was there? She lifted it from the box and held it up to herself. It smelled like candle wax. Her fingers slipped over the cool satin fabric. She spread the skirt out and looked in the standing full length mirror. Her princess dress. She felt tears creeping up; they were in the back of her throat.

Then she thought of her "prince" who'd run off with the village wench and wanted half the kingdom, even though Maggie'd footed more than half the castle bills.

No crying, she lectured her reflection. *This was a happy reminder at one time, but now it's an albatross. I'm going to do it. It'll be cathartic.*

"Kona," she called, tossing the dress in a heap on the guest bed. "Walkies. Let's hit the drug store. Momma needs some red dye."

Chapter 20: That Really Gets My Goat

The five of them had agreed to meet at Maggie's before the party. She'd just finished putting Kona's devil-horn headband on him, which he seemed content enough to wear, when the doorbell rang. She opened it to find Andy Warhol and Marilyn Monroe. Raul wore a black suit with narrow tie, large glasses. His black hair hid under a white wig that he'd ratted up so that it framed his face in wild tufts. Helen, in a white halter dress, voluminous blond wig and lots of blue eye shadow, fluttered her false eyelashes.

"You guys look fantastic," Maggie said. She gave them each a quick hug while Kona whined and wiggled for some attention.

"Thank you," Helen said in a breathy voice. She struck the classic bent-knee, hands on thighs Marilyn-over-the-street-grate pose while Raul patted the dog. She stood straight again and added in her normal voice, "Andy here wanted to come as Van Gogh, but I nixed the idea when he wanted me to be a Potato Eater. I was never an Atkins believer; I mean, I love potatoes in any form, but I'm not going to a party dressed in a drab getup like that."

"No, Marilyn's much more you, although you sort of look like an anorexic version of her. I think she had more meat on her bones," Maggie said.

"She definitely had more boobs. I had to stuff my bra to fill out this halter."

"I helped," Raul grinned and winked as he grabbed at Helen. She beat him back with her purse and he held up his arms in defeat. He took Maggie's hands, held them out and assessed her costume. "You look great too; Chagall right?"

Maggie spun for them. She'd tie-dyed the dress, gathering bunches of it in loops of twine before plunging it with rubber-gloved hands into the laundry room sink filled with dye, as if it were a living thing she needed to hold under until it went limp. She'd felt a slight pang as the dress turned from white to peach, but as it deepened to pink she began to enjoy the transformation. By the time it was dark red she was smiling. It came out perfect; some parts of the dress darker red than others, streaks of lighter sections here and there. It looked painted.

She held up her goat to show him off. She'd remembered that one of the zoo gift shops carried a huge selection of stuffed animals. She'd used her membership card to go find a goat; then, searched online for a miniature shop where she'd found a cello. She'd adhered it to his hoof with a hot glue gun. A long white veil trailing down her back and a bouquet of white daisies and Baby's Breath completed the look.

"*C'est fantastique*," Helen said.

Before Maggie could reply, there was a knock. She opened it and couldn't help letting out a gasp. Kona growled.

Brian looked like something that had barely survived a nuclear apocalypse. He wore black pants and a long-sleeved T-shirt, both streaked with muddy shades of brown, gray and orange paint. He'd slicked back his thinning hair with gel. He'd covered his face in pale pancake makeup with splotches of gold and orange and painted the backs of his hands, which he held at the sides of his face, to match. His lips, outlined in black, formed the circle of a silent scream, just as in the painting. He looked horrifying. At first Maggie thought it was the makeup and the pose, but the final touch, making him look truly petrified and petrifying, was the gold contact lenses he wore.

"Trick or Treat, Beautiful," he dropped the pose and smiled. He held out his hands as if to hug her.

"Don't you get that makeup on me." She backed up, as did Kona. "Eeesh, you look so creepy. You're even freaking out the dog."

"It's OK, boy." Brian held out a hand and Kona sniffed it

tentatively. His tail wagged and Brian ruffled his ears. Brian said hello to Helen and Raul and added, "No shaking hands for me tonight." He displayed his painting job. "The right hand was the hardest part. Difficult to paint with your left hand."

Brian had brought his camera along and asked Helen to take a picture of him with Maggie. "I told my mother about the party and she wanted to see our costumes," he said.

As they all finished posing for pictures, the bell rang and Kona barked.

Maggie opened it to find Russell, wearing a shaggy St. Bernard costume and holding a fan of five Bicycle playing cards in his hand. The dog suit came up over his head in a hood with floppy ears. His nose was covered in brown makeup and he chewed the stub of a cigar.

They all laughed and Maggie asked, "*Dogs Playing Poker* is your favorite painting?"

"It's close. I was going to come as Elvis, but couldn't figure out how to do a black velvet background. This was the next best thing."

Maggie introduced Brian and Russell, then Russell surveyed everyone's outfits. "You guys all look great." He sized up Maggie. "You're a bride? I have no idea why you're holding a goat, but you look nice."

"It's a Chagall painting, *La Mariée*." Maggie had prepared for this in case someone didn't know what she was. She'd printed a picture of the painting, folded it up and slipped it in her sleeve. She set her goat on the kitchen counter, then pulled out the picture. "See?"

Russell looked at Maggie's dress again, then at Brian. "So, love and . . . fear. Good combo. Those go hand in hand. You guys plan that?"

Maggie felt herself blush. *Maybe this was a bad idea. I didn't mean to come as love personified. I just like the goat.*

Brian chuckled. "No, we didn't plan it, but you're right. There's always a certain amount of anxiety that goes along with falling in love." He made a move to take hold of Maggie's hand, but she moved away again.

"Uh-uh," she waggled a finger, "You don't want to mess up your hands and I don't want you to mess up my dress." She certainly did not want to talk about falling in love; not here, not now, not anytime soon. Besides she hadn't meant for the costume to represent love. Quite the opposite. She was aware some cultures get married in red dresses, but not her Irish ancestors, so she thought of the costume as a sort of anti-bride; a statement that she was over and done with her marriage. She had told Helen on Tuesday at yoga about dying her wedding dress—causing Helen to state, "You rock"—but the boys didn't need to know. *Time to end this conversation.* "OK, let's go. We're fashionably late enough." She hooked a thumb toward the door. "I'll be the designated driver. Hey, wait. Where's my goat?"

They all looked at the kitchen counter, where she'd set it, then turned as one when they heard Kona's toenails clicking quickly out of the room.

AT THE PARTY, a rush of warmth hit them as they came through the door. The room was packed. It was a chilly night, so few of the party-goers wanted to be outside, and the impeccable minimalist great room was wall-to-wall with artists and their works. There was a simply dressed, older balding man in the foyer who Maggie guessed was Picasso, as his companion had painted her face blue with spare eyeballs adorning the sides of her head. Further in, another couple, the man carrying a pitch fork, was dressed as *American Gothic.* In her first look around the room Maggie saw a woman in black as *Whistler's Mother;* unfortunately for Raul, several Andy Warhols; at least two versions of *Girl with a Pearl Earring;* and a Frida Kahlo, with mono-brow, and her portly date who Maggie assumed must be Diego Rivera. Dozens of other guests talked and laughed over the music. Maggie couldn't wait to walk around and see everyone's costumes.

Brian found the host, Jens, who was dressed as Van Gogh with a bandaged ear, causing Maggie and Helen to exchange looks with

Raul, and introduced them all.

Jens admired their costumes, laughing at Russell's. He asked Maggie if he could see her goat (Raul had managed to catch Kona on his way out of the room, and Maggie traded her little devil-dog the stuffed animal for his peanut-butter filled Kong) and inspected its cello. They all chatted until Toulouse-Lautrec and a French can-can dancer walked in, and Jens excused himself to go greet them. "Help yourselves to drinks in the kitchen, and there's food in the dining room," he said as he clapped Brian on the back and walked off.

They moved to the kitchen for drinks, then split off in different directions. Helen and Raul went for some food and Maggie and Brian saw Lani, the chief curator from the museum, and went to say hello. Russell flirted with a Degas ballerina at the bar, shaking a martini for her.

Lani, with her olive skin, long black wig and floral print sarong, might have just stepped out of a Gauguin painting of Tahiti. They chatted for a while, but when the conversation turned to a problem with one of Lani's staff at work, Maggie excused herself to get some food.

In the dining room, she was circling the table, her plate in one hand and her goat and bouquet tucked under her arm, when a couple entered in dramatic fashion. God, a stocky man in wild white wig, full graying beard and flowing gauzy tunic, and Adam, his partner, in a beige body suit with painted muscles, walked through the dining room entryway. They abruptly stood apart and gazed at one another as their outstretched hands met at their finger tips. Everyone laughed; a few applauded.

"Luckily there aren't too many rooms in this place," God said, digging into the salmon mousse. "We only had to make our grand entrance twice."

Adam sidled up to Maggie, waiting for his turn at the plate of prosciutto-wrapped melon. He whispered to her, "Never let your boyfriend play God." He rolled his eyes. "Even for a few hours." He raised his voice a bit so God would be sure to hear, "He's been insufferable."

"Are you telling that young bride there lies?" God asked from the other side of the table.

"You tell me," Adam said. "Aren't you the all-knowing one here?"

Maggie asked if they were both freezing.

"Well, I can only speak for my mere mortal self, but, yes, I froze my fig leaf on the walk from the car."

God plucked a bright red apple out of the centerpiece, a cornucopia of fruit. "You," he said to Adam, holding it aloft, "Stay away from these."

Adam gave Maggie a "see what I mean" look.

"Good luck with him," Maggie smiled, picked up her sparkling water and plate of hors d'oeuvres and looked for a spot to set down her accoutrements while she ate. Although she shivered at the thought of Adam in his thin bodysuit, she felt warm in her long dress. She decided to go out on the balcony, and was instantly refreshed by the wind off the water. The smell of the sea was strong and she could hear waves crashing, but it was a dark night with little moon so she could barely see the ocean shimmering in the distance.

Thick white candles in hurricane lamps lit the patio, where groups of party-goers huddled under tall stainless steel heaters spaced evenly along the balcony. Maggie noticed an empty table at the end of the deck and went and set her plate down. A woman, dressed as *Mona Lisa* in a dark velvet gown, asked if she could share the table.

"Please," Maggie said, then introduced herself.

"Nice to meet you. I'm Diane. I work for Jens managing one of his galleries."

When Diane learned of Maggie's volunteer work at MAMA, she said, "I've been meaning to come see the Hidelbaum exhibit."

"It's amazing. It's here until Christmas, so you've got some time to come see it."

They became engrossed in a discussion of art as they ate. From Maggie's seat she had a view into the kitchen and she noticed Russell mixing himself another martini. She watched as the ballerina appeared at his furry brown elbow. She held her now empty glass out like Tinker Bell with her wand; they laughed together. Maggie tried to concentrate on what Diane was saying about a trip she'd taken to Germany for the gallery. The petite dancer stood *en pointe* and whispered in Russell's ear.

"Sorry, what was that?" Maggie asked.

"I asked if you've been to Germany."

"No, but I'd love to go." Maggie shifted her chair, as if adjusting her alignment with the heater, but really having seen enough of the flirtation inside. She gave Diane her full attention, and they spoke about various trips they'd each taken until Maggie felt chilly.

"I think I'll go back in. My hands are so cold I can't feel my goat."

"You go ahead; it's too hot for me in there in this velvet robe," Diane said. "It was nice talking to you. I'll try to come see that exhibit on a Thursday night so I can say hi."

"I'll keep an eye out for you." Maggie went in to a welcome wave of body heat. The serene crashing of the waves was replaced by the thumping bass of the music and buzz of the crowd. She decided to go wash her hands before looking for Brian and was about to go in search of a bathroom, when she saw Dave and That Woman standing by the stereo.

She froze. *What the hell are they doing here? And what the hell are they wearing?* She shot them a look she usually reserved for people who ran red lights or cut in line at the movies. Dave wore a Yankees uniform. Stupid Slut (true to her nature, Maggie thought) was dressed as a French maid. *If she wanted to dress like a slut she could have at least been an art-themed slut. A topless Venus de Milo or something. And I know just the person to rip her arms off.*

Dave saw her and did a double-take. He whispered something to his date and marched over to Maggie. "What are you doing here?"

"I was about to ask you the same thing."

"Jessica's brother works for the guy that owns this place, Vince or whatever his name is."

"His name is Jens. And you're not even dressed right. You're supposed to be wearing a costume related to art."

"We can wear whatever we want. What are *you* doing here?"

Maggie threw her shoulders back. "My boyfriend," she stressed the word and saw the muscles in Dave's jaw tense, "happens to be good friends with Jens. And he's the director of the modern art museum." *Hah. Take that. He's super brilliant, has a great career, and . . . oh hell, he looks really weird tonight. How am I supposed to rub in how young and good-looking my boyfriend is when he looks half-bald and . . . half-dead? Crap. Stupid costume party. And where the hell is he, when I need him here fawning over me?* She scanned the room for Brian.

"Wait a minute, is that your—" Dave pointed at her dress, then shook his head and snorted. "Never mind." He ran a hand through his hair. "Look, as long as you're here. I've been wanting, well, I've been meaning to call you." He swallowed. Maggie wondered if there might be a tear bulging at the corner of his eye. "I . . . I miss Kona. I wanted to see if I could visit him once in a while. Maybe I could take him running sometimes. I miss that."

"My boyfriend takes him running now."

"Oh. OK, well, something else then. Maybe we could work out some visitation."

"No." Maggie shook her head. "No way. You're the one who walked out. And you haven't even tried to come see him once in all this time. I can't believe you're even bringing this up now. It's been months. You don't even care about Kona."

"I do too. It's not me. I've wanted to see him. I miss him. It's Jess." He glanced at Jessica and Maggie followed his eyes. Jessica watched them over the top of a CD case she pretended to read in the dim light. He lowered his voice, as if she could hear over the hum of the crowd and the music. "She's afraid of Kona." *Good! But, what an idiot. Who's afraid of Kona? He's a big sweetie.* He went on as if he knew what Maggie was thinking. "It's just that, he knocked her down, that . . . well, that time she was at the house." *Good boy, Kona! You knew that slut wasn't supposed to be in Momma's house. You are getting a huge treat when I get home.* Maggie had been tortured by the thought of Kona aiding and abetting Dave's introduction of that slut into her home. She'd pictured the three of them cuddled on the sofa together. But now she knew how it had really been; Kona had been her champion. Her knight in sheddable armor. "I finally convinced her to give him another try. Please, Maggie. I miss him."

"No; never gonna happen. You are totally out of sight, out of mind to him, and I'm not going to let you confuse him. Get another dog. You replaced me easily enough; I'm sure it will be just as easy for you to replace Kona. You'd better go; there's a Musketeer after your maid."

She turned and stormed off to find Brian. *What nerve. I can't believe him. God, I could use a drink. Why did I offer to be the designated driver?* She headed down a dark hallway and had just rounded the corner when she heard Jens' German accent through a half open door.

"It doesn't worry you that your girlfriend is dressed as a bride?" he asked.

She stopped short.

"Why should that worry me?" Brian's voice asked.

"She is maybe sending you some sort of signal, yes?"

"No, I don't think . . . It's her favorite painting. Do you think it's a signal?"

Oh God, why did I wear this?

On cue, God walked up behind her. "Eavesdropping is a sin, my child," he whispered. She glared at his back as he swept past her on down the hall.

Better bust this conversation up. "Brian," she called out as she pushed the door open and walked in. "I've been looking for you. Thought I heard your voice in here."

"Sorry. Jens was showing me a piece he just bought, and I lost track of time. Let's go back out to the party." He put his hand gently at her elbow, careful to not smear makeup on her.

When they were in the hallway, she stopped him. "I have to warn you; my ex is here."

"Oh, I need to get a look at the idiot who was stupid enough to walk out on you."

"Aww. I'd kiss you if you weren't covered in makeup."

"I'll take a rain check. Come on."

From a corner of the great room, Brian pretended to casually check out the other guests.

"Let me guess, the jock and the tramp in the fishnets skulking over by the stereo," he said. When she nodded he added, "He does look like an idiot. Especially dressed like that in this crowd."

Damn right. He is *an idiot!* She put her arm around Brian's waist, leaned into him and said, "You're good at making me feel better. I'm glad I'm here with you." He beamed at her, his white smile incongruous in his orange and gray face. *That darn makeup. Oh, what the hell. He's earned it.* She gave him a slow, tender kiss.

"That was nice," he said. "But now your lips are all black."

Maggie excused herself to go find the bathroom. On her way, she saw the Degas ballerina feeding the poker-playing dog an olive from her drink. He pretended to snap at it ferociously as she pulled her delicate fingers away, then giggled and scratched his belly.

Chapter 21: Plan B

"Shit, shit, shit." Maggie sat up straight in Brian's bed. Peaches ran in and looked around, perhaps hoping to catch Kona getting in trouble again. But Maggie wasn't cursing at Kona. She was alone.

The party had progressed on. She'd wanted to leave after her run-in with Dave, but Jens had insisted Brian meet some people, so they'd stayed. The four of them had left at one o'clock, minus one hound dog who said he wasn't ready to leave yet and would get a ride home with a certain ballerina.

They'd driven back to Maggie's to drop Helen and Raul at their car, picked up Kona and headed to Brian's. When they got to the condo, Maggie had planned to carefully bring up the subject of her costume. She'd wanted to make sure Brian was clear about her anti-bride stance behind it, but then he'd dragged her into the shower with him, saying he needed someone for quality control to make sure he got all the paint off, and one thing had led to another and the subject of her costume never came up.

That morning, Maggie awoke to Brian leaving a breakfast tray by the bed. No croissants this time, but juice, whole wheat toast, coffee and the paper. He'd said he hadn't meant to wake her; he was going for a quick run with Kona and, after, would she be willing to whip him up a smoothie before heading out for her bike ride. She'd said she needed to check her messages and make sure Russell would even be there, but, yes, she'd love to make him a smoothie.

After he left, she'd sat back against the pillows sipping her juice, then dug the Business section out of the big Sunday paper. There on page one, below the fold, the headline read: *BioHealth CEO Remains*

Positive as FDA Pulls Plug.

The headline had caused her to sit up straight, spilling some of her juice on Brian's T-shirt that she had slept in, and swear like a teenager who just learned how.

She scanned the article—an interview with BioHealth's Chief Executive Officer, Ian Camfield. It said it was a follow-up to Friday's news that the FDA was not going to approve the company's heretofore "promising" drug, as clinical trial patients had displayed a "significantly higher" incidence of heart attacks than the general populace.

"What article?" She hadn't read the paper on Friday or Saturday. Busy working on her costume, she'd tossed the papers in the recycling untouched. She'd figured if she missed any big news she'd find out soon enough. And soon enough had arrived this morning on a silver tray.

The stock had tanked on Friday and was down to $3.10. The CEO was trying to save his company and his investors' confidence; he hyped other drugs in BioHealth's pipeline, claiming this one drug wasn't the only "trick in our bag." But a Wall Street analyst was quoted, saying, "The other therapies BioHealth is working on are in the earliest stages, and it could be almost a decade before they're ready for commercial release." He added that his firm had downgraded the stock from "hold" to "sell," and acknowledged rumored news that a large pharmaceutical firm might try to acquire BioHealth at a deep discount for its technology.

"Holy crap. How can this be happening?" Maggie said aloud. *$3.10. A possible buy-out by a pharma company. For what, maybe $4 a share? Maybe $4 and change?* She did the math—$200,000 sounded like a nice chunk of money, until taking out Dave's half and the IRS's . . . what? A third? She'd be lucky to have $75,000 left over. Not exactly the stuff comfortable, cushy nest eggs are built of.

She crumpled the paper and threw it on the floor. She felt bone-tired and a little nauseous, hung over except for the fact that she hadn't had a single drink at the party.

"Craaaaaaappppp!" She got up and paced the bedroom. Peaches, prancing back and forth behind her, darted out of the way each time Maggie headed the opposite direction.

There goes my grand plan. Again. First Dave screws it up and now BioHealth. Damn Dave. Damn Ian. Damn researchers who had everyone convinced the drug was the best thing since Prozac.

She stopped in her tracks. *Wait a minute. On the plus side, this means no big windfall for Dave and Stupid Slut. Hah! No early retirement for* them. *No dream vacation to some romantic tropical beach. No diamond ring paid for on the back of my hard work.*

"Hah," she said aloud.

The dull silver lining to her big, black BioHealth cloud didn't help.

She walked in circles around the condo thinking, thinking, thinking. Realizing that Peaches seemed upset and confused, following close at Maggie's heels, she finally sat cross-legged on the living room rug and pulled the little dog into her lap. She stroked Peaches' head while she thought some more from a stationary position.

When Brian and Kona came home, they found her sitting on the rug. She didn't look up. Kona trotted over, excited to have her at face-licking level and more than happy to sponge up her tears with his thick wet tongue.

"Oh, Buddy," she said. She put her arms around his neck and hugged him.

"What's wrong?" Brian asked.

She told him about the article. He'd known about her plan and had been a sounding board when she'd take different professions out for a theoretical spin. He was good at helping her list the pros and cons of various positions.

"I'm going to be stuck doing accounting forever," she was still holding on to Kona and rested her forehead against his. Peaches stood in Maggie's lap and gave her delicate artist's paint-brush kisses on her chin. "Thank you, sweeties," Maggie said to the dogs.

She wondered if she should get to a mirror to stop the crying. Dark thoughts circled her mind, like vultures. The idea of sticking with a job she didn't love—and never would—made her feel wrapped in chains. Weighed down. Rooted to the spot. Although even that wasn't right, she realized. Roots implied growth and there was no growth for her in accounting. Sure there was *career* growth. She was on a track that was easy for her to run. Certain and steady and lucrative. And since she was on her own, she needed to make the most of that. From a practical standpoint, it made no sense to quit. She didn't have anyone else to rely on. She had to save for retirement; she needed decent benefits. What if she got sick or became disabled? She didn't have kids who could take care of her someday like Mom did. She needed her job. She needed accounting. But why did it have to make her feel so empty? It fed her bank account, but starved her soul.

Brian held out his hands and pulled her up off the floor. "Come here." She let him hug her, even though sweat soaked his shirt. "You'll be fine." He stroked her hair. "Lots of people hate their jobs. I read an article about it the other day. I was going to email it to you. It said something like just under half of all Americans aren't satisfied with their jobs."

"Oh. Right." *Does he think I'm just being a big whiner? After all, he's right; I'm in good company. Probably hard for him to relate. He's lucky enough to love his job.*

She thought of all the people just scraping by. People who couldn't afford to even think of anything else other than the job they hated, but still felt lucky to have. Plenty of people were getting by paycheck to paycheck and hoping that someday, somehow, their savings and Social Security would be enough once they finally stopped punching the clock; that satisfying, final swift punch in the face of that damned clock.

Her misery, however, was not loving the company at the moment. In fact, her misery didn't even like the company. Her misery just wanted to get out of there and be alone for a while.

She pulled away and said she was going to get dressed.

"Hey, you OK?" Brian called after her.

"Yeah, fine." She tried to make her voice sound normal. "Look,

I'll make you a smoothie, but then I've got to run and meet Russell."

She wanted to get out on her bike. She hadn't checked her messages yet, but she hoped Russell wouldn't show up. She wanted to be alone with her pumping legs and heart. Just ride and think. Or ride and forget.

SHE ROUNDED THE corner to their agreed meeting spot and saw Russell waiting for her. He waved and called out an entirely too hearty, "Good morning."

She was tempted to ask what was good about it; it was cold and the sky was as gray as the skin on a corpse. Instead she just said, "I wasn't sure you'd be here. Thought you might have a private dance lesson this morning."

"No. Not me. Not much of a dancer. And I look terrible in tights." He zipped his cycling jacket up to his chin.

"Seriously, what happened with your Tiny Dancer?" They pulled out and began slowly pedaling side by side along their standard route.

"Nuthin'. We counted the headlights on the roadway, she dropped me off and that was that."

"Highway," Maggie said.

"You want to ride on the highway?"

"No, the lyrics. It's not 'roadway,' it's '*high*way.'"

"OK. Sorry, Mr. Lennon. Didn't mean to screw up your lyrics."

"*Lennon?* It's Elton freaking John."

"OK. Good grief. That's who I meant. Boy, somebody got up on the wrong side of her boyfriend's bed this morning."

Maggie coasted and reached down to yank the Velcro strap tighter on her cycling shoe. "Let's get going. I feel like riding hard." Without waiting for a reply, she changed gears and pulled out ahead of him, stamping down on her pedals.

"Works for me." Russell whipped in behind her to draft off her back wheel.

When they got to Torrey Pines she beat him up the hill by a good thirty seconds. They reached their resting spot overlooking the ocean ten minutes quicker than usual.

"Alright, what's wrong?" Russell asked.

"What makes you think something's wrong?" She fought with the slick foil wrapper on her PowerBar, supplied by Russell. "Why do they make these things so goddamn hard to open?"

"Give it here." He took it, found the notch in the wrapper and pulled it apart. "Obviously you are not yourself today." He handed the nutritious-but-not-so-very-delicious brick back to her and pulled another out of the back pocket of his jersey. "You and Brian have a fight?"

"No, we didn't have a fight." She worked over the chunk she tore off the bar with her molars. "It's my damn BioHealth shares. And my damn job." She told him about the stock.

"Oh, wow. I didn't see today's paper yet. I know you were counting on those shares. I'm really sorry, Maggie."

"Thanks." She looked out toward the churning ocean, a steely blue under the gray sky.

"Have you had time to think about Plan B yet?"

"Sort of. Wouldn't you think I'd be the type to already have a Plan B all mapped out? But *no*; I believed the story they were selling at BioHealth. I really thought that was going to be my golden ticket. I was so stupid." She shook her head. "Anyway, I'm thinking I'm pretty much stuck with accounting now. I'm not really at an age where you can take a lot risks, you know? I mean, I need health insurance. I need a steady paycheck." Maggie thought of her mother, who had some savings, but also counted on Medicare and Social Security. Maggie knew it was possible Mom might outlive her money, but if it came to that, she could count on her kids for help. But who did Maggie have?

"I guess. I mean, you talk like you're so old, but I think you're probably looking at this from a worst case scenario view." He took a drink from his water bottle. "What if you worked as an accountant, only at a place you could be passionate about. I mean, the whole green cleaning products thing is nice and all, but I know it doesn't exactly have you jumping out of bed in the morning. What if you worked at a museum or for a chain of galleries or something like that?"

She sighed. "Yeah, you're right. I can try to find a more fulfilling job somewhere else. And in the meantime, at least I'm not working insane hours anymore. And I have some actual hobbies." She took in a deep breath of the salty ocean air and pounded her gloved fist on her handle bar. "I can get my enjoyment out of life after five and on weekends . . . right?"

"There you go. Let's drink to that." They thudded their water bottles together and both threw back their heads.

They finished eating in silence, except for the sounds of smacking lips as they chewed the hard bars.

She tucked the wrapper in her pocket and said, "Thanks for making me feel better."

"Sure." He smiled and gave her a light punch on the arm. "And now I'm going to make you hurt, cuz I'm going to beat your butt back home." He readjusted his helmet, got back on the seat of his bike and started rolling out onto the street.

"I'd like to see you try," she scoffed, jumped on her bike, and pulled out after him.

LATER THAT AFTERNOON, while she and Kona napped, the phone rang.

Brian said he was worried about her and wanted to check in. "I hope you don't think I wasn't very understanding before. I know you must be really disappointed about the stock."

"No, it's OK. You were right. I'm feeling better. I mean, it sucks, but I'll get over it," she said, hoping to convince herself as well as him.

"I was thinking that what you need is an accounting job at the museum, or something like that. I know we don't have any openings now, but if something comes up you're certainly the first one I'd think of."

"That's sweet. And I thought of that too, but it's probably not a great idea for us to work together. Anyway, don't worry about it. I'll think of something."

When she hung up, she lay back down and patted Kona. She thought that maybe when you're depressed it's not necessarily such a good idea to try to act like your dog. After all, they spend a lot of time eating and sleeping—probably the two highest ranking activities of any depressed person.

"Come on, Buddy. Let's get up. Take me for a walk."

Chapter 22: "Mantic" Meals and Madmen

The weeks leading up to their Boston trip alternated between creeping along and racing by. Time crept while Maggie was at work, but had a tendency to move at the speed of light, the speed of fun, on her days off and weekends.

Maggie tried settling into Plan B. The "enjoy life outside of work" part of her Plan was going well. She went to yoga and the gym with Helen, biked with Russell, took long walks with Kona in the crisp fall air, and enjoyed the "finer things" with Brian. They went out for meals at restaurants overlooking the ocean and drank expensive bottles of red wine; he took her to another play and a jazz concert; they explored the galleries in La Jolla and Del Mar. Sometimes they would "slum it," as Brian joked, and stay in with a movie (usually sub-titled) and a pizza, always covered in something exotic; the last one they'd had was fig and prosciutto. Maggie would have been happy with pepperoni, but she had to admit it had been tasty.

The "just get through the day at work" part of Plan B was tougher to take. Things were stressful at Clean N' Green. Stephen had been negotiating with Wal-Mart to carry their products, but the dealings hit a snag when a competitor came along with a cheaper line. The retail chain had given Clean N' Green a chance to rethink their pricing. Stephen had her analyzing different strategies. He was feeling pressure, and she was doing her best to not let him outsource too much of it to her. She went in, did her work, and tried to leave at a reasonable hour. She told herself, "It'll be OK." And she remembered what Mom always said whenever she'd complained before heading to work at Orange Julius in high school: they don't call it "work" because it's fun.

The last week before Thanksgiving her phone hardly stopped ringing. Unfortunately, it was almost never her realtor. She'd called once to assure Maggie things were only slow because of the holidays and would pick up soon. No, instead, it was one family member after another.

Kevin wanted to know where she and Brian were staying. He called another day for her opinion on a wedding present for Annie. Shay and Annie both called to discuss dresses. Shay called again when she found a Smurf bride and groom cake topper on eBay. She knew Kevin would get a kick out of it, but worried Annie would kill her for sending it to him. (They decided she should go for it.) Mom called several times about the Thanksgiving menu. She'd offered to cook at Kevin and Annie's. Maggie tried to convince Mom they should just go out, but Mom wouldn't hear of it.

She also talked to Gram, who confessed being unsure about bringing Humphrey. Although having her own qualms about Brian, Maggie was surprised.

"Why?" she asked. "Everyone's looking forward to meeting him."

"Oh, I know, sweetie. It's just such a big event for the family, and maybe it would be better to go on my own. I don't want to have to be worrying about whether Humphrey's having a good time." Maggie wondered momentarily if this was Gram's way of letting her know she didn't think it was a good idea to bring Brian, but realized Gram didn't operate that way. Mom, maybe; but not Gram. She must honestly be concerned.

"I'm guessing Humphrey's probably adept at taking care of himself, so you don't need to worry about him every minute. You can have some family time." They were both silent for a moment. "But, to be honest, I've been thinking the same thing and wondering if I should un-invite Brian. I know that'd be rude, but—"

"No, no, no. I'm very much looking forward to meeting your gentleman friend. Please bring him," Gram said, her voice perking up.

"I want to . . . what is it you young people say? I want to check him."

"You mean check him *out?*" Maggie grinned.

"Oh, right; check him out. I thought the other way sounded too much like a hockey game."

"OK, I'm bringing him. And you can check him out. But, if I'm not allowed to second-guess inviting my gentleman friend, neither are you."

SHAY WAS RIGHT; what was I worried about? Maggie smiled as she sat at Thanksgiving dinner with her family, her boyfriend, and Annie's parents.

Earlier that afternoon, in the final throes of dinner prep, Maggie and Shannon had finally had a moment alone in the kitchen. Shannon had asked if Russell was always so funny; he'd had them all laughing talking about his horrible flight, folded in his tiny seat like an origami swan and trying to sleep on the aptly named red-eye that had brought him to town that morning.

"Yes, he is always that funny, although hopefully he'll be serious during the wedding." Maggie tasted the potatoes Shannon had mashed. "But what about Brian? What do you think?"

"I like him," Shannon had told her. "He seems great, and, honestly, if you hadn't told me how much younger he is, I never would have guessed."

Maggie realized now she'd blown their age difference out of proportion. Brian had been right—their ages were just numbers. *Kona wouldn't have worried about it; I shouldn't have either.* She looked around the crowded table. *Everyone seems to really like him. And he looks so handsome tonight. Of course, he ought to. He took longer getting ready than I did.* Brian had spent forever ironing. He'd said he wanted to look his best for meeting her family and wished he'd had room to pack his own iron, since the one supplied by the hotel was "an abomination."

Other than Brian fretting over the sad state of the crease in his pants, the first twenty-four-plus hours of their trip had gone very well. They'd landed on time Wednesday afternoon and gone out for a relaxed dinner. Then today, she and Brian had taken her niece, Beth, and nephew, James, out to play in the snow.

They'd bundled up and driven to a spot Kevin had mapped out for them. Maggie, who had as much experience with snow as she did with power tools, had enjoyed watching Brian help Beth and James make perfect snowballs, which had precipitated a huge boys-versus-girls war. Then the four of them built a snowman almost as tall as Maggie. They'd brought along bananas and cinnamon cookies for a snack with a thermos of cocoa and used one of the bananas for the snowman's nose. Brian, always so mature, never once tried to use the banana for *another* snowman appendage when the kids weren't looking, but the idea had crossed Maggie's mind. When Beth asked Brian to make a snow angel for her, Maggie had smiled watching him make a big show of flapping his arms and legs. *He's so great with them.*

Now, at dinner, Maggie sat between the kids. They'd both wanted to sit by her, which pleased her since she'd worried they wouldn't really remember her since their visit to San Diego last year. Maggie struck a deal with Beth that as long as she tasted everything, Maggie would smuggle any uneaten portions of whatever Beth didn't like onto her own plate when Shay wasn't looking. Shay sat on the far side of James, and she and Maggie took turns coaxing him to eat.

Maggie looked around the room, lit by the glow of several tall white tapers. James declared it "mantic." Shay explained that any cause for lit candles was the definition of romantic for James, for example calling his last birthday cake "very mantic." Maggie agreed with him.

The windows were fogged against the cold night. She drank in the flushed faces, whether from the candlelight, the wine, or the body warmth of fourteen people at a table designed for ten, she didn't know. It was a boisterous crowd that passed plates and ate elbow-to-elbow. Mom talked to Annie's parents about the weather and how she hoped it would be a beautiful, brisk day on Saturday like it had been today. Russell flirted with Gram, who blushed and batted his shoulder; Humphrey (who was droopy and adorable as a basset, just like Gram had said) and Shay's husband, Michael, told fishing stories. Annie and Kevin whispered together, beautiful and in love. And

Brian oohed and aahed as Beth told him the plot synopsis of *The Little Mermaid*, including passages of dialog she knew by heart. It was possible she would soon break into song.

Maggie turned back to James and Shay, "I've missed you guys. I can't believe I'm all alone on the West Coast now."

"You should move out here too," Shay said. "I know I'd love it if you were closer, and so would the kids. James, please eat your green beans."

"I love *The Little Worm-maid*," James said very seriously to Maggie, his mouth ringed with sweet potatoes.

Maggie smiled. "I love her too, James. Now listen to your mother and eat a bean." She looked back at Shay and said, "I don't know if I could handle the cold weather here."

"I know. I always thought of myself as a Southern California girl, but now here I am; I've got a windshield scraper, a snow blower, and more down in my wardrobe than a flock of geese. But, it's nice." She shrugged. "Different, but nice. And there's more to life than great weather. Besides, I bet Kona would love the snow. James, please at least *try* a bean."

Maggie took advantage of the green bean struggle to change the subject. She didn't want to talk about moving, and the reasons for or against it, while her boyfriend sat an arm's length away, probably trying to listen in over the second act of *Finding Nemo*.

AFTER THE DISHES were done, Brian suggested a walk around the block. Everyone but Maggie opted to lie around the living room moaning, so it was just the two of them.

"You were very cute with Beth. I hope she wasn't making you crazy, with that all-Disney, all-the-time talk."

"No, not at all. I like kids. And I adore your niece. She looks like a miniature version of you." Brian squeezed her arm tighter as they walked arm-in-arm, hunkered down in their coats. "Your whole family is wonderful."

Maggie peeked over the upturned collar of her wool coat. "I'm glad you're having fun." She rubbed the end of her nose with a mittened hand. "It's freezing out here. Let's go back."

"Not until I do this," he ducked under the eave of a building they were passing, out of the pale orange glow of the street lamps, and kissed her.

She pulled away after a moment. "It's too cold," she protested. "Our lips will stick together. Let's go back. Besides, I want to call Helen and make sure Kona's being good."

"Wait, I want to tell you something."

"Tell me while we walk. My toes are numb." She tugged at him.

"No, wait. I want to—." A muffled *Beethoven's Fifth* came from under layers of pants pocket, dinner jacket and overcoat. "Probably my mother," he said. He yanked his glove off with his teeth and fought through the layers to answer before it went to voicemail. He motioned for her to go, and they started walking as he said hello.

He stopped.

Maggie watched his expression change. His eyebrows, raised in anticipation as he'd answered the phone, began a slow slide down his forehead and did not stop until they were crouched together over his eyes.

"Ohmygod. Tell me *exactly* what happened." He stood silent for a minute. "No."

Maggie put her hand on his shoulder and searched his face. Horrible thoughts came to her. She heard a woman's voice, but couldn't hear what she was saying. She hoped it wasn't his mom with bad news.

"I guess that's good at least . . . Of course . . . I'll get the first flight back in the morning."

"What happened?" Maggie asked when he hung up. She was still holding his shoulder with one hand, the other over her heart.

"That was Lani. She was calling from the museum. A rep from the security company called her when they couldn't reach me at home. Some maniac threw a construction block through the front glass and broke in."

"Oh no. Did he take anything?"

"No, I almost wish he had. We might have a chance to recover it. He vandalized the Hidelbaum's in the foyer." He searched the cold, black sky. "I can't believe this is happening."

"Where was security? Why didn't they stop him?"

"They did stop him, but one was watching the monitors; the other was making the rounds at the back of the building. They said it took them less than a minute to get to the front, but you can do a lot of damage in seconds."

"Oh, this is awful." Maggie thought of the huge, serene, pastel-colored paintings and felt sick to her stomach. "All three of them?" Brian nodded. "Are they ruined?"

He told her everything the curator had said. The guards had managed to catch the guy, who raved like a madman and brandished his knife. No one had been hurt, but he'd had time to slash the three paintings in the entryway. Brian started to walk back.

"I've got to get to the hotel and make some calls. They've secured everything for now, but I've got a million things to do. I need to call Hidelbaum's agent first. He's always so reluctant to display his works, and now this."

"I can call the airline and find you a flight back while you make your work calls."

Back at Kevin and Annie's, they explained to everyone what had happened. Brian addressed the room, "It was lovely to meet all of you, but I'm going to have to fly back to San Diego first thing tomorrow." Maggie was touched by the fact that he took time to say goodbye to everyone individually, even though she knew his mind must be racing.

He said goodbye to her mother last and hugged her.

"I'm so sorry you have to leave," Mom said. "Maybe we'll see you again at Christmas?"

Maggie glared at her mother as she moved in for her own hug, and said, "Can't really think about that right now, Mom. We've gotta go. Thanks for the lovely dinner." She waved goodbye to the crowd, "I'll see you all tomorrow." Then they went back out into the night.

Maggie thought about how she'd have to go to the wedding alone now and an image flashed through her mind as they walked to their rental car. She felt guilty for thinking of something so trivial and self-absorbed while Brian was completely stressed and hundreds of thousands of dollars worth of art hung shredded back in San Diego. But she couldn't shake the picture of her and all the other single women, her mother included, being rounded up at the wedding reception, like beagles for the hunt. They were all dressed in long-sleeved white gowns with big brown and black patches; little tri-colored hounds on the scent, barking and baying as they waited for the glowing bride to cast her bouquet, and perhaps a bit of good luck, in their oh-so-anxious direction.

Chapter 23: Sitting by Dippy

"And now, by the power vested in me by the Internet," Russell drew a soft chuckle from the guests, "I pronounce you: husband and wife. You may kiss the bride."

Maggie watched Kevin, who looked so handsome and so . . . grown up in his tux that when she'd first seen him tears had filled her eyes, take Annie, runway-model-meets-Grace-Kelly beautiful in her blush gown and upswept hairdo, in his arms and kiss her.

Everyone applauded. Russell clapped loudest of all. Maggie caught his eye and winked. She was proud of him, standing there looking tall and handsome in his dark suit. His little Internet power joke was the only one he'd snuck in; he'd been very solemn, more serious than she'd ever seen him. He'd coaxed more tears from her when he spoke so eloquently about loving someone and wanting to share the rest of your life with them, every last bit of it, from the greatest joys to the deepest sorrows to the smallest tasks of getting through everyday life. The tears began as little salty hints of regret over her own botched vows, but she squeezed them back. She focused on the happy couple, determined to only let through tears of joy.

While they posed for the photographer, Maggie thought to herself that they made a rather attractive wedding party: Annie in her sleeveless pale pink gown and bouquet of cream-colored roses; Kevin and Annie's brother, Jeremy, so dapper in their tuxedos; and Maggie in her shimmering empire gown with its deep garnet color. The photographer played up the brother-as-bridesman and sister-as-best-woman angle, and snapped shots of Maggie and Kevin smoking cigars and Jeremy fussing with Annie's veil. He also posed the happy couple behind their Smurf-topped cake. (Annie confessed to her new sisters-in-law that she'd been irritated when the box first arrived in the mail; but since it was the only thing Kevin had asked for in all the wedding planning she couldn't say no. She'd decided to run with it and surprised him by having the cake frosted in white and Smurf-blue fondant.)

They were in a small inn outside Boston. Except for the immediate family and Russell, all staying at a hotel near Kevin's, the wedding guests filled the rooms of the inn: Annie's family from California, Mom's sister and her family, Annie's and Kevin's friends. The reception was in the dining room, which had large windows that overlooked the snow-covered grounds. Bouquets of pink Gerbera daisies and cream-colored roses brightened the tables.

As Maggie walked in to the dining room, she ran into her Mom's sister.

"It's so good to see you," Aunt Deirdre said as she squeezed Maggie. She was enveloped in Aunt D's blue polyester suit and Jean Nate scent. It had been almost five years since she'd seen her aunt, who placed her white-gloved hand on Maggie's arm and whispered, "How are you doing? I mean, really? With Dave gone and all."

"I'm fine; great actually." She grabbed a champagne glass off the tray of a passing waiter.

"You look a little tired." Her aunt patted her arm and nodded.

Maggie gulped the champagne. Of course she was tired; she'd been up until one the previous night playing poker with Russell, Jeremy and her brother at his mild excuse for a bachelor party. They'd cleaned him out; Russell was right—Kevin had no poker face. They'd stayed up way too late laughing as Kevin's chips dwindled. They'd hoped, for his sake, it was true that lack of luck at cards meant he'd be lucky in love.

"I mean, you look good, dear. A little thin and tired, but good. Your Mom says—"

"I don't mean to interrupt, but I promised Kevin I'd check that everything was OK with the dinner service," Maggie lied. "I'll talk to you later, OK?" She downed the champagne and headed toward the kitchen as a follow-through on her lie.

At the far end of the room she turned and saw Deirdre grab Shannon and whisper to her. *No doubt asking how I'm really doing. Oh well, Shay'll set her straight.*

When Maggie turned back, there was Mom, eyes still damp. "Wasn't that a lovely ceremony?" Mom asked.

"Yes, it was. I'm glad everything went so well." Maggie reached into her evening bag and pulled out a tissue for her mother.

"My baby's all grown up and married," she said as she dabbed the corners of her eyes. She sniffled, then brightened. "Do you think they'll have kids?"

"Ma, they just got married like ten minutes ago. Let's give them some time, OK?"

"They'd have such gorgeous babies." Her mother was practically salivating at the thought of getting her hands on those lovely grandbabies she was imagining. "Has he said anything to you?" Maggie wondered if this was how junkies looked at their dealers.

"No, he hasn't. And, yes, they're the most beautiful people I know and their offspring would no doubt be the same. But, let's just enjoy today." She took another swig from her glass.

"I am. I am enjoying today." She smiled at Maggie. "You look so pretty, honey. A little thin and tired, but so pretty." She played with a spiral of Maggie's hair.

"Thanks," Maggie said. She excused herself to go mingle as her mother no doubt said a silent prayer for a brand new little O'Connell come next fall.

When it was time to sit down to dinner, the seating was a free-for-all. In keeping with the carefree vibe of the wedding, no one had assigned seats except the happy couple. Still, Maggie figured she'd be at the head table with Kevin, Annie, Jeremy and his wife, and Russell. The tables were set for eight and sure enough, there was Russell, waving her over. At the final two seats sat Deirdre's oldest daughter, Debbie, and her husband.

Aunt Deirdre and her husband Dan had thought it would be

cute to name all their children with D names: Debbie, Doug, Davey, Drew and Delfina. The O'Connell children, who had never been overly close to their McMaster cousins, thought this was anything but cute. Years ago they'd come up with their own secret names for the clan: Dippy, Dud, Dopey, Droopy and, well, Delfina they just called Delfina since they thought going through life with that name was punishment enough.

Kevin hadn't wanted to invite them, but Mom was very close to Deirdre, and that was the one time she'd put her foot down with Kevin about the wedding.

As Maggie approached the table, she could tell by the look on Kevin's face that he was now regretting not having assigned people to their seats. She widened her eyes at him in a silent signal that she hoped communicated: *At least you're not stuck sitting next to Dippy like me.*

Dippy stood as Maggie reached the table and said, "It's so great to see you." This smaller version of Aunt Deirdre pulled Maggie into a firm hug. No polyester suit, but the same curves padded her short frame, and a similar hairdo encircled her head like beige cotton candy.

Now Maggie felt guilty. This would probably be fine.

They sat down as the waiters served their salads and more champagne.

"How is every little thing? I mean, I heard about Dave," she leaned in as if indicating that she knew, but would not mind a personal recitation, of every sordid detail.

As she'd done with Aunt D, Maggie tried again to say how great she was. But Dippy continued, undeterred, talking about how horrible the whole thing was. Maggie tried steering the conversation to other topics. Dippy moved on to telling stories of friends who'd also married "cheating, lying dogs." Maggie tried telling Dippy point blank that it probably wasn't right to talk about adultery and divorce at a wedding. Dippy nodded in the direction of her husband and whispered, "If he ever cheats, I'll cut him, if you know what I mean." She raised her eyebrows and made a little scissoring motion with her fingers. Maggie tried to turn and talk to Russell. But there was no stopping Dippy, who went on all through the meal. The only saving grace was her soft voice, which Maggie prayed couldn't be heard by the other side of the table.

"And look at you. It doesn't make sense that he'd leave you. I mean, you're pretty *and* skinny. Too skinny if you ask me. Are you eating?" She lowered her tone even more, "Are you depressed? Is that it? I notice you're hardly eating your salmon."

"I'm not depressed. I'm fine. Really." Maggie took another drink of champagne and sought a way out of this conversation. Russell was asking Kevin and Annie about their upcoming honeymoon trip. Debbie's husband was telling Jeremy and his wife all about the corrugated box business.

Why the hell isn't Brian here to save me from this? Just my luck. What good is having a handsome boyfriend if he's not here to keep these crazy women out of my hair? She finished her drink and excused herself, saying she needed to freshen up before the toast.

Maggie checked her makeup in the dismally lit bathroom mirror. *They're right. I do look tired.* She patted powder under her eyes. Shannon stuck her head in the door and said, "I've been looking for you. They're ready for the toast." Maggie took a deep breath and followed Shannon out.

Maggie grabbed her refilled glass from her place setting and went to the front of the room. She clutched the microphone in one hand and her champagne flute in the other.

She wished the couple all the best. She told a story about Kevin, in his youth, declaring all girls "totally gross" and how their dad had told him he should keep that quiet since they were out-numbered in the house. At the mention of Dad, she made blurry eye contact with Mom and Shay who were both crying. She tried to keep her voice steady as a tear sky-dived off the apple of her cheek and she looked at Kevin. "I'm glad you reversed your position on girls, because I can't imagine a more beautiful woman, inside and out, for you to share your life with." She held up her glass and everyone shouted, "Here, here," and drank to the couple.

Later, Maggie was sitting with Beth and James watching the couples dancing as the DJ played *Someone to Watch Over Me.* Kevin snuck kisses from Annie; Shannon and Michael shared a laugh; Dippy steered her husband like a remote-controlled car; and Humphrey guided Gram across the floor with stately grace. Maggie had just finished her champagne and started to look around for a waiter, when Russell walked up.

"I love this song," he said. "Will you dance with me?"

"Sure," she said taking his proffered hand.

The dance floor felt slick under her heels, or maybe it was the three glasses of champagne that made her feel a little uncertain on her feet. She hoped she wouldn't fall, but Russell felt solid as they moved in time to the music, so she let herself relax in his arms. His hand warmed the small of her back.

"Nice wedding, huh?" he said.

"Yeah. Very."

"It's a bummer Brian couldn't be here."

"Yeah." At the mention of Brian, Maggie realized that she'd never danced with him. It also occurred to her that other than wishing he was there to save her from Dippy, she hadn't thought about him much today. Not at all really. She felt a little guilty about that, but then, it had been a very busy day. OK, I'll think about him now, she told herself. *I should make him take me out dancing sometime. I wonder if he's a good dancer. As good as Russell* . . . She glanced up at Russell who smiled down at her until she looked away. She noticed Annie's younger sister, Trisha, sitting alone. "You should ask Trisha to dance."

"Oh, yeah. Maybe."

"Did you meet her yet? She's nice. And obviously gorgeous. And she's single. *And* she lives in San Diego."

"You want me to dance with her or marry her?"

"I'm just saying she's a single, good-looking person. What more do you need?"

He looked over Maggie's head in Trisha's direction. "I guess she's kind of a cute kid."

The song ended and the DJ put on *Lady in Red*. "I hate this song," they said in unison and walked off the dance floor. Maggie saw James about to drop a big Smurfy blue bite of cake on his little rented tuxedo pants and hurried to intervene.

The rest of the reception passed in a bubbly blur. Maggie danced with her brother twice, and later with Humphrey to *Blue Moon*. She did the twist with Russell and, during the faster numbers, danced by herself or with Shannon. She tried, unsuccessfully, to avoid Deirdre, Dippy and Delfina. She hugged her mom and grandmother repeatedly, both of whom commented on how bony she was getting. She threw herself gratefully, if somewhat sloppily, into Annie's arms when the bride announced her intention, after being pressed on the issue by Delfina, to *not* toss the bouquet. Annie said it was too lovely, and frankly too heavy ("It could hurt someone"), to throw and she planned to have it dried as a keepsake. As Maggie drank toast after toast, she knew she was quickly passing from tipsy to buzzed to flat-out drunk, but she didn't care. It felt good to let loose and, after all, it wasn't every day your little brother got married, right?

When Mom said she was tired, Grandma and Humphrey said they'd escort her back to the hotel.

"If we didn't have to get up and start driving home so early tomorrow, you'd know I'd be here, dancing, all night, right?" Gram said to Kevin as they all said their goodbyes.

When Maggie hugged her mother goodbye, Mom whispered, "Honey, I think you've had enough champagne. You should go into the kitchen and see if they have any saltines."

At the end of the night, when the music had stopped, the women had kicked off their high heels, and only their best friends and siblings were left, Maggie heard Kevin, through a fizzy haze, ask Russell to make sure she got back to the hotel OK. There were more tears as she said sniffly, sloppy goodbyes and told everyone she loved them. Only she said, "I luf you guys."

On the cab ride back, when she finally had time to sit and be quiet, except for periodic sniffling, she realized her head was pounding.

"I think I mida had too much champagne." She pressed her cold fingers to her temples.

"You are gonna have one heck of a headache, my dear." Russell watched her slump against the seat, sinking deep into her coat. "But I'll get you some aspirin when we get back."

Good as his word, Russell saw her to her room and sat her down on the bed. He went to the bathroom and came back with water and three ibuprofen.

"Take these," he held them out to her.

"I woulden be in this mess if Dave're here," she started to cry after she swallowed the pills. "Owww. My head."

"Well, don't cry. You're just going to make your head hurt worse. Boy, you are way drunk. You said 'Dave.' Don't you mean 'Brian'?" He sat beside her and the bed sank with his weight. She fell toward him, but decided against fighting momentum. She leaned into his chest and he put his arm around her.

"No, *Dave*," she said. "Dave knows I c-can't handle champagne. He woulda never let me drink sumuch." She sat up and wiped her nose on the back of her hand. "Dave knew everything 'bout me. And now I g-gotta start all over. Go through the whole 'here're my ugly s-secrets and my b-bad habits and I h-hope you'll still like me' thing. It sucks." She put her head back on his chest and snuffled into his shirt.

"I know," he pulled a strand of hair that clung to her wet cheek away from her face and tucked it behind her ear. "Getting your heart broken does indeed suck."

"Whadda you know about it?" She sat up, her eyebrows knitted.

"Contrary to my devil-may-care façade, I've had my heart broken before. Really, it's true," he added when she looked at him, disbelieving.

"What happened?"

He sighed. "I was young. Young and in love. Wow, it's almost ten years ago. My older brother, Adam, introduced me to this girl in his study group. He was taking the bar exam."

"You have a brother? I didden know that." She stopped crying.

"Yeah, I do . . . Anyway, Adam introduces me to his friend, Kate. We hit it off and started dating. Before I know it, she's moved into my place. I'm stupid-happy. I'm thinking, 'How did I get this lucky?' So I decide to ask her to marry me. I set up this whole elaborate thing; tell her I'm going to L.A. for the day for work, but really I took the day off, and I'm getting everything rolling for the big surprise." Maggie thought back to the things Russell had said during the ceremony about wanting to share the rest of your life with someone, and her heart ached for him, knowing his story was about to end very badly.

"I pick up the ring; go to our favorite restaurant to set everything up; I even talk to the chef about the best place to hide the ring where she won't accidentally swallow it. The whole nine yards. Ten freaking yards, even. Only I'm the one that gets the surprise."

"Uh oh."

"Yeah, uh oh. I come home that afternoon, thinking she won't even be there and I find her . . .," he paused for a moment and licked his lips. Maggie knew he was seeing the image as clearly as that day ten years ago. "I find her in bed with Adam. My own goddamn brother. She didn't love me. She *never* loved me."

"That's awful." She started to cry again. "Whyda people have to be so awful? W-why do they have to cheat?" She hunted for something to wipe her nose on. She'd reached for the end of the thick gold and beige bedspread when Russell grabbed a tissue off the nightstand and handed it to her. She blew her nose loudly. She started to sob now, an ugly, hiccupping cry accompanied by shuddering gasps for breath.

"W-why did Dave have to be such a r-rat? W-why did he have to leave me? What's wrong with me? I m-make more money than what's-her-name. I even make moh . . . more money than *him*. I have bigger boobs than her. I've seen her. It's true. And I'm c-cuter than her."

"Maggie, you are cute like the Sistine Chapel is cute. Like the Grand Canyon is cute." He pulled her back to his chest and tried to quiet her. "Dave's a complete and utter idiot. You're better off without him."

"I'm sorry." She took a deep breath as she sat up.

"What? You've got nothing to be sorry for." He looked into

what she knew were red, blood-shot eyes with his clear blue ones.

She pointed at his shirt. "I got your nice shirt all wet . . . and . . . I sorta w-wiped my nose on your tie." Her face wrinkled and she started to cry once more.

WHEN RUSSELL LEFT, she lay in bed with one foot on the floor. Her head spun, not just from drinking too many drinks, but thinking too many thoughts.

She thought about how they'd both been betrayed. But at least she'd had years, decades even, of mutual love. Poor Russell, though, had never experienced that. Were you really experiencing love if you only felt the one side of it? The one-directional flow? No, she didn't think so. That was a kind of love, but certainly not the best kind.

It reminded her of a poem they studied in one of her college Lit classes, something about love being like a river. *That's just stupid. Love's not a river. It doesn't go one way on a set path. Unless . . . it's unrequited love, I 'spose. Maybe that's what the poet meant? But, that's dumb, cuz if your love's a river, nothing's ever going to come back at you. Unless . . . your lover's in a boat maybe . . . Anyway, it's stupid.*

Her drunken mind tried to come up with a better metaphor, her own metaphor for love. *Real love isn't one way—it goes back and forth. And it's involuntary. Maybe . . . like . . . a tornado. No, that's no good. Too destructive. That's wrong. No, it's like . . . a dog's tail. That's it! True love goes back and forth, and you can't control it. You find that person you're in love with, and it's gonna wag. And there's no stopping it.*

Chapter 24: At Least the Flight Was On Time

On the long flight home, Maggie had a lot of time to think. Resting her still throbbing head (she could feel her pulse in her eyeballs) on the pathetic dumpling-sized standard issue plane pillow, she closed her eyes.

First she thought about Russell and his story. The poor guy. He'd been burned pretty damn badly. She'd been scalded in the third degree herself, but at least she hadn't walked *in* on them. And . . . *ick*. It made her shiver to think of walking in on Dave with her own—no; that was too horrifying to even contemplate. Besides, it was ridiculous. *Shay would never in a million years* . . . Last night, thinking about the enormous double betrayal Russell had suffered and her empathy for him *and* all that alcohol had made her more than a little tempted to comfort him. She'd actually thought that in her head, "comfort him;" only what she meant was: "kiss the hell out of him." She'd wanted to hold him and make him forget he'd ever known that horrid Kate. And Adam as well. *What a rotten brother. No wonder he never mentioned the rat bastard.*

But now, in the harsh light of day, she was relieved that she hadn't made a pass at him. That was just a crazy, drunken thought. Everything was embarrassing enough as it was. She groaned inwardly thinking how much worse she'd be feeling if she'd thrown herself at him. He'd have no doubt turned her down while looking into her tear-, snot-, and drool-smeared face.

No, he'd been a total sweetie. After she'd ruined his tie, he'd softly said, "It's OK," and taken it off. Her heart beat hard as she realized she was hoping he'd take his shirt off next, but he'd stood up, picked up her pajamas off the nightstand, and told her she better get some sleep.

He'd waited while she got ready for bed, (horrified by the red Rorschach splotches on the face in the mirror, she'd stayed in the bathroom as long as possible) and then tucked her in. He'd applied his cool lips to her hot forehead and left.

How embarrassing. But that was the other great thing about Russell. She'd seen him at the hotel this morning, looking bright-eyed while she hid behind dark sunglasses, and he'd told her there was nothing to be embarrassed about. She'd told him she couldn't believe she'd gotten so worked up again over Dave. "I don't even really think it was Dave so much as the idea of Dave," she'd said as he helped her carry her luggage out to her rental car. "The idea of thinking I was happily settled. I don't know. I thought I was doing really well with the whole divorce thing, but maybe not so much."

"Weddings are always hard to get through after a breakup, not to mention the holidays. And, in case you weren't aware, alcohol is a depressant. And that cousin of yours, holy cow. I heard her grilling you all through dinner. Talk about a depressant." He'd waited by the trunk while she fumbled in her purse for her keys, trying to function without taking off her gloves.

"Did you hear all that? I couldn't get her to stop."

"I didn't hear all of it, but I heard enough."

"Well, thanks. That makes me feel better." She'd held up the keys to show her success and opened the trunk. "I better get going. Thanks again."

Russell was on a later flight out that day so he'd hugged her goodbye and said he'd see her back in San Diego.

She thought about what he'd said, about the alcohol and Dippy and the wedding combining to make her depression mount a sneak attack. She really had thought she was doing so well, so "great," as she kept insisting to her aunt and cousins. But now she realized there was still this dark spot, deep within her. She pictured it like a growth, or a lump, wiggly and amorphous. *Like that nasty sourdough starter. A slimy lump of sour-Dave-starter. Just add alcohol and the yeast gets going and next thing you know you've got a full-on loaf's worth of depression to deal with.*

Good grief, what's Christmas going to be like? And New Year's . . . Maybe I should swear off alcohol for the holidays. Especially champagne.

Next she thought about one incident at the reception that stood out crystal clear, even though most of her party memories were fuzzy around the edges, like out-of-focus photographs. After the toasts and cake-cutting were done, she'd avoided the empty seat next to Dippy and gone to sit by Gram and Humphrey.

"Your toast was very nice, sweetie," Gram had said. "And I've been meaning to tell you that you and your young man make a lovely couple." As she said this, she'd nodded her head towards Russell still seated at the head table. "I'm glad I got to meet Russell."

"Gram, Russell's not my boyfriend. Brian's my boyfriend. Brian, you know; he had to leave after Thanksgiving dinner?" Maggie was thankful when recognition had flooded the old woman's lined face; recognition tinged with embarrassment.

Gram had put her parchment-paper hands to her face. "Oh, I'm so sorry. I got confused. Of course, Brian. I don't know what I was thinking."

Maggie had joked, "Too much champagne for you, young lady. Humphrey, she's cut off. Don't let her operate any heavy machinery. Keep an eye on her."

"I never take my eyes off of her," Humphrey had said. He rubbed Gram's arm and smiled.

Yep, he's a keeper, Maggie had thought.

Thinking back on it now, she realized it was the first time she'd ever seen any sign of confusion or forgetfulness from Gram, who was always so sharp. It worried her.

Next she thought of the things she was leaving behind: she started with Gram, who wasn't getting any younger. Then there were her siblings, her mom (*OK, Mom makes me crazy, but I still love her*), and especially Beth and James. Knowing she'd never have kids of her own, she wanted desperately to have a close relationship with them. She loved them so much. She couldn't wait until they were old enough to come and spend summers with her, but she worried that maybe by then they'd hardly know her. *Will they want to spend time with me? I'll have to try to stay close over email and the phone and fly out as much as possible. It could work . . .*

Then she thought of the things she was heading back to.

Her dog, but he didn't count; not because she didn't love him to death, but because he'd go with her wherever she went, so wasn't really part of the equation.

Her soon-to-be-ex-husband and ex-home. Not fun things to head back to. She just wanted the stupid house to sell already. She was anxious to be on to something new. Once the house sold, everything could be finalized with the divorce and she'd never have speak to Dave again.

Her job. There was another thing she wasn't looking forward to returning to, she thought as she shifted in her seat. The place was doing OK, but they needed to swing a deal with one of the big chains if they were going to make real money. Stephen had the R&D team re-working the formulas into something cheaper as he and Maggie hunted for other ways to cut expenses. He was in a bad mood most of the time. It was stressful and generally no fun at all.

What else? Hmmm. Brian. Finally, here was something worth heading home for. *My Golden Boy. Boy . . .* Or was she excited about heading home to him? She felt guilty now, thinking about that wave of lust she'd felt for Russell last night. *I wouldn't have cheated on Brian though. That was just a champagne-induced whim . . . Thank God I didn't* do *anything.*

Thinking of Brian made her wonder what he'd wanted to tell her when he'd pulled her close on the street, right before the call from the museum. Maybe she was reading too much into things, but she worried that maybe he was going to tell her he loved her.

She was trying to be like Kona, go with the flow, enjoy the ride, and she had . . . for a while. But now she suspected the ride might morph from the merry-go-round into the tunnel of love. She wasn't ready for that. She wasn't in love with him.

I wish I was. He's practically perfect. We love the same things. Well, most of the same things. I wouldn't mind going to a ball game or eating something greasy once in a while. And maybe just once it would be nice to hang out in our sweats . . . watch something mindless on TV; just blob. I always feel like I have to be so perfectly dressed and pressed with him.

But maybe I'm being too nit-picky. It's early on; we haven't been together all that long. I could maybe fall in love him. Maybe. He's a great guy— thoughtful, super smart, kind. She thought about how her whole family seemed to like him; remembered how adorable he'd been with Beth.

Wait a minute . . . I wonder . . . does he want kids? If he does, that would definitely be a problem.

She knew she didn't want them; and now, when she thought about it, really examined her feelings, she also knew she didn't want *him.* She realized, right there, crammed between the window and the large man on the right leaning into her space bubble, that even though she was fond of Brian, she would never fall in love with him.

He's sort of like accounting. They're both perfect for me, on paper, but I'll never love accounting and I'll never love him. I'm stuck with accounting, I need it too much, but Brian . . . I've gotta break it off. If he was falling in love, she wanted to end it right away, before he got in deeper. She didn't want to hurt him.

Or, maybe I could wait; see how things go . . . Maybe I'm all wrong. What makes me think this brilliant guy is falling for me? He probably just wanted to tell me something else. Invite me on a trip or something. Maybe he's . . . thinking about moving. Or getting another dog. Or he's planning to take Samba lessons. Yeah, I'm making way too big of a deal out of this. I'll just let things continue on the way they've been. We'll go out and keep having great sex, well . . . pretty good sex. I'll just keep . . . enjoying the ride.

Only, that wasn't how she operated. She'd always thought it was better to be by yourself than be with someone you weren't one hundred percent crazy about. Of course, she'd never actually had to put that into practice before.

This doesn't feel right anymore. I can't just "pass the time" with him. Sure, I like him, but I'll never be in love with him. Deep down, I'd be waiting for someone else to come along, someone special. Then when (or if) he does, Mr. Special will think I'm already with someone.

She felt terrible thinking these things. Brian was special; just not *her* special.

She punched the pillow and stared out the window at the blanket of clouds below. *Swell. I'm heading home to a house I need to sell, a job I can't stand, and a boyfriend I need to break up with. Ugh.* And depending on how things went with Brian, she might need to stop volunteering at the museum as well. Hopefully he'd be OK with being friends. Or at least leave work early on Thursday nights when she came in.

Her head pounded worse than before.

Finally, she thought of her friends; something she was excited about heading home to. Russell and Helen had been so great. She didn't know how she would have gotten through the last few months without them. Maggie looked forward to heading straight to Helen's after she landed to pick up Kona. She could use a hug from her friend and that I-missed-you-more-than-you'll-ever-know look from her dog.

Thank heaven Brian wasn't meeting her flight. He'd called last night while she was at the wedding and left a message saying he'd be at the museum all day Sunday, trying to get everything finalized so they could re-open on Monday. He told her he hoped she was having fun, wished he was there, and asked her to call when she got in on Sunday.

She figured she'd tell him she was tired from the flight, too exhausted to get together tonight, and she'd see him Monday after work. She couldn't deal with seeing him today.

I'll break up with him Monday. How depressing.

She squirmed in her seat. Breaking up with Brian was bad enough, but she'd never been this blue heading home from a trip before. But then, this was the first trip she'd taken since her separation from Dave. Before, if she traveled alone, there was always Dave to go back to. And if they went away together, Kona, their home, and their life waited for their return.

She weighed the balance of the things she was leaving behind and going to miss against the things she was not looking forward to returning to. She was going back to nothing more than a couple of great friends and glorious weather.

The pilot came on over the intercom: "This is Captain Sattler. We should be landing in San Diego in about twenty minutes. The weather is . . . well, for those you of coming to San Diego for the first time, it's going to be little disappointing. It's only forty-three degrees on the ground and raining. But we'll be getting you to your gate on time."

When the plane landed, she turned on her cell. There was a voicemail from Helen.

"I know your message said you'd take a cab to my place, but look for me at the curb. You know I don't believe in that ESP bullshit—in fact, I'm going to start calling it *BSP*—but, I just had this feeling you could use a hug sooner rather than later. I'll be circling, *amiga*."

She'd hate me calling her this, but she is so sweet.

It was drizzling when Maggie stepped out of the airport, but she brightened as soon as she spotted Helen's yellow Beetle. She waved and Helen pulled up; it was even better to see her there than Maggie had anticipated: Kona was in the passenger seat. He saw Maggie and stood up and started his happy-to-see-you dance, which was tough in the confined space.

Helen shoved him into the backseat so Maggie could get in. Once in her seat, he tried to squeeze in with her, covering her with kisses and whipping Helen with his tail.

"No one's ever that excited to see me," Helen said, shoving on the dog's hindquarters.

"There's nothing like one of Kona's greetings to make you feel loved."

Chapter 25: Black Monday (And Tuesday's Forecast Ain't Great Either)

"I missed you." Brian wrapped her in a hug. She heard his "mellow" playlist in the background and noticed the dim, romantic lighting over his shoulder. He kissed her, but she pulled away after a few seconds.

"How are you?" he asked. "Tired?" He held her shoulders and looked into her eyes.

"Yeah. Very."

"Me too. It was a stressful weekend, dealing with the police, the museum board, Hidelbaum, the insurance company. I didn't sleep much."

And I'm about to add to your list of troubles.

"And, the worst part," he continued, "is that I lost out on spending the long weekend with you. I wish you could spend the night." He'd invited her to bring Kona and stay over, but she'd lied and said she needed to be at work early the next day so she couldn't. "I'd like to show you how much I missed you."

He moved in for another kiss, but she pretended not to notice and took her purse off her shoulder to deflect him. She set it on the table in the foyer. "No greeting from Peaches?"

"Poor Princess is still at the kennel. I knew I'd be at the museum and wouldn't have time for her so I called and asked them to keep her until Tuesday. It's been very lonely around here." He moved toward the kitchen. "Wine?"

"Yes, please." *Oh no; no Peaches to pour his troubles out to when I'm done with him.* She flashed on the comfort she'd felt at least having Kona there when Dave walked out, and felt even more guilty. *But maybe he'll be fine. Maybe he's not that into me. Maybe this will all be a big relief.*

He handed her a glass of cabernet. "Tell me all about the wedding." He put his hand on her back and steered her to the living room. He'd lit a dozen candles and set them about.

Oh God. "It was really nice." She sat on the sofa, took her shoes off and pulled her feet up under her.

"Nice? That's it?" He tried to sit close, but it was awkward with her legs between them.

She gave him the *CliffsNotes* version of the weekend, wanting to get as quickly as possible to the reason she'd come.

"We need to talk," she said.

"I don't like the way you say that." He set his glass on the coffee table and inched closer.

"Brian," she set her glass down as well, "You know I like you, a lot . . ." She sought the words she'd rehearsed with Helen, then again in bed last night, all day at work, and in the car driving over.

"There's a 'but' coming, isn't there?" He slumped against the cushions. "You're about to give me the 'let's be friends' speech aren't you?"

"I *do* want us to be friends." Now she moved closer to him. She put her feet back down on the floor and reached out to touch his arm. She felt the sharp crease of his shirtsleeve as he put his hand over his eyes.

"I can't believe this." He dragged his hand down his face; shook his head. "I thought . . . You just took me to meet your entire family. I really . . . loved meeting them. I thought—"

"I know." No, she didn't know what he thought. She was afraid to hear what he thought. "But I didn't mean to send any signals. I wanted you to come with me to the wedding, but I—"

"You what?" His eyes narrowed.

"I didn't mean for it to . . . mean anything."

"You didn't want it to mean anything? Just a casual jaunt cross-country for Thanksgiving and this huge family event. Introduce me to everyone. But I'm not supposed to see anything in all this, or *feel* anything. I thought you invited me because . . ." He pushed himself up off the couch. The candles winked and mocked them. He reached the other side of the room and spoke without turning to look at her. "I, I'm just a complete idiot, aren't I?"

"No, you're not. It's me. I'm the idiot. I should've realized; I should've gone by myself. But I . . ."

"You just didn't want to go alone. Am I right? You didn't want to be the 'single one' at the party. I was just someone to have on your arm. I could have been anybody. How could you be so . . . selfish?" His voice caught on the words. He looked up at the ceiling and she saw that he tried to fight back tears.

Oh God, this is not going well. This was not the touching "We'll always have Boston" scene she'd rehearsed in her head. *Say something nice; try to make him feel better.*

"You're right. I was selfish. But I really did like you. I *do* like you—you're brilliant and handsome and sweet and . . ."

He looked back at her. His forehead was crumpled, but his lop-sided smile, that she'd always found so adorable, struggled to come out.

OK—this is better. Keep going. "I'm so sorry. I'd never intentionally hurt you."

He went to sit beside her again. His sad eyes glanced at her, then he looked down at his hands. *Come on, Brian, say something. Show me that you're OK with all this.*

"Maybe . . ." he started, then stopped. *Say "maybe we can be friends."* She willed him to say it. He cleared his throat. "Maybe . . . it was too soon for me to go meet your family. Maybe that was just a bad idea on both our parts." *There you go. See; it's not all my fault. Come on now, say it . . . "let's be friends."* He clutched her hands. "Maybe we were just moving too fast. Maybe . . . you could give us another chance." *Oh, crap.* "Maggie, I think I'm . . ." He licked his lips and searched her eyes. "I could be really good for you. Can't you give this a little more thought?"

"Brian—," she started, but he buried his head in her lap before she could say another word. At least he'd let go of her hands, which he'd been crushing. *Ow,* she mouthed over his bent head as she shook her hands out. "Look, Brian . . ."

"No!" His words were muffled by her skirt. "Don't say anything yet. You're tired. It was a long, emotional trip. You should go home and think about it and . . . and . . . in the morning, you'll see that I'm right. We're good together."

"Brian, I have thought about it. I thought about it for hours on the flight home. I thought about everything, especially how adorable you were with Beth. And I have a feeling you want kids—and you know I don't. We, we just don't want the same things."

"No." He looked up, a tear streamed down his face. "I don't *have* to have kids."

"Brian, listen to yourself. That's crazy. Things are just not going to work out for us. Please, you see that, right?"

"No, I don't understand any of this. I thought everything was great. You invited me on that trip. Your mom asked me if I'd be there at Christmas. My mother thinks you sound great."

"You talk to your mom about us?"

"I talk to her about everything. And she thought it sounded like you liked me. She wanted me to bring you home at Christmas. She—" He sank to the floor and wrapped his arms around her legs. She felt wet tears on her bare feet.

Oh God. I've got to get him pulled together and get out of here. She struggled to slip her legs out of his grip. "Please, sit up. Talk to me. Up here, on the sofa." She pulled at him, then gave up and rubbed his back as he wept.

The phone rang. She heard his greeting on the answering machine, then a woman's voice. "Hello, Bunny! I guess you're not at home . . . I know you said your Magpie's back, so I suppose you're out on the town with your lovebird. I'll speak to you later."

Magpie? Lovebird? She calls him "Bunny"?!

Brian lifted his head from the floor. He sniffled. "I need you to leave. I need to call my mother." He got up and moved toward the phone.

She grabbed her shoes and purse. She looked back from the foyer. *OK, I guess we're done here . . . but, he's not even going to say goodbye to me? After all that?* She heard him dial and choke out the word, "Mother."

She opened the door and harsh light flooded in from the hall. He looked up; put his hand over the phone. "Wait, Maggie . . ." *Finally. He's going to say goodbye at least.* "You shouldn't come to the museum anymore." He turned back to the phone, turned his back on her.

THE NEXT MORNING, her phone rang at 5:30. She felt like she'd only fallen asleep minutes ago, after tossing and turning most of the night. She'd never broken anyone's heart before and she lay in bed for hours thinking about it. *Was there a better way I could have handled it? A phone call? 'Dear Brian' email? Sure, that would have been easier for me, but . . .* Of course, the pain was nothing like being the broken-hearted one, but it was no fun being the heart-breaker either. *And now I can't even go to the museum anymore. Crap.*

When she'd finally fallen asleep, she dreamt she was standing naked in the main gallery. She tried to cover herself with two exhibit pamphlets as a patron asked her to please go tell a loud, rude man to get off his cell phone. The man morphed into Brian, sobbing into his phone. He dropped the phone when he saw her, only it didn't clatter as it hit the floor; it rang. Loudly.

Now, realizing it was her own phone, her heart pounded as if she'd actually just run naked through the museum. She bolted up and grabbed it.

"Sweetie?" Gram sounded faint and fragile.

"What's wrong?" Maggie felt panic rising in her.

"Your Mom, she's on her way to the hospital." Gram started to cry. "I think you need to come, as soon as possible."

Maggie told Gram to take a deep breath and tell her exactly what was going on. Gram told her they'd gotten home from their two-day drive back from Boston the night before. Mom had decided to spend the night at Gram's. She was tired from all the driving.

"Thank God she was here. If she'd gone home, I don't know what might have happened."

"What *did* happen? What's going on?" Maggie tried to stay calm and keep Gram focused.

Gram said she'd gotten up this morning and was making coffee, when Mom came out, weaving a little. "Her face was ashy; she fell and I called 911 right away. They just left. They're taking her to emergency. I haven't even gotten dressed yet."

"OK, Gram, take a cab to the hospital. Have Humphrey go with you. When you know something, call Shay. I hope I'll be in the air by then. Shay can leave a message on my cell."

They hung up and Maggie started making frantic calls. A United flight was leaving in three hours. She could make it if she hurried.

She called Shannon while she threw clothes in her suitcase, still open on the bedroom floor from Sunday. Shannon wanted to fly down too, but Maggie suggested she wait to hear more. If the worst had happened, they'd all be too late anyway, but hopefully they would get her to the hospital in time and everything would be fine.

"Don't call Kev yet," she told Shannon. "There's no point interrupting their honeymoon until we know more. Shit, I've got to figure out what to do with Kona." She realized she should probably take him along, since she had no idea how long she'd be away. Besides, they'd flown with him before and she knew the drill. She had a crate and some doggie-downers they used to calm him on long car rides. "I've gotta call United and make sure Kona can get on the flight. I'll call you when I land."

On the way to the airport she called Stephen and left him a message that there'd been an emergency and she'd check in later.

Finally she called Dave. He expressed concern for her mother, but she cut him off. "Someone's got to water the plants in case the realtor shows the house. Can you do it?" She hated to ask him for anything, but, after all, it was his house too and he should have to help with some of the hassle of selling it. When he agreed, she added, "I, uh, didn't really sell your stupid TV. Go ahead and take it." She hung up without waiting for his reply.

On the plane, heading cross-country for the third time in a week, she was faced, again, with several hours of thinking and worrying. She worried about what she'd find when she got there. Worried about Gram, if the worst did happen. Worried about Kona, who was probably at this minute trying to claw his way out of his crate. She couldn't be certain, but she thought she'd heard howling coming from the belly of the plane when she'd gotten on board.

Chapter 26: We Also Have Great Elbows

Maggie and Kona, his crate filling most of the cab's backseat, had no choice but to go to Mom's house first. She was anxious to get to the hospital, but there was no way, since she had to get Kona settled.

She knew Mom had made it through surgery; there was a message from Shay on her cell when she landed, and she'd also called Gram. Gram had gone home to rest once the triple by-pass was done. Things were still dicey and Mom was in ICU. The nurses promised to call Gram if there were any changes.

Maggie asked the cab driver to wait. She put Kona out back so he could go potty, then set down food and water. She took the cab to Gram's, went up for a thorough hugging and the car keys, and then headed to the hospital in Mom's car with directions scribbled on a torn envelope.

She wound through the hospital maze to ICU. A nurse showed her to Mom's room.

Maggie put her hand to her mouth. Luckily she saw Mom's chest lift as she slept or Maggie would have thought there was just some delay in moving her to the morgue. Her face was gray as an old tennis shoe. Her skin sagged; her mouth hung open.

The nurse told her Mom was resting comfortably and the surgery had been successful. *This is the look of success? What would she look like if it'd gone badly?* The nurse said the doctor could tell her more and would be by shortly, then went back to her station.

When the doctor came in, with his thick dark hair and glasses, he looked every bit the made-for-TV doctor. Maggie wondered if all his patients fell in love with him. Until he spoke.

"You the patient's daughter?" he asked without looking at her. She said yes while he flipped the pages of Mom's chart, she assumed just for show. *How could he really be reading any of it that fast?* He checked his shiny gold watch and said, while scribbling notes, "When people have blockages as bad as your mother's, most of them drop dead before they make it to the hospital. And even then, the majority don't last forty-eight hours."

It's only been like twelve hours. What's he saying?

"But we fully expect her to recover. The surgery went extremely well." Maggie half-expected him to exhale on his fingernails and polish them on his blue scrubs. "If she takes better care of herself, she could live another twenty or thirty years." He walked out before Maggie could ask any questions.

She realized she'd been holding her breath. She let it out and dropped to the hard chair next to the bed, with its bleach-masked-by-artificial-citrus smell. She reached for her cell. *Gotta call Gram with the update first, oh, and remind her to call Aunt D; then I'll call Shay and Kev.* Mom stirred.

"Ted?" Her voice was hoarse, her eyes unfocused.

Oh God, she's calling for Daddy. "No, Mom, it's me, Maggie. You're in the hospital. You're gonna be OK." She felt for Mom's hand under the sheet. "Mom?"

But she'd already shut her eyes and dropped under again.

While Mom slept, Maggie made her calls. She talked to Kevin for some time. At first he insisted he and Annie should fly back right away, but Maggie finally convinced him there was no need to cut their honeymoon short. He promised he'd check in again soon. When she'd called everyone, she tried to read an old *Good Housekeeping* she found on a stand. She was mindlessly flipping pages when the nurse came in.

"Need to check on your mom." The plump nurse, in lavender scrubs and a matching hair-scrunchie, smiled at Maggie. She untucked the blankets at the end of the bed and felt Mom's feet. "Need to see if her feet are warm; check her circulation," she explained. She shook her head enthusiastically. "These are not the feet of a sixty-six-year-old woman.'"

Maggie wasn't sure how to respond to that. *Thank you? Or: "We O'Connell women are known for our youthful feet."* She just smiled back.

"Really, your mother has the most beautiful skin. I can see you got that from her, you lucky thing. She doesn't look a day over sixty."

"Thanks," Maggie said. She reassessed her mom. She really did look much younger than her sixty-six years, well, when she was outside of a hospital bed anyway and had a bit of color in her cheeks. Maggie wondered if any men were chasing after her.

A steady flow of staff breezed in and out that evening, checking on Mom, performing tests, all of them telling Maggie not to worry. *What an insanely hard job. I could never be a nurse. Although it would be nice to have a job where you made people feel better.*

When the nurses assured her Mom would be fine through the night, she went home to Kona and crashed. It was only eight o'clock back in San Diego, but she was exhausted from all the drama of yesterday and today. She was still half on East Coast time anyway, having just left Boston on Sunday, although that felt like it was weeks ago.

The next morning, Mom was awake when she got to the hospital.

"You gave us quite a scare, Mom. But you're going to be fine."

Mom still looked out of it, but at least her face had gone from gray to beige. She barely turned up the corners of her mouth and reached feebly for Maggie.

"Everybody's been really worried. And you've had quite the stream of folks through here. About five different nurses, the pulmonary physician, the cardiologist, the hematologist, the neurologist, and I think maybe even an ichthyologist."

Maggie hadn't expected her mom to laugh, but she was hoping she'd say *some*thing.

"Mom, how are you feeling?" She squeezed Mom's hand and felt her squeeze back.

"Your father came for me," Mom said in a sandpaper voice.

Maggie blinked. She didn't want to cry in front of her mom while she was trying to lift her spirits. But now Mom was talking about a whole other kind of spirits.

"Well, he's just going to have to wait. You're not going anywhere yet, Mom."

"I was ready. You should have let me go."

Even now, she tells me I'm doing it wrong. "Mom, they didn't really give us the option."

THE FOLLOWING SUNDAY they let Maggie take Mom home. Maggie was surprised how chilly it was that early December day. She brought Mom a cheerful wool cardigan embroidered with holly for the car ride and cranked up the heat. It was the first time Maggie had driven from the hospital that she'd registered the fake pine boughs and Happy Holidays banners on the lampposts.

Mom must have noticed them too. "You'll have to help me finish my Christmas shopping, honey." Her voice was hoarse from so little use. "I did most of it last month, but I need a few more things."

"Mom, you need to concentrate on getting well. We'll worry about Christmas later."

That night, after Maggie had Mom settled in bed and asleep, Shannon called and offered to drive down with the kids and help.

"No," Maggie insisted. "I'm fine here alone. Besides, you can't really bring the kids right now. They'd be too much for Mom. She needs quiet."

"But it doesn't seem fair. You're doing everything. And what about work?"

"Shay, it's OK. Work's getting along without me. I've been calling them and doing some work over email on Mom's computer."

James screamed in the background and Shay said, "Better go; chaos reigns. I'll come with the beasts when she's stronger. Call you tomorrow."

The next day began the trial and error process of figuring out what she could feed Mom that didn't make her gag. With the mix of prescriptions she was on, she constantly felt sick to her stomach. Nothing sounded good, and since she couldn't eat, she grew weaker and light-headed.

After several days and several cans of "nutritional" drinks down the drain (which Mom said tasted like chalk and Maggie thought were a joke—sugar, corn syrup, and a list of things she couldn't pronounce being key ingredients), she discovered the only thing Mom could keep down was one of her smoothies. She went to the health food store for protein powder and brewer's yeast to build up Mom's strength. She tempted Mom's taste buds with different flavor combos: strawberry-banana, orange-mango, kiwi-raspberry. She snuck some spinach and cucumber into the last one, taking advantage of the sharp, tart taste of the berries to mask the spinach flavor while upping the iron and Vitamin C.

Soon Mom was strong enough for sitting up in bed and, the highlight of her week, having Maggie wash her hair in the kitchen sink.

One day Maggie blended together a smoothie with Asian pear and a hint of cranberry. She took it to Mom's room at lunch time, followed by Kona. Mom asked Maggie to sit with her. The shades were still down so Maggie flipped on the small table lamp beside the bed.

"Do you know what day it is, honey?"

"Sure, Wednesday, December fifth."

"No, that's not what I meant. It's the eve of Saint Nicolas Day."

"I used to love Saint Nicolas Day; used to love putting my shoes out the night before."

"I know. Your father loved it too."

"I couldn't wait to wake up and find all the little presents in my shoe."

"Your Dad bought those presents. It was all his idea."

"Really? I never knew that."

"Really. It was a tradition from his grandma, and he wanted to share it with you kids."

"Daddy was the best." Maggie sat watching Mom sip her smoothie through the red and white straw. "Can I ask you something? Did you ever want to get remarried?"

"No, honey, I never did," she said without hesitation. "Not that

I didn't have the opportunity. Especially with one man, Alfred. I guess about six or seven years after your father died. Must have been six, because I started seeing him right after Kevin moved away to college. Remember him? He came to Thanksgiving dinner that year."

"I remember." Maggie nodded. "He was short and had glasses."

"He was very sweet."

"I remember he seemed nice. He brought that huge centerpiece. We had to put the turkey and mashed potatoes on the hutch because it took up so much room on the table."

"That's right. I'd forgotten about that centerpiece." Mom smiled, then continued. "He liked you kids."

"He did? Wasn't that the year Kevin made Shay laugh so hard cranberry sauce came out her nose?"

Mom made her duck face. Maggie had never been so happy to see that face; it meant Mom was well enough to get irritated.

"Yes, that was that year. But he liked you all *anyway* . . . He asked me to marry him shortly after that." Maggie opened her eyes wide at her mother. "He said he loved me and wanted to take care of me. He said I could sell my shop if I wanted. He owned a string of furniture stores. He had such a beautiful house," she added wistfully.

"How come you said no?"

"Well, I cared for him, but I didn't love him."

"Weren't you tempted to *try* to love him? You sure would've had it a lot easier." Mom had worked until the shop was too much for her weakening heart. Eventually she'd sold the store and moved to Jacksonville where real estate was cheaper and she could be near her own mother.

"I might have grown to love him. He was tender, thoughtful. But, it wasn't like with your father." She looked down at her hands and fingered the simple gold wedding band she'd never stopped wearing. "I couldn't forget what it was like with your father."

Maggie's eyes brimmed with tears. "Daddy was one in a billion."

"He was, honey. He sure was." A tear rolled down Mom's cheek. Maggie plucked two tissues out of the box on the nightstand and handed one to Mom.

"But, do you think it's possible to love more than one person? Or is it just the one shot? Did I screw up my one shot?" She wiped away a tear about to plunge from her chin. She felt other little lemming tears lined up behind it.

"Maggie, unfortunately, Dave was not like your father." Mom shook her head. "Your father and I had some tough times, too."

Maggie blinked at her.

"I know, I never told you kids." She folded and unfolded the tissue, smoothed it with her hands. "We didn't have much money at first, and with you and Shannon born so close together, well your father was under a lot of stress trying to provide for us, and I wasn't always very patient. I could get so wrapped up in you kids. Sometimes I'm amazed he didn't just walk out. But he stayed. He loved me and he loved you kids. And I know it seemed like Dave was the love of your life and you'd always be together, but he wasn't worthy of you. Things got a little tough, and what did he do? He turned to another woman. Good riddance to bad rubbish, I say."

"Really? But I thought you wanted me to work it out with him?"

"I did, at first. I thought maybe he'd just made a mistake and with some counseling you two could work things out. But, there was nothing you could do. He made a mistake, all right. Walking away from someone as smart and beautiful and caring as you."

Maggie's chin wobbled. She put her head down on the patchwork quilt over Mom's legs. She closed her eyes, hoping to stop the tears. She felt Mom's fingers running through her hair. She must have been in grade school the last time Mom stroked her hair as she cried.

"There's someone out there for you who's going to love you unconditionally."

"You mean besides Kona?"

Mom laughed, "Yes, I mean besides Kona."

Kona sat up at the sound of his name and rested his head on Maggie's leg. She sat up too. "I made mistakes too though, Mom. I see that now. And if I'm lucky enough to meet someone else, I'm not going to take that person for granted like I did with Dave."

"You just have to remember what's important. I know you're going to be OK. And I know I said I'd be content when all my kids are happily married, but, I really just want the 'happy' part. You know, I'm very proud of you, Maggie." Mom reached for her hand. "I know I've pushed you hard sometimes, but I wanted you to get your degree and have a good career. And now you do. It makes me feel good, knowing you can take care of yourself, no matter what happens. I . . . I didn't want you to be like me."

"What do you mean 'like you'? You had a good career. You ran your own store. You did great. It can't have been easy raising us after Dad died. And you got us all through college." Maggie studied the road map of veins on Mom's hand. "I'm proud of you too, Mom."

They sat in silence for a moment, then Maggie stood and kissed Mom on the forehead. "I think I've worn you out enough for one afternoon. You'd better take a nap. In fact, I think I'll take one myself." Maggie shut off the light and called Kona, who followed her out of the room.

Maggie snuggled on the sofa under the pale green and pink afghan Gram had crocheted ages ago. She finished her smoothie while running her conversation with Mom over in her head.

I am going to be OK. If I find another man to love, who loves me too, I'm going to work harder. Make sure he always knows he's the most important thing in the world to me. Even if I get a little crazy and caught up in work now and then, I'll make sure he knows he's my top priority. And if I don't meet someone, well, that'll be OK too. I'll figure out what I want to be; what I want to do. And it'll be something I can get excited about. If I can get excited about it, then I know I can make it a success—no matter what it is.

She thought about how accounting was like cleaning the bathroom. Sure, she could do a really excellent job at it. She could make the bathroom sparkle, but it was just another chore. It wasn't something she could put her heart into. She'd been successful at accounting without even really trying, so imagine what she could do if she loved her work? And now she needed to figure out what that thing was . . . She needed to think.

When Mom's well, I'll go back and work at Clean N' Green until I figure out what I want to do. Or . . . maybe I should just go for it. Quit. Really *give myself time to think.*

It was a scary thought, quitting, just like breaking up with Brian had been scary at first.

She looked at Kona, sitting next to the sofa, waiting for her to give him the glass to lick.

"Buddy, this is one time when I haven't been able to take my cues from you," she said.

Kona was a slut who would give his love to anyone who wanted it. He would *always* choose to be with someone, anyone, over being alone. That was fine for dogs, but somehow just not right for humans. She extended her theory about relationships—that she shouldn't simply pass the time with someone who was great on paper, that she didn't love—to her work.

She knew quitting was the right thing to do now, just like breaking up with Brian had been the right thing. She couldn't keep hanging on to this career that was perfect, in theory, while waiting for her dream to happen by. She was going to have to take a risk. Then she'd be able to put the necessary time and effort into figuring things out. She'd open herself up to the possibilities; be ready and waiting when she and her dream job found each other.

She pictured herself and some personification of her dream, a little like the Invisible Man, running towards one another on an empty beach, into each others' arms. She smiled at her silly vision, and at her decision, then rolled onto her side and set her empty glass down on the floor.

She closed her eyes and floated into the blissful state between wakefulness and sleep. She heard the soft laps of Kona's tongue reaching into her glass. As she drifted off, Kona gave her a darting lick on the end of her nose. His breath smelled of the bacon treat she'd given him earlier, mixed with the sweet fruity tang of the smoothie.

She slept deeply and dreamt she was putting bacon in the blender while Kona stood on the kitchen countertop next to her, nodding his encouragement.

Chapter 27: This Could Be My Mailman

Maggie woke from her nap with the seed of an idea. She watered and fed it the rest of the day. That afternoon she got on Mom's computer and downloaded a template for a business plan. Maggie stayed up late after Mom fell asleep, filling page after page of Mom's stationery with ideas: business names, pricing, promotions, revenue and cost estimates. She searched for commercial real estate online to see what rents were like. She wanted to be sure she had good numbers in her plan. When she was done with commercial real estate, she checked houses. She knew they would be less than in California, but she was shocked at just how much cheaper they were. She'd already estimated long ago what she expected to clear from the sale of the house. *It wouldn't go far on my own in San Diego, but here . . .*

She transferred all her scribbled calculations into Mom's computer to check her math. It added up. It all made sense. Next she dashed out a "pro" list that filled an entire page. She made a "con" list that was much shorter, but also much more frightening, so she scratched it out.

Kona slept on the floor by the desk while she worked. At one point he awoke just long enough to roll onto his back and stretch. He fell back asleep, paws in the air, underbelly exposed.

Look at him. Not a care. He could be content anywhere. And . . . so can I.

She finally went to bed at two, thinking she should sleep on it. When she woke Thursday morning, she was just as excited about the idea. All day, in between taking care of Mom and running to the drug store to get her new prescription filled, she would duck into the guest bedroom and look at her calculations, her plans, her "pro" list.

This could really work.

FRIDAY, AFTER GETTING Mom's breakfast and helping her shower, she told Mom she had errands to run. Said she'd stop at the grocery store; she wanted to get some frozen peaches and pomegranate juice to try out a new smoothie flavor.

She took Mom's car and drove around different neighborhoods, trying to imagine what it would be like to live in Jacksonville. She tried on locations like she'd once tried on occupations.

She saw a For Sale sign on a small, brick house with ivory trim and flower boxes full of pink geraniums and thought, We could live there. She passed a lush, green park where a woman was walking a golden retriever. *Kona would love that park.* Everywhere she drove, she thought: *That could be my gym; I could go there for pizza; that's where my business could be.*

At the grocery store, she thought, This could be my Salvation Army Santa. As her handful of coins clattered into his red bucket, Santa kept ringing his bell and smiled and thanked her.

It'd feel so good to start over. She walked into the chilly grocery store. *Somewhere closer to the family. Somewhere less expensive. This really could actually work.*

Maggie stopped short with her cart. There, next to the kumquats in Publix Super Market, she knew for certain: she would quit her job, move to Jacksonville, and start a smoothie business.

Now she was too excited to shop. She grabbed the peaches and pomegranate juice out of the cart, forgot about the rest of the groceries, and raced home to tell Mom and Kona the news.

Mom didn't seem to believe it at first when Maggie outlined her plan. Maggie said, "I know we might make each other crazy, but do you think I could live here? Until I find my own place?"

Mom smiled. "I know what you really mean. What you really mean is, you know *I'll* make *you* crazy, but, yes, if you can stand it, I'd love to have you here, for as long as you need."

Mom was smart. That was what she'd meant.

"OK, then. You're stuck with me." Maggie knew moving in

temporarily with Mom was the right thing to do. Shay and the kids could come and stay for a bit, take over while Maggie went back to San Diego and got her things in order, but Shay couldn't stay for an extended period. And the doctor had said it would be at least four to six weeks, maybe more, before Mom could drive again. Mom was going to need someone there with her until at least mid-January.

Mom said she wanted to call Gram and tell her the good news before taking a nap. Maggie got the phone for her, then went into the other room and called Shay on her cell.

She told her sister everything, going into great detail about her ideas for names, flavors, even how she wanted to decorate the shop.

"It'll be great! I can still use all my accounting and business skills to run the place, and my wanna-be-creative side to come up with the flavors and the décor, and I'll be doing something I can feel good about—providing healthy treats." She talked non-stop another ten minutes, then said, "Or is this totally crazy? Maybe I should sleep on it some more. Run some more numbers? Do some more research?"

"I don't think it's at all crazy. If you want the truth, I haven't heard you this excited since . . . well, honestly, I don't think I've ever heard you this excited before. I think you should go for it. And I can't wait for all of us to be back on the same coast again. The kids'll be excited too. This is so great. Now, when do you need me to come down there so you can go home?"

"Gosh, I don't know. Soon. I've got a million things to do." Maggie rattled off a list of things, until she came to: "Ohmygosh, I've got to quit my job." She told Shannon she better hang up and call her soon-to-be-former boss right away. Get it over with. "I'll call you back and we'll look at our calendars and figure this out."

I'd better call Stephen before I lose my nerve, she thought. But she knew it all felt right. *I don't think I will lose my nerve.*

She sat cross-legged in the middle of the bed with her cell, and dialed Stephen's line.

"You mustn't quit *now*," he said in his lovely British accent, when she told him. "Things have gone rather well this past week with Wal-Mart. We're quite close to signing with them."

"Well, that's great, Stephen. I'm happy to hear that. I mean, I'm happy for *you*."

"But I was going to ask you to go full time when you get back. I've got big plans for this company, Maggie. I want to take it public. You've got the experience with that. I need you; need your help. And we're all going to make scads of money."

Scads of money. For a moment, Maggie thought of her bank account, her IRA, her broker, her future retired self. Scads of money sounded very good for all of them. Very good indeed. And the absence of scads of money had been precisely at the heart of every item on her "con" list.

Maybe I should go back, go full time, maybe for like another year or two . . .

The thought flickered through her head for a moment. Just long enough to crush the joy she'd been feeling moments before; crush it like an apple in a cider mill. She recognized that feeling, that soul-wrenching feeling. She thought of the inevitable stress, the never-ending SEC deadlines, the long days (and nights) trapped in her office under the fluorescent lights. *Buzz kill, your name is accounting.*

"No, Stephen." She sat up straighter, still cross-legged on the bed. "It's tempting. And I'd really like to help you out, but I can't. I've got to do what's right for me."

He tried to convince her for several more minutes, but finally gave up. She warned him that between her Mom and the move, she wouldn't be able to give much of a notice period, but said she'd come in one day when she was in town next week and help out over email until they found someone else.

She hung up. She'd done it. She wasn't going to be an accountant anymore. Well, except for keeping her *own* books, but that would be totally different. She wanted to scream for joy, but knew Mom was trying to nap. She flattened herself on the bed and kicked her legs into the mattress and shook her hair wildly back and forth. She rolled over and let out a muffled, "Eeeeeeee" into her pillow.

Kona heard the commotion and jumped up on the bed. She rolled back and lay smiling at him as he stood, looking down at her.

She held onto his big, square head and pulled herself up to kiss the end of his nose.

"We're going to be very happy here, Buddy," she said. "I just know it."

His tail wagged, but he seemed to look confused. She wondered if he was thinking, "But haven't we always been happy?"

She sat up and hugged him, then decided to call Helen and Russell; break the news to them. This was the one hiccup in her plan; the part she didn't like. *I know they'll both be happy for me, but will they think I'm crazy? Try to talk me out of it? God, I'm going to miss them.*

She started to dial Helen's number, when she remembered that Helen had emailed the other day saying she'd be in Spain until the weekend.

She was dialing Russell when another call came in. She recognized Dave's number. Maybe someone had made an offer on the house.

"Hey," she answered. "Do you have some news about the house?"

"Um, yeah," Dave said. "How's your mom?"

"She's better; thanks for asking. But let's hear it. Do you have good news for me?"

"Well, I'm not sure you'll think it's good, but . . . now promise you'll think about this before saying anything."

Oh God. What's coming?

He seemed to be waiting for her.

"OK, whatever, I promise."

He rattled his news off as if it were one crazy-long multi-syllabic word: "Jess-and-I've-been-thinking-and-we'd-like-to-buy-the-house."

Maggie could feel the phrase, "No way in hell" sliding up from her throat, pushing at her teeth. She'd hated the thought of them in *her* house. She held the phone away from her ear for a moment, but heard him continue on.

"You promised you'd think for a sec. Look, we'd buy out your half. You can have the furniture if you want, or we'll buy that from you, too. Well, except the TV, cuz you said I could have that."

"Dave, are you—"

He interrupted. "I know you think I'm insane or unfeeling or whatever, but when I came over here the other day, I remembered how much I always liked this house. And the neighborhood's great, and it's really close to work for both of us. The commute from her apartment's been killing both of us, and—"

"Dave, wait. I wasn't going to say 'are you insane?' I was going to say: are you going to pay me market value?" *I don't need to ask if you're insane. You are insane. But whatever.*

Dave let out a huge sigh. "Really?" He rushed on as if afraid she's change her mind. "Yeah, we'll work it out with the realtor or the appraiser or whatever. And if you want to take the furniture, that's cool."

"You can have the furniture." *Especially that leather couch I never wanted, and our bed.* She thought of the expensive memory foam mattress they'd bought a few years back. She hoped the memories of her locked in that mattress would haunt them, maybe every night for the first month or two . . . or six. *You'll be wishing we'd bought forgetful foam.*

When she hung up, she lay back again. She couldn't believe living in the house wasn't going to be an issue for either Dave or Jessica; but then she realized it didn't matter any more. She wanted, no, needed, to be rid of the place.

It actually is ideal—for me anyway. For them, it's nuts. She sat up and shook her head, while she dialed Russell's number.

"Hey," he said. "Got your email the other day. Glad to hear your mom's doing better. I knew those super smoothies of yours would fix her up. But I was kinda surprised about that Brian news." She'd emailed a bare-bones mention that she and Brian had broken up. "I thought you guys were tight. You sure seemed that way on Thanksgiving."

"I don't know. Things were OK still on Thanksgiving, but then . . . I dunno." She flushed with guilt again, thinking about her desire to kiss Russell, hold him that night of the wedding, while she was still technically dating Brian. She had to admit to herself now that

that brief moment with Russell, even if just a flicker brought on by too much alcohol mixed liberally with depression about her divorce, had influenced her thinking about Brian on the flight home the next day. It had been the start of her questioning their relationship. The beginning of the end. "It just was never going to work out between us. I don't really want to talk about it."

"OK." They were both silent a moment. "So, since your mom's doing better, are you coming home soon?"

"Yeah. I have to work it out with my sis, but hopefully Monday or Tuesday."

"Great, I've missed our rides. Give me a call when you get in. Maybe we can do dinner."

"There's another reason I called. I quit my job today. I finally thought of something else I want to do."

"That's great! Congratulations. I know how much you've wanted to make a change."

Then she told him exactly how big of a change she had planned. She explained that she'd only be back in San Diego about ten days or so. Just long enough to get her things together. She needed to do some packing, ship whatever wouldn't fit in her car, and then drive back to Florida in time for Christmas.

"Whoa. You're moving? To Florida? Like, the other side of the country?"

"Yeah, *that* Florida."

"But . . . What about . . . What about the hurricanes in Florida?"

"What about the earthquakes in California?"

"OK, well, what about that horrid humidity?"

"What about that horrible drought and the fire danger?"

"Have you thought about the bugs in Florida? The bugs in Florida are insanely huge."

"What I've thought about is the mortgage payments and the rents in California. *Those* are insanely huge. And, besides, Kona can kill the bugs for me."

"Well, you've just got this all figured out. I guess with your brother gone and Brian out of the picture, you've got no ties here anymore. But, aren't you going to miss . . . California?"

Maggie felt a little stab. Could she do this? Could she leave her friends? Could she leave *him*? Yes, she needed to. Financially, it made sense to move. And her mom and her grandma needed her.

"Yes, of course I'm going to miss California." She felt a lump the size of Kona's tennis ball in her throat. "And I'm going to miss you . . . you guys. But I'll come back for visits. And you can come and visit me. You and, and Helen." Maggie heard her Mom calling her. "I've got to go, OK? We'll talk when I get back."

SHAY AND THE kids arrived late Monday afternoon to take over nursing duties, and Maggie and Kona flew out the next morning. She'd thought about leaving him there. She hated to make him get on a plane again, but Shannon was going to have her hands full enough with Mom and the kids. And besides, Maggie was a little nervous about driving cross-country by herself. She wanted to have her furry friend and guardian there with her. He'd be good company; help her feel safe. So, when she'd mapped out their route back, which she figured would take four days, she'd been sure to look up dog-friendly motel chains along the way.

The long flight back was a variation on her flight home from Boston, only now the things she was leaving behind had switched places with the things she was happy about returning to. After the move she'd be back near her family again. Selling the house, the divorce, accounting—it was all going to be behind her. She was excited, nervous but excited, about her new career and fresh start in Jacksonville. But then she thought about Helen and Russell. She was going to miss them so much. Miss how they always made her feel better; made her laugh. She thought about how she'd been so lonely and depressed before she met them both.

They've been so supportive of me. Especially Russell. Helping me with the house. And always telling me how smart I am; how I could be successful at anything. She smiled and looked out the window as the fun times they'd spent together replayed in her mind. She saw him primping on their bike rides; showing off the single time he beat her up the hill;

belting out show tunes in her back yard while he worked on her fence. She thought about the huge smile that would spread over his face every time he saw her—it was almost as good as one of Kona's welcome-homes. She thought about how Russell could always make her laugh. She realized now that the day she'd found out her BioHealth stocks weren't going to be worth much, he was the one who'd made her feel better. *My own boyfriend made me feel worse, telling me I was in good company with all the other job-haters. Russell was first at trying to help me come up with a constructive plan. He's really very sweet . . . And setting me up with Mark. That was pretty sweet too—even if the guy was a complete and total jerk. I'm still not sure what Russell was thinking, trying to fix me up with that loser, but . . . he* thought *he was doing a nice thing.* She thought back to that night again. Her hand went to her hair. *God, he made me feel so self conscious about putting my hair up. But then, he did tell me I have "really beautiful" hair. That was nice to hear . . . God, I'm going to miss him.*

She drifted off to sleep. She dreamt Russell was washing her hair. It started out very tender, even though he was washing it in the big red plastic tub she used to wash Kona in the backyard. When he was done, her hair was instantly dry. She thanked him with a quick hug, but said she had to run. "Wait," he said. He reached up and ran his hand through her hair. She thought he was going to pull her close and kiss her; she longed for it. But then, a pair of scissors flashed in his other hand and he cut the handful of her hair off. He looked at the locks in his hand while she burst into tears. She woke with a start as the plane bounced off a patch of rough air.

The pilot announced that everyone should be sure their seatbelts were fastened as the turbulence was going to be bad on their approach to San Diego. She felt unnerved by the bizarre dream and sick to her stomach from the jostling. She didn't have a chance to spend any more time pondering how much she was going to miss Russell, how much he meant to her. She was too busy clutching the armrests and holding the plane up for the rest of the flight.

BACK IN SAN Diego, the week was non-stop: working out details with Dave, the lawyers, the realtor; figuring out what would stay in the house and what would come with her; arranging for shipping for her bikes, books, artwork, dishes, all the things that wouldn't fit in the car. Each night Maggie collapsed into bed, where Kona already waited sound asleep. Normally one to toss and turn while obsessing over to-do lists and second guessing her decisions, Maggie felt oddly calm. She chalked it up to sheer exhaustion—that and an innate sense that she must be doing the right thing; there was no need, no time for second thoughts. She slept dreamlessly, often waking up hours later, still splayed in the same position.

At the end of a long Saturday filled with sorting, packing, labeling and throwing things out, she met Helen and Russell for dinner at Alfonso's in La Jolla; the spot where the pros had given her their tips for dating all those months before.

As usual, Helen was late, but Russell was there, waiting. When he saw her walk in, he gave her a sad smile. It was nothing like that first beaming grin he'd given her that day they met at Bandito's, nothing like his usual smile. He stood up and greeted her with a warm hug. A very warm hug. A border-line searing hug. The thoughts she'd started thinking on the plane came back to her in a flash; the thoughts of how much she would miss him, of what he meant to her. She realized at the scent of him, the scratch of his shirt on her cheek, the heat of his strong back under her hands, that she was in love with him. *No . . . In love? Can that be possible? Does he . . . make my tail wag?*

Yes. Holy crap; yes.

She was aware of the deafening beat of her heart. It sounded like her ribs were playing hacky sack with it. She thought he must hear it too.

"I can't believe you're leaving us," he said into the top of her head.

She swallowed, hard. "I—" was all she could manage to say.

"*Amiga!*" Helen came through the door. Russell released Maggie and she hugged Helen. After the hug with Russell, Helen's cheek felt cool on hers.

Maggie felt for her chair while Helen and Russell peppered her with questions. They lapsed into silence and studied their menus. Maggie couldn't read any of it. She kept glancing up over the list of specials, to look at Russell, concentrating on his menu, laid flat on the table before him. She looked at the deep crinkles around his eyes; the bits of gray in his brown hair; the spot where the collar of his shirt lay open against his tan neck.

How long has this been going on? she grilled herself. *When did he start making my tail wag? Was it that kiss in his condo? . . . No . . . it was before that even. Maybe the first time he showed up on my doorstep with his toolbox. But, back then, I was still the walking-wounded. No way was I ready for a relationship.*

When she finally *was* ready to date again, he'd already met Natalia, and by the time they broke up, Maggie was with Brian. Besides, she'd convinced herself that Russell wasn't interested in being in love—maybe wasn't even capable. But, in Boston, when he'd told her his story, she realized he *was* capable; he was just leery of opening up again. Like a dog whose tail had been slammed in the door, he wasn't planning on going through that door again if he could help it. She pictured him bubble-wrapping his heart and storing it in a lockbox he'd built himself.

And just as she'd realized that day on Mom's couch, that she hadn't given herself enough time to think about her career, she realized, now, as he argued the merits of burritos versus soft tacos with Helen, that she hadn't had time to consider her *feelings* either.

She managed to get through dinner; she wasn't sure how. Helen and Russell both commented that she must be jet lagged, tired, from everything—taking care of her mom, getting ready to move, but, really she was just distracted. She couldn't focus.

She kept thinking: *How's this going to fit into my plan? He lives in San Diego. And I'm about to move two thousand miles away.* She told herself she couldn't just calmly say, "Gosh, it occurs to me that I'm in love with you. Now, please move across the country with me." That was a lot for a person to absorb. And she didn't want to risk losing their friendship. He was her best two-legged, non-furry, male friend.

She lay awake all night, trying to think of what she should do, what she could say. In the wee hours of the night, when all ideas seem like good ones, she'd decided to try hinting at her feelings. She could gauge his reaction. She reasoned that if she glimpsed any sign of his tail wagging back at her, then full steam ahead: she'd go for it; tell him she thought she might be in love with him. But, if he ignored her cue, well, then . . . it would be best to keep her mouth shut.

She knew she wouldn't see him that week though. She'd been hoping they'd go on one last bike ride that Sunday, her last ride in San Diego, but he couldn't make it. He told her he had to fly out Sunday for three days of meetings with customers in Oregon. But he said he'd be back late Wednesday and they'd see each other Thursday night for her going away dinner.

She told him he better not miss it. Because the next day, first thing Friday morning, the twenty-first of December, Maggie planned to load her dog into her Honda and they'd be off. With a four day drive, that would put her back at Mom's on Christmas Eve. Shannon's husband, Michael, would be there by then, and so would Kevin and Annie. They'd all be together for Christmas for the first time in years. It was something to look forward to, at least, while she worried about driving off with her heart still sitting on the curb in San Diego.

AT HER GOING away dinner, Maggie cried when Helen, Raul and Russell toasted her and wished her success in Jacksonville. They all lingered over their meal, over the wine, over dessert. No one wanted to be the first to say goodbye. But finally, Maggie said she had to get up early the next day to get on the road. Besides, she needed her chance to talk to Russell. She'd dropped her car at his condo and ridden along with him to Il Fornaio in Del Mar where they'd met up with Helen and Raul. That way she knew she'd be alone with him when they went back for her car.

She cried again as she hugged Helen goodbye on the street in front of the restaurant. Others walking by stared at the women sniffling into each others' hair and swearing they'd visit.

She was silent in the car on the way home with Russell. The

goodbye with Helen had worn her out. She wondered how she'd get through the next one. But, she hoped, it wouldn't *be* a goodbye. She hoped she'd drop her hint, and he'd pick it up and hand it back to her. They'd hug, kiss, laugh, then make love. They'd talk for hours about how their long distance romance was going to work until he could be with her in Florida. She'd still have to drive off in the morning, counting on Kona and coffee to keep her awake, but their goodbye would be a "see you soon."

At least, that was the way she'd imagined it last night. And again this morning. And now, as they pulled into his parking garage. Of course, in between each imagined scene of the tender revelation of their mutual feelings, she'd think, *Is this crazy? Am I crazy? Is this all too sudden?* As soon as she'd tell herself it was indeed all too sudden, she'd realize, no, it felt right. She thought it again as they got out of the car: *Yes, this is insane. Kinda. But it's still* right. *It's all happening crazy-fast, but I want to be with him. I can't help it. And I need to let him know. I can't leave town without knowing what he's thinking.*

"Do you want to come up for some tea?" Russell asked. "I've got decaf. I know you probably don't want to drink anything more, since you have to get up early. Anyway, you have to come up, because I have a little Christmas present for you."

"A present? You didn't have to do that." *Shoot, why didn't I think to get him something. But, if all goes well, maybe I'll be his present . . .* She blushed at the thought and looked down to hide her red cheeks behind her hair.

Upstairs he handed her a shiny silver and gold gift bag. She held it up to her ear and shook it. It weighed very little and she asked for a hint, but he said there'd be no hints, no peeking, and no opening it until Christmas.

They talked over their orange spice tea. He asked her the same questions she'd already answered about the drive and where she planned to stop along the way.

As she came to the bottom of her teacup, she worked up her courage. She readied her hint. Pulled it out in her mind and practiced it, polished it one last time; her hint, which she thought had all the subtlety of a granite boulder.

"I feel like Dorothy in the *Wizard of Oz,* saying goodbye to the Scarecrow," she said. "She told him she was going to miss him the most of all."

This was not the sum total of her hint. She assumed he would have seen the movie and therefore know that Dorothy and the Scarecrow shared a platonic love. (*They were just friends, right?* she'd wondered the night before. *Could there have been a roll in the hay? Hmmm, with a man* made *of hay? No, that seems unlikely, if not downright physically impossible.*) So she'd added an extra clue, which she thought showed that she was *not* taking the role of Dorothy, eternal platonic friend.

She reached for her pendant. "I've always had a wicked, no, uh, no pun intended, crush on the Scarecrow." She threw in the "no pun" business at the last minute, just in case, to keep the mood light.

After dropping her two-ton hint, she kept her eyes on her cup. She was afraid to look up. *What's he thinking? God, is he ever going to say something?* She glanced at him, her heart pounding.

He studied his own cup. He chewed his lower lip, then looked at her from under his eyebrows. His features were tight, she couldn't read them, but then a slow half-smile began to spread across his face.

Oh God, I think he gets it. I think he gets my hint. She held her breath.

He cleared his throat with a single, short cough and said, "Are you saying I don't have any brains?"

She looked down at the table, blinking rapidly. Her temperature spiked with the effort to hold back her tears. The back of her neck flamed hot; her chin trembled. She felt bright red patches bloom around her nostrils. *Well . . . guess he doesn't want to hurt my feelings. Make a joke. Act like I never said anything. OK . . .* She was glad the lights were dim. She hoped he wouldn't see how upset she was. She pushed away the last of her tea and stood up. "No, I'm not." She forced a smile and glanced up at him. "Better go." She busied herself with her purse.

She let a few silent tears seep into his shirt as they hugged at his door.

He kissed the top of her head and murmured, "I promise I'll

come see you."

"Better." She opened her lips only enough to slip the single word through.

He offered to walk her to her car, but she shook her head. She peeled herself away from him, flashed a goodbye wave one last time, and ran down the stairwell. She didn't want to stand there, feeling miserable and crying while she waited for the elevator. She cried in her car until she felt calm enough to manage the drive home.

The next morning at six, after a night of almost no sleep, she loaded Kona into her packed Honda, and they drove off toward the rising sun and their new life in Jacksonville.

THEIR FIRST EVENING on the road, at the Best Western in Lordsburg, New Mexico (where Kona was supposed to be staying off the furniture, but she'd given up and laid out a blanket she brought in from the car so he could get up on the bed with her), Maggie released a long sigh. She sat on the wild multicolored polyester bedspread and poked at her cashew chicken from the Happy Palace with her chop sticks. Kona lay next to her, dutifully staying on his blanket, but at the ready in case she dropped a morsel.

She stared at the TV. *Miracle on 34th Street* was on, but she'd turned the sound off. On top of the TV sat the silver and gold gift bag from Russell, the crumpled white tissue paper lay on the floor below it. Next to the bag was a burgundy wool scarf, curled upon itself like a nest. She couldn't wait until Christmas. She had missed him, missed home, wondered again if she was making the right decision, and had decided to open the present. When she did, she'd smiled, pulled out the scarf and rubbed the soft material against her cheek. The card read, "Merry Christmas. Thought this 'Russell Original' would look pretty with your hair." She wished things had gone differently last night. Wished they were together and imagined his large, rough hands wrapping the scarf around her neck. She'd held it to her nose and breathed deeply, hoping to find his scent on it, but no trace of him lingered.

She looked at the scarf now, on top of the TV set, and gave the cashew chicken one last poke. She held the remains of the takeout box for Kona.

"I'm glad you're here, Bud. This trip would be a total nightmare otherwise. I don't think I could make it without you." She stroked his head. "In fact, I couldn't have made it through this past year without you."

He finished licking the takeout box and looked up at her.

"I love you, Buddy."

He held her gaze with such a tender, solemn look that she swore he understood what she had said. Or, he might have been thinking, "Are you going to eat that fortune cookie?"

Chapter 28: We've Got Bacon, Chicken, Cheese or Peanut Butter

Maggie noticed the time/temperature sign at the bank across the street flash back and forth between nine a.m. and seventy-five degrees as she unlocked the door to Kona's Smoothie Shack. Kona followed her into the cool, dim space. She hadn't expected the Jacksonville weather to already be this hot by April, and in fact the locals assured her the stretch of eighty-five degree days they'd had was unusual. But she wasn't about to complain, since the weather kept the customers coming in droves. Business had been great ever since she opened this location in mid-March, following in the footsteps of the original Shack ten miles across town, but now the heat wave was really driving sales through the thatched roof.

She was helping out, opening the store every morning this week while her manager was on vacation. She liked opening. Get there early, do the prep, enjoy the quiet for a bit. And she wanted to try out a new flavor. She'd had an idea to add a few gourmet selections to both the human and pooch smoothie menus and wanted to try out a bacon and sweet potato combo for the dogs. In testing at home, Kona had given it an enthusiastic six-lick rating. Maggie would judge flavors by how many times Kona would continue to lick his lips after she'd taken the cup away. Now she wanted to try making a large batch with the equipment at the shop and see how that went. Kona had come along to make sure the batch was up to snuff. She'd have the staff give samples away today and see if the average canine liked it as much as her personal taste-tester.

She straightened the framed newspaper article on the wall above the work station (*New Biz Brings Cool Treats to Dogs & Their Humans* it said in bold type at the top) and then got busy slicing potatoes. She'd read it so many times she practically knew it by heart. The photo of Kona and her in front of the original Shack always made her smile. The picture included the outdoor seating area, enclosed by a low, white picket fence and filled with the tables, umbrellas and the "hitching post" where customers could tie up their dogs while they came inside. The neon sign was also visible over the top of Maggie's head: a volcano spewing pink smoothie while a Labrador sat under it catching drops on his tongue. The lettering underneath read: "Smoothies for Pooches & Their People."

The article explained that this was no ordinary smoothie shop, for in addition to "nutritious and delicious concoctions, including many lo-cal options," customers also received a free Dixie-Cup-sized "pooch smoothie, specially designed for the canine palate." The article quoted Maggie saying, "We've already got lots of regulars. Folks take their dogs for a walk and stop by to get a smoothie for themselves and their fuzzy friends." The reporter had asked what was the "most popular flavor with the four-footed set," and Maggie had told him it was "bacon—hands, or rather *paws*, down over the other flavors." Although there were lots of customers who liked the cheese, chicken, and peanut butter flavors as well.

The article also described the Hawaiian-themed décor and mentioned the local artist Maggie had hired to paint the interior murals. The walls were vivid blue and green tropical island backgrounds, with larger-than-life dogs of all breeds wearing Hawaiian shirts and sipping smoothies. At this second shack, Maggie had hired the same artist and had him paint dogs in leis and grass skirts. She looked around at them now and smiled.

The publicity had certainly helped bring people in, as if Gram wasn't already drumming up enough business for her. Gram had turned out to be quite the pusher, getting all the seniors and staff from her building hooked on Maggie's smoothies, whether they had dogs or not. Mom had been coming by pretty regularly as well, along with her new beau, George, whom she'd met while on side-by-side treadmills at the cardiac rehab center.

One day in early March Mom brought Gram by the original shack and Maggie had left her staff in charge while she went out and sat with them in the sun for a bit.

"Can you believe how well this is going?" Maggie had asked, after telling them about the sales growth she was seeing and her progress on opening the second Shack by the university.

"Of course we can, sweetie," Gram had said.

Mom had added, "We've always known you'd be a huge success, no matter what you decided to do."

"Come on, though, you had to think I was crazy when I told you I was going to start a smoothie shop that would include flavors for dogs, didn't you?" She'd grinned. "Maybe a little?"

Mom had given her that new variant on her duck face that she'd been doing a lot lately, mostly since meeting George. It was the same stretched yet pursed lips, but with an added move: the corners of her mouth turned up. Maggie interpreted it as her "I don't really want to smile, but can't help myself" face. Mom had made her happy duck face and said, "Well, maybe a little."

Maggie checked the boiling sweet potatoes and decided they were tender enough. She glanced up at the clock as she drained the water. She had about an hour to finish up here, then by the time the staff got in and took over, she'd still have enough time to go home and get cleaned up for the meeting with Collin.

Her lawyer meetings now were nothing like the ones she'd had in San Diego. Collin was a sharp dresser, witty, erudite. They always chatted pleasantly for a while before getting down to business. Twice they'd gotten so carried away, Collin had had to stop and look at his online calendar and say, "What we were supposed to be talking about again? We might have to carry this conversation over into lunch." And they'd done just that.

No, meetings with Collin were much different. His office had huge windows with a view of the water, and *he* wasn't hard on the eyes either. It also helped that the reason for their meetings was so much more pleasant: he was drawing up a franchising contract for her business, which was his area of expertise. Two of her regulars, Lawrence and Ethan, wanted to take her idea with them when they moved to Miami next month.

Maggie had met Lawrence through Gram; he was Gram's favorite nurse at the senior complex and one of the people she'd gotten hooked on Maggie's smoothies. He and his partner, Ethan, lived near the Shack and would come by a couple of times a week with their pug, Yentl. Yentl would do just about anything for the peanut butter flavor, and the three of them were some of her first, and most loyal, customers. In fact, Lawrence and Ethan had been the ones who convinced her to start selling T-shirts and hats with her logo, which were selling surprisingly well.

They'd ended up becoming good friends. The three of them would often try out new restaurants or visit art galleries. Maggie wanted to start volunteering again and they'd been going to various museums around town with her. So far, the Museum of Contemporary Art was her top pick, but Lawrence and Ethan wanted to be sure she found "the one with the best energy."

She'd been sad when they told her that they'd decided to move to Miami, but thrilled when they had then asked about taking her business idea with them. They thought Kona's Smoothie Shack was "fab" and wanted to use her recipes, the logo, the name, everything.

Swell. Two more names for my long-distance-friends list. As she cooked the bacon, she thought of the two she missed so much on the West Coast—Helen, who continually claimed to not believe in "that BSP," but somehow always knew exactly when Maggie most needed a phone call; and Russell . . . Russell.

She sighed as she thought back on it all now. She'd seen both Helen and Russell once since she moved. Helen had flown out in early January to help scout locations; Russell had been out in February for a business trip, but also stayed the weekend to install shelves in the newly-opened Shack's storage room. She'd felt that same spark at seeing him (and tortured herself with a sleepless night wondering how he didn't feel it too—it seemed so palpable, so intense), but no more hint-dropping for her. As he'd hugged her goodbye and said "see you soon," she'd replied "hope so," while telling herself to finally accept it; they'd never be more than friends.

As she tossed the ingredients into the large blender, Maggie stopped thinking about her old friends and looked forward to seeing her new ones, "her boys" as she called them. Lawrence and Ethan were meeting her at Collin's office to go over the franchise paperwork. She crumbled in big handfuls of the crispy bacon slices and threw Kona a chunk. She flipped the switch on the powerful machine; the ingredients melded into a lovely dark orange shade. She was pouring some into a small cup (in addition to Kona, Maggie also tested the dog smoothie flavors—after all, it was all good, high-quality ingredients) when her cell rang.

"It's me, Russell. How are you? Is this a bad time?"

"No, it's perfect. I'm good." Maggie smiled the second she recognized his voice. Just like Helen, Russell also had a knack for calling when Maggie was thinking of him. "How are you?"

"I'm good, too. I wanted to talk to you about something, though, if you have a minute?"

"Sure. I've gotta get cleaned up for a meeting later, but I've got plenty of time. What's up?" She held the phone to her ear with her shoulder while she finished topping up the cup. She dipped her pinky in and licked it. *Oh, that's good.* She nodded her head and gave herself a thumb-up rating.

"It's been, what, about two months since I was there?" Russell asked.

"Yeah, two months too long. When are you coming again? Is that why you're calling?"

"As a matter of fact, yeah. I've been talking to my boss about—"

"Russell? Are you there?" Maggie looked at her phone. The call had dropped.

She put the phone down to wait for him to call back and drank the small cup of smoothie. *That really is good.* She picked up a dish towel and wiped her hands.

She spun around as she heard someone rap on the glass front

door. He was back-lit, but she recognized his tall figure and broad shoulders instantly. She let out a little yelp of glee and she and Kona ran to open the door as Russell leaned into the glass, his hands cupped around his eyes against the glare. He smiled as he saw them bounding across the floor at him.

"It's so great to see you." She opened the door and he came in. He gave her a quick, firm hug and rubbed Kona's back. He was tan as ever in his white polo shirt with his company's logo and navy blue shorts. She noted his legs looked like he'd kept up with the cycling after she left.

"I'm here." He held his hands out as if he'd completed a magic trick.

"Your grasp of the obvious is really top notch," she said as they grinned at one another. "I can see that you're here." She looked him up and down.

"No, I mean, I'm here—Jacksonville. For good. I moved here."

"What?" Maggie screamed and hugged him again. "Why didn't you tell me?"

Kona wiggled, responding to their energy.

"I wanted it to be a surprise."

"Mission accomplished. I can't believe this. How did this happen? It's for your work?"

"Yeah, I've been talking to our company's owner about starting a branch office ever since I was here in February. He loved the idea. He's been wanting to expand and there are boat-loads of doctors' offices here. So, that's why I'm here; to start up our new southeast branch."

"When did you get here? I can't believe you've been keeping this from me." She hit him on the arm with her dish towel.

"I moved a couple of days ago. I'm in a furnished temporary rental for now." He pointed his thumb in the general direction of his apartment. "Wanted to figure out exactly where the office'll be before I settle into something more permanent."

"This is insane. I can't believe this." She bounced up and down like a child. Kona danced from foot to foot. She pictured them riding their bikes every Sunday. There was a great Cuban restaurant near her house she wanted to take him to. Maybe they could go there tonight. She had tons of ideas for great locations for his office and knew just the neighborhood he should move to . . . OK, it was her neighborhood . . . but it really was a *great* neighborhood.

"There's something else." He rubbed the back of his neck. "I moved here with someone. We're living together."

Maggie stopped bouncing. Kona sat down. "Oh." The brakes were applied rather harshly to her happy image of them on their bikes. "Well, that's great news, too. You're just . . . full of surprises today, aren't you?" Her hand went to her jade pendant. *He's finally committing to someone. And they're going to be right here, under my nose.*

"I want you to meet her. I know you'll like her."

"I'm sure I will. We'll all have to get together—real soon," she started to head back around the counter. "I was, uh, working on something back here. I kinda need to finish it up before that meeting I mentioned, um, when you were on the phone."

"You can meet her right now. She's outside. I've told her all about you. And she's one helluva gorgeous blond, so we should get out there before someone steals her from me."

Ohmygod. He wants me to meet his new beautiful, blond girlfriend and I look like hell. I haven't taken a shower yet this morning. I don't even have any makeup on. Of course, Russell had seen Maggie unshowered and makeup-free many times on their weekly rides, but that didn't mean she wanted to meet his new girlfriend when she wasn't looking her absolute best.

"Come on," Russell held the door open and motioned for her to follow. "She doesn't bite." He called out, "Honey, here's Maggie. The woman I've been telling you about."

Maggie walked toward him. When she got close enough, he grabbed her hand and pulled her through the door; Kona tagged along.

There, tied to the hitching post in the shade, was a beautiful yellow lab puppy. Her tail wagged furiously when she saw Russell.

"Maggie, this is Dorothy," Russell said as he bent and scratched the top of the dog's head.

Maggie felt as though her bones had turned to mashed sweet potato. The dog provided an excellent excuse to collapse onto the rectangle of Astroturf in front of the hitching post.

"Dorothy, it's *so* good to meet you," Maggie said as she received several dozen kisses from the wiggly puppy. Kona peered at the small dog over Maggie's shoulder. Russell crouched down next to them.

"You got a dog."

"Your grasp of the obvious is really top notch." He grinned at her.

"But . . . I thought a dog was too much of a commitment."

"I never said that. *You* did. I said I couldn't have a dog because I'd have to be home every night. Remember me—traveling salesman?"

"Oh, yeah." Maggie thought back to their conversation all those months ago. Maybe she *had* put words in his mouth. "But, aren't you still going to be traveling?"

"No, not much. I'm going to run the office. I'll hire all the salespeople, and they'll report to me. I'll have to go to San Diego once in a while, but I'm hoping Dorothy and Kona here will get along and maybe you can dog-sit for me."

The dogs sniffed each other, tails wagging.

"Looks like they're going to get along great," Maggie said. "So, Dorothy, huh?"

"Yup. You remember what you said to me your last night in San Diego?" he asked.

"Of course I do," she kept petting the yellow dog while he spoke. She didn't look at him.

"And then I asked you if you thought I didn't have any brains, which I guess I didn't, since I kinda ruined the moment there . . . Anyway, now when I look at Dorothy, it reminds that I need brains, heart *and* courage if I'm going to get what I want out of life."

She looked up and said, "The brains alone don't cut it, do they?"

Two tails were already wagging. Two more joined in.

They were both silent for a moment, until Maggie stood up. "Wait one sec, I have something I want Dorothy to try."

She ran inside and poured two cups of the bacon and sweet potato smoothie. Once back outside, she crouched down between the dogs and held a cup for each of them as they lapped up the contents. Dorothy never took her big brown eyes off of Maggie.

"Well, that's done it," Russell said. "I think she's in love with you."

"I think maybe I'm in love with her, too." Maggie left the cups on the ground for the dogs to finish working on and stood up. She put her arms around Russell's neck, and he held her tight.

They both laughed as Kona squeezed in between their legs, but they did not separate.

There was his intoxicating smell: soft leather, ginger, and rain on the ocean.

She smelled like bacon.

~ *The End* ~

25356122R00185

Made in the USA
Middletown, DE
27 October 2015